THROUGH BULLETS AND THUNDERSTORMS

A HOLOCAUST SURVIVAL PACT

JANINA SCARLET

ALSO BY JANINA SCARLET

Fiction

Therapy Quest

Dark Agents: Violet and the Trial of Trauma

Comics

The Pain Diaries

Pain Diaries, Volume 2: Medications and Pain

Super Kids

Paths to Recovery for Military Sexual Trauma

Family Support for Military Sexual Trauma

Hunger Action Heroes Unite!

Non-fiction

Superhero Therapy

Harry Potter Therapy

Supernatural Therapy: Hunting Your Internal Monsters IRL

Super Survivors

Superhero Therapy for Anxiety and Trauma (Clinician's Manual)

Super-Women

It Shouldn't Be This Way

Unseen, Unheard, Undervalued

PRAISE FOR THE BOOK:

"A story so unbelievable it shouldn't be true. *Bullets and Thunderstorms* starts off with a horrifying bang and doesn't let you breathe until the very last page. This incredible survival story reminds us that when hate and bigotry are given permission to grow, brave heroes will always rise up against it.

The beautiful, personal details that Scarlet weaves into her family history bring to life the suffering and perseverance of her grandmother's remarkable story. Shocking, unflinching, and true, this book should be required reading—as both a warning, and an inspiration. Hope is embroidered through every page."

- Lora Innes (author of *The Dreamer*)

"Janina Scarlet takes an unflinching look at the Holocaust but serves as a reliable guide through some of history's darkest moments. Compelling, heartbreaking, and uplifting in equal measures. Highly recommended!"

THROUGH BULLETS AND

THUNDERSTORMS:

A Holocaust Survival Pact

BASED ON A TRUE STORY

Janina Scarlet

Divine Feminine Publishing

Text copyright © 2025 by Janina Scarlet
Divine Feminine Publishing
www.divinefeminine-publishing.com
For information about special discounts for bulk purchases,
please contact the publisher using the contact form:
www.divinefeminine-publishing.com/contact

Cover illustration by: Sasha West and Paul G. Miehl

Acquisition editor: Erin Michelle Gibes

Copy Editor: Paxton Alyssa

ISBN: (paperback): 979-8-9929404-0-4

ISBN: (e-book): 979-8-9929404-2-8

Publisher: Divine Feminine Publishing

Copyright © Janina Scarlet, 2025

Subjects: World War II—Holocaust |Historical Fiction | Women's Historical Fiction | Jewish Biographies | Jewish Holocaust History | Holocaust Survivors | Survivor Stories |

To my grandparents and to everyone who survived the Holocaust,
and especially to those who did not.

GLOSSARY

Anhalten (German) – dog command - Stop

Askorbinka (Russian) – ascorbic acid (Vitamin C)

Auf Deutsch (German) – in German

Babulya (Russian) - granny

Babushka (Russian) – grandmother

Balalaika – a musical instrument

Bozhe (Russian) – God

Bozhe Moi (Russian) - my God

Dacha (Russian) – vacation/summer house

Danke Schön (German) – thank you very much

Davai (Russian) – let's go

Devochka (Russian) - girl

Dobroye utro (Russian) – Good morning

Dorogaya (Russian) – dear

Es gibt zwölf Monate im Jahr (German) – There are twelve months in the year

Fass (German) – a command for dogs, meaning "attack" or "bite"

Frau (German) – Missus

Guten Morgen (German) – Good morning

Herr (German) - Mister

Ja (German) – Yes

Kasha (Ukrainian) – buckwheat porridge

Krasavitsa (Russian) – beautiful lady

Kotyonok (Russian) – kitten

Lebensborn (German) – fount of life (an SS-initiated breeding program)

Malchik (Russian) – boy

Mamo (Ukrainian) - mom

Moya dorogaya (Russian) – my dear

Paskudnik (Yiddish) – vile person; son of a b**ch

Platok (Russian) – a headscarf

Politsei (Russian) – police

Setzen (German) – dog command - Sit

Slava Bogu (Russian) – Thank God

Tateh (Yidish) - Dad

Tato (Ukrainian) - Dad

Titka (Ukrainian) – Aunt

Wie viele Monate gibt es in einem Jahr? (German) - How many months are there in a year?

Ya ne znayu (Russian) – I don't know

CONTENT WARNING

This book is based on a true story of the author's grandmother, and as such, it depicts real events that occurred during WWII. This book contains some graphic depictions of violence, death, and sexual assault, specifically in chapters 8, 18-22, 35, 38, 41, and 56-57. Some readers may find these chapters upsetting. Please utilize caution when reading these chapters.

PROLOGUE

pril 12, 1995, 11:50pm, on the train from Moscow

I LEARNED a long time ago that people show up at their best or their worst when facing the barrel of a loaded gun. Tonight is no different. I wake from a deep sleep when our train cabin door flies open.

"Border patrol," a man's voice says, and someone flicks on the light.

Two men enter the train cars. They wear official Russian military uniforms—full fatigues. A gold star-shaped pin glistens on the front center of their fur hats. One of them has a dark unibrow. Each guard sports a leather belt around his waist and a machine gun in his hands.

My lips twitch and I suck in a breath at the sight of them. Even at seventy-two years old, I know that I could still pack a punch if it came to it.

"Babushka!" My 11-year-old granddaughter, Jana, shouts, hops down from her bunk, and sprints toward me.

As if hunting a rabbit, Unibrow sharply turns his gun on the little girl, his finger on the trigger.

"Don't move," he barks.

Jana freezes; her eyes open wide.

My body pulsates with rage.

"Hey," I shout, clenching my tiny, wrinkled fists at the guard.

It works.

The guard shifts his gun away from my granddaughter and points it at me instead.

"What?" Unibrow asks me.

"What is it you want?" I demand.

"Border patrol. This train is leaving Russia and about to cross the border into Ukraine. Do you have any weapons, drugs, money?"

"Oh, you know, just a machine gun," I reply, rolling my eyes and overemphasizing the sarcasm.

"Don't make us search you, *babulya*," Unibrow threatens.

"C'mon, she's just a little old granny," says his comrade. "She's harmless."

"They're Jews. *Ukrainian Jews*," Unibrow says, inspecting everyone's passports and frowning. "We should search them."

Try me, I think but say nothing out loud.

"Let's go. They don't have anything," the second guard says.

Unibrow stands still for a moment, his gun and his eyes resting firmly on me. But my gaze is unflinching in return.

He spits on the floor and the two guards walk out.

IT TAKES me over two hours to fall back asleep, my heart pounding, my mind playing out what I would have done if the guards hadn't left.

Scream to get other passengers' attention.

Bribe them with cash.

Hit the Unibrow, he's closer.

Take his gun and point it on the other one.

They might shoot me, but the family would be safe. And the documents—our refugee papers from the American Embassy—would be safe.

I take a big breath and slide my hand under my pillow. I tug my cotton purse and pull it toward me. My fingers glide over the fraying thread. Even in the dark, I can make out the embroidered shapes—four roses, a tiara, a music clef, and a spade.

I slip my hand inside the purse and feel around. Moving my wallet and passport aside with my fingers, I focus on the most important items and count.

Button. One.

Ribbon. Two.

Tassel. Three.

I exhale in relief and turn my attention to my sleeping family, their faces lit by the moonlight. I watch them like a mother bear watching over her cubs. Inside me is a silent roar that only I can hear.

No one will ever hurt them, not while I'm still breathing.

As I finally begin to drift to sleep, I am awakened again by a familiar exploding sound.

A firefight.

I jolt up with a gasp, my pillow covered in sweat.

"Are they shooting again?" I ask.

Jana looks over at me in surprise. "No, Babushka. It's the thunderstorm."

I exhale, trying to steady my breath. I close my eyes and try to rest, my heart still pounding.

"Babushka?"

My eyes fly open once again. "Yes, *moya dorogaya*?"

"Who did you think was shooting?"

"No one, *dorogaya*." I say, my heart still pounding. "No one. Now, go back to sleep."

CHAPTER 1
THE NIGHT WITCHES

J*une 1941, Vinnytsia, Ukraine*

IN THE QUIET moments before sunrise, I stand at the edge of our pasture, clutching my shawl tightly against the encroaching whispers of the war.

Yesterday, my classmates were buzzing with speculations before our chemistry final. Some said that the fascists are coming to Ukraine. Others said that they are already here.

I don't know what to believe. I take a breath and try to focus on the sounds of crickets around me, the damp of the morning dew dripping through the holes of my sandals, and the first rays of the sun kissing my cheeks.

I recite the days of the week in German in my mind.

Montag. Dienstag. Mittwoch. Donnerstag. Freitag. Samstag. Sonntag.

The German final is in just a few hours and once I'm done with it, I can graduate.

I inhale again, breathing more deeply now.

I am the first in my family to graduate from upper school.

And when I'm finished, I will teach.

Somewhere in the distance, a rooster crows. And then another.

Somewhere else, a dog barks and a cow moos.

But not Moo-Moo.

Moo-Moo is older now, but the pain in her eyes is the same as it was the day that Mamo died. She knows. She's always known.

It's been eight years, but I still see Mamo's face in everything she touched and everyone she ever loved, including Moo-Moo.

The neighbors have always said that Moo-Moo is an obedient cow, but I know better. There is a difference between obedience and resignation—the former is a choice.

This morning, Moo-Moo looks like a prisoner, the kind that has given up all hope of freedom. The kind that doesn't try to escape long after the prison doors are open.

Moo-Moo's once luscious auburn-and-white skin is sagging and the sparkle in her eyes has completely gone out.

She doesn't move as I walk up to her. Her head is bowed low to the grass, but she is not eating. Her once perky ears droop, resembling those of a lamb.

"Just hang on, *moya dorogaya*," I murmur to her, gently stroking Moo-Moo's drooping flank.

The old cow's bones are brittle under her sagging

skin, and I try to shake the image of my mother's thinning flesh during the last weeks of her life.

Yesterday, Papa again threatened to put Moo-Moo down. Says she's getting too thin and too old.

I won't let him.

I lean my head against Moo-Moo's and whisper in the old cow's ear, "I know, my girl. I know you're tired."

The cow doesn't move.

"Please, Moo-Moo. I need you," I whisper.

She doesn't respond.

"I don't want to lose you too."

Moo-Moo looks up at me and tilts her head to one side.

My face breaks into a smile. "You're willing to try it?"

And although Moo-Moo doesn't answer, I hop to my old cow's side and place one of the buckets under her. Then I gently wipe Moo-Moo's udder with a wet cloth and oil, and squeeze.

"Thank you, my girl," I keep repeating as each of the buckets fill with fresh milk. "Thank you."

When the buckets are full, I take a deep sigh of relief. Moo-Moo will live another day.

As I reach for the buckets, I glance down at the marigolds at Moo-Moo's feet. Or what should have been marigolds but are now wilting fernlike leaves. I bend down to look at them more closely, being careful not to touch them—any plants, pollen, or fresh earth cause my eyes to swell for hours.

I hate gardening. I would rather clean cow dung all day than spend even a few minutes planting seeds. Everything I plant always dies. And yet, my grandmother insists I keep trying.

Babushka is wrong. I'll never be able to keep a garden.

7

I shake my head at the marigolds and then pat my cow. "I'll see you tomorrow, Moo-Moo."

Moo-Moo lifts her head and nudges at my hand. I grin and kiss her on the cheek, pick up the two milk buckets, and head home.

I climb the steps of our cottage, place the buckets on the wooden floor of our porch, and push on the front door. It creaks as it opens. I carry the buckets inside and lock the door behind me.

Careful not to wake my father, who is snoring in his corner bed, I pour the milk from the buckets into small glass jars through a cloth strainer, just like Babushka taught me.

I then leave three jars on the table next to my father's bed and bring the rest down to the cellar.

By the time I climb back up, Yakov, my father, is just getting out of bed. He has his fraying grey shorts on, a matching stained shirt, and a frown.

"Good morning, Papa," I say.

My father grunts at me in a familiar response.

I gather the empty clay jars from under the table and set them aside to rinse later. They still reek of homemade vodka.

Six days to Mamo's birthday.

I swallow my tears, pushing the grief away. I hand Papa one of the milk jars and then straighten his blanket over his bed.

As he drinks his milk in silence, I try to choose my words carefully. "Papa, I am sorry, I just wanted to let you know that I don't think I can make supper today."

"It's six in the morning, Maria," he replies, finger brushing his greying black hair. "What are you worrying about supper for?"

"I have a test today."

He frowns at me. "A test?" He sits on the corner of his bed and reaches for the pitcher of water and a cup, nearly spilling it as he pours.

My heart pounds in my chest. "Yes, Papa. A final exam. In German. I told you yesterday about my exams, remember?"

A stern expression comes over his long, bony face as he takes in a shivering breath. "You said you're done with your other classes. Makes no sense for you to be going just for one stupid test." His bottom lip curves like he just drank soured milk. He shakes his head and glares at me. "You're not going."

My throat tightens at his words.

I expected some resistance from him, but not that he'd outright forbid me from taking the exam, especially after I'd worked so hard to graduate. If I can only graduate, then I can work. If I can work, then I can be free.

I take half a step toward him to argue but his gaze makes me step back. I've never seen him look at me in this way. His nostrils flare with anger but his eyes—his big brown eyes are pleading.

No, I realize, *he has looked at me this way before*. When I was getting ready for school the day after Mamo died. He forbade me from going to school that day and for the entire week after.

This grief, it's never gone, is it?

I used to think that if I could just do enough, care for him enough, be a good enough daughter, then I could help him through it.

But time does not heal all heartbreak. How can it? After all, grief is both a silent scream and a love that's bursting out of you with nowhere to go.

"Papa," I try again, softening my voice as if speaking to a child, just like Babushka taught me. "Please understand. I have to go. It's my *final* exam. I graduate tomorrow, if I pass it. I have been working so hard and—"

I jolt with a gasp as he bangs his fist on the kitchen table.

"I said NO!" he shouts.

His chest is heaving. He wipes foaming saliva from his mouth.

My chest and stomach are thumping, and tears burn as they run down my cheeks.

It's never enough. Nothing I do is ever enough.

"But Papa...why?" I whisper.

He glares at me, his finger shaking as he speaks.

"Why? WHY? Where's your mother?" he spits.

I step back as Papa raises his fist in the air, slamming it onto the table again. The wood creaks and buckles. Splinters fly in every direction.

"DEAD!"

"Papa..." I whisper again, choking through my tears.

"And where's your brother? Huh? Where's Pavlik? We haven't heard from him in months!"

He stands up, in all his height, towering over me for a moment, and then paces around our tiny kitchen and muttering under his breath. "*German* final... I'll give you *German final*... The goddamn fascists are coming, and she wants to go do some *German final*."

Papa. My poor Papa.

I run toward him, take his large, calloused hands in mine, and look at him, speaking from somewhere behind my tears.

"Papa! Look at me! I know Mamo's birthday is always hard for you. I miss her too."

His lower lip twitches, and he tries turning away but I squeeze his hands in mine, "I know you are scared, Papa. I know you're worried about me. About Pavlik. But it's going to be okay."

I don't even know if what I'm saying is true, but I am trying to comfort him, nonetheless.

He rips his hands away from mine. "I have to get ready for work."

"No, Papa, wait," I start again.

But Papa interrupts me, "Not now."

Something inside me swells larger than my pain. "Papa!" I shout. "You're not even listening to me."

A familiar flash of anger in my father's eyes.

He shakes his finger in my face. "How many times do I have to tell you? Good girls don't get angry. You want to get yourself killed? Remember—if you're nice to people, then people treat you nice."

I pinch my lips together to keep myself from saying what I really want to say and take a slow breath.

"Papa, I'm sorry," I try again. "Please listen. Pavlik is out on the front lines. He can't write. You know that. But he will be back. You'll see."

Papa grunts.

I think it's working. I continue, careful to keep my voice even, "And the fascists—they're in Poland, Papa. They're not coming here. It will be okay."

There is a knock on the door. I take a step toward it, but—

"Don't open it," Papa orders. "You don't know who it could be."

I stop mid-step staring at my father and awaiting his instruction.

A knock comes again and then my grandmother's voice, "Yakov? Maria? Open the door."

I rush to open it, letting my grandmother in. "Babushka!"

My shoulders settle in relief. *Maybe he'll listen to her if he won't listen to me.*

Babushka must have just returned from a trip to the well because she is carrying two buckets full of water, splashing all over her green floral dress and brown sandals.

"Babushka! What are you doing with those?" I say. "You shouldn't be carrying those. They're heavy! Here, let me."

I grab the water buckets and hoist them onto the table.

Papa leans on the wall behind him, his arms folded across his chest. "You forgot your keys again, Mamo?"

Babushka nods. "Yes, sorry." She walks over to the table and rummages through the drawers. "They must be here somewhere."

"That's the third time this month," Papa says. His voice sounds calmer now. He walks up to her and helps her look. "You should see a doctor, Mamo. I worry about you."

A moment later, Babushka pulls out a set of keys with a small pink ribbon from the bottom drawer. "Found them. And you worry too much, *dorogoi moi.*" She boops Papa on the nose and giggles to herself.

Papa smirks at her as he always does, but his shoulders have dropped, and his growl has softened now. "Mamo, tell her she isn't going to school," he says nodding toward me. "She's eighteen already. She needs to focus on finding a husband anyway."

"I will not," Babushka replies, opening one of the milk jars. She takes a sip and then continues, "You have to understand, son, that times have changed. Women aren't just meant to be housewives anymore. They can teach. Or work in a factory, just like you. Some even fly planes for the Air Force. Fighting the fascists. Night Witches, people call them."

"Bah!" Papa waves at her.

But Babushka ignores him and turns toward me. "I mean it. Anything men can do, you can do too."

"Oh, so, this is where she's getting these ideas," Papa says. "I keep telling her that she needs to be a good girl. Respect her elders, and all that. And here you are, undoing everything I've been teaching her," he grumbles and then turns toward me. "I'm off to work. I expect to find you here when I get home."

I sigh and nod. "Yes, Papa."

He nods back. "That's my good little princess." He gives me a kiss on the forehead and walks out the door.

"How are the marigolds coming along?" Babushka asks, adjusting the hair in her loose grey bun.

I lower my head to stare at an old burn stain in one of the floorboards. "Not good. I hate gardening, Babushka. I'm no good at it."

"Nonsense." Babushka puts down her milk jar and walks over to me.

She pats my head the way she'd always done, as if petting a teeny precious kitten. "Look at me, *moya dorogaya*."

My heart warms as I look into Babushka's brown, adoring eyes. She cradles my cheeks with her small, wrinkled hands, smelling of warm bread and fresh honey.

"Remember that gardening isn't about being *good* at

it," she says. "It's about creating life and helping it grow. It's about talking to the plants and caring for them, the way that you care for Moo-Moo."

I don't think I'll ever like gardening, but I don't argue. Instead, I nod. "I'll try again."

Babushka squeezes my cheeks, and then walks over to her bed. She pulls a bundle of cloth out from under her pillow and presents it to me. "Here, *dorogaya*. I made this for your final exam and graduation. Now, go wash your face and put it on."

I unravel the cloth to reveal a black dress embroidered with four scarlet roses and emerald-green leaves around the sleeves and collar. It looks just like the one my mother used to wear.

I run my shaking fingers over the hand stitched flowers, as both warmth and a chill go through my spine.

"Thank you, Babushka. It's beautiful," I sniffle through my smile.

Babushka gently smooths out my hair. "Anything for you, my precious one." She kisses me on the forehead. "Now, go get ready. You don't want to be late for your exam."

My heart jumps in my chest. "But Papa said-"

Babushka puts her hands on my shoulders. "Listen to me and hear me. You always have choices. And when it comes down to it, I hope you'll choose to be more like the Night Witches."

My voice trembles. "But Papa—"

"Don't worry about your father, *dorogaya*. I'll handle him. Now, go change. You still need to drop off some milk for Yuriy Mihailovich and then hurry to school."

I let out a quiet exhale of relief. "Thank you, Babushka."

After washing my face in cold water from the well, I put on my new dress and inspect myself in the mirror. The dress is a little tight around my chest and hips, but it still fits, nonetheless. The embroidered flowers on the sleeves and collar make it look more formal than any of my other dresses. It looks regal.

I smile at my reflection in the mirror. With my long charcoal braids, my big brown eyes, and my short, thin structure, I do look a lot like my mother.

"You like it?" Babushka asks.

"I love it," I beam at my grandmother. "Thank you, Babushka."

I give her a kiss on the cheek, grab the remaining milk jar from the table, and skip out the door.

CHAPTER 2
SERGEI

The sun beams through the clouds as I make my way through the neighboring streets. Radiant light highlights the emerald green of the lush summer leaves. I close my eyes for a few moments to listen, allowing my muscles to settle in relief. The birds chirp in a discordant chorus. I breathe in the sweet smell of strawberries and freedom.

I open my eyes and grin. The sunlight caresses and warms my cheeks like Babushka's touch.

I almost slip on the rocks protruding from the unpaved ground along the dirt path but manage to gain my footing again. I keep walking past a patch of unruly grass and wildflowers, and then climb the familiar wooden steps of our neighbor's cottage, just a few hundred meters away from our own.

I knock.

"Who is it?" Yuriy snaps as he yanks open the door.

His furrowed eyebrows are louder than his voice. His disheveled light-brown hair has streaks of silver in it. He smells like sweat and vodka. I don't know why, but I always feel nervous around him.

"Yuriy Mihailovich, I brought you some milk," I mumble as I hand him a milk jar. "You can leave the empty jar outside the door, like last time. I'll pick it up later."

Yuriy's expression softens. "Thanks."

"You're welcome," I say, but Yuriy has already slammed the door.

I shake my head. "Typical."

I run down the path and nearly bump into Rosa, another elderly neighbor, also widowed, like Yuriy. "Sorry, Rosa Viktorovna. *Dobroye utro.*"

"Good morning, Maria," Rosa says. She yanks at the leash in her hands, which is connected to her small dog, a mutt. "Malchik, stop pulling," Rosa scolds, and turns toward me. "Congratulations on your graduation." She looks around to make sure no one can hear us and then adds quietly, "Listen to me, Maria. The fascists are coming."

A chill runs through my body, as Rosa continues, "If you see any Germans, don't let them know you are Jewish. And whatever you do, do not under any circumstances let them see your documents. Do you understand?"

I nod at her, unsure of what to say.

She nods back. "Good. Now, hurry to your school."

I nod again and run off.

My mind is swimming with images of what I would do if I was to encounter a German soldier. *Would I lie about being Jewish? What would I say?*

I'm so lost in thought that I don't notice the man

walking behind me, until he says, "*Debroye utro, krasavitsa!*"

My stomach hardens as I hold my breath.

And then I speed up. *Please leave me alone,* I think. *Not today. Of all the days, not today.*

His footsteps accelerate behind me. I try to walk even faster. I look down at my sandals, trying not to trip over the uneven patches of grass and gravel.

His feet shuffle even louder and closer.

Don't look up, I tell myself. *Don't turn around.*

Harsh fingers wrap around my arm.

I jerk and spin around, and there he is.

Sergei towers over me. A twig protrudes from his unruly blonde hair, like a horn on a charging bull.

I can't believe I used to think he was handsome.

Years ago, his chin-length blonde hair and sky-blue eyes reminded me of the prince I read about in *Cinderella.* But now, his hawk-like towering posture makes me shudder.

"What do you want, Sergei?"

"You have no manners." Sergei huffs, still squeezing my arm. "When someone wishes you a good morning, you need to say *good morning* back. And when someone calls you beautiful, you need to say *thank you.* I would think your father raised you better than that. Even if he is a Jew."

I bite my lip.

He's in one of his moods today, I realize. *I need to be careful about what I say and how I say it.* I try to pull my arm away, but Sergei squeezes it further.

I take a quiet breath and try to keep my voice as steady as possible, "I'm sorry. Good morning, Sergei. Please, let me go."

He smirks and lets go of my arm, "Relax, you cow! I'm just playing around with you. I know you like it when I play with you." He grabs a hold of one of my braids now.

I shudder. "You mean like when you take my shoes and I have to chase you to get them back?"

He chuckles, staring into my eyes with a half-smile, "I like you, stupid. And you know that you like me too." He slides his hand down my braid, twisting the bottom of it around his finger.

I let him. I know it's pointless to argue.

Placating him isn't working. I just need to get away.

"I'm late for school," I say, trying to keep my voice calm.

"No, you're not. Your school doesn't start until eight. It's what, seven kilometers away?"

"How do you know that? You don't even go there."

He ignores my question but is no longer smiling. He just squeezes my braid in his fist, and tugs at it, before throwing it away like cow manure. "I don't understand why you're doing this. You finished primary school like the rest of us. Eight years is plenty, if you ask me. Why walk seven kilometers each way to do even more school?"

"I want to finish my upper diploma," I say and try to walk past him, but he runs in front of me, blocking my path.

His eyes shine now, like they did when he played with the neighborhood German Shepherd, Grey. More than once, I witnessed Sergei pretend to feed Grey by making a motion with his hand like he was tossing food to him, and when the old dog would sniff around the ground and whine, Sergei would laugh, teasing repeatedly, before he would finally feed him.

Is everything a game to him? I wonder, but I say nothing.

Sergei folds his arms across his chest, still blocking my path, "Why do you want your diploma anyway? Only ugly girls need those, the ones who can't get husbands to take care of them."

I try to go around him again, but he blocks my path once more. "You're eighteen now," Sergei continues, "not getting any younger. You should be thinking about marriage now."

I leap to the other side, but so does he.

I stop for a moment to collect myself, and Sergei's grin widens. "You know, I would be happy to take you as my wife. What do you say?"

"Please move out of my way," I respond.

"You didn't answer my question," he says, taking a slow step closer to me, his nose almost touching mine. I can smell his morning breath and yesterday's supper.

"Please leave me alone!" I hiss.

I try to get around him once more, but Sergei grabs both my shoulders, squeezing them with force.

For a moment, I just stare at him. Then, with a sharp exhale, I push him backward onto the grass.

Sergei falls but not without taking me with him.

"Oh, I see. Is this what you wanted, Maria?" he laughs when I land on top of him.

His laugh makes me nauseated, and I stifle a furious scream.

I push myself off him and run, lest he see the tears of frustration in my eyes.

He runs after me, circling me now, like a hungry dog, until he blocks my path again.

"Just stop and listen for a minute, will you?" He is

21

panting now. With his usual smirk gone, his face looks more serious than I've seen him before. He starts over enunciating his words, "They are *killing* Jews. They're sending them away to die." He takes a breath and lowers his voice again, "Now, if you were my wife, they might not care that you're a Jew. Just think about that."

He quiets, no longer laughing, his eyes piercing mine.

Is this true? Would I be safer with him? The thought makes me want to vomit.

"So, what do you say?" he asks. "Be smart. Marry me. Let me save you."

My head is swimming with thoughts. *Are the fascists actually going to come here? To Ukraine? Are they going to kill us? Has something happened to Pavlik? Will I ever see my brother again?*

"Hey! Are you ignoring me?" Sergei roars, shaking me by my shoulders. "Answer me!"

My hands tighten into small fists. I once again push his hands off me. "Get. Away." I hiss through gritted teeth.

He scowls but I don't wait for the rest of his reaction. Instead, I turn around and run to school.

"Oh, that's fine!" he shouts after me. "You keep running! See what happens when the Nazis walk through our streets like they're doing in Poland! I was going to marry you to save you but now"—he gives a frenzied laugh—"now you can die just like the rest of them. Kikes! All of you!"

I keep running, unable to stop the tears now.

CHAPTER 3
SONATA

I am panting by the time I get to school – a single-story red brick building with large, rounded windows. At the entrance, a scarlet red flag with a gold hammer and sickle waves on the flagpole.

I step inside and walk through a narrow hallway, which smells of chalk, wood, and dust. Two of my class-mates are sitting on a long crimson hallway bench and reviewing class notes. The girls are so caught up in their studies, they don't acknowledge me as I walk past them.

I wipe the sweat from my brow and peek through the door of my classroom. Andrei, my classmate, is napping, his head resting on his arms atop of one of the two long desks. Aside from him, the classroom is empty.

I don't own a watch but the large brown clock on the wall indicates I am thirty-five minutes early.

I take a breath, part out of relief, partly to steady myself. I step back out into the corridor and look down the hall toward the music classroom.

Should I go in? I wonder, glancing at the music room door.

23

My heart still pounds from running and from Sergei's words: *They are killing Jews. They're sending them away to die.*

I take a determined step away from my classroom and past the two girls studying in the hall.

Just for a little bit.

I dart down the empty hallway toward the large wooden double doors. I tug at one of them.

It opens to a cluttered room. Dust particles dance along the elongated sunrays that seep into the room through two side windows. Two balalaikas are propped against a light blue wall, although one of them is missing a string. There is a dusty poster on the wall, picturing Lenin, speaking to two young people at the bottom of the poster, stating, "The task is to study."

Below the poster is a row of wooden chairs that face a small brown oak piano. I take a step, and then another, creeping toward it, afraid of getting into trouble for being in the music room without a teacher present. The piano may be old, but illuminated by a sunbeam, it looks so majestic, it might as well be superb.

I settle down on the old bench in front of it, lift the wooden fallboard, and caress the keys with my shivering fingers.

I close my eyes.

It is a different piano, but it's still similar to the one my mother taught me to play—the one at my primary school.

I haven't played at all in eight years.

Not since my mother died.

The first time I ever touched a piano, I was seven. I sat on my mother's lap, too short to reach the floor pedals and the more distant keys.

24

I remember her whispering into my ear, "When you play music, it's like you are transported to another world. A world where everything's okay. A world where you are safe."

I swallow the bittersweet memory deep into my throat and align my fingers. The first note makes me shiver.

Another world.

My fingers instinctively play a familiar tune.

What is it?

Beethoven perhaps?

That's right. The Moonlight Sonata.

I press the keys harder, trying to stomp out the memory of Sergei from my mind.

A world where you are safe.

My fingers slip as Sergei's voice replays in my mind, *Kikes! All of you!,* and I frantically realign them again and continue, trying to escape into *a world where everything's okay.* My mother's hands guiding me now.

I jerk upwards when the sound of the bell drowns out the last note I play, and with it, my mother's touch as well.

CHAPTER 4

THE GERMAN FINAL

The classroom looks as it always has—two long brown benches on either side of two decrepit wooden tables. Rusty nails stick out on some of the sides of the backless seats.

A black chalkboard is mounted on the wall at the front of the class. It still lists the days of the week in German from last week's lesson.

Montag. Dienstag. Mittwoch. Donnerstag. Freitag. Samstag. Sonntag.

A single square window illuminates the space, casting an oppressive tone throughout the cramped classroom. The instructor's desk rests in between the window and the blackboard, creating an aura of stoic authority.

The teacher, Ivan Ivanovich, is slouching in his chair like a dehydrated plant. His face looks as withered and empty as the classroom walls. His black jacket matches his pants, both covered in dandruff and animal fuzz. Most of his greying hair seems to have migrated from his scalp to his rather impressive beard.

When I walk in, Ivan Ivanovich sighs and shakes his

head, as he does whenever any student enters his classroom.

Why does he continue to teach if he hates it so much?

When all the students have settled down, Ivan Ivanovich reviews the rules of the examination in his usual monotone.

"Each of you will come to the front of the classroom. I will ask you one or two questions *auf Deutsch* and you must answer me *auf Deutsch*. You will be graded from one to five. You need at least a three to pass. Now, let us review."

A large German textbook lies open on his desk, looking as worn and intimidating as the person holding it. Ivan Ivanovich reads straight from its pages, going over the phrases and concepts, and never looking up from his book.

As he continues to drone on, someone elbows me on my right side. I turn.

My classmate, Natasha, leans close to me and whispers, "Maria?"

Natasha's waist-long blonde hair is braided with silky scarlet lace and bows. Her dress looks as if it was made in the factory rather than homemade—with its matching buttons and colors, not a single stitch out of line, not a single stain nor a wrinkle. Her family has helpers to do the manual work, and unlike mine, Natasha's hands and nails are manicured and clean. She is the only girl in town who owns lipstick, which she sometimes shares with her friends.

I am not one of them.

Except for Andrei, the only other Jewish person in my class, most students avoid me, as if being Jewish is something contagious.

So, why is Natasha talking to me now?

I open my mouth, unsure of how to respond, close it, and then try again. "Yes?"

Natasha waves for me to lean in closer and then whispers in my ear, "I'm getting married next week."

I turn around to make sure Natasha isn't addressing the girl on the other side of me. Natasha has never shared her personal information with me directly, although her updates somehow always become class news.

The girl on the other side of me, a member of Natasha's posse, is staring at me as well, as if awaiting my response.

So, Natasha is indeed talking to me.

I figure that I should probably nod, so I do, and say, "Oh. Congratulations! Are you marrying Kolya?"

Natasha shakes her head. "No. I got bored of Kolya. I'm marrying Oleg."

Natasha often grows bored of things. I sometimes wonder if Natasha is only finishing higher schooling to try and outrun her boredom. Unsure of how to reply, I wait for Natasha to continue.

"Well," she says. "I need to receive my diploma tomorrow. I won't want to have to come back and take this class again next year when I'm pregnant, will I?"

I look at her in shock. "Wait, you're pregnant?"

Natasha snorts. "No, stupid! I'm getting *married* next week! Which means we're gonna do stuff and I will probably be pregnant soon, too." She raises her eyebrows at me. "You *do* know how women's bodies work, don't you?"

My cheeks burn and my stomach drops from embarrassment.

"Okay?" I manage to get out, just wanting the conversation to end.

"Well, as I said, I don't want to be coming back here next year while I'm pregnant. This is my last class. I'm failing, but if I pass the oral exam today, I can still graduate tomorrow…" She trails off as if waiting for me to finish her sentence.

When I don't, Natasha groans, exasperated, "Oh, *Bozhe Moi*! I need your help, Maria!"

This shakes me awake.

"You want me to help you *with* the final exam *during* the final exam?"

"YES! So, will you do it? Or will you be a kike about it?"

My shoulders stiffen at this word. "What did you say?"

Natasha waves me off. "Oh, you know what I mean— because Jews are greedy."

I just stare at her.

Natasha rolls her eyes. "Oh, *Bozhe*! Learn how to take a joke, Maria. I was just saying… Look, will you help me or not? I *need* to pass this test!"

I sigh. "Why me?"

"You have the top marks in German." Natasha moves closer and puts her hand on my arm. "So, will you help me? Please?" she asks again.

Papa's voice echoes in my mind, *Good girls are supposed to be nice.*

I glance at the teacher, who is still reading the textbook.

But if I help her, I will be breaking the rules. I'll get in trouble.

I glance back at Natasha's pleading face and remember my grandmother's words. *"You always have choices. And when it comes down to it, I hope you'll choose to be more like the Night Witches."*

I sigh, "Um...yes...okay..."

"Good!" Natasha claps her hands together. "So, what's the plan?"

I look around the classroom. Just behind Natasha, I spot a rag mop leaning against the wall.

"Hand me that mop over there," I say. "You can reach it behind you."

Natasha raises her eyebrows again. "A mop? Why?"

"You'll see."

Natasha reaches behind her and grabs the mop handle.

As Ivan Ivanovich continues to read aloud from the enormous textbook, the rest of the class now shifts their attention to our mission.

"What are you doing with the mop?" Andrei asks, his large blue eyes opened wide.

I glance at him and then back at the teacher, but Ivan Ivanovich keeps on reading aloud without looking up. I put my finger to my lips. Andrei nods in agreement.

Natasha hands me the mop and whispers to Andrei, "She said she needs it."

"Ooh, for what?" whispers Olga, who also sits nearby, and looks far more interested in this than in the exam review.

"You'll see," I say and peek again to make sure that the teacher isn't paying attention. Then I write the days of the week on a piece of paper and rip it into seven pieces, so that each piece has a separate day of the week on it.

"I can use the mop handle to feed you the answers," I whisper to my classmates.

"How?" Andrei asks.

I demonstrate. I open the clasp of the mop handle and remove the filthy rag that is attached to it. I then clip one of my answer sheets to the mop handle and snake it under the table and toward Andrei so that he can read the answer sheet.

Andrei beams, and Natasha claps her hands.

"Will you help me too?" Andrei whispers.

"And me!" Olga says, tugging on my sleeve.

"And me!" other students wink and whisper.

"Looks like you're going to be taking this exam for the whole class," Natasha giggles. "Perhaps after we graduate tomorrow, we can all celebrate at my house. You should come too, Maria."

I grin at her. *Papa was right. If you're nice to people, then people treat you nice.*

It takes another hour before the exam begins, which gives me plenty of time to write out as many answer sheets as I can think of. Ivan Ivanovich still sits at his desk, droning on. But at 9:30, he glances up at the clock, slams the textbook shut, and pulls out the test questions and the gradebook from his desk.

"Andrei Alterman. Come up," Ivan Ivanovich orders.

Andrei pales as he stands, shaking as he approaches the teacher's desk, his back to the class.

"Face your classmates," Ivan Ivanovich commands.

Andrei turns to face us, standing in front of the teacher's desk, gulping, and staring at me with pleading eyes.

I sigh and crawl under the long table toward the front

of the class, my mop handle and numerous answer sheets by my side.

"*Wie viele Monate gibt es in einem Jahr?*" the teacher asks and turns the hourglass to get started.

Andrei glances down, his lower lip quivering, and his cheeks blushing.

I pull out the appropriate answer sheet and attach it to the mop handle with the proficiency of a sniper securing a scope to a rifle. I extend the small tip of the mop handle with the answer sheet from under the desk and toward Andrei.

He looks down and reads out loud, "*Es gibt zwölf Monate im Jahr.*"

"Sit down. Five," Ivan Ivanovich states without looking up from his desk. He records Andrei's grade in his gradebook.

Andrei returns to his seat, grinning, as the teacher continues. "Next. Natasha Belyakova."

Natasha winks at me and goes up to the front.

One by one, student by student, question by question, the magical mop handle receives more use in one day than it has the entire previous year. Ivan Ivanovich never looks up from his desk, focusing only on his roster and on his grade book. At the end of every student's answer, he responds with only, "Sit down. Five."

I DON'T JUST WALK into my house that evening. I dance into it. My father isn't home from the factory yet and Babushka must have gone out, so I have the house to myself. Holding onto the hem of my new dress, I twirl around the room.

I have friends. And tomorrow we'll celebrate and—

There is a knock at the door.

I rush to open it. "Did you forget your keys again?"

But it isn't Babushka.

It's Natasha, standing there with two men in military uniforms.

Their uniforms look grey. Or are they green? It's hard to tell in the nighttime. Each man is carrying some kind of a submachine gun, although I don't know what kind it is. An Iron Cross medal and an eagle symbol with its wings spread over a swastika leaves no questions about their identities.

Fascists.

In a lazy, matter of fact way, both men remove their guns from their shoulders and point them at me.

Oh, Bozhe! What's happening?

Natasha smirks and points at me. "Here she is, officers. Here's the kike."

CHAPTER 5
DOCUMENTS

For a second, I just stare at the two SS officers like a mouse watching a coiling snake—aware of the present danger but unable to move. Then I squeeze my eyes shut, preparing for the sound of the firing gun.

But it doesn't come.

I jerk when one of the officers speaks in Russian, with a thick German accent, "She says you are a Jew."

I open one eye and then another.

My heart pounds somewhere in my throat.

I swallow.

"No," I respond in German, knowing that Natasha wouldn't be able to understand. "She is mistaken. I'm a Ukrainian National. I'm not a Jew."

The two SS exchange glances and then look back to me, still pointing their guns in my direction.

"Documents," one of them demands. He has four *silver pips*—collar patches—on one side of his collar badge and two lightning bolts on the other.

"What?" I ask not because I don't understand the question but to take time to figure out my options.

"Documents," the one with four pips repeats. "Show me your birth certificate."

My heart is pounding so hard that I think I'm going to be sick.

What do I do? What do I do?

I can kick the one closer to me and wrestle out his gun. I can run inside and climb out the back window. I—

The man aims.

"Don't shoot!" I shout in Russian and then switch back to German. "Don't shoot. I have my birth certificate inside. Please, just let me go and get it."

The first man still aims his gun at me and then instructs the second, "Hauptsturmführer Weber, you go with her, I'll stay here."

"Yes, Sturmbannführer," Weber says. He lowers his weapon, straps it around his shoulder, and says, "Go ahead. Get your papers. I will follow you."

"Oh, and Weber," Four Pips says. "If she tries to run, just shoot her."

"Yes, Sturmbannführer Schmidt." Weber nods and follows me inside.

My heart races, my breaths are so shallow that I'm suffocating, and my stomach twists like it's being turned inside out.

Weber's heavy footsteps thunder behind me, each one like a death sentence.

A million possibilities race through my mind, but it's impossible to disentangle a single thread. My eyes frantically dart around my cottage—*my home*—searching for an escape. Despair grips around my throat like a chokehold as I realize there is nowhere to hide.

My papers are hidden behind the stove, along with my father's and grandmother's certificates. And I know that under *Nationality* instead of *Ukrainian* like the documents of most people that I know, our papers read, *Jew.*

Weber clears his throat and plops down on the wooden bench Papa built last year.

I shiver, trying not to look at the stove, and pretend to search under the pillow, the blanket, and under the bed. Then, I walk over to the kitchen area. I pull open one of the kitchen drawers. The butcher's knife glints at me.

My mind floods with violent thoughts once again.

Should I stab him? But what about the other one? Should I take this one's gun after I stab him and then shoot the one outside? And shoot Natasha?

I shake my head as if talking myself out of it.

I can't kill them. But maybe… maybe I can stab myself.

I glance up to the cracked ceiling in a silent prayer.

Mamo? Mamo, if you can hear me, please help me.

The scraping sound of the moving bench against the floor makes me jump. Weber stands up, red lines in his eyes suggesting that he has not slept for days. He rubs his temples. "Have you found it yet?"

"Are you getting a headache?" I ask, ignoring his question. "I have some aspirin if you'd—"

"No!" he snaps, glaring at me. "I do not get headaches."

I outstretch my hands at him. "Okay. Okay."

I pull open the medicine drawer, take out two aspirins, and hand them to him. "Please take them. You know. Just in case."

He stares at me for a few seconds and then snatches the pills from my hand and swallows them dry. "You say nothing of this."

I nod. "Yes, of course."

The door creaks open, and Natasha walks in, followed by Sturmbannführer Schmidt.

"You live in this?" Natasha asks pointing at the bare walls of my cottage.

I don't meet her eyes.

How could she do this?

Natasha's lip curls in disgust. She turns to Schmidt. "If I may, I thank you and thank the Führer for liberating all of us from Stalin's regime and for relocating the Jews away from us. Now we can live and raise our children in safety. Heil Hitler!" She salutes.

"Quiet, girl!" Schmidt says in Russian and then addresses Weber in German. "Find her papers yet?"

Weber shakes his head.

"Alright," Schmidt says.

He pulls the rifle off his shoulder and aims it at me again as nonchalantly as if he is about to clean the dirt off his shoes.

I fall to my knees, pleading in German, "No! I have them. I swear, I have them. Please don't shoot. Please come back tomorrow and I will show you. I'm a Ukrainian National. I'm not a Jew."

Schmidt cocks his gun.

"Wait, what's going on?" Natasha asks in Russian, looking from Schmidt to me and back to Schmidt again.

"Silence!" Weber snaps at her in Russian and then addresses his superior in German. "I believe her, Sturmbannführer Schmidt. Our orders were to kills the Jews, not the Ukrainian Nationals."

Schmidt lowers his weapon, but he doesn't look convinced. "But she doesn't have her papers."

"With all due respect," Weber argues, "if you're right, we can always shoot her tomorrow, but if you're wrong, we can't un-shoot her."

Schmidt sighs. "Fine, I suppose you're right."

He slings his weapon back around his shoulder, and addresses me directly, "You'd better have them tomorrow because if you don't—" He pantomimes shooting me with his fingers. "Bang!"

I jump and then nod, still kneeling.

"Find them," Weber says to me and walks out the door.

"Bang." Schmidt motions again and follows Weber outside.

Natasha looks down at me. "What did they say? Why did they keep pointing a gun at you? And why didn't they relocate you?"

I just stare at her, screaming at her in my mind.

How could you?

But no words come out of my mouth.

Natasha shakes her head and storms out, slamming the door behind her.

I jerk at the loud sound and wipe my face.

All of a sudden, my vision blurs. The walls of the already tiny cottage seem to be moving closer to me. I try to get up but fall back down again.

"Help," I whisper.

And then I shake.

Violently.

I dry heave.

Cold chills spread over me.

What's happening to me?

There is a knock on the door, and everything comes

back into focus. In fact, everything suddenly feels sharper, brighter, and louder than just a moment ago.

Are they back to shoot me?

"Maria?" A man's voice sounds on the other side of the door.

I jump up to my feet and run toward the door. "Papa?"

I fling the door open.

It isn't Papa standing on the other side of it. It's Yuriy, my neighbor.

He steps inside.

I tense up all over again. "What do you want?"

Yuriy walks in, closes the door behind him, grabs my arms and inspects them. "Are you okay? Did they hurt you?"

I shake my head.

Yuriy exhales in relief. "Good. Grab your stuff. We need to move. Now."

I pull my arms out of his hands. "Go where? Where's Papa? And Babushka? I need to wait for them."

Yuriy grabs my shoulders and shakes me. "Look at me. I know you're in shock, but I need you to think clearly. The Nazis took your father and grandmother this morning. I saw it happen. I don't know how you're still standing here. Some guardian angels must be watching over you. But we need to move because whatever you did to make them leave, it won't last for long."

My lips tremble. I hold onto Yuriy's arms to steady myself because my legs threaten to give out. "My... Papa? And Babushka? They were taken?"

I look up at him, barely able to see his face through the film of tears over my eyes.

Yuriy sighs and his grip softens.

"Yes," he says, his voice quieter now. "They were taken while you were in school. I guess it's lucky that you went."

I swallow and Yuriy continues, "I need you to get your things and come with me. We have to move quickly."

CHAPTER 6
YURIY

I n less than ten minutes, I pack my things into a pillowcase—two pairs of stockings, two pairs of underwear, a white cotton handkerchief, a small glass bottle of aspirin, a loaf of bread that Babushka baked yesterday, and two wooden spools—one with black thread and the other one indigo, with a needle wrapped inside of it. I then roll up my birth certificate and stuff it inside my stockings.

Should I leave Papa and Babushka's birth certificates here?

Will they need them if they come back to the house?

No, if the Nazis find these, then we're all dead for sure. Better if they are missing.

I roll up the birth certificates and shove them inside my other stockings, burying them all the way down inside my pillowcase.

I pick up my coat from the nail on the wall.

Should I bring it?

The thought of being gone long enough to need my winter coat makes me weak in the arms and I drop my coat onto the wooden floor. I hurry to pick it up and hang it back on the nail again.

Better to pack light.

I examine the dress I am wearing.

This is my new dress. Babushka made it. I need to take good care of it. I'll keep it on and pack one more.

I stuff my old blue dress into the pillowcase too.

I pick up an old yarn doll that my mother made for my sixth birthday. I squeeze the doll to my chest and then place it back on top of my bed.

I'll be back for you.

I think of Moo-Moo.

I'll check on her in a few days. She has enough hay and water to last a little while.

I try to think of what else I might need, but my mind comes up blank. I give my house one final look.

I was born here. There is a part of me that believed I would always live here. Now I am not sure what to think or where I will be.

"We have to hurry," Yuriy says.

I sigh and walk toward the door.

"Wait," Yuriy says. "Let me check first."

He opens the door a small crack and peeks through it. Seemingly satisfied, he opens it wider, but also raises the palm of his hand, instructing me to wait.

Yuriy brings his finger to his lips, and I nod in understanding. I stay silent as a mouse, awaiting his orders.

Yuriy pokes his head out and looks left and right. The sound of countless crickets fills the cottage. Somewhere in the distance, a dog barks. Aside from that, all is quiet.

Yuriy motions for me to come closer and follow him. I tiptoe behind him in silence for several minutes, the kind of minutes that feel like hours.

When we approach his house, Yuriy motions for me to stop again. He looks around and then walks inside and closes the door. The lights flicker on inside, and his shadow moves about his cottage. A cold chill runs down my back despite the sticky-warm summer heat.

I jump when Yuriy opens his door again. He nods at me and motions for me to come inside.

I have been bringing him milk every day for eight years, but I've never been inside his house before.

I tiptoe inside and glance around. In some ways, it is similar to our own—a small, single-room cottage with a giant masonry stove and a perch for a bed. A crooked, handmade wooden table stands at the corner opposite the stove, surrounded by two wooden chairs.

His kitchen is similar to ours as well—a simple, unpainted wooden cabinet for spices, plates, and towels, as well as a bucket full of fresh water for cooking and washing. Unlike our kitchen, however, his features curtains hung in the doorway next to the cabinet to divide the kitchen from the sleeping area.

The masonry stove with a sleeping perch has a curtain too.

He waves me closer, and I obey.

"You're too compliant," Yuriy says to me. "Being the good, obedient girl you were raised to be could get you killed now. You need to start thinking like a survivor instead."

I just stare at him. I am not sure what I am supposed to say, so I don't say anything at all.

Yuriy lights his pipe before addressing me. "We don't have much time. Give me your documents."

I suck in some air and back away from him. "What do

you want from me? Where is Papa? And Babushka? What will happen to them?"

Yuriy exhales a puff of smoke and nods. "Good. *Good.* Maybe there's hope for you."

I stare at him, trembling, panting, blinking.

What does he mean by that?

Yuriy puffs his pipe for a few moments in silence and then continues, "I have known you since you were nine years old. I remember when your Mamo died." I hold my breath and swallow the memory down as Yuriy continues, "When my wife, my Olechka, died, it was you who brought me bread, salt, and milk. And you've been bringing me milk ever since. It's time for me to repay the favor."

"What are you saying?" I ask, squeezing the pillowcase of my belongings to my chest.

"I'm saying that I'm going to fix your papers for you. But you will still need to leave town. Too many people know you in Vinnytsia." He extends his hand to me but does not approach. "Now, let me see your documents."

As if pulled by an invisible string, I walk up to him without taking my eyes off him. I then fumble around in my pillowcase and pull out the rolled-up papers from my stockings.

Yuriy puts down his pipe, grabs the documents, unrolls them, and inspects them under his kerosene lamp. He separates my father's and my grandmother's certificates. "Right. We must hide these."

He unrolls the third one. "Now, let's look at yours."

He pulls my birth certificate closer to him and examines it. "So, of course, we'll need to change *Jew* to *Ukrainian* but that won't be enough."

I gape at him. "Change? Change how? And what do you mean that it won't be enough?"

Yuriy holds the paper between us, pointing to the relevant lines in the document. "Well, for starters, it would be better for you to have a nice common Ukrainian name that won't stand out. Like," he looks up to his spider web-covered ceiling, "like Natasha, for example."

"No," I say in a sharp tone. "Not Natasha. Anything but that."

Yuriy smirks. "Okay. Not Natasha. How about Anna? That's a pretty common girl's name."

I nod, though I'm still confused by all this. "Okay."

Yuriy points to the next line. "Then there's your last name."

"What's wrong with my last name?"

"Are you kidding me?" He laughs. "Furman? It practically screams Jew. We need to change it to a more Ukrainian or Russian sounding surname."

He sits down at the table puffing his pipe and points for me to sit too.

I sit opposite him. "Like what?"

Yuriy rubs his chin, "Like... Like Furmanova."

I nod, starting to understand now. "Okay."

"And finally," he points to my patronymic, "it says Yakovlevna, so daughter of Yakov. You might as well call yourself a Jewish princess with that in your birth certificate."

I place my palms on the table and look up at him. "So, what should I do?"

He puffs again. "Change it to an everyday, common patronymic. One so common that you become invisible. Like Ivanovna, for example, daughter of Ivan. So,

Furmanova, Anna Ivanovna. Nationality: Ukrainian. That's what your birth certificate needs to say."

I open my mouth to speak but can't, so I close it and then try again. "But—but that's *illegal*." I whisper the last word and look down at my palms, which are gripping the edge of the table now. "It's against the law."

"Look at me," Yuriy says. And when I do, he continues, pointing his index finger in the air for added emphasis, "If there's anything you take away from this madness that's happening here, remember this." He leans closer and continues in a hushed voice, "What's right by the law isn't always the right thing to do. And the right thing to do isn't always the most legal. People aren't meant to be caged or slaughtered like cattle. You're a human being. Not a mouse to be stamped out. And that is why we're doing this."

I swallow the flurry of emotions that are threatening to erupt again and nod at him. "Okay. But how? How am I going to change my birth certificate?"

"Don't you worry about that. I'm going to forge it for you. Years in the city clerk's office taught me a thing or two. Now, why don't you go get some sleep on the stove perch and I'll wake you up when it's ready."

He puts on his glasses and adjusts them on the bridge of his nose, and I play with the skirt of my dress as Yuriy sets out a set of inks, papers, and funny tubes that smell like chemicals when he opens them.

Will it work? Can he actually change my papers?

I was six years old the first time I realized that Jewish people are not listed as Ukrainian Nationals, even if they are born in Ukraine. I was sitting on the stoop outside my house with my friend, Katya, when she asked me, "Is it true that you're a kike?"

I had never heard the word until that point but based on the look of pure disgust on Katya's face, I gauged that it was not something I wanted to be.

I shook my head. "No."

"Let me see your papers then," Katya said.

"My papers?"

"Yeah, your birth certificate. Let me see it." Katya outstretched her hand, waiting for the documents.

I shrugged. "Okay."

I walked in and disappeared inside my house. A few minutes later, I reemerged with my birth certificate, excited to prove Katya wrong. I glanced over it when I fished it out from behind the stove and studied it. Nowhere on my birth certificate did it say the word "kike."

"Here," I said, handing the paper to Katya.

Katya inspected the paper and smirked. "I knew it! You are a kike!"

My cheeks were cold and hot at the same time. "What? It doesn't say that. What are you—"

"Here." Katya pointed to the line that listed my nationality. "It says Jew."

"And?" I asked, confused.

"Jew means kike."

I yanked the paper away. "And what does yours say?"

Katya stood up and tightened her blonde ponytail. "Mine says Ukrainian because I'm a Ukrainian National."

I stood up as well, tears welling up in my eyes. "But... I'm a Ukrainian National too. I was born here."

Katya shook her head. "Nope. You're a Jew. That's your nationality."

She turned away from me and walked toward the fenced door.

I ran after her. "Wait! Where are you going? I thought we were going to play today?"

Katya turned around and shook her head. "My mother doesn't allow me to play with kikes."

After that, Moo-Moo was the only friend I had.

Yuriy coughs and my attention snaps back to the present.

I chew on my lip. "Um, Yuriy?"

"What?" Yuriy says without looking at me.

"What about Moo-Moo?"

He peers up at me from above his glasses and smirks. "You're unbelievable, you know that? The world is falling apart, and you're worried about your cow."

"Please," I manage to whimper as my mind finishes my sentence, *I can't lose her too.*

Yuriy shakes his head. "Fine. I'll take care of your cow. Now get some sleep. You'll need all your strength tomorrow."

CHAPTER 7
THE PREMONITION

*B*abushka hands me the new graduation dress, her face stern and focused.

"Put it on and leave," she says, "and do not come back home. You hear me? Don't come back home!"

A loud bang wakes me, and I jolt up with a start. Another one makes me jump off the perch.

"What was that?" I whisper to Yuriy, squinting from the morning sun.

He puts his finger to his lips instructing me to keep quiet.

Did he sleep in the chair all night?

Another loud bang makes both of us jump.

"Is that … a thunderstorm?" I ask, afraid to know the answer.

Yuriy shakes his head. "No."

My heart jumps.

Another shot fires in the distance.

"Oh, *Bozhe!*" I shout and bolt out the door.

"Wait!" Yuriy yells.

His footsteps close behind me as he shouts, "Wait! Come back, you stupid girl!"

But I pretend not to hear him.

I don't want to hear him. Don't want any of it to be true.

I run toward my home, ignoring the damp grass on my bare feet, then stop a few meters short.

Moo-Moo's body lies motionless, coloring the green grass crimson.

I collapse on my knees and cover my mouth to stifle my scream. I bury my head in Moo-Moo's velvety hide. My head spins and my toes curl all at the same time.

"No! Please, no," I mutter, my body shivering, flashing back to the moment I buried my head in my mother's chest moments after she took her last breath.

"Maria!" The word is more of a hiss than a whisper.

I turn my head and through the thick of my tears manage to make out Yuriy peeking from behind a tree. His wide eyes, his pale face, and a harsh scowl under his drooping mustache are all screaming at me in silence.

He waves at me to come closer.

But I refuse.

Rage boils inside of me. My vision both blurs and narrows at the same time. My pulse pounds in my ears.

I jump up, back away from Yuriy, and run, barely able to see where I am going.

Behind me, Yuriy hisses for me to stop and to come back, but I don't care anymore. I run toward the main road, past the market, and in the direction of my school until I run into a crowd in the middle of a dirt road.

I elbow my way to the front.

What I see makes my knees tremble.

Two women lie dead on the ground. I don't recognize

them. A German militiaman with the SS insignia on his collar stands behind nine other people kneeling in a line, facing the crowd.

The militiaman holds a handgun.

I choke when I recognize Babushka among those kneeling.

Our eyes lock.

Wisps of Babushka's long silver locks have fallen out of her bun. Her usual sparkle is replaced by dark shadows in her brown eyes. Babushka shakes her head at me, silently instructing me to stay quiet, to do nothing, as the SS takes a step towards her.

CHAPTER 8
VICTIMS AND SPECTATORS

Everything around me buzzes with confused words and whispers, but the glance between me and Babushka freezes in time, separate from the commotion of the crowd.

Babushka's eyes are pleading. I can hear her sweet, elder voice, deep inside my heart.

Leave. Run. Save yourself.

I want to scream at them to leave her alone, I want to grab her hand and run.

Bang!

An elderly man, about a meter away from Babushka, falls into the morning grass. I cover my mouth and swallow to keep myself from retching.

I look around me, desperate for someone to do something—for someone older or stronger than me to make things right—but nobody moves.

Someone whispers in Ukrainian, "This isn't right. We should do something."

Someone else says, "What can we do? They have guns."

My eyes dart toward Rosa Viktorovna. She's here, in the crowd too. She is trembling and she is covering her mouth as well.

Several children cry, clinging to their mothers.

But nobody moves.

Is no one going to do anything?

I glance back at Babushka. There are two realities unfolding side by side in front of me—the moment yesterday morning when Babushka tenderly kissed my forehead—and the horror of the present moment.

In the former version, I can still see Babushka—relentless, eternal as she argued with my father, telling him that times for women have changed. Now, in front of my eyes, Babushka looks small, vulnerable, frail and —

Bang!

The man who was kneeling next to Babushka, just a moment ago, collapses onto the grass.

The man who shot him steps behind Babushka and raises his gun.

Bang!

Babushka falls.

I scream.

Or at least, I try to. I open my mouth, but nothing comes out.

I try to move, but I'm frozen. My gaze is transfixed on a set of keys with a pink ribbon in the dirt next to Babushka's hand, mere centimeters from her fingers.

I stare at the ribbon and then close my eyes. Babushka's voice from my dream replays in my mind, *"Do not come back home. You hear me? Don't come back home!"*

I open my eyes and squeeze my fists.

Good. I can move again. I have to leave—but then I see him. My classmate, Andrei Alterman.

He is kneeling in the line too, just a few meters from where Babushka lies motionless on the ground.

Bang!

Another person falls.

Andrei's impossibly long eyelashes seem even longer now, his blond hair disheveled and sticking up in peaks. Andrei's mother kneels next to him; her hands are clasped against her chest, right over left. Her eyes are closed, and her lips are moving, seemingly in prayer, while the SS inserts a new clip into his gun.

Bang!

When the man next to her falls, Andrei's mother opens her eyes and grabs her son's hand. And as Andrei turns his head to face her—

Bang!

I stand motionless but wanting to shout at everyone there—at the SS, at the spectators, at those who are whispering, and at those who remain silent.

Don't you know that these are human beings?

I take a tiny step forward, unsure of what I am doing. Something in me wants to be closer to Andrei, something unwilling to let him, in his last moments, feel alone.

Andrei stares at his mother's body. He is still clutching her hand. He is blinking so fast, as if to try to stop time, or to make it go backward. His expression reminds me of a small, confused child.

The SS behind Andrei points his gun at the back of the boy's head.

"I'm so sorry, Andrei," I whisper.

I squeeze the palms of my hands against my pounding heart.

Bang!

Someone puts a hand over my mouth.

"Don't scream," Yuriy whispers.

I nod. At this point, I can't scream even if I want to.

Yuriy turns me around. "Let's go."

Bang!

The crowd parts to let me and Yuriy through.

Bang!

"Aww, that's it? I thought there would be more," someone says.

And something inside my soul bursts open.

I rip my arm out of Yuriy's hold. "Leave me alone!" I shout and run.

I hear Yuriy cursing behind me.

But it doesn't matter. I just keep running. I run with all the fury and grief inside of me.

Someone steps in front of me and I stop, panting.

I glance up to find the hollow barrel of a handgun pointed between my eyes.

The gun's owner is a tall, wide man in a German uniform with the same kind of double lightning SS insignia on his collar as the man who just slaughtered Babushka, Andrei, and all those people.

"Documents," the man says in Russian.

I shake my head in defiance.

"Stop!" Yuriy yells.

The SS glances in his direction, and I use this moment of distraction to run.

I don't stop when I hear the shouting behind me. I don't stop when there are gun shots behind me, or when a glass bottle laying on the ground, less than a few centimeters away from me, shatters.

Tears fly from my eyes as I run barefoot on the muddy roads, past the thorn bushes that scratch at my knees and thighs, and all the way to the Southern Bug—a long, narrow river, deep, dark, and ominous.

When I get to the shore, I fall to my knees in the sand, shaking, and let out a guttural sob. I don't just cry. I heave. My body trembles with the violence of it. I am sick with anguish that guts my insides.

A few minutes later, I stop shaking. My breath steadies but my thoughts swarm like a hive of bees.

Those people, the ones who stood by, they watched like it was a circus show.

I get up and start walking toward the river.

Did they not know that Babushka was a person?

My steps are more determined now and more purposeful with each thought.

Did they not see Andrei as his mother's son? Don't they realize that we're just like them?

I think of Andrei—shy, kind, and delicate. Andrei, who would sometimes get stomachaches, just like any other kid. Andrei, who feared speaking in front of others more than death. And Babushka, who cheered along with everyone else whenever Dynamo won the soccer match on the radio.

We are all the same. The only difference is the one word stamped on our paperwork the day we were born.

I wipe the snot and tears from my face and dart toward the river.

And if this is a world where they could kill Andrei, kill my neighbors, kill my Babushka — then I don't want to be a part of this world anymore.

I cough and my chest aches, but I don't stop.

If I am going to die anyway, I'd rather it be MY choice.

I race toward the water, ready to put an end to my life.

The only problem is that someone else is already here.

CHAPTER 9
SURVIVAL PACT

A tall, slender figure wearing a long, grey dress marches into the water. I can't see the woman's face, but I can hear her crying.

I scan the beach. Despite the midsummer heat, there is no one else at the river shore this morning, either because it is too early or because of the executions.

The figure in grey advances further into the water.

I curse under my breath.

Girls here often aren't taught how to swim, which is why drowning in the Southern Bug is a common method of suicide for us. I counted on it to put an end to my suffering. Even knowing that it was a popular method, I did not count on it being someone else's plan as well. And something about that gives me pause.

I have to stop her.

"Wait!" I shout, stepping into the cold river.

The girl turns to face me. She looks about twenty, or perhaps slightly older. Like me, she has dark braids, pulled back with a summer handkerchief. Her face is pale and covered in dirt. There are twigs in her hair and blood-stains on her dress collar.

"Hold on just a minute," I shout over the sound of the current and run toward her. My bare feet ache, as I step on sharp gravel. My dress is now wet and heavy, but I keep walking toward the other girl. "Just wait for a moment," I call again, panting.

The girl shakes her head. She is shivering. Her lips tremble and as I step closer to her, I notice a large green bruise under the girl's eye.

"Just leave me alone!" she shrieks over the tumul-tuous rushing of the current. She turns away from me and charges deeper into the river.

"Wait!" I pant after her. "I can't swim."

"Neither can I," the girl says without turning around, "that's the point."

"You can't kill yourself!" I shout, advancing after her. The water is now above my chest.

"Actually, as it turns out, I can," the girl spits back. "Now, get the hell out of the water or you'll drown too."

"Look—" I say, trying to catch my breath, "I'm Jewish. And I think you are too."

The girl stops walking and turns around. She is chest-deep in the water now, like I was a moment ago. "And?"

I stop walking too. "You can't kill yourself." The water is up to my lips now, and I get a mouthful of it when I speak. I spit some of it out and get on my tiptoes to avoid any further ingestion.

The girl rolls her eyes. "Why exactly?"

I bite the inside my lip before responding. "Because... because that's what I was going to do."

The other girl stares, pressing her lips into a white slash. She takes a long breath and then speaks again.

"Look, kid. I came here for a reason, and I just need you to get out of my way. So, how about you go over there—" she points to her left, "and I go over here—" she points to her right, "and we won't have a problem."

"No!"

"Don't you see?" the other girl says, her voice breaking. "They've already taken everything from us. This is the one thing we still have control over. It's the one thing they can't take away."

I take a tiny step toward her, balancing on very tips of my toes, barely clinging to a rock that's slightly higher than the ones around it. "For a moment I thought that too. It's easy to think that. It's easy to lose hope. It makes sense that we want this suffering to end. But at the same time, this is also the one gift we have left that's ours. And maybe by staying alive—" I take another step toward the girl and reach for her.

But the current intensifies and sweeps both of my feet off the rock I have been standing on.

My head slips under the water.

I try to get back up but can't find my footing on the slippery rocks.

I can no longer tell which way I need to stand, which way is up, and which way is the river floor. I squeeze my eyes shut. A new kind of panic spreads through my body like quick poison.

This is it. This is how I'm going to die.

Two strong hands grip my arms, pull me up, and help me to get on my feet again.

I wipe my burning eyes, cough, and spit out the water from my mouth.

When I am finally able to open my eyes, I see the same girl standing in front of me, shaking her head. "This has got to be the most embarrassing suicide attempt in history of the world," she says and then bursts out laughing.

I exhale in relief and find myself laughing too, mostly from nerves.

"C'mon. Let's go," the girl adds and pulls me by my arm.

The closer we get to the shore, the heavier my dress is and the more my feet ache. I trip several times, but the other girl grips my arm tighter, helping me to secure my balance.

When we reach the shore, we fall onto the sand, panting.

For a few minutes, neither one of us speaks. Then the girl asks, "What's your name?"

"Maria. You?"

"Lyuda," she says.

"I'm glad you didn't kill yourself."

Lyuda snorts. "It seems like I just can't die today."

I stare at her. "What do you mean?"

Lyuda sits up, her face looking grim and somehow much older than it did a minute ago. "My mother tried to have mercy on us last night—me, my two younger sisters, and my grandma. She turned the gas on and said that it would be more peaceful than what was waiting for us."

My heart pounds again. "What did you do?"

Lyuda shrugs. "What could we do? We all wrestled with her to turn the stove off. Then, we all cried."

"And then?" I ask.

"And then my mother begged me to leave. I refused." Lyuda spits on the ground. "They all got taken when I went out to the well this morning."

Oh, Bozhe! We are the same. We are both alone now.

I sit up and kneel in front of Lyuda. "Do you realize that we are all that we have now?"

Lyuda rolls her eyes. "Kid, I just met you. That doesn't make us friends. I tried to protect my little sisters by staying here and look where that got me. Besides, one or both of us will probably be dead by evening. Our papers make it very clear who we are, and we are just as dead without them as we are with them."

"Not necessarily." I tell Lyuda about Yuriy's offer.

Lyuda listens carefully, then tilts her head to the side in thought after I have answered all her questions. "And you think he'd be willing to do that for me?"

I nod. "Just promise me that we will both look out for each other."

Lyuda shakes her head. "Kid, I can't promise you that. I'm in no place to take care of anyone."

"Don't call me a kid," I say, pouting.

Lyuda laughs. "Fine. I will call you *Mouse*. Better?"

"Why *Mouse*?" I ask, brushing the sand off my dress.

Lyuda shrugs and smiles. "It seems fitting. You're very short and timid." She gets up. "We should go somewhere where we are not in such an open view."

I get up too.

I need her. But I think she needs me too.

"Promise me that we will survive together," I say. "Promise me, Lyuda."

Lyuda, who towers nearly fifteen centimeters over me, looks down, shakes her head, and gives an exasperated sigh, but not without a sideways smile. "Fine. I promise."

We shake on it.

CHAPTER 10

INSPECTION

Lyuda and I spend the day hiding out by the cliffs. When I take off my new dress to dry it in the sun, I gasp. Patches of wet sand and mud span across it in multiple spots. To make matters worse, several stitches on the embroidered roses have come loose. My fingers caress the scarlet threads as if trying to comfort them, as if trying to hold Babushka's hand one more time.

I'm sorry, I say to Babushka in a silent prayer. *I'm so sorry. I will fix it just as soon as I am able.*

It must be well past nine o'clock by the time we sneak toward Yuriy's house. The sun has just set, and we move quickly to take advantage of the nightfall. I just hope that my stomach isn't growling loud enough for us to draw attention to ourselves.

Yuriy opens the door and gives me a sideways glance.

"Ah, if it isn't the wayward girl. And oh, look. She brought a friend."

Yuriy looks over my shoulder at Lyuda. He stares her up and down, scowling.

Is he angry? Will he not let us in? Did he change his mind?

"Yuriy, this is Lyuda," I whisper gesturing back at my new friend and trying to keep my voice as calm as possible. "I'm sorry, Yuriy. I shouldn't have run. I panicked."

"Oh, just get inside already before someone sees you," he snaps.

I sigh with relief.

Yuriy lets us in and locks the door behind us.

Lyuda's shoes, still wet from the river, squish as she walks across Yuriy's floor. She approaches his wooden table and takes a seat at one of the chairs in front of it. I sit at the chair opposite her and slip on the sandals I left here this morning.

"Oh, sure. Make yourselves as home," Yuriy says with sarcasm in his voice.

He walks toward the masonry stove and pulls out my stuffed pillowcase. "Catch," he says and throws it at me.

I reach for it and miss. The pillowcase collapses onto the floor, its contents spilling on the ground.

My cheeks burn.

"Not good at catching, are you, Mouse?" Lyuda says and gets up to help me pick up my belongings.

My heart leaps at the sight of a package wrapped in brown paper.

Bread!

I pull out the loaf and place it on the table. The three of us surround it, eyeing the bread as if it were made of precious stones.

"Here," I say and split the loaf into three.

I hand each one of us a piece.

I bite into my portion and my eyes well with tears.

It's *our* bread. It's the bread that Babushka baked two days ago. No one else could bake like her.

It tastes sweet. And salty. And crunchy. And chewy.

It tastes warm, even though its actual temperature is not.

It tastes like home.

I close my eyes and chew in silence. We all do.

Yuriy is the first to speak. "Right. Okay. I assume you came here for this."

He takes out a folded piece of paper from his back pocket and hands it to me.

I unfold it and read:

Surname: Furmanova
Given Name: Anna
Patronymic: Ivanovna
Date of birth: 20 March 1923
Place of birth: Vinnytsia, Ukraine
Nationality: Ukrainian

I read the paper over and over again, unsure how to feel. Having the *right* birth certificate weighs against the bitter taste of disgust in my mouth at having to deny my true heritage.

"Thank you," I say to Yuriy, forcing myself to smile.

"Don't mention it," Yuriy says. "And I've got something else for you."

He hands me a small pink ribbon. "Someone must have grabbed your grandmother's key. Perhaps hoping to loot your house? Who knows? But I found the ribbon outside on the ground and figured you might want it."

My hands tremble as I reach for the ribbon. I cradle it

in my hands and pet it as if it were a newborn kitten, just as Babushka used to pet me.

"I can wash it for you if you'd like," Yuriy offers, pointing to the mud stains on the ribbon.

I shake my head. "No. No, thank you."

I sniff the tiny pink band. It still smells like Babushka's blintzes.

It's all I have left of her. This and my dress.

I squeeze the ribbon one more time and then tuck it into my pillowcase.

Yuriy turns to Lyuda. "I assume you'll be needing documents too?"

"No, I'll just trust the nice Nazi men to take my word for it," Lyuda says with obvious sarcasm in her voice.

Yuriy folds his arms. "You wanna try that again?"

Lyuda rolls her eyes and shoves her papers at him.

Yuriy snatches them and grunts at her, "You're welcome, your majesty."

A knock on the door makes all three of us jump.

"Open up. Inspection," a man's voice demands in German.

CHAPTER II
RATS

There is another knock, a louder one this time. "Open your door! Inspection!" the same voice roars, this time in Russian with a thick German accent.

"Don't make a sound," Yuriy whispers and then shouts toward the door, "Just a minute! I'm getting dressed."

He motions for us to follow him. We all freeze when Lyuda's shoes squish again. She slips them off and carries them under her arm.

My heart pounds so loudly that I'm sure the SS outside can hear it. I get on all fours and crawl on the floor to avoid making any sound. Lyuda follows my lead, her earlier surly demeanor suddenly gone, replaced by silent obedience.

Yuriy beckons us toward the center of the room and pulls back a dusty striped rug to uncover a tiny hook underneath it. He carefully pulls the hook up to reveal wooden steps. They lead down to an underground cellar.

Someone pounds on the door again. "Open up or we'll break the door!"

"Coming!" Yuriy shouts and turns toward us. "Hurry. Get down there and don't make a sound," he whispers.

He closes the trap door behind us, and we step into darkness. Above us, we hear Yuriy's footsteps leading out to the front door, as the two of us creep down the six wooden steps to the bottom of the cellar.

I extend my hand to feel for the shelving and use my other hand to guide Lyuda behind me.

Above us, someone says, "Documents," and then after a quiet pause, "Anyone else here?"

"No, officer. Just me," Yuriy says.

I hear heavy footsteps thudding on the cabin floor above us. Yuriy and whoever was at the door. Dust from above seeps into our eyes and noses as they walk. I pinch my nose so as not to sneeze and focus on breathing through my mouth.

"The neighbor girl, have you seen her?" a gruff-sounding man with a German accent asks.

"Can's say that I have," Yuriy says. "Why? What'd she do?"

"She's a Jew," the same man says, his footsteps stopping somewhere right above our heads. "And anyone hiding Jews will be treated the same way as the Jews themselves."

"She brings me milk every morning," Yuriy says. "Try coming back tomorrow morning, 'round six. You might catch her then."

There is a pause. And then slow movement of footsteps again. "Well, if you see her, detain her."

"Understood," Yuriy says.

Something brushes past my foot. Something bigger than my foot. Something with a tail.

I gasp and kick it away from me. The rat squeaks and knocks over a low-standing glass jar.

The glass shatters.

Strawberry jam judging by the smell of it.

I suck in a breath.

"What was that?" the German man asks from above.

I squeeze Lyuda's hand, and she squeezes back. Whatever is going to happen, it's going to happen to both of us.

Above us, the German man asks in Russian, "What was that? Do you have a basement in here?"

"No. No basement," Yuriy replies.

There is a shuffling of feet and then, "What is that? A door? You said no basement."

"I did," Yuriy says. "I do not have a basement. Just an old moldy cellar."

"Let's have a look then."

I take a big breath and pull Lyuda's hand behind me. The two of us feel our way around the shelves in the dark.

They're going to find us. We're dead.

The cellar door flies open above us and soft light floods the cellar.

"Be my guest," Yuriy says, "but I'm warning you, it's full of rats down there. You're welcome to exterminate them, in case you provide that kind of service."

There is a long, quiet pause.

I imagine the SS staring Yuriy up and down before he speaks again. "That was your first and only warning. The next time you speak with disrespect, we will shoot you."

We, I think in horror. *There's more than one of them.*

"My apologies," Yuriy says.

The SS ignores him and addresses someone else in German, "You two. Go check the cellar. If you see anyone down there, shoot them."

"Yes, Oberscharführer Krüger," another man says, and two sets of footsteps descend the creaking steps. I count each one of them in my mind.

One.

Two.

Three.

The steps creak louder, booming in my ears.

Four.

Five.

I hold my breath.

Six.

As the first SS comes down the stairs, all the senses in my body become hyper focused. It is as if everything moves in slow motion while my brain functions at triple the usual speed. Each time the SS men take a step forward into the cellar, Lyuda and I take a step back into the shadows, taking care to match our steps to those of the SS men to mask any sound.

When we turn the corner around one of the shelves, I pull Lyuda's arm down, and we both crouch down on the ground.

Babushka, help us, I pray silently.

Backlit by lantern light, the dark shadows of the SS tower on the wall right next to us like a nightmare. The outlines of their guns are so long, it seems impossible they could fit in the cellar at all.

Lyuda wraps her arms around me and I hug her back. I can feel Lyuda trembling, both of our hearts pounding in harmony.

I look up, shaking.

I see the barrel of a gun emerge on the other side of the shelf, inches from my face. I also feel something scurry over my feet.

There's a loud gasp.

Bang!

Bang!

Lyuda and I huddle together, clinging to one another, each covering the other's head with her arms. But neither one of us screams.

"What was that?" Krüger demands from upstairs.

The SS closest to us curses under his breath and the other roars with laughter.

"Brauner shot a rat," the one further back manages to report over a fit of laughter. "He got scared of a rat."

"It caught me by surprise," Brauner retorts before adding, "No matter. There's no one here. Let's go."

Moments later, two sets of footsteps ascend. The trapdoor slams shut with a bang, wrapping the cellar in a thick layer of darkness like a soothing blanket on a cold winter night.

I let out a long breath, and only now realize that Lyuda's nails have been digging into my arm the entire time. I place my hand on top of Lyuda's and the other girl loosens her grip.

We squeeze our hands and breathe together, both shaking and panting in relief.

Above us, voices are still conversing, but my brain is too flooded to make sense of what they are saying now. A few minutes later, the footsteps march above us again and then the front door opens and slams shut. I count the seconds in my mind, just to give my brain something to focus on.

Three hundred and eighty-two seconds later, the

trapdoor above us opens once again and Yuriy peeks inside.

"They're gone," he whispers. "You two okay?"

"Yeah," Lyuda whispers for both of us.

"Good," Yuriy says. "Stay there. I'll tell you when it's safe to come out."

And with that, he closes the trapdoor again.

CHAPTER 12
PARTING WAYS

The first thing I see are Babushka's big brown eyes. My eyes lock with my grandmother's as everything else blurs by us, running at triple the speed. *Babushka kneels in a line, staring at me.*

She speaks directly to me, so that I am the only one who can hear her: "Promise me that you will survive."

I bite my lip before responding, "But Babushka, I can't promise you that."

Suddenly everything goes dark and cold, and it's just the two of us in a dank, gloomy cellar.

Babushka shakes me by my shoulders, the contours of her body barely visible in the light of the cracked open door. "Promise me, Maria. Look me in the eyes and promise me that you will survive."

I feel a chill running throughout my entire body. My voice quivers as I speak. "All right. I promise."

"Good," Babushka says, the outline of her body barely visible now.

"Don't go, Babushka," I beg, tears running down my cheeks, "don't go."

"Mouse." Someone is shaking me. "Hey, Mouse."

I jerk awake in the darkness.

Lyuda's arms are around me. "I think you had a bad dream."

I shake my head, even though Lyuda can't see it. "No. Not a bad one. Just... just sad."

The trap door above us creaks open.

We both jump up and hide behind one of the shelves until we hear Yuriy whisper, "Come on up. Quietly."

I sigh in relief and Lyuda does too. We climb up the creaking stairs and into Yuriy's kitchen.

Lights from the kerosene lamps dance in their containers, casting long shadows on the walls. I squint my eyes, the brightness making me wince after many hours in the dark.

Lyuda yawns. "What time is it?" She rubs her eyes, and I notice that she is squinting too.

"A little after two in the morning," Yuriy says. He's carrying a bundle in his arms. He gives me my pillowcase, then he hands us several apples and a handful of walnuts, as well as twenty rubles for each of us. "Take these. For emergencies."

We stare at him, but neither of us moves. Yuriy extends his arm toward us. "Go on. Take them."

My chest swells. "Thank you. But this is too much."

"Shut up and pack them," Yuriy orders.

I give him a smile. "Thank you again." I pack my portion of the food and the money into my pillowcase.

Yuriy also gives Lyuda a pillowcase for her belongings.

"Thanks," she says and stuffs her things into it.

"And here, take this too," Yuriy says, handing her a piece of paper.

Lyuda holds it near the light and reads it silently. I peek over her shoulder to read it as well. In her hands, Lyuda holds an official birth certificate with *Ukrainian* written next to her nationality, right below her new name, *Romanova, Lyudmila Aleksandrovna.*

"Hey, how come she gets to keep her first name, and I don't?" I ask.

"Her name is more Russian sounding than yours," Yuriy explains and then addresses Lyuda, "What do you think?"

Lyuda takes a few breaths as if to steady her nerves. Then she looks up at Yuriy. "You don't even know me, but you saved my life. Thank you." Her voice breaks as she speaks.

Yuriy waves her off. "Ah. Don't thank me yet." He leans in closer. "Now, listen to me very carefully, both of you. You need to leave Vinnytsia immediately. Whatever you do, do not come back here until this is all over. You can't risk being recognized."

"Where should we go?" Lyuda asks.

"The Nazis are coming from the West," he says, "so, you need to go East. Go into a small village. Use your papers to get work and to make sure people know you with your new identities. This way, should the Nazis go there, you'll have many people to vouch for you without risking their lives. Besides, some say that the SS are checking city clerk records to find out where Jews live. Most villages don't keep birth records. Not yet anyway. So, go to a village and stay there. Try not to move around too much. Don't attract attention to yourselves."

Both of us nod.

"Yuriy? How long do you think this will last?" I ask, unsure if I want to hear the answer.

"How long what will last?" he asks.

"All of it. The occupation. The executions," I say.

Yuriy shakes his head. "Hard to be sure, but I imagine somewhere around three, maybe four months. Six at the absolute most."

"That's such a long time," I whisper, grasping at my chest. "And in that time, they will continue to kill all the Jewish people they can find?"

Yuriy lowers his head and nods but doesn't say anything. The three of us sit in silence for several minutes. When he looks up again, I am surprised to see some wetness in Yuriy's eyes.

He takes a big breath. "You two need to leave now, so that you can get as far as you can. If anyone stops you, tell them that you two are cousins, going to visit your sick aunt in Uman."

"Got it," Lyuda says.

"One more thing," Yuriy adds, "your new identities—memorize them. Your new names, surnames, and your patronymics, know them better than your own."

We both nod.

"Now go," Yuriy says.

I feel a strong urge to hug him the way I would hug Papa before his long trips. But I am not sure how proper it would be to hug Yuriy, so I don't.

"Thank you, Yuriy, for everything," I say instead and walk out the door.

Lyuda follows me. And when I turn around, Yuriy waves at us one more time before he goes back into his cottage and closes the door behind him.

"Ready?" Lyuda asks.

I nod. And together, we walk into the darkness.

CHAPTER 13
NEMYRIV

The unyielding sun swelters and burns my skin by the time we reach the Nemyriv Village. My feet are blistered and swollen. We have passed several farms. I am depleted, and unable to walk much further, but I don't dare say anything. I don't want to give Lyuda any reason to leave me behind.

"I need a break," Lyuda finally says and collapses in the shade of a weeping willow.

"Me too," I say, relieved, before collapsing next to her. I only intend to close my eyes for a second, but soon I am drifting off to sleep.

A mooing sound startles me awake.

"Moo-Moo?" I mumble, rubbing my eyes. My vision is still blurry.

Someone elbows my side.

It's Lyuda.

I stare at her for a moment, the events of the last two days etching themselves into my brain like razor blades.

A cow moos again, and I turn in its direction.

Not one, but four cows graze a few dozen meters from

where we are resting. A small boy of about six years old watches the two of us with his mouth open while he picks his nose.

Lyuda gets up and approaches toward him.

"Hi, little boy. What's your name?" she asks in Russian.

The boy stares at her, still picking his nose, but doesn't respond.

"Try Ukrainian," I suggest.

"What's your name?" Lyuda asks in Ukrainian.

The boy stares at her but doesn't say anything.

"His name is Kostya, and he can't hear." A man's voice comes from behind me.

I spin around. A tall, thin, older man, wearing brown trousers stained with grass, and a sweat-covered white shirt is walking toward me.

The man swats a few flies away from himself and takes another step toward me before he stops. He looks me up and down and then Lyuda.

"You're not from here," he says in Ukrainian.

"No, we're not," I say.

He nods at us. "City girls, are you?"

He's onto us. Will he sell us out to the Nazis?

I force myself to nod. "How did you know?"

He points to my dress. "Your clothes. These aren't farming clothes. What are you doing here?"

I stare down at my dress. The skirt of it is so wrinkled, it is as if a cow has chewed it.

Babushka would be so mad if she could see me now. I've had the dress for not even three days, and it's already wrinkled, fraying, and—I bend down to examine the bottom flounce—is that a stain?

I rub the darker black circle on the bottom of my dress. It's hard and sticky at the same time.

I sniff it. It smells sweet.

It's the jam from the cellar.

The dress suddenly feels as heavy on me as it did when I stepped out of the river.

I stand up straight and take a slow breath to recenter myself before responding, "We are looking for work. Do you know anyone who is hiring?"

The man pulls a blue Belomorkanal cigarette pack out of his pocket. He takes out one of the cigarettes, lights it, and takes a long, lingering inhale before he replies, "What are your names?"

"I'm Anna," I say, careful to use my new name, just like Yuriy taught me. "And that's Lyuda. What's your name?"

"Fyodr Stepanovich," he says, sending a cloud of smoke toward me. "You can call me Fedka. Anyway, I hear the Germans are hiring. Good jobs in Germany for young people."

Is this a joke? Does he know that we're Jewish? Or am I just being paranoid?

"We were hoping for something a little closer to home," Lyuda says and walks back toward me.

Having her next to me steadies me, and I exhale some of my fear.

Fedka clicks his tongue. "Too bad. I hear they're good jobs too. So much the Germans have done for our country."

"What?" I snap before Lyuda elbows me to keep quiet.

Fedka puffs his cigarette again. "Didn't you hear? They're getting rid of the Soviet rule in Ukraine." He points to his cows. "I raised these cows. I take care of them. But the Soviets say that they're communal cows and therefore, I must give *them* my milk. But the Germans—they say we get to keep our cows. And our land too. Thank the Lord for capitalism and the Germans for liberating us." He takes another puff. "Now, you were asking about work?"

We both nod.

"Got any papers?" Fedka asks.

Lyuda and I exchange glances and hand him our documents. My heart pounds when Fedka inspects them.

Will this work? Will these pass for the real ones?

Fedka nods and hands the papers back to us. "Happy birthday, I guess," he says to Lyuda.

"Huh?" Lyuda asks and then catches herself, "Oh, that's right. It's my birthday. Silly me."

"I tell you what," Fedka says. "You two take care of my chickens, my cows, and my stable today and I'll give you each a piece of bread with salo. After that, we'll see."

"One slice of bread with a measly piece of beef fat?" Lyuda snaps.

"Pork fat," Fedka corrects her. "Take it or starve."

"We'll take it," I say before Lyuda argues any further. "And might we possibly ask for a place to sleep?"

Fedka eyes me before he points toward a stable. "You can sleep in there. Plenty of hay for the two of you."

"Thank you," I say and pull the disgruntled Lyuda with me to the stable.

CHAPTER 14
POTATO JUICE

The sun has long set by the time we are done for the day and have settled in the haystack inside the stable. The moon glints through the cracks in the wood, the only source of light we have. I shudder to think about how cold it will be if we have to stay here through the winter.

The barn door creaks open, and the twinkle of light dances as Fedka walks in, carrying a plate in one hand, an oil lamp in the other.

"Here," he says and hands us the plate, which holds two slices of black bread, each topped with a piece of thin, raw salo. "And also, here." He hands Lyuda a small, uncorked glass bottle from his trouser pocket. "Happy birthday. My wife, Olena, won't let me drink it. It's our last one but you might as well have it."

"Um, thanks," Lyuda says.

We exchange glances and Lyuda shrugs.

Fedka nods and hands us the lamp. "Don't start a fire now, hear?"

We both nod and Fedka limps out of the barn.

"What are we going to do?" I ask.

"About what?" Lyuda asks picking up her sliced bread with salo.

I point to the salo on top of my piece of bread. It looks oily and smells like cooked meat. "That." My stomach growls. I am not sure if I am disgusted or hungry. Or both.

Lyuda raises her eyebrow. "What?"

I point to the salo. "It's pork fat." And when Lyuda doesn't respond, I say, "It's *pork.*"

Lyuda shrugs. "What are we going to do? We are going to eat it." She eyes me and adds, "Look, we just need to survive right now. Don't you know anyone who died in the Holodomor?" She asks, referring to the famine.

I shiver at the memory. "My Mamo."

Lyuda sighs. "My condolences. And I'm sure that she would have wanted you to survive in any way possible."

I feel a tug inside my stomach. "But... but we aren't supposed to eat pork."

Lyuda glances up at me. "There are a lot of things people aren't supposed to do. Not all rules are meant to be followed. People aren't supposed to be executing people either but here we are," she says reminding me of what Yuriy said earlier. "Besides, salo is high in nutrients. We need as many of those as we can get right now."

I stare at her. "I don't know."

Lyuda rubs the tiny piece of salo over her entire bread slice as if painting a delicious meal with her finger. I notice that the exposed parts of Lyuda's bread are now coated with a thin layer of fat.

Just like Babushka's freshly baked buttered bread.

Lyuda bites into the salo-covered bread. She closes her eyes as she chews and lets out a satisfied moan.

"Good?" I ask, feeling my own mouth water.

"So good," Lyuda says. "You should try it."

I weigh out my options. *What would Papa say if I do it? What would Mamo have said if I don't?*

My mind flashes to the last moments of my mother's life —seeing Mamo's ribs protruding from her dress. *How did I not notice how thin she'd gotten?*

Eat, moya dorogaya, Mamo would say to me on countless evenings.

And you, Mamo?

I'm so full, I will burst, Mamo always said, although I could have sworn that I heard her stomach grumble.

After a few minutes of reminiscing, I sigh and rub my own piece of salo around my slice of bread. I then slide the salo off the bread and bite into the "buttered" slice. It tastes chewy, oily, and deliciously crunchy at the same time.

I'm a bad Jew. I should not be enjoying this.

I hand my salo slice to Lyuda. "Take it, I don't want it."

Lyuda nods. She breaks off a small piece of her remaining bread and hands it to me. "Fine, then you take this. We'll trade."

I wave her away. "No, no. That's yours."

Lyuda shoves the bread into my hands. "Take it. Besides," she holds out the bottle of vodka, "we need some food in our stomachs if we're going to drink this."

I scrunch my nose. "I don't know about this. Do you even like vodka?"

Lyuda shrugs. "Never had it. You?"

I shake my head. "Me neither. Papa tried to get me to taste it once, but it smelled terrible, and I didn't want to."

Lyuda snorts and points to the bottle. "Well, now's

our chance to try something new. Happy birthday to me, I guess."

I chuckle. "When is your actual birthday anyway?"

"September twenty-eighth," Lyuda says.

She brings the bottle up to her lips and takes a small swig. "Bleh." She scrunches her face as she swallows it. "Oof. That's disgusting."

She makes a gagging motion and then hands me the bottle. "Have some."

"Are you insane? You just said that it was disgusting."

Lyuda shoves the bottle into my hands. "You need to try it. We need all the calories we can get."

"I thought vodka doesn't have many calories," I say.

"Don't argue with your elders," she says and burps. "Besides, vodka is essentially potatoes—just very processed ones."

I grin. "Very processed." I bring the bottle to my face. "Ugh. It smells terrible."

"Try it."

I sigh and take a small sip.

As soon as I swallow it, I cough and gag. My entire mouth stings. My throat stings. My eyes water. "Eww. It's revolting. Why would anyone drink that?"

"Gimme," Lyuda says and pulls the bottle away from me. She raises the bottle as if giving a toast. "To potatoes!" she says and takes another swig.

She squints her face and shakes her head as if trying to shake the disgusting taste out of her mouth. She grunts and hands the bottle back to me. "We need the calories. Trust me. Drink."

I sigh again and raise the bottle. "To potatoes."

I take a larger sip this time. This one doesn't burn as

much as the first one, and it feels warmer going down my throat.

By the fourth sip, I am starting to giggle. "It's like I'm eating bread and I'm drinking potatoes. Not a soup. But like... like a juice! Potato juice. With alcohol." My eyes tear with laughter.

Lyuda sneers, "Is this what you always dreamed of when you were little? Sleeping in a stable and drinking potato juice?" She takes another big sip.

"No, silly," I say, pulling the bottle toward me. I take another big swig. "I always—" I accidentally spill some of the vodka on myself. I ignore it and continue, "I always wanted to be a princess." I smooth out the pleats of my dress. "A royal princess." I hiccup. "I know it's not very communist of me to want to be a princess, but don't worry, I'd share all my wealth. And all I actually want is to wear a tiara."

"Is that all?" Lyuda asks, starting to slur her words.

"Yep." I hiccup again.

"Well, why didn't you just say so?"

Lyuda gets up and nearly falls over in the process. She stumbles toward the opposite wall of the stable.

One of the horses neighs as she passes by.

Lyuda shushes it with a finger to her mouth, "Shh. Don't be rude. Others are trying to sleep. You have no respect for other people."

"A horse is not a people," I giggle.

"You have no respect for *people*," Lyuda corrects herself and makes her way toward the opposite wall, swaying as she walks.

"Where are you going?" I ask in a loud whisper, clutching the empty bottle to my chest like a teddy bear.

"It's a surprise," Lyuda whispers back.

She returns a few minutes later with several newspapers she must have dug out of the trash.

"What's that for?" I ask.

"You'll see."

Lyuda folds the newspaper sheets several times to make a long, thin band. She bends it into a circle and folds the corners together.

"There," she says, placing the newspaper circle on top of my head. "You have a tiara. So, now you're a princess and all of your wishes have come true."

I feel my eyes water again. "A princess? Me? Really?"

"Yep," Lyuda says and plops down in the hay next to me. "You're Cinderella. And I guess that makes me your fairy godmother."

"Pfft." I burst out laughing. "A fairy godmother. A *Jewish* godmother to a Jewish communist princess," I shout in Yiddish.

"Shh," Lyuda says. She sits up, looks around, and whispers, "Quiet. They'll hear us."

I tense up all over and look around as well. "Who?"

"The evil stepsisters."

"Pfft!" I fall back into the hay, laughing.

It's the most I've laughed since the day Mamo died.

CHAPTER 15
I CAN FEEL THE EARTH MOVE

T hey are all lined up on their knees. *Behind them towers a man with short, blond hair, a stern expression on his pale face. His ice-blue eyes are devoid of pain or empathy for any of the human beings he slaughters.*

One. By. One.

What is going through his mind?

What is going through the mind of every person this man stands behind right before he pulls the trigger? Do they remember the birth of their first child? The angst of their first date? The fear of failing a final exam? Do they remember running to their mother for comfort after scraping their knee on the harsh earth? Do they long for someone to hold their hand right before—

Bang!

The blazing flash from the gun barrel burns into my eyes. Everything is too bright. And then too dark.

I sit up with a gasp.

Did I get shot?

Am I blind?

"Mouse?" Lyuda's voice sounds groggy in the darkness. "What's the matter? You okay?"

I clutch the top of my head with my palms. "Did I get shot?"

"What? No." I feel Lyuda grab my hand. "Did you have a nightmare?"

I open my mouth to answer but excruciating throbbing in my head stops me from being able to make a sound.

Did I get shot?

The sound I heard felt so real that my ears are still ringing from it. My head is pounding over and over as if a woodpecker is trying to hammer a hole in it.

I groan and squeeze my hands over my eyes. My whole body convulses and contorts, and I collapse down on the hay again.

"Whoa," I hear Lyuda say as she pulls my hands off my face. She looks blurry; the image of her is going in and out. "Seriously, are you okay, Mouse? What's the matter?"

I am starting to tremble now. "My head...hurts." All of a sudden, I can't stop my body from shaking. I gasp for breath. "What's... happening...to me? Am I... dying?"

Lyuda wraps her arms around me and cradles my head to her chest. "You're okay. You're just a little hung over. And I think you're having a bad attack of the nerves right now."

I squint open one of my eyes at her, still shaking. "A what?"

"It's okay. It's an attack of the nerves," Lyuda says in a soft, calming voice. She pats my head as if petting a small kitten. "You'll be okay. It happens. And it will pass. Try to get some sleep. Everything is going to be okay."

I keep shaking but feel my body calm as Lyuda

soothes me, holding me in her arms and stroking my head just like Babushka used to do. My whirlwind of thoughts is slowing down with each pet.

Am I dying? … Am I losing my mind? … Will Lyuda leave me?

I keep shaking until sleep takes over once again.

When I wake, my head still hurts but it no longer pounds.

"She's alive! It's a miracle," Lyuda proclaims, standing over me. Her voice booms over the raucous sounds of the midsummer crickets.

I groan and sit up.

The ground spins under me, and I grab onto Lyuda's ankle for stability.

"I think I can feel the Earth move," I mumble. "It's spinning."

Somehow, I am both nauseated and hungry at the same time, wanting to gorge on food but also repulsed by the thought of it. My lips are cracked and dry.

"Water," I groan.

Lyuda crouches down next to me. "Here." She shoves a metal mug of water into one of my hands and an aspirin into the other. "Take it."

I place the pill into my mouth and chug the cold water until the mug is empty.

I wipe my mouth and fall back down into the hay. "Thanks." I let out a long breath. "Where did you get the water?"

"There's a well about two kilometers away. I borrowed the mug from Fedka," Lyuda says. "Now sit up. I need you to eat."

I prop myself up onto my elbows. "Huh?"

Lyuda unwraps a small newspaper package she had

on her lap and takes out a piece of rye bread and a small, boiled potato. She breaks each food item into halves, and hands me my portions. "Eat."

I gawk at the food and then at her. "Where did you get these?"

Lyuda grins at me. "Where do you think? Fedka paid me."

The pain of realization hits me like a sledgehammer. "I slept all day. And you—" I gape at Lyuda, "you worked all day. For the both of us."

My stomach drops. *She should just leave me. I'm just a burden. A sick, stupid burden.*

Lyuda snorts. "I suppose instead of Cinderella, I should call you Sleeping Beauty."

I don't respond at first because the huge lump in my throat makes it difficult to speak. Instead, I hug my new friend as tight as I can until I am able to conjure up the energy to whisper, "Thank you."

Lyuda pats me on the back. "Don't mention it."

The two of us eat in silence, trying to eat as slowly as possible, trying to pretend that we are eating more than we are.

It doesn't work, and that night we fall asleep with our stomachs rumbling.

CHAPTER 16

MONSTERS IN
THE PALACE

"Hey, we got to celebrate my fake birthday, but we never got to celebrate your real one," Lyuda says to me on a hot August afternoon.

She is holding a white enamel basin in her hands as the two of us pick raspberries for Fedka. My mouth waters at the sweet smell of the ripe and juicy berries, a stark difference to the scratchy bushes they grow on.

I sneeze and wipe my face with my sleeve, careful not to touch my face with my sticky hands.

"Oh, it's no big deal, it was back in March," I respond and sneeze again.

I pull out my handkerchief from the sleeve of my dress and blow my nose. I try to ignore the fact that my dress hangs looser around my arms and waist now than it did two months ago.

It looks different now too. There are several stains on it and more of the embroidery is fraying. I patched up some of the loose scarlet stitches with black thread since I don't own any red. It makes the dress look more macabre than it did when Babushka first made it for me, but I don't mind. It still reminds me of her. It's still a part of her.

I sneeze again.

"How long do your allergies last?" Lyuda asks before she sneaks a couple of berries into her mouth. "Your eyelids look like you've been stung by bees."

I sneeze again. "Most of the summer, especially if I'm in the garden. Part of the reason why I always hated gardening, really."

"All right, that's enough. You hold the bowl now. I'll pick the rest," Lyuda says and sneaks another berry into her mouth before shoving the bowl into my hands.

"You need to stop eating them," I say, trying to ignore the sweet smell of the raspberries. It doesn't matter if I am congested, I can always smell raspberries. "Fedka will notice. He pretty much counts them."

Lyuda shoves another berry into her mouth with a look of defiance. "It's not like he's paying us. We work way too hard for a slice of bread, a measly potato, or an occasional piece of salo every other week, which you don't even eat. So, the way I see it, allowing us to eat a few berries before he has to give the stack to the Germans is the least Fedka can do."

"But—"

Lyuda shakes her head. "Don't argue with your elders. Now, be a good girl," she winks at me, "or should I say a naughty girl, and enjoy a few berries. Live a little."

I giggle and sneak a berry into my mouth, feeling naughty and excited at the same time.

She's right. It's just a few berries.

"I meant what I said earlier," Lyuda continues. "Let's celebrate your birthday."

My cheeks flush. "I don't need to—"

But Lyuda isn't listening. "I didn't know you when you had your last birthday, and we don't know if either one of us will be alive for your next one. So how about it, Mouse? What would you like to do for your birthday?"

I sigh. "Fine."

My mind flashes to the times that Babushka and I would pick sunflower seeds together. We would gather the flowers, bring them home, and hang them out to dry. Then we would rub the sunflower heads together over a bucket and collect the dried seeds. My favorite moment was when the four of us—Babushka, Papa, my brother, and me—would eat the sunflower seeds together in our front yard and gaze at the stars.

This memory makes my chest ache. *My poor Babushka. She didn't deserve to die like that. And my brother, is he still alive? And Papa? What happened to him?*

I would do anything to have one more moment with them. One more memory.

I glance up at Lyuda. "For my birthday, I would like to have some sunflower seeds."

Lyuda nods. "Got it. Anything else?"

I shake my head. "Nope. Just been craving some sunflower seeds and, maybe, a picnic."

"Craving, eh?" Lyuda teases. "Are you having your period or something?"

"No," I respond. "I haven't had my period since—" I lift my gaze to the sky, trying to remember, "May? I think. So, over three months now."

Lyuda whistles. "And I thought it was just me."

I feel a cold chill traveling down the middle of my back. "What does it mean?"

Lyuda puts her hand on my shoulder. "Don't worry about it, Mouse. It happens sometimes."

But something about the way that Lyuda avoids my gaze makes me feel uneasy.

"Do you think we're sick?" I ask, feeling my heart speed up in my chest. "Is this because we're not eating enough? Are we going to die?"

Lyuda grabs both of my shoulders now and gives me a big smile that doesn't reach her eyes. "It means that we are going to get you some sunflower seeds." She hands me the bowl. "I'll be back in a bit. Don't ask questions."

I nod and don't ask anything further. Lyuda nods back and walks out of the garden.

LYUDA WALTZES into the stable later that night. "Hey. Guess what?" Her eyes shine in the moonlight.

"You've been gone for hours, where have you been?" I snap, feeling guilty and self-righteous at the same time.

I put down the cup I've been polishing over and over with my hankerchief for the past four hours. "I thought the Nazis got you."

Lyuda giggles. "You were worried about me."

"Was not!"

Lyuda snorts. "Whatever you say, *mom*!" She grabs my hand and pulls me outside. "C'mon. I have something to show you."

I sigh and follow Lyuda up the moonlit road.

"Where are we going?" I whisper after fifteen minutes of silence between us.

"You'll see," Lyuda says, her voice pitched high in excitement.

My heart pounds in my chest again, but I don't ask any more questions. The cacophony of frogs and cricket songs drowns out the sound of our footsteps. We turn a corner and get on one unfamiliar road, and then another.

We turn one more corner and I gasp.

There, in front of us, is a real-life palace. Royal white columns support the snow-colored balconies. Round arches outline enormous windows fit for a queen. White marble lions sit atop marble pedestals as if guarding the entryway.

"Whoa. What is that?" I ask.

Lyuda grins. "Surprise! It's a palace. A real princess used to live here. Princess Maria Scherbatova, from what one of the local kids told me. Anyway, it's a museum now... Was... Technically, the Nazis live there now."

I tighten my fists. "The Nazis live there?"

Lyuda nods and plays with her long braid before answering. "Yeah. Moved in a few weeks ago, apparently. Makes me wonder if you and I should start thinking about going East toward Kyiv. Mamo used to tell me about this cathedral, the Kyievo-Pecherska Lavra. She said it has these underground caves, and chapels, and even living quarters. I thought we could maybe live there."

I stare at her. "Leave here? Go to Kyiv? Why?"

Lyuda shakes her head and tosses her braid behind her. "Forget I said anything. We're fine here."

But my stomach clenches like it always did right before Papa would yell at me. Something isn't right. "What aren't you telling me?"

Lyuda waves me off. "Honestly, don't worry about it. I just wanted to show you the palace. You said that you always wanted to be a princess, so I thought that as a princess, you should see a real palace in real life." She grins. "Happy birthday, Mouse."

I feel an uneasy warmth of gratitude spreading across my chest. Lyuda found this palace just for me, but she won't tell me why she's thinking of Kyiv, of leaving, and that makes me nervous.

"Thank you," I manage to say, still wrestling with trying to understand my conflicting feelings.

Lyuda beams at me. "Don't mention it. Now, sit."

She plops down onto the grass under a nearby bush and pats the ground next to her. "Sit, silly. We are having a royal birthday picnic for you."

I kneel next to her and squint. "Not with potato juice though, right?"

Lyuda laughs out loud. "Not with potato juice."

She reaches over to the bush next to her and pulls down two sunflower heads that she must have hidden in there earlier.

"Happy birthday, Mouse," Lyuda says with a big grin and hands one of the sunflower heads to me.

My eyes burn from gratitude. *I can't believe she did this for me. No one has ever done so much to celebrate my birthday.*

I grin back at her. "Oh. Thank you." I squeeze the sunflower to my chest like an old friend. "Thank you so much."

We lean against each other, and I chew on the raw sunflower seeds, which taste sweet, oily, and nutty all at the same time. My body feels less tense with each seed.

Snuggled under the stars next to Lyuda, I watch the moonlit palace that once belonged to a princess and try not to think about the monsters that live there now, or the secrets I suspect Lyuda is keeping from me.

CHAPTER 17
HOPE AND PILLOWCASES

The chill of the crisp September night still lingers in the air. It makes me shiver, even though I still feel the warmth from the spot next to me in the hay where Lyuda was sleeping earlier.

The air smells of damp earth, old straw, and horse manure. My vision is still coming into focus as Lyuda is storming around the stable.

"Pack your pillowcase, we're leaving," Lyuda says.

I sit up and rub the sleep out of my eyes. "Huh?"

But Lyuda darts around the stable and doesn't answer. A mouse scurries by her, but Lyuda doesn't seem to notice. She is frantically grabbing her things from around the barn—hair pins, an extra pair of stockings Fedka's wife, Olena, gave her, other things that I can't see from my angle—and stuffing them into her own pillowcase.

I force myself to get up and shift from foot to foot to stay warm. The cracked wood floor feels like ice even in my stocking-covered feet. Still groggy, I slide into my sandals and smooth out the bottom of my blue dress. I try to use my graduation dress as little as possible now, lest it get any more stains or holes in it.

I shiver again and plunge my hand through the film of ice in our wash water and splash my face.

"What's happening?" I ask Lyuda from across the stable. "What's wrong?"

Lyuda grabs my pillowcase and throws it to me. "Pack. Now. We're leaving."

I run toward her and grab her arm. "Lyuda? What is it? What's happened?"

She grunts but doesn't respond. She tears my pillowcase away from me and shoves my graduation dress inside it, as well as my extra socks and stockings.

I get in front of Lyuda, grab her arms and pull her in for a hug. Lyuda pushes me away, dropping both our pillowcases, their contents spilling out onto the floor.

Lyuda curses under her breath, bends down and starts reloading the pillowcases. I sigh and watch her silently. A few moments later, Lyuda answers without looking at me, "More executions. In Vinnytsia. It's all over."

I feel sick to my stomach. "Oh, *Bozhe*! How do you know?"

Lyuda stands back up and faces me. "Fedka's cousin, the one that can read, he had a newspaper. Anyway, we're going to Kyiv. Right now. We'll find that cathedral. The caves. We'll hide out there for a while."

I gape at her. "Go to Kyiv? Why? You said we wouldn't have to—"

"I didn't want to worry you," Lyuda interrupts.

I fold my arms across my chest. "So, you *have* been keeping secrets from me."

Lyuda rolls her eyes. "Don't start. Pack."

I don't move. "Yuriy said not to travel much and to stay where people know our new identities."

Lyuda grips both of my arms and shakes me. "Mouse, the Red Army is in Kyiv." Her eyes shine as she speaks. "It's our only chance." She picks up my pillowcase off the floor and throws it at me. "Finish packing."

My hands are trembling so much that I almost drop the pillowcase with all of my possessions.

Will it work? What if the Nazi's catch us before we get to the Red Army? Even if we make it, will things be any better when we get there? What if things are worse?

I'm not sure leaving makes sense, but Lyuda is so determined I'm afraid she might leave without me if I don't hurry.

Mirroring Lyuda's energy, I grab my sewing kit—my needle and my two spools of thread. I stick the needle inside the black thread spool, which looks much thinner now from the numerous times I've had to patch my clothes and Lyuda's.

If we are going to see the Red Army, I'd better put on my best dress.

I change out of my plain blue dress and into my graduation one, still my best dress even though most of the red roses now have black thread in their stitching. The dress also features several new carefully embroidered black and blue designs to cover the rips and tears it has gained since Babushka gave it to me.

Each new design I've added is a loving message to my family. I've stitched a blue clef note over a small black threaded square to honor my mother. I added a black spade over a blue patch to remember my brother Pavlik, and all the card games we played together. I added a small black tiara over one of the roses as a tribute to my father to remember the time he called me a princess. And I sewed my grandmother's key ribbon into the dress, folding it to become a single pink rose.

I smooth over some of the wrinkles and run my fingers over each of the new stiches.

It's like I'm wearing a hug from each of you, every time I put it on, I think, trying not to let Lyuda see my eyes well up with tears.

"Hurry up, Mouse," Lyuda snaps. "Why are you just standing there?"

I rush to fasten my dress. I am stretching my hands behind my back to push the single black button through the wide eyelet, but my hands tremble so much that I keep missing the hole.

"Let me," Lyuda says and buttons my dress behind me before spinning my arm to turn me around. "This dress hangs on you like a potato sack."

I glance down and frown. She's right, the dress is indeed a much looser fit now.

How embarrassing. I will be meeting the Red Army looking like this. Maybe there's a way I will be able to take it in a little.

I grab the walnuts Yuriy left us and stuff them into my pillowcase as well.

My head is spinning. *This is happening so fast.*

"What about Fedka?" I ask Lyuda. "What about our job? And food?"

"Already took care of it," Lyuda says as she continues gathering our belongings. "I talked to Fedka. He wasn't happy about it, but I said we're going to visit a sick aunt, just like Yuriy told us. Fedka won't be able to hold our jobs, but he was nice enough to give us some bread and potatoes to bring along."

She points to a bucket filled with a loaf of bread and six raw potatoes. She empties the contents of the bucket into her pillowcase.

"He gave us all of that for free?" I ask.

Lyuda shakes her head. "Not exactly. More like in exchange for money."

I feel a storm bubbling up inside me. "You mean the money that Yuriy gave us? You spent our money without asking me?"

Lyuda snaps her head in my direction. "Yes, because one of us has to make the adult decisions around here."

"What is that supposed to mean?" I fire back.

Lyuda takes a step toward me. She takes a big breath. "Look, I'm sorry. Okay? I shouldn't have said that, and I should have consulted you first. But this is our best bet. We're malnourished. It will only get worse in the winter. Our summer sandals won't do. And where will we get winter clothing?"

I feel my toes numb from the cold. "And you think the Red Army will help us?"

Lyuda shrugs. "I don't know."

I fold my arms across my chest again. "Then what is the point?"

Lyuda takes another step closer to me. "Look, Mouse, I know you're scared. I'm scared too. I won't lie, this is a big risk. But I think we are taking a bigger risk by staying here."

Memories of the executions flash before my eyes.

Whatever might happen has got to be better than that.

I take a big breath and nod. "Okay. Survival pact?"

Lyuda smiles. "Survival pact."

CHAPTER 18
KYIV

I t takes us four and a half days to reach Kyiv. We stop at random villages to do barn work in exchange for a place to sleep.

"We will rest when we get to Kyiv," Lyuda says on the third day of our journey. "We will get all the sleep and food we need. Because once we get there, Mouse, when we get to the Pecherska Lavra Cathedral, we can hide out there. When we get there, we will be free."

I grin at her, my entire body warming despite the chilly air at this one word, *free.*

I imagine playing cards with my brother like we used to when we were children, *free*, without worrying about being executed for a single word written on our birth certificates.

Free to sleep, play, and be.

Free.

"How will we find Pecherska Lavra?" I ask. "Do you know what it looks like?"

Lyuda glances up as if trying to remember. "My

Mamo told me that it's almost 100 meters high, so we can't miss it."

We learn more about Pecherska Lavra along the way.

"If I remember correctly, it's close to the Dnipro River," an elderly man tells us when we stop him in Zolotukha. "It's got a big golden tip and an enormous bell tower."

"So, once we get to Kyiv, we should be able to see and hear it?" Lyuda asks.

"Should be," the man says and limps away.

During the next morning, I notice the golden, green, and scarlet leaves are becoming scarcer, dry leaves crunching under our sandals as we walk, and the small houses are more densely clustered together.

"We must be getting close." Lyuda grins.

Free, I recite silently to myself and smile back at my friend.

But as the sight of smoke comes into view, my stomach tightens and I feel dizzy, as if I'm about to fall out of a tree. "Something is wrong."

We continue walking into town. Soot and ash cover what at one time must have been sunlit streets, smoke now blocking out the sun and making the late September morning feel like the dead of night.

"What happened here?" I ask.

"I... I don't know," Lyuda says with a stutter. She clears her throat, rolls back her shoulders, and grabs my hand the way my Mamo used to do when I was little. "Let's go. Let's find Dnipro. Once we find the river, we'll find the cathedral."

We speed up toward the river. And there, glinting in the pools of sunlight, I see the golden tip of the bell tower.

My heart springs in my chest. I can barely breathe.

We made it. We're free.

"There it is!" Lyuda shouts. "I told you we would find it. Quick!"

We run toward it, but as we get closer, we stop short.

The cathedral's entrance has been blown out. Large columns that must have once stood upright lay strewn about like fallen tree-trunks, their depictions of Eastern Orthodox Saints cracked and broken. The ornate stained-glass windows are shattered into a million shards, like a stadium of bloodied glass. One of the massive golden domes has collapsed onto the pavement, cracked into tiny sparkling pieces.

No!

I gaze up at Lyuda and am shocked to see tears in her eyes. "What do we do, Lyuda? What do we do?"

Lyuda stands up taller, sniffles, as if inhaling her own tears, and says, "We will figure it out. Let's go."

I allow her to lead me away.

My world feels suddenly hazy, like stepping into a waking dream. I feel detached from my body, as if I am watching my life from a distance. Terrifying thoughts crawl into my mind as I ask myself over and over: *Is it real? Or am I losing my mind?*

Many of the buildings we pass are also in ruins. We pass structures that have been decimated—huge, gaping holes where apartments should have been, walls replaced by chunks of rubble, foundations laid bare. Others look unscathed but have swastika flags hanging in their windows instead of people's curtains.

But what strikes me the most is the deafening silence all around us. No children playing in the streets. No adults chatting on the boulevard corners. No dogs chasing one another through the alleyways. I can only hear the shattered glass from blown windows crunching under our sandals as we walk.

As we continue along the main road, I glance off to the side at what I guess must have once been a majestic opera house. Now, it is barely the frame of a building. Charred pieces of a grand piano are scattered throughout the rubble.

Several meters from us, lying in the middle of the street, next to someone's abandoned shoe, is a bloody sleeve. Flies buzz around it. I step closer to it.

The sleeve isn't empty, I realize. There is still an arm inside it.

"Don't look at that," Lyuda says and pulls me away. "C'mon, let's get off the streets."

We turn the corner and walk until we find a narrow alley. We are both coughing from the soot and I try not to stare at a lump down the alley, which is probably a decomposing corpse. The quick glance I do spare in its direction makes it clear that it is partially eaten. *By rats, maybe?* I think.

Lyuda looks around. I follow her gaze to a small figure hunched over a few hundred meters away. The figure gets back up and then crouches back down again.

"Let's go," Lyuda says to me and runs toward the person.

"Wait!" I shout and run after her.

As we get closer, I realize that the figure is a very thin girl of no more than fourteen. She has long, lanky limbs, thin brown hair that barely reaches her shoulders, and a gaunt face. Her tattered green dress hangs off her narrow shoulders. She has her back to us as she digs through the remains of one of the bodies, pulls something out, and shoves it into a dusty brown pouch.

"Hey," Lyuda calls after her.

The girl freezes. Then she slowly turns to face us, her hands up in surrender.

"We're not going to hurt you," Lyuda says. "We don't care that you're looting. We just want to talk. What's your name?"

The girl lowers her hands and nods. "Vera."

Lyuda takes a step toward her but when Vera flinches, Lyuda backs away again. "Okay. Don't worry. I won't come any closer."

Vera nods.

"We just want to know if you know where the Red Army is," Lyuda says.

My thoughts are racing. *Oh, Bozhe. Why did Lyuda ask her that? What if that girl works for the Nazis or for the politsei?*

Vera stares from me to Lyuda and back to me again. "You don't know?"

"What?" Lyuda and I ask at the same time.

I suck in my breath as Vera explains, "The Red Army surrendered earlier this week. Kyiv is under German control now."

CHAPTER 19

SCORCHED EARTH

My vision blurs again. Lyuda's and Vera's voices fade in and out, and I feel like I am battling a persistent dream.

Vera says something about, "The tanks ... aircrafts" and then Lyuda says something I can't make out.

The two voices blend and blur, and I am struggling to follow.

"Bombs ..."

"Surrendered ... looting"

Is that still Vera talking? Or Lyuda? I am no longer sure.

"Red Army ... Scorched earth"

"What does that mean? How is the earth scorched?"

I really thought it would be over. I thought we would be free. How could I have been so naïve?

I close my eyes. It hurts too much to keep them open.

There's a familiar gentle whisper in my ear. "When you play music, it's like you are transported to another world. A world where everything's okay. A world where you are safe."

I place my tiny hands above my mother's and together we begin to play.

It's the Dog Waltz.

The silliness of its tune makes me giggle. I glance up at my mother, who sticks out her tongue at me, making me laugh even more, as we keep on playing. We split out hands and share the keys, where I am playing the higher right side as my mother takes the left.

"Mouse! Mouse, can you hear me?" My mother's voice sounds urgent all of a sudden.

I jerk up.

A distorted face stares back at me.

There is a nose.

Eyes.

The lips are moving.

"Mouse! Talk to me, are you okay?"

The strange facial features morph together. They look familiar.

Mamo?

No, not her.

Lyuda.

"Lyuda?" I whisper.

Two firm hands guide me to sit down on the ground. My vision and my hearing are still going in and out.

What's happening to me?

The voice sounds like it's coming from underwater. Or from another world. "Mouse? Mouse, look at me."

Lyuda's face is still going in and out of focus as she speaks. "Look at me. Follow my finger with your head if you can hear me."

Lyuda's index finger comes into focus as the rest of her is still blurred. It takes all my strength to follow it.

I turn my head once from left to right. For a moment,

my vision comes back, and things come back into focus, and then blur again.

I'm going to be sick.

"Stay with me, Mouse," Lyuda says. "Try it again."

Again, I follow Lyuda's finger and turn my head from left to right.

Once. Twice. Three times. Four times.

I take a big breath.

Everything comes back into focus again, including Lyuda's worried face with her wide-open brown eyes.

"Better?" Lyuda asks.

I nod. "Much."

Shaking my head four times. I have to remember this technique.

Lyuda takes a long sigh of relief. "Good."

I take in our surroundings. We are alone again. "Where's Vera?"

Lyuda whistles. "She left about 20 minutes ago. Where did *you* go in your mind?"

I shake my head, unsure of how to answer that. "Nowhere."

I scan around, desperate for some signs of life.

A large sign posted on the wall of one of the standing buildings catches my eye. My head is still in a fog, but I force myself to walk over and read it.

The sign depicts the same information in both Russian and Ukrainian:

All the kikes residing in Kyiv and the nearby regions must appear on Monday, 29 of September 1941 at 8 in the morning on the corner of Melnikov and Docteriv Streets (near the cemetery).

Bring with you your documents, money, and valuables, as well as warm clothes, undergarments, etc.

Any kikes who do not follow this order and are to be found in another location will be shot. Any citizens who sneak into the empty apartments left by the kikes and try to loot any items left behind will be shot.

My mouth falls open as I read the sign over and over. I am not sure exactly when Lyuda comes up next to me. I don't realize that I've grabbed Lyuda's arm and have been digging my fingernails into her flesh until she cries out, "Watch the nails!"

"Sorry," I mumble, easing my grip.

I watch Lyuda's lips move as she reads the sign too and watch her face pale.

I gaze back at the sign and read the date again. *Twenty-ninth of September. That's tomorrow!*

A cold chill runs down the middle of my spine. "Where are they taking them?" I ask.

Lyuda shakes her head. "I don't know. The work camps maybe? Or maybe Siberia?"

I glare at her, but I can barely see her through the rage in my eyes. "They're sending them away. From their homes. From their loved ones. Sending them to death camps."

"You don't know that," Lyuda protests.

"Are you serious?" I snap in a loud whisper. "Do you not remember what happened to your family? And mine? Even the children?"

"Shh," Lyuda whispers, grabbing a hold of my arms. "You're right, okay? It's terrible. And in this very moment, there's nothing we can do about it. So, let's find a place to stay for the night and then we will figure out what to do."

Does she actually care? She might be able to carry on like nothing happened, but I still have a soul.

116

"Fine, whatever," I retort, break free of her hold, and start to walk away.

Lyuda grabs my arm and spins me around. "Are you seriously throwing a tantrum right now in a city crawling with Nazis?"

"I don't even care anymore." I fire back.

I realize that I am being unreasonable, but I can't help it. I'm angry and I just want to leave. To run away. From everything. Anywhere but here.

Several options for taking my life flash in my mind again but before I can entertain them, Lyuda puts her hands on my shoulders.

I open my eyes to look up at her. I didn't even realize that I'd closed them.

Lyuda leans down, so that we are eye to eye now. "I get it. Okay? This is hard for me too."

I throw Lyuda's hands off me. "Is it? It sure doesn't seem like it."

Lyuda takes a slow breath, looks around to make sure there isn't anyone around who could hear us and then leans in to face me again. "I know that I put on this *act* like I'm fine. But that's just how I cope. The truth is that I'm *never* fine. Only a heartless monster would be fine right now.

"I don't know how I'm going to make it from one day to the next. This war! These executions—they make me want to kill myself every single day. But I don't. And you know why? Because of our survival pact."

Oh, she does care. She suffers too. But she hides it to keep living.

My chest swells and warms, although I also feel guilty that Lyuda's suffering is comforting for me. Maybe it's just knowing that I'm not alone in this. It's not that I'm weak. She struggles too.

The two of us stay still for a few moments before I break the silence. "I'm sorry."

"Don't mention it," Lyuda mumbles and then looks up at the sky. "We'd better find shelter soon. It looks like it's going to rain."

Dark, violent clouds fill the sky, invading the sun and pillaging the stars, consuming them one by one, like a vicious curtain, covering up even the smallest glimpses of light, or hope.

CHAPTER 20
ACES AND WALNUTS

The two of us walk up to a small wooden cottage. It's the last house on a long dirt road.

Lyuda knocks.

There's a shuffling sound, and then an elderly woman opens the door a few centimeters. She is wearing a green *platok*, a stained floral long-sleeve dress, and a frown.

"I'm not hiring," she says.

"But you don't even have to pay us," Lyuda argues. "We just need a place to stay."

The woman shakes her head. "You need a permit to employ people now, especially if you're hiring workers for more than a week. The Germans are knocking on everyone's door. Checking everyone's papers."

Lyuda and I exchange glances.

What are we going to do?

"Please, just for one night," Lyuda pleads. "Can't you just say we are your granddaughters if anyone asks?"

The woman eyes us up and down in suspicion. "I don't know you. For all I know, you could be trying to trick me and get me into trouble."

119

I bite my lip, pleading with the woman with my eyes, just as Lyuda is pleading with her words. "Please. Just for one night. We are just two young girls trying to survive."

Tears form in the old woman's eyes. Her tone is softer now. "God forgive me. I can't. I have a sick husband to take care of. My neighbor's husband was nearly lashed to death for being too sick to go to work. The other neighbor, Borya, got his leg shot off by an angry German. He had a limp, you see, Borya, and the German must have thought he was trying to get out of working." She shook her head. "They're strict. Too strict. I can't risk it."

She slams the door in our faces, making both of us jump.

THIRTY MINUTES LATER, we still have no luck finding a place to sleep—the residents are all too terrified to take in strangers and unregistered workers.

Thunder rolls again, making my heart leap. My legs ache in my summer sandals and my head is so heavy that I expect it to fall off my neck and roll down the hill we are currently climbing.

"Maybe we should just find a place to sleep in one of the alleys?" I suggest, trying to stifle a yawn.

Lyuda shakes her head. "We'll get cold and wet and probably die of pneumonia." She looks around. "Maybe we can sneak into one of the stables."

I stop walking. "You can't be serious," I whisper.

"Completely serious," Lyuda says and pulls me by my arm. "C'mon, let's go."

I want to protest but can't find the energy. I follow

Lyuda as my vision starts to blur again. Nothing seems real anymore.

Was any of it ever real? Is this a dream? A nightmare?

It doesn't seem any more or less real than when I was still in my family home, playing cards with my brother. It was ten years ago, but it seems like both much longer ago and much more recently, as time blends the seams of my memories.

"So, the Ace beats the King?" I ask.

Pavlik nods. "In Durak, the Ace is always the highest, except for the trump suit, so Spades in this case."

"So, which card from the trump suit beats the Ace of another suit?" I ask, squeezing the corner of the Six of Spades card between my fingers.

"Any of them," Pavlik says with a smile.

"Ha!" I exclaim placing my Six of Spades over his Ace of Diamonds.

"Well played," Pavlik says with a smile, as he scoops up the cards and places them in the discard pile. "This game is about strategy, about knowing your opponent. And so long as you play the cards in a smart way, you can win just about any match."

I grin back.

"Did you hear what I just said?" Pavlik asks, his expression becoming serious now.

"Huh?"

The memory of him dissolves like a wispy cloud.

"Did you hear what I just said?" Lyuda asks, squinting at me.

I blink at her but don't understand what is happening.

What was that technique again?

Oh, right.

I shake my head left to right and count. *One. Two. Three. Four.*

Lyuda shifts into focus again.

"Sorry," I say and stare down at my toes, which are starting to turn blue from the cold.

Lyuda takes another big breath. Her tone reminds me of the one Babushka used when she was trying very hard to remain patient. "I said that it was very nice of Olga Mihailovna to let us stay here."

"Who?" I ask. "I thought we were going to sneak into a stable?"

Lyuda lets out an exasperated sigh. "We *were* until Olga Mihailovna here," Lyuda points at a middle-aged woman I haven't noticed until now, "caught us and said she'd let us stay in her stable for a night if we cleaned it."

I give Olga Mihailovna a half-smile. "Thank you."

"Follow me," Olga says and leads us to the stable. She is thin and pale, and her coat seems too big for her. "Quickly, before the storm starts."

We follow her into the stable and I sigh with relief. *We have a warm place to sleep.*

There's a pig pen in one corner and beautiful horses in another. Olga points to the black horse in the back. "That's Amur, and the brown one is Indrik. I expect you to take good care of them. You can sleep in the hay."

"Thank you," Lyuda says. "That works for us."

"I'm sorry I can't feed you," Olga says. "The Nazis took most of our food away. I barely have enough for me and my kids. My husband was taken to the front a few months ago. This is all I can offer." She points to the stack of hay and hands us a kerosene lamp.

"We understand," Lyuda says. "This is perfect and very generous of you."

Olga nods and walks out of the stable, as thunder rumbles in the distance.

I plop down in the hay and try to rest. A few minutes later, I can feel my toes again, and with them, a sense of reality returns as well. I feel the tension release from my shoulders. I didn't even realize how tense I was.

I pull my pillowcase closer to me, untie it, and pull out one of the walnuts Yuriy gave us two months ago.

"Happy birthday, Lyuda," I say. "Your actual birthday, that is."

Lyuda whistles. "I didn't even realize that it was today." She looks from the walnut back to me. "Wanna split it?"

CHAPTER 21

BULLETS AND THUNDERSTORMS

Thunder rumbles in the sky like enemy fire. Lightning flashes and fills the stable with an eerie, piercing light.

Twice when I am awakened by the roaring thunder, I could swear that I see the figure of a man—but whenever I sit up to get a closer look, the figure vanishes.

"Listen to me, Maria," an urgent voice says to me in Yiddish.

I jerk up again. Now, I see him—Pavlik.

My brother.

I gasp. "Pavlik? Is that really you?"

There is a bloody stain in the middle of his chest, but Pavlik does not seem to care or notice. "Maria, whatever you do, stay here. Hide. Stay until the thunder stops. And then, you run."

"What?" I ask, blinking so much that it makes me dizzy.

"Promise me," he says. Blood gushes down his chest.

I feel a rising panic in my own chest.

"Pavlik!" I scream.

"Are you okay?" Lyuda's sleepy voice sounds right next to me.

"Was it a dream?" I ask and look frantically around the stable.

It must be morning, because the sun beams through the windows, but the air is still cold. I hop out of the hay, walk across the stable, and step out the door. Raindrops fall onto my face from the tree branches swaying in the wind even though the rain itself seems to have stopped some time ago.

Lyuda walks up next to me. "Mouse? What is it? What's going on?"

I pull my friend back inside the stable and share my dream with her.

"What do you think it means?" Lyuda asks when I'm finished.

I am shivering all over. "I don't know. He said to wait until the thunder stops. And it already stopped. So, does this mean that we should go now?"

Lyuda shifts from foot to foot. "What if it was just a dream? What if it doesn't mean anything?"

I shake my head. "No. It was real. It was *too* real." My eyes widen in realization, and the horrible feeling in my chest feels like I am drowning all over again, just like the first time I met Lyuda. I collapse onto the floor. "Oh, *Bozhe!*"

Lyuda kneels next to me. "What is it? What's wrong?"

My lips tremble as I speak. "Pavlik! My brother. I think... I think he's dead."

As soon as I utter the words, I know them to be true.

My own chest and my own heart feel like they are bleeding too. Like a part of me is dying with him. I close my eyes as tears burn my cheeks, a scream stifled deep in my throat and chest.

The tight pressure in my chest is so familiar. When Mamo died in the Holodomor famine eight years ago, my chest felt like this too. I had bronchitis at the time and couldn't stop shivering from grief and fever.

While Papa and Babushka were at work, Pavlik made me potato soup, boiling our last potato.

"Eat," he said, bringing a wooden spoon to my lips. Red cherries and golden leaves were painted on the inside of the spoon and its long handle was painted the color of gold.

"What about you?" I asked.

My throat hurt when I spoke, but the warmth of the hot soup made my chest feel better.

"I ate earlier," Pavlik said, his growling stomach betraying his lie.

I tilted my head, trying to make sense of it. "When did you eat? You've been at home all day and we don't have—"

"I said I ate," he snapped, making me jump and spill some of the soup on my dress. He sighed and continued in a softer tone but without meeting my gaze, "And in any case, you're really doing me a favor. If you don't finish the soup, it will go bad, and Papa will be angry." He glanced up at me. "Now, come on, eat. You need your strength."

Lyuda wraps her arms around me and the two of us rock back and forth, because this grief is too violent to allow me to be still.

"I really think he's dead," I say once I'm able to speak again.

"I believe you," Lyuda says. "And if he came to you like that with a warning, then we need to listen to him. The thunder stopped, so we need to—"

The rumbling sounds of submachine guns interrupt her words.

The two of us gape at each other, our eyes wide with fear. Keeping our heads low, we run to the furthest corner of the stable and hide behind a giant stack of hay.

"The thunder," I whisper into Lyuda's ear. "I think this is what he meant."

Lyuda nods and we huddle together, feeling each other's hearts pounding in our chests.

CHAPTER 22
BABIN YAR

Thirty-six hours.

I've counted each second in my head. It's the only way to keep my mind occupied while all we can do is to hide out and wait.

Thirty-six hours and fourteen minutes until the gunfire stopped. And although I suppose the actual shooting took place somewhere about a kilometer away, my ears are still ringing, making it difficult to hear what Lyuda is saying.

Lyuda's hands cradle my face, forcing me to look up at her. Her eyes are wide, her pupils fully dilated, reflecting the light of the kerosene lamp. I can see her lips moving but it's impossible to make out what she's saying over the hissing and ringing sounds in my ears.

Once again, it feels like I am drowning. Like I am underwater, seeing through a filter. Everything is blurry and distant, and nothing is real.

Stop. Do the technique again, I remind myself.

I shake my head left to right, and count. *One. Two. Three. Four.*

Slowly, things come back into focus and my hearing stabilizes, though some of the buzzing remains.

Lyuda shakes me by the shoulders again. "Mouse? Girl, look at me. Can you hear me? Are you okay?"

I look up at my friend again and nod. "Yeah. I think. I dunno." I am shivering again, when a horrendous realization hits me.

I jump up, still shaking. "Did they kill them? Did they kill them all?"

Lyuda takes a big breath. "I'm sure we're going to find out soon enough but right now, we need to get ourselves together and get the hell out of here."

I shake my head again, trying to snap out of the strange feeling taking over my entire body. My vision is going in and out of focus again.

Am I losing my mind?

"I dunno. I dunno," I keep muttering.

"Maria," Lyuda says, addressing me by my real name. "Remember what your brother said."

It works. My vision clears. I take a big breath and nod. "Okay."

We leave Olga's kerosene lamp, grab our pillowcases of belongings and creep outside. The sun has already set, and the moon isn't out yet. We tiptoe around the stable, to avoid waking anyone or drawing attention to ourselves.

We turn the corner.

And I gasp.

Several meters in front of us, I can make out a shadow of a figure, swaying in the darkness. The figure stumbles and whispers, "Help me," before collapsing on the ground.

Pavlik's face flashes in my mind, and I rush over

toward the figure. Lying in a heap in front of us is a young woman, naked and covered in blood and dirt.

I shake her. "Hey. Are you okay?"

Lyuda pulls my arm, "Mouse, leave her. We need to run. Let's go."

Images of bystanders watching the executions in Vinnytsia flash through my mind. People who watched and did nothing.

I won't be like them.

I shake the woman again.

"I said, let's go," Lyuda hisses.

"No," I say. "We can't just leave her here."

Lyuda folds her arms across her chest. "Are you serious?"

"Yuriy risked his life to help us," I remind her. "I won't just stand back and let her die. We need to do our part too."

I feel Lyuda's eyes glaring at me in the darkness. "Listen to me. This might be our only chance to leave. And besides, we need to listen to your brother. He told you to leave right after the storm."

I glare back at her in defiance. "Pavlik would never have left an innocent person to die."

After several minutes of whispered deliberations, Lyuda reluctantly agrees, and the two of us drag the unconscious woman inside the stable.

"You know, for a mouse, you are damn stubborn sometimes," Lyuda says, heaving, as we carry the woman toward the haystack.

"I guess sometimes even a mouse needs to roar," I reply and somehow find myself smiling.

Something about this interaction feels different. I feel

something I've never felt before. I feel my own power, or a small semblance of having it.

I wet my hands in the bucket of drinking water for the horses and rinse the woman's face and neck.

The young woman bolts up, gasping. Panting. Her eyes are bulging.

"Whoa! It's okay. Shh. You're okay," I say, my hands in front of me as if trying to tame a wild horse.

The woman stares at me and then at Lyuda. She is still panting, and as her breath starts to slow down, she begins to shake. She curls into herself, holding her chest and stomach as her body trembles, reminding me of my own attack of the nerves when the Nazis came to my house and after my hangover.

The woman is still shivering.

She must be freezing. I should give her some clothes.

I grab my pillowcase, untie it, and examine its contents. I pull out my spare blue dress, stockings, and underwear.

But I need these.

I glance back at the naked woman in front of me.

But she needs them too.

I squeeze the sleeve of my blue dress in a silent farewell. I hand the dress and my spare stockings and underwear to the woman. "Here. Put these on."

"Thanks," the woman whispers through chattering teeth.

Her hands shake, making it difficult for her to get dressed, but she refuses my help.

"What's your name?" Lyuda asks when the woman is finished.

"F-f-frida," she says, stuttering.

"You're Jewish," I say.

Frida's eyes bulge again. She wheezes.

I put my palms up again. "It's okay. You're safe. We're Jewish too."

Frida lets out a big sigh of relief. "*Slava Bogu.*"

Lyuda sits next to Frida. "If you don't mind me asking, what happened out there today?"

Frida takes a big shaky breath, her eyes shining with terror, lit up by the dancing flame of the kerosene lamp.

Frida shakes her head the entire time that she speaks. "It was terrible. There were notices all over the city that all the Jewish people were to congregate by the Jewish cemetery."

"Yes, we saw those," Lyuda interrupts.

Frida nods. "Right. So, we all brought our papers, valuables, and warm clothes. I thought we would be relocated."

She shakes for a few moments before she is able to continue. "They checked all our papers and turned away anyone who wasn't Jewish. Families were separated. Husbands and wives pulled apart; children torn away from their parents. It didn't seem to matter to them."

She takes another big shaky breath. "And then they sent us to walk forward in groups. We were told to take off all our clothes and put them into the clothes pile. Then, we had to place our valuables into another pile, and our winter clothes into another pile. By the time it was my turn, the piles were mountainous."

"Oh, *Bozhe,*" I whisper.

Frida continues, stuttering as she speaks. "They brought a group of twenty-five people at a time to step toward the ravine, the Babin Yar Ravine, and then—" She breaks off.

My mind is playing out the details of everything Frida

describes as if I am right there next to her. In line with every innocent person, having no other choice but to wait in line to be slaughtered.

Like animals. Like vermin. Deprived of respect, kindness, and dignity.

Not one of us is able to speak for a while until Frida is able to continue, "Once they were done with the first group, they pushed forward the next group of people to the edge of the ravine. Then they shot them to have them fall on top of the previous corpses... It was like a game for them. A sick, twisted game."

She takes a few more breaths. "They killed the adults. And they killed the children, some of them—torn from their mother's breast."

Another breath. "When it was my group's turn, I jumped into the ravine a split second before they started shooting and buried myself underneath some of the bodies..." She shudders. "And when they would throw in more bodies on top of me, I'd wait a little, and then throw them off of me, so that I wasn't fully buried but was also covered."

She sits motionless for a little while, staring into space.

She's shaking. I'm shaking too. I want to comfort her, to save her, to do something for her and all those other people.

But instead, I just feel helpless and stupid.

I remember what the bystanders in the crowd in Vinnytsia were saying during the executions. *What can we do? They have guns.*

Is this how these bystanders felt too? Did they also want to help as much as I do right now, but felt powerless? Somehow, this realization wipes away any anger I felt toward them, because we are all the same. We are all scared. We all feel powerless to change anything right now. Even if we really want to.

"And then?" Lyuda asks Frida, breaking me out of my reverie.

Frida swallows. "And then they buried us."

My head jerks up at her. "What do you mean, *buried*?"

Frida looks up at me. "They covered us with a thin layer of dirt." She shudders again. "There were people next to me. And underneath me. And on top of me. Most of them dead. Many had their blood on me. But some... some were still moaning in pain, gasping, suffocating."

"What did you do?" Lyuda asks.

Frida takes another big breath. "I waited until I couldn't hear the Nazis above me and then started to dig myself out."

She pantomimes digging with her fingers, and I notice the dirt and dried blood on her fingertips. I imagine Frida pushing the bodies off her, as she had to crawl out of the mass grave. All while Lyuda and I were safe here in the stable. My stomach twists from guilt.

It should have been me. Why did all those people have to die? And why do I get to live?

Frida shakes harder now. I put my hand on her shoulder. She jerks at the touch, but then seems to relax. She shakes her head from side to side several times, just like I did earlier.

She does it too. Just like me. And just like Lyuda taught me. Is this what everyone does to manage this nightmare?

"Once I dug myself out, I ran," Frida says. "I heard gunshots behind me and fell on the ground, both from fear and to pretend to be dead, just in case they were shooting at me.

"As I lay down, pretending to be dead, I saw some of them returning, shooting at the people in the mass grave I just crawled out of, through the dirt. And then the moaning stopped."

My voice shakes as I dare to ask the question I don't actually want to know the answer to. "How many Jewish people did they just kill out there over the last thirty-six hours?"

Frida's lip quivers and her voice breaks. "I'm not sure exactly, but if I had to guess—" She shakes her head again. "Over thirty thousand."

CHAPTER 23
BEHIND THE HAY

For a while, none of us says anything because there are no words, in Russian, Ukrainian, Yiddish, German, or in any other language, to express the anguish of what has just happened. Not something that happened in some scary storybook, but happened right here, in our home country. To our people. To our families. To real human beings.

Finally, I reach out my hands to the other two girls. We all clasp hands and squeeze tight, a gesture that says more than any words ever could.

Suddenly, Frida lets go of my hand and spins toward the stable door.

"Frida? What is it?" I whisper.

"Shh." Frida crouches down to the ground and crawls toward the entryway.

My heart pounds as I follow her, Lyuda close behind us both. And then I hear it too—voices.

A man with a gruff voice and a thick German accent is asking Olga Mihailovna for her paperwork, the paperwork for her children, and whether anyone is hiding at the house or the stables.

"See for yourself. We've got nothing to hide," Olga says. "I have two Ukrainian girls helping me."

"I will need to check their paperwork too," I hear the German man say.

"I checked it already," Olga replies. "If you want to check it again, fine. Check them and leave. And keep your voices down. You're scaring my pigs."

Lyuda and I exchange glances.

She's so brave, I think of Olga.

I hear the man switch to German, addressing someone else, "Sturmscharführer Klein, you check the stable and I'll check the house."

"Yes, Untersturmführer Hermann," another man's voice responds.

"We need to hide," I whisper.

Lyuda grabs my hand. "No. We shouldn't hide." She points at Frida. "We only need to hide her."

She pulls me and Frida toward the large stack of hay we were just sitting on. "Get under there," she tells Frida.

Frida takes a big breath but doesn't argue. She buries herself in the hay with Lyuda and me helping to cover her. Then Lyuda and I plop down on top and pretend to be asleep.

I can't even imagine what Frida is feeling right now, having to bury herself under the hay after what she just went through.

A bright light appears in the doorway, making me squint. The long, menacing shadow of an SS officer and his submachine gun appears before I can see the rest of him enter the stable. His square face and squared shoulders make him look intimidating, but it is the malice in his eyes that makes me tremble throughout my entire body.

"Who is here?" Klein asks in broken Russian.

Lyuda and I sit up and raise both our hands.

I can't seem to find my breath but Lyuda, thankfully, is able to answer for both of us in Russian. "It's just me and my friend, Anna, here."

Just like his shoulders, Sturmscharführer Klein's shoes are also square. Even his stiff movements seem to be square. There isn't a part of him that doesn't have an angle. He holds out his kerosene lamp in front of him and takes a few steps closer to us, his gun pointing at Lyuda's head.

As he approaches, I can see two silver pips and two silver stripes on one side of his collar, and two bolts of lightning on the other side. He wears an Iron Cross medal pinned to his chest and one around his neck, and I shudder to think what he must have done to earn them.

"Let me see your papers," Klein demands and takes another step toward us.

I nod.

Lyuda and I both reach into our pillowcases, careful to go as slowly as possible, so as not to be shot. We pull out our forged documents and hand them to Klein. He brings his lamp closer to our faces, leans down and examines each document without taking the papers from our hands, and without taking his finger off the trigger. He squints, trying to make out the words.

"All seems to be in order?" Untersturmführer Hermann's voice comes from the outside, and a moment later, he walks in.

Klein straightens up and turns to face his superior.

Like Klein, Hermann is also broad-shouldered, and is

139

also sporting an Iron Cross, but unlike Klein's uniform, Hermann's features three silver pips instead of two.

"All seems in order," Klein responds in German.

Hermann nods. "Good. Check to see if anyone else is here."

"Yes, Untersturmführer Hermann," Klein responds.

He clicks his heels together and stalks around the stable, his gun pointed in front of him, while Hermann stands like a statue, with his hands behind his back, observing Klein and Lyuda and I, all at the same time.

Oh, Bozhe. What if they find her? What if they discover Frida?

I stare down at Hermann's bloodstained shoes so that I won't accidentally give away Frida's presence.

How many people did you personally kill out there today, you paskudnik!

I grip my fists and keep my gaze down, listening for the clinking of Klein's shoes as he walks around the stable. Klein's steps are heavy, thudding on the wood like each step is a hammer blow. There is an air of painstaking malice with which he knocks over buckets and cans as he walks, not because they are in his way, but simply because he can.

I jump when the horses whinny, startled by the force of Klein's footsteps, but I am determined to stay right here—in the hay next to Lyuda, shielding Frida as much as possible.

As Klein circles around the stable, I sneak a quick glance at Hermann's face. His eyebrows are knit together, and his jaw is clenched like he is one word away from slaughter.

"All seems clear, Untersturmführer Hermann," Klein finally says, and I let out the tiniest bit of an exhale.

"Check behind the hay," Hermann orders.

My jaw locks with such pressure that my eyes water from the searing pain. I am certain that my pounding heart will give us all away. I hold my breath, bite my lip, and jam my fingernails into my arm to keep myself still. I lower my gaze once more, listening for the sound of Klein's deliberate footsteps to gauge exactly where he is, as he walks behind the hay, behind where Lyuda and I are sitting, hoping that there is no trace of Frida.

Finally, I hear Klein's booming voice declare in German, "All seems in proper order, Untersturmführer Hermann."

I glance up to see Hermann nod at Klein, and the two march out of the stable without another look at us.

Lyuda and I let out a simultaneous long exhale. We sit motionless for a few minutes, just staring at each other and taking deep breaths.

"Frida!" Lyuda whispers to me, and we dig her up from under the hay.

"Are you okay?" I ask.

Frida nods. She is still shaking, and her cheeks have lost all color again.

"Shh, it's okay. They're gone now," I reassure her.

I lie down in the hay next to Frida and wrap my arms around her, just like Lyuda did when I was struggling in the past.

"We need to get out of here," Lyuda says after a few minutes.

Frida and I sit up, neither of us shaking now.

Frida sighs. "I don't think I can go anywhere. If anyone asks me for my papers, and I don't have them, I'm dead."

Lyuda nods. "That's why we need to bring you to Yuriy."

"Who?"

Over the next half an hour, Lyuda and I take turns filling in Frida about our journey in animated whispers. My heart warms as Frida's eyes begin to shine with hope.

"And you think he'd be willing to help?" she asks.

"I think he'd be happy to help," Lyuda says.

A dark thought occurs to me. "But how are we going to get back to Vinnytsia? Even if Yuriy can forge her birth certificate, Frida doesn't have her paperwork *now*, in order to get there."

Lyuda thinks about it, chewing her bottom lip. Then she smiles. "I think I have a plan."

CHAPTER 24
MUSICAL DOCUMENTS

All three of us huddle in a circle next to the pig enclosure while Lyuda explains her idea.

"So, essentially, we'll be playing a game of musical chairs with the documents," Lyuda says. "We are going to rotate every day. So, Frida, you will use Maria's documents to travel with me to secure a one-day job with a place to stay. We won't be looking for pay or food as those places would be harder to find. We'll only be looking for shelter."

"What will I do?" I ask, pinching the hem of my black graduation dress between my fingers.

"You, Mouse, will stay here for one more day. I think Olga Mihailovna will be okay with that. Besides, since they checked this place last night, I imagine they won't check again today or tomorrow."

"And then?" I ask. The thought of being left behind in Kyiv without Lyuda and without my documents makes my mouth go dry.

"And then I will come back for you with your papers, and we will both travel to where Frida will be waiting for us. Since her papers will have already been checked, it is unlikely that they will be checked again the next day."

I nod, as Lyuda continues, "Then, the following day, we'll switch. Frida will stay behind since her paperwork would have been checked already, and Mouse and I will travel to find the next job with our documents. After which, I will then return for Frida. We'll rotate like this until we get to Fedka's house. We'll plead for our jobs back. I'll stay and work, and, Mouse and Frida, you two will take the papers and go to Vinnytsia to find Yuriy."

"There are a lot of things that can go wrong," Frida says. Her voice trembles again.

Lyuda nods. "Exactly. And that's why we are going to practice."

OVER AN HOUR, we rehearse over and over again, as Lyuda tests Frida while holding my birth certificate in her hands. "What is your name?"

"Furmanova, Anna Ivanovna," Frida recites.

Lyuda nods. "Good. Date of birth?"

"Um," Frida starts.

But Lyuda interrupts her. "No *ums*! This has to be perfect in order to work. Try again."

AFTER LYUDA AND FRIDA LEAVE, I begin cleaning the stable, taking special care to stay out of sight.

A few hours later, Olga Mihailovna walks in, her stern face and long fingers making her look like she is ready to fight anyone in her way. She is wearing a white dress that looks similar to one that Babushka used to wear, with traditional red and black stitching around the sleeves and curving around her skirts, and topped with a black vest, buttoned at her waist. Between the several rows of red beads around her neck and long blonde braid that wraps around her head like a crown, Olga looks like a Slavic queen.

"Hi, Anna. I'm sorry I didn't check on you sooner. These last few days were—well, you know what they were." I notice she is carrying two steaming cups of tea in her hands. She glances around the barn. "Where is your friend?"

My stomach clenches and rumbles as I imagine how a cup of warm tea would feel going down my throat into my empty belly. I gulp.

"Good morning," I reply, with a slight head bow. "Lyuda went to the well to get some more water for the horses."

"Oh, that's nice," Olga says, and hands me both cups of tea. "How are the animals?"

One of the horses whinnies as she walks toward him.

"Amur has been groaning all night, and I saw Indrik cribbing at the bucket this morning," I respond. "The pigs seem okay."

Olga pets Amur and tusks at Indrik, who is indeed still biting at the rim of his bucket. "Those damn Germans scaring my animals, not to mention what they did to all those poor people."

I fiddle with my skirt. "Right."

"How long do you two plan to stay in my stable?" Olga asks.

I shift my feet and take a long gulp of my tea before answering, "We're probably leaving either later tonight or early tomorrow morning, if that's all right." I have rehearsed this part of the story with Lyuda too before she left with Frida.

Olga shrugs. "Doesn't bother me. Just know that if you plan to stay longer than a week, I'll have to register you. And I'd rather deal with the Germans as little as possible."

I force myself to keep my eyes on the floor. "Of course. We understand completely and thank you so much for your hospitality. We'll be gone tomorrow."

"Don't mention it." Olga starts to leave and then comes back. "And Anna, you just make sure you and your friend always have your paperwork with you. I hear the Germans and the auxiliary police are checking everyone's papers now. If you don't have them, you could get shot like those poor people yesterday."

I glance up at her. The woman's brow is knotted in concern. "Don't worry, Olga Mihailovna, I have my paperwork right there." I motion to my empty pillowcase.

"Good." Olga shakes her head, her eyes glazed over in a memory. "I still can't believe those Germans killed all those people. Monsters is what they are. Fascists." She sighs. "Well, I suppose I should let you get back to work," she says, and walks out of the stable.

I peek out of the stable door. I even get onto my tip toes and peer out as far as I can see.

No signs of the Nazis. But no signs of Lyuda either.

I pace around the stable. *What if it didn't work? What if they got caught? Did they get killed?*

Images of my friends being executed flood my mind. I stop pacing but my heart is still racing inside my chest.

"No!" I say to myself out loud, and then shake my

head four times from side to side, and then silently add, *Don't go there. Stay in the present.*

I pace again.

What if they don't come back? What if they run away without me?

I shake my head.

No. Lyuda wouldn't do that.

I stop again.

But what will I do without my paperwork if they don't come back? Stay here and starve? Try to sneak back to find Yuriy? Take my chances with the Nazis?

A familiar voice comes from behind me. "Ready to go?"

I spin on my feet to find Lyuda smiling in the entryway. She holds out my birth certificate. "Here you go."

I run toward Lyuda and hug her as tightly as I can. "You came back! You came back for me!"

Lyuda sniffles and gives me a small squeeze back. "Of course, I did, silly. Did you think I would leave you here by yourself?"

"For a moment," I admit, finally letting go of her.

"You're not getting rid of me yet. Or ever, perhaps." She winks at me. "Now, grab your pillowcase and let's go."

I grab my belongings and follow Lyuda out.

"Where is she?" I whisper.

"Boyarka."

I stop. "Are you serious? That's where a hundred Jewish people died in the pogroms."

"More like three hundred," Lyuda replies.

She appears unfazed, but I know better now than to believe her façade. Still, the news gives me pause. "I don't know."

Lyuda bends down to be eye level with me. "It's true that they killed hundreds of our people there twenty years ago. And because of that, the city isn't crawling with Nazis at the moment, so you've gotta pick your battles, Mouse."

I sigh and follow Lyuda, feeling myself slipping into hopelessness again. *It doesn't matter. None of it matters anymore. What is the point of it anyway?*

I take a big breath. *No. Remember the pact. You made the pact, and you need to honor it. And you promised Lyuda. And Pavlik. And Babushka.*

I nod to myself and speed up to walk next to Lyuda, with a little more determination in my step.

CHAPTER 25

GREED AND JEALOUSY

It takes us six days to get back to Nemyriv, rotating and sharing our birth certificates along the way. We finish the last of our bread and potatoes on the third day. For the rest of the trip, we survive on water and any milk or raw eggs we manage to "borrow" while working on farms along the way. The only food we have left are three remaining walnuts that I keep in my pillowcase, for an absolute emergency.

By the time Lyuda and I get back to Nemyriv, the sun has already set, and I can see my breath when I shiver. I can barely feel my toes in my summer sandals and the numbness spreads throughout my entire body.

Lyuda knocks on Fedka's front door.

He opens it a few minutes later, a cigarette attached to the corner of his mouth. "Well, if it isn't the two lost lambs." The smoke from his cigarette stings my eyes.

"Fedka, we're sorry," Lyuda says. "Look, things got really rough in Kyiv."

Fedka raises his eyebrow, "Kyiv? I thought you were visiting your sick aunt in Uman?"

I curse under my breath, but Lyuda doesn't miss a beat, "Look, we are desperate. Can we please have our jobs back?"

Fedka shakes his head and puffs some more. "Can't. Already hired two others."

"But... where are we supposed to go?" I manage to ask.

Fedka tuts, "Don't know what to tell you. You were gone too long. Left at the worst time. I needed workers for the harvest."

There's an empty feeling deep inside my stomach, and not from hunger. The last string of hope I was clinging onto is now unraveling.

Lyuda is pleading now. "How about just one night? Please? It's freezing and it's getting really dark out."

Fedka shakes his head again. "Can't. Don't have enough food to pay you with the Germans taking most of it away."

I thought you were happy that the Germans were here, I think bitterly. *It didn't matter when they were killing Jewish people but now that they are taking your food and treating you worse than the Soviets did, now you care all of a sudden.*

"Please," Lyuda says. "You don't even have to feed us. We just need a place to sleep for one night. Please, Fedka. It will cost you nothing and you will have double the labor."

Fedka chews on his lip considering this. Then he holds out his index finger. "One night. And I want you both out by the morning."

"Thank you so much!" Lyuda says.

"Yes, thank you," I say without looking at him.

⁓

FEDKA LEAVES AS SOON as he introduces us to the other girls at the stable. Vika, the younger of the two, is plump and short, but still taller than I am. She has light brown hair, which she wears in two loose braids. Olessya, the older one, is slender and has black shoulder-length hair. The two of them shoot me quick glances and then whisper to one another and giggle. This reminds me of Natasha and her school flock.

"I have to go check on my uncle," Lyuda says to me, loud enough for the two other girls to hear. "I'll be back soon."

"I'll walk you out," I say, matching Lyuda's volume.

When we are outside and out of earshot, I grab Lyuda's hand and whisper, "What are we going to do? We can't bring Frida here."

Lyuda squeezes my hand back. "Don't worry. I'll think of something. I think best when I'm walking anyway."

I sigh and nod. "Okay." I hand my birth certificate to Lyuda. "Be safe."

Lyuda hugs me. "You too, Mouse."

I watch Lyuda walk farther and farther away, and only when I can no longer see her do I return to the stable.

Vika and Olessya are sitting next to each other, each eating half a cooked potato, still in its skin. I stare from one to the other and swallow the saliva that forms in my mouth from hunger.

"Fedka didn't feed you?" Olessya asks.

"No."

"Wow. What a kike!" Vika says and giggles to herself.

"Fedka is Jewish?" I ask.

"Huh?" Vika raises her eyebrow. "Oh. No, obviously.

You know what I mean. 'Cause Jews are greedy," she says, now reminding me of Natasha even more.

Vika takes another bite out of her potato. A small piece of it falls on the ground. Vika picks it up and shoves it into her mouth.

"Right," I say.

I sigh and start scrubbing the floor, trying to ignore the loud rumbling in my stomach.

I FEEL Lyuda's firm hands shaking me awake. It must be after midnight.

"Mouse, wake up. Come with me," she whispers.

Shivering from the fierce autumn cold, I sit up. My toes are numb, and my only stockings are dirt-stained and full of holes.

We've got to get winter clothes somehow, I think as I follow Lyuda outside, careful not to wake Olessya and Vika.

Frida waits around the corner. She is trembling and is still wearing my spare dress.

"It's so cold." Frida's teeth chatter as she speaks.

"It's October, what do you expect," Lyuda replies dryly.

I look around to make sure no one else is nearby. "So, what's the plan?"

Lyuda yawns. "Well, I'm going to finally get some sleep in the stable here. It will just look like I'm getting a late start in the morning. And you two go find Yuriy and then come back for me with my papers."

Lyuda hands her birth certificate to me. "Here. You use this. You know my information better than Frida does. And she should keep using yours until she gets her own."

Frida and I both nod as Lyuda continues, "And Frida, once Yuriy makes your papers, the three of us can look for a job together."

Frida shakes her head. "You two have already done so much for me, and I can never repay you for that. But I think us three traveling together will make it more difficult to find a job. I have some distant family in Cherkassy. They aren't Jewish, but I think I can trust them. Once I have the paperwork, I'll be able to travel there."

Lyuda nods. "Then I guess I won't be seeing you again."

Although her face remains stoic, Lyuda's lips curve downward in a small frown.

Frida wraps her arms around Lyuda and hugs her, her voice breaking as she speaks. "Thank you, my dear. Thank you for everything." The two girls cling to each other for a moment as Frida wipes a few loose tears from her face.

For a fraction of a second, I feel a twinge of jealousy in the pit of my stomach.

Does Lyuda care about her more than me? They've spent so much time together. Does she wish that I would leave so the two of them could stay together?

Then I silently kick myself. *Stop it! What is the matter with you?*

I don't even notice that Lyuda and Frida have stopped hugging until I am nearly knocked off my feet by Frida's tight embrace. "And you! You saved my life. Thank you."

I grin at her, feeling even more sheepish about my jealousy, and hug Frida back. *We are all in this together.*

CHAPTER 26
VINNYTSIA

Frida and I rush to Vinnytsia in order to stay warm. I try to ignore the aching blisters I've developed from the sandals rubbing against my stockings.

"I've never walked so much in my entire life," Frida says, panting.

I nod but say nothing, looking up ahead. I can just make out the familiar wooden sign on the road ahead that reads "Vinnytsia," and my heart leaps in my chest. Like forbidden love, it is excruciating to be so close to home and to know that I cannot stay here. Not now. Possibly not ever.

As we approach my old neighborhood, my heart feels like it's being put through a meat grinder, and my mind flutters with rapid fire thoughts.

Can I go home just for a minute? Is Papa there? Is someone else now living in my house? Can I sneak in and get more clothes? Maybe my coat? Maybe we can sleep there?

But when we turn onto my home road, my knees buckle at what I see ahead of me. Where my house used to be, there is now just a black, charred piece of dead land.

My vision blurs and the familiar sound of a piano invites me to slip away.

No! I shake my head to remain in the present. My vision refocuses and blurs again.

"It burned. All of it," I mumble, blinking away my tears.

I shake my head again. Hard. Counting this time. *One. Two. Three. Four.*

"Oh, Maria. I'm so sorry," Frida whispers, taking my hand in both of hers.

I take a few long breaths to steady myself. And then a sudden realization floods me. "Oh, *Bozhe*! Yuriy!"

I bolt in the direction of his house, Frida's footsteps sounding closely behind me. And a few moments later, I see it—a charred, gaping square of nothing, just like the one where my own house stood before.

Frida runs up to me. "Oh, *Bozhe Moi.*"

"Burned down two weeks ago," a creaking voice sounds behind us.

I spin around to my neighbor, Rosa Viktorovna. She wears a green winter coat and a grey *platok* around her head and neck. Malchik, her dog, is pulling on her leash, but Rosa holds firm.

Before I can stop myself, I rush over to the old woman and hug her. She smells so familiar—like soup and *kasha*.

Rosa hugs me back, her embrace reminding me of Babushka. "So good to see that you're alive."

I smile at her through my tears. "You too." I nod at Frida. "And this is my friend, um... Lyuda."

"Nice to meet you, Lyuda," Rosa says.

"What happened here?" Frida asks, pointing to the burned square where Yuriy's house used to be.

Rosa shakes her head. "What do you think happened? The damn Nazis burned all the houses down that belonged to Jewish people, or those who supported them, or protested the Nazi regime in any way."

I take a few slow breaths and ask, "Do you know what happened to Yuriy?"

Rosa sighs. "He was sent to Germany to become an Ostarbeiter."

"A what?" Frida and I ask at the same time.

Rosa pulls her dog toward her and beckons the two of us to come closer as well. She looks around and then whispers, "The Ostarbeiter program is a conscription of Soviet people sent to Germany to work. The German slogans claim it pays well and that the Ostarbeiter get to live in great conditions, but I don't believe it."

"Wait, they're *forcing* people into it?" Frida asks. "As in forced labor?"

Rosa nods. "Exactly. See, in July, they were looking for volunteers. My son, Ilya, he volunteered. I haven't heard from him since."

I suck in a breath and Rosa continues, her voice breaking several times as she speaks, "In August, they started forcing young people to go. Now, they're sending just about any able-bodied people they can find, as young as twelve and as old as fifty, from what I hear. With all the men in the Army or imprisoned, and all the women being conscripted, pretty soon it will just be old people and the Jews left. And you know what the Nazis have been doing with them."

I swallow and nod. "So, they took Yuriy to this Ost—what's it called again?"

"Ostarbeiter," Rosa says. "And yes. He wasn't happy about it, but they just threw him on the train to Germany and that was that."

"So, there's a chance that he's still alive?" Frida asks.

Rosa shrugs. "Who knows? My advice is for you both to leave Vinnytsia immediately. Stay away from here. People here know you, Maria, and even if they don't recognize you, you're more likely to be conscripted to become an Ostarbeiter from a major city than a smaller village."

I sigh and hug her again. "I will. Thank you, Rosa Viktorovna. Stay safe."

"You too, dear," Rosa says, sniffling. "Now go. Run. Both of you. The sun is almost all the way up, there will be more people up and about soon."

The two of us run but my thoughts run even faster.

How can this be happening? What's going to happen to us? How can people allow for this to happen? How can God allow this to happen?

We run until we reach the edge of the city. When we stop, we are both panting and sweating.

Frida rubs her hands together and then takes out my birth certificate and hands it to me. "Thank you. For everything."

I bring my hand to my chest in realization. "Really? You're not coming? But what are you going to do?"

Frida nods. "If I make it to my relatives' house safely, I'll be okay."

I bite my lip. *What should I do? Will she be okay if I leave her without any paperwork? But what choice do we have? If Lyuda was here, she would have known what to do.*

As if sensing my uncertainty, Frida puts her hand on my shoulder. "It's okay. I'll be careful."

I nod and hug her. "Stay safe."

"I promise," Frida says.

"Hang on," I say, realizing there is one more thing I can do to help Frida. I untie my pillowcase and take out the remaining three walnuts I've been carrying since the last time I saw Yuriy. "Here. Take these. For the road."

Tears mist in Frida's eyes as she accepts them. "Thank you," she says. "Thank you."

CHAPTER 27
KOLO-MYKHAILIVKA

After I return and Lyuda and I leave Nemyriv, we search for work in smaller villages for two full days, with no luck. Most places offer shelter as payment but not food. Everywhere is the same—"The Germans take all our food and give us back only rations, so I have no food to offer you."

"If this continues, we're going to have to request food from the Germans," Lyuda says.

I clench my jaw, feeling my cheeks flush with fury. *Is she joking? Requesting food from the Nazis? After everything they've done?*

"Fascists," I correct her. "These are fascists."

She holds back from saying anything and the two of us walk in silence until Lyuda points to a sign posted on a nearby pine tree—*Come to Germany to help with household chores.*

The poster displays a picture of a smiling woman, an Ostarbeiter, cutting up food for a happy German family—a mother and two small children. The poster also includes a quote from the Ostarbeiter, "I live with a German family, and I feel just fine."

Lyuda scoffs, "Maybe we should volunteer."

I stop mid-step. "Are you serious? I told you what Rosa Viktorovna said to me and Frida."

Lyuda holds up her hand. "Relax, Mouse. I'm joking, obviously."

I clench my fists. "Well, don't. They took Yuriy, okay? Rosa's son volunteered and she hasn't heard from him since. No letters. Nothing."

Lyuda steps closer to me and places her hands on my shoulders. "I know you're worried but that doesn't mean anything. Mail is hard to get now. You said that you hadn't heard from your brother in a long—"

"He's DEAD!" I shout in Lyuda's face. My lips are trembling, but I won't let Lyuda see me cry right now.

I wait for her to argue, ready to yell at her again, but she doesn't give me the chance. "Okay," she says in a stoic but calm voice. "Let's just try to find something to eat."

I growl but do not reply. A part of me wants to fight with her right now. *Why? Why do I feel the need to yell at my only friend?*

Lyuda spins around, checking out our surroundings. "Where are we anyway?"

All around us are never-ending pine trees, leading into an ominous-looking forest. There's also an abandoned church, an old mill, and several dilapidated houses in the distance.

"Let's try there," Lyuda says, pointing at one of the houses.

I grunt and try to take a step, but it feels like someone struck both my feet with a hockey stick. They burn and throb, but also feel numb at the same time. My legs tremble and give out.

I fall onto my knees. For a split second, my vision blurs but returns again a moment later.

I have nothing left. No energy. No strength. Nothing.

Lyuda runs over to me. "Hey, are you okay?"

I shake my head. "I'm not okay. Obviously! We've been walking for days now. Nothing is working out. Nothing is getting better. And nothing will ever get better."

Lyuda takes a slow breath and nods. "Okay. You stay here and rest. I'll see what I can find us."

I scoff. *How can she be so calm about this?*

I reposition myself to sit on the frost-covered ground, barely able to feel the cold anymore. My vision comes in and out as I watch my best friend wander from one house to another.

Guilt rolls over me like a thick cloud. *Lyuda should just leave me here to die. I'm so weak. And I am so rude. She deserves a better friend. Like Frida.*

My eyelids feel heavier than any milk buckets I've ever carried. I'm not sure when they close all the way, as the scenes of the last few months flash in my memories.

Guns.

Screams.

Bodies.

Is this real?

I reach my hands out for the long, smooth keys of the school piano. One of the keys has a small scratch on it, I can feel it with my index finger.

It's like you are transported to another world. A world where everything's okay.

I play Vivaldi's *Winter,* my hands swiftly caressing the keys.

"Agit iz apliz!" Someone shouts.

"Huh?" My eyelids fly open, but my vision is still blurred. I shake out my head. Left to right.

"Agit iz apliz," Lyuda repeats.

I shake my head four times and Lyuda's words finally become coherent. *I got us a place.*

"You... you did?" I manage to whisper.

Lyuda is already helping me up. "Yes, a woman in one of the houses there took pity on us. Said she'd let us stay for one night and share some food if we help with supper."

I am sure I am hallucinating. "Did you just say food?"

Lyuda laughs. "You definitely could use it. You're starting to slur your words."

Lyuda wraps my arm over her shoulder and lifts me up by my waist. She drags me up to a small cottage home, where a middle-aged woman with a long brown braid is bringing in laundry from a clothesline.

She turns toward us and gasps when she sees me. "Dasha? Dashenka, is that you?"

"Her name is Anna," Lyuda says, glancing sideways at me. "This is my friend that I was telling you about. And Anna, this is Margarita Sergeevna."

"Call me Rita," the woman says. "*Bozhe Moi,* she looks just like my Dasha. My daughter. She was taken to the Ostarbeiter a month ago. But it feels like forever ago now." Rita's eyes well up. She sniffles and points to her door. "Please, go inside. Warm up by the fire."

"Many thanks," Lyuda says and drags me inside.

Rita walks in after us and closes the door.

My feet are still throbbing but the heat from the stove

is helping them to warm up again. It's the same kind of masonry stove that we have at home.

Used to have, I silently correct myself, swallowing the memory of my burned house deep down, to cry about later.

Lyuda drags me to the stove and plops me into the chair in front of it. "Here. Sit. Rest," Lyuda orders and addresses Rita. "Can you please tell us what city this is?"

Rita has just finished flinging the laundry over the masonry stove perch to dry. She walks across the room to a table surrounded by four chairs with a bucket of vegetables on it.

"You're in Kolo-Mykhailivka," Rita says, and begins separating vegetables. "Help me with these please?"

"Yes, of course," Lyuda says and then turns to me. "You rest. I got this."

I nod and Lyuda nods back at me before she goes to help Rita.

I stare at my best friend, as my ears buzz and my vision blurs again. My body fluctuates between rest and trembling.

Six potatoes. One bucket. Two pots.

The counting helps. My vision snaps back into focus. I shake my head for good measure.

One. Two. Three. Four.

My ears stop ringing and my breathing slows.

"Here. Peel the potatoes," Rita says to Lyuda as she hands her a small knife.

"No problem," Lyuda says. She grabs a potato from the bucket and starts peeling.

A few peeled potatoes later, Lyuda asks, "Rita, what is that forest that's by here?"

Rita raises her eyebrow at Lyuda. "You mean the Stryzhavka forest? You don't want to go in there."

"Why not?" Lyuda asks.

Rita slides her blade into an onion. She chops it into quarters and then wipes her eyes with her sleeve. "The rumor is that's where the Nazis are holding most of the Soviet Army prisoners and are forcing them to do labor." She chops up one of the onion quarters, while putting the rest aside.

"What kind of labor?" Lyuda asks, reaching for the next potato to peel.

Rita shrugs. "No one knows for sure. But they say that it's going to be something bad." She bites her lip. "And there's another thing."

"What?" Lyuda asks with curiosity in her voice.

"I don't know how true this is, but they say that there's some kind of a monster that lives in those woods."

"You mean aside from the Nazis?" Lyuda asks.

Rita drops her onion quarter onto the floor. "Shh, don't let anyone hear you say that." She picks up the onion and blows on it to clean it, before wiping it against her apron. She takes a breath and continues in a whisper, "But yes. I overheard my husband talk about some kind of a wolf. A big, terrible wolf that kills people."

I picture a giant wolf. *Is the wolf eating people? Are the Germans training wolves to do their dirty work?*

My body is starting to vibrate. I've rested enough, and now I need to move, to do something. Still a bit woozy, I force myself to get up and walk up to Rita. "How can I help?"

Rita points at a large pot sitting on the counter next to the stove. "Fill that up with water. We're going to make soup."

I nod and fill up the pot from the bucket of water on the floor and join Lyuda and Rita at the table. Over the next half an hour, we cut, chop, and slice potatoes, onions, and carrots and add them to the pot, along with a pinch of salt and dried dill weed.

As we wait for the soup to cook, Rita walks up to me. She gazes deep into my eyes, her own still misty even though she's long done peeling the onions.

"Thank you, Dashenka," Rita says softly. "Good girl." She sniffles and walks out, into another room.

My chest tightens. This grief, it's so familiar, like a visit from an old friend.

"What do I do?" I whisper to Lyuda.

Lyuda shrugs. "Just go with it, I guess."

A minute later, Rita reenters the kitchen, humming a lullaby. The same lullaby Mamo used to sing to me. I gulp and bite my lip to keep the sadness away.

"Don't worry, Dashenka, I won't let anyone harm you ever again," Rita says. She cradles my face in her hands for a moment, then returns to the soup.

I exchange glances with Lyuda, who shrugs again.

"Sit, please. Dinner is almost ready," Rita says.

A little hesitant, Lyuda and I walk over to the table and sit down. The table wobbles when we rest our arms on it.

Rita brings over the steaming soup, still in the pot, and sets it on the knitted trivet in the center of the table. She lays out four spoons—traditional Ukrainian wooden spoons—red cherries painted over a black background, with a golden handle and a red tip.

Just like the ones we used to have.

"Please eat," Rita says, and sits at the table across from me.

I nod at her and look down at the soup. *I never liked soup before. Babushka always had to coax me into eating it.*

Right now, however, I don't need convincing. I would have eaten just about anything, but this soup smells like home, and I have never felt more ready to eat.

I pick up one of the spoons and submerge it in the still-steaming liquid, trying to breathe and calm my pounding heart. The steam coming off my spoon warms my hands, cheeks, and forehead. It's only now that I truly realize how cold I've been. And for how long.

I blow on the spoon and watch the steam dance away from me. I can't remember the last time I've had a hot meal. I blow on my spoon again and take a slow, careful sip.

I close my eyes, feeling the warmth spreading from my mouth, down my throat, and warming my entire body from the inside out. I haven't eaten anything like this since last spring. It stirs an emotion that feels bittersweet and somehow familiar: hope.

The front door swings open and a tall man steps inside. He wears a black uniform resembling that of a police officer, but it isn't quite right. He is wearing a military-like garrison cap and at its center is a golden pin of an eagle perched over a swastika. Two machetes and a handgun are holstered to his belt, and a rifle hangs around his shoulder.

Does he work for the Nazis? I wonder, my heart pounding somewhere in my throat.

The man stares at us, his arms folded across his chest. "Who are you?" he demands.

Rita jumps up from her chair. "Vlad, honey. This is Anna and Lyuda. They are going to stay here tonight."

Vlad doesn't look at her but addresses Lyuda and me directly. "Documents."

We pull out our birth certificates and Vlad extends his hand, then holds the documents up to the light of the kerosene lamp, near the edge of the table.

"Why do you need to see those?" Rita asks, rubbing his arm now. "You are home now. You can stop working for one minute—just sit down and have some dinner."

"Protocol," he says without taking his eyes off the papers. "Need to make sure they're not Jews."

He examines the papers for a few more moments before handing them back to us.

I breathe out a sigh of relief as quietly as I can.

"And now, you will need to be evaluated for fitness for the Ostarbeiter," Vlad says. "Come with me."

CHAPTER 28

DINNER NEGOTIATIONS

I want to gasp but can't take a single breath. I squeeze my eyes shut and then open them again.

No. This is not a nightmare, at least not one I can wake from.

Vlad is still standing in front of us, his face cold and lifeless.

Lyuda is the first to break the silence. "Actually, we were already evaluated. In Vinnytsia. Just last week. They said we were too weak, scrawny, and not a good enough fit to be a proper Ostarbeiter in Germany."

I glance from her to Vlad. The man narrows his eyes and is glaring at her now.

"Even if you're telling the truth, it doesn't matter," he says without blinking. "I was told this morning that Germany is very short on workers, and they need all the people they can get."

I look to Lyuda for guidance, but for the first time since we met at the Southern Bug River, she doesn't seem to have anything to say.

Vlad nods. "Right. I thought so. You two are going to have to come with me."

The sound of the breaking glass makes all three of us jump and turn. Rita is standing in the far corner of the kitchen. *When did she get there?* Her hands are trembling. And on the floor next to her feet, the broken pieces of a glass bowl sparkle in the light of the kerosene lamp.

"No." Rita says with finality in her tone.

Vlad raises his eyebrow at her. "What do you mean, *no*?"

Rita approaches her husband. Her chest rises up and down and she breathes heavily, glaring up at him in defiance. "I mean that you're not taking them."

Vlad spreads his arms wide, gesturing as he speaks, "What do you care? You don't even know them."

Rita points at me. "That one looks just like our Dasha."

I wish that I could hide. Or run. But neither is possible at the moment.

Vlad's nostrils flare. He draws in a long breath and releases it before he responds. "Look, Dasha was sent there to work. To make money. I'm sure she's very happy in Germany."

Rita charges toward him, shaking with wrath. "Then why doesn't she write?"

Vlad rubs the inside corners of his eyes with his fingers. "We've been over this before. She's fine. You're just hysterical." He walks toward a wooden cabinet, pulls open a drawer and takes out a small, brown, glass vial. He then walks up to Rita and hands it to her. "Here. Take some Valerian. Calm your nerves."

Glass shatters again as Rita smashes the vial on the ground.

"What are you, crazy?" Vlad yells. "Why did you do that? That was our last vial. You made me go to Vinnytsia last year to get that for you."

Rita glares up at him again, her eyes wide with fury. "Do not think you can keep placating me," she says with a low growl. "Our daughter is hurt. Or dead. Or worse."

Vlad squints at her. "What's worse than being dead?"

Rita shakes her head. "You're not a woman. You wouldn't understand."

What does she mean? I wonder. *What's worse than death?*

Vlad rubs his temples and then takes a big breath, speaking in a calmer tone now, "Look, for all we know, those two could be kikes. There've been reports of people forging documents."

I glance at Lyuda, who shakes her head slightly, as if to say, *Don't react.*

"I don't care," Rita rages. "They're *people*. They're girls. Just like our little girl. You can't take them."

Vlad rolls his eyes. "You're being ridiculous. I'm an auxiliary. I have to follow the law."

Rita pokes at his chest with her finger. "The law and the right thing to do aren't always the same. The law is supposed to protect people, not order their executions or deportations."

Vlad takes a step back, away from her, raising his arms in the air. "I don't know what to tell you. I have a job to do."

"And so do I!" Rita shouts. "And if you bring them in, I swear to God, I will volunteer for the Ostarbeiter too."

Vlad's eyes bulge. "You? You can't." His voice has softened. "You can't go."

Rita folds her arms again. "I thought you said that they need all the people they can get."

For several moments, neither one of them moves or blinks. Only their chests heave up and down as they stare at one another.

Lyuda and I look at each other, waiting for whatever will happen next.

Finally, Vlad nods toward us as he addresses his wife. "Fine. They stay for one night only."

Rita takes a big breath, and then smiles and claps her hands together, as if nothing happened. "Wonderful. Now, let's eat, the soup is getting cold. Everyone, grab a spoon and we will share the pot as one family."

She sits down, pulls one of the spoons toward her, and begins to eat. Lyuda follows her example, and I do as well, afraid that the food will be taken away from us at any moment.

Vlad sighs and sits down on the chair next to his wife.

The four of us dine in silence.

CHAPTER 29
COAT AND BOOTS

S omeone shakes me. I jerk up.

"Shh," Rita whispers. "Don't say anything. You and your friend have to leave. Hurry. Before my husband wakes up."

I see Lyuda across the room. She is already up and getting ready.

I sigh. Rita allowed us sleep in her daughter's bed, and it's the first time I've slept in an actual bed in over four months. It actually has a sheet, a pillow, and even a blanket. For the first time since June, I don't have to brush the hay out of my hair.

I sigh again more deeply and force myself to get up. I pull the blanket over the sheet to make the bed and fluff the pillow, longing to take it with me.

If only we could stay. I'd work for the rest of my life just to be able to sleep in a bed with a blanket and a pillow.

I look over to Lyuda, who is also staring at the bed we just slept in with a kind of parting sorrow.

"Here, take this," Rita whispers.

I turn to find Rita holding a bundle of cloth and a pair

of warm winter boots made with black wool and red rubber slips for the snow.

Rita shakes out the fur bundle, and I gasp at the sight.

It's gorgeous!

It's a *kozhukh*—a coat made of white sheepskin with a thick black fur lining inside of it. This one is embroidered with red, purple, and pink tulips, and green leaves on the collar and at the hem. Four red tassels hang around its waistline.

Rita hands me the coat and gives the boots to Lyuda. "Take these. They were Dasha's. She's always been so kind and generous. She'd want you to have these." Tears bubble up in her eyes. She sniffles. "I'm sorry that I only have one set of each. Divide them how you see fit."

"Thank you," Lyuda whispers, her eyes wide.

"Yes. Thank you," I whisper, running my fingers over the soft sheepskin of the coat, barely able to contain my own tears.

Rita eyes the two of us. "Whatever happens, do not under any circumstances volunteer for the Ostarbeiter, no matter how hungry or desperate you get. If you go, you will not come back. No matter what they promise you, don't go. Avoid being taken at all costs. Promise me."

I nod. "I promise."

"I promise," Lyuda repeats.

Rita nods. "Now, listen to me. A couple of kilometers west of here is a mill."

"Yes, we saw it yesterday," Lyuda says.

"Good," Rita replies. "I heard that they are looking for workers because all of theirs were taken for the Ostarbeiter. They might be able to hire you, and hopefully they can feed you. If you get in, then just do your jobs, keep your heads down, and stay out of everyone's sight. Do not bring attention to yourselves. Do you understand?"

Lyuda and I both nod.

"Good," Rita says and walks us out the door.

The first snow of the year covers the ground. Except for the pines, the trees are naked and lifeless, their branches swaying in the icy breeze.

I feel my cheeks burn with the familiar annual frost. "So cold," I mumble. I can see my breath as I speak.

"Yep," Lyuda agrees.

Lyuda's cheeks are scarlet, and based on how much my own cheeks burn, I suspect that they are the same shade.

"So, how do we divide these?" I ask, pointing to our new clothes.

"Hmm," Lyuda says. "We might be able to share the coat. If you wear one sleeve and I wear another, we can snuggle inside it together. We might not be able to button it but we'll both be warm."

I nod. "And the boots?"

Lyuda sighs. "We're going to have to take turns." She hands me the boots. "You first. We'll switch every ten minutes."

I nod and remove my sandals, shoving them into my pillowcase. Then I pull on the boots, nearly losing my balance in the process. And when I straighten up, my feet are warm for the first time in months. A heating sensation spreads from my feet all the way up to my chest.

"They fit perfectly," I grin.

Lyuda laughs. "Alright, Cinderella, now it's time to try on your royal gown."

I giggle and insert my left arm into the coat sleeve. "Ready."

Lyuda smirks. "Well, this will be a whole new experience."

She steps closer to me until our sides touch. We put our arms around each other at the waist, and Lyuda slides her right arm into the remaining sleeve. "We probably look ridiculous."

"At least we're warm," I say and grin at her.

And indeed, the coat and the boots make me feel so good that I am almost giddy. I am warm, safe, and close to my best friend.

Everything is going to be okay, I say to myself with a renewed sense of optimism.

Careful to step together, the two of us make our way toward the mill.

CHAPTER 30

THE MILL

"Like I said, I don't have much food to go around," Ruslan says. He is balding, his remaining greasy brown hair combed over the bald spot at the top of his head. "I can offer you shelter at the mill. It's warmer there than outside."

Lyuda and I both shake our heads.

"That won't work," Lyuda says. "We need food to survive. And you need workers."

Ruslan shifts uncomfortably. "I *do* need workers, but I also need food." He nods at a little boy of about three years old. "It's just me and my son now. The Germans took my wife as an Ostarbeiter last month."

Oh, Bozhe. They separated this little boy from his mother. They're tearing families apart. That means that they can take anyone.

"We can work at the mill and help you to take care of your son," Lyuda says.

Ruslan bites his lip. "I don't know."

"And the household," I add. "We can work at the mill,

take care of your son, and take care of the house. We'll cook, clean, and wash your clothes. All for a share of the food and shelter."

Ruslan sighs. "I need to think about it." He takes a breath, pauses, and raises his eyebrow. "Wait, how come you two weren't selected for the Ostarbeiter?"

"Like I said, you need workers. And a nanny," Lyuda says, dodging his question.

Ruslan's eyes shift, likely considering his options. Finally, he says, "Fine. I'll give you what I can and in return you'll work the mill, take care of the household, and watch Pavlik."

I gasp. "Pavlik?" I stare at the little boy. "His name is Pavlik?"

Ruslan furrows his thick eyebrows. "Yes. Is that a problem?"

I shake my head. "No. No problem at all."

My heart aches and warms at the same time. I walk up to the little boy. His blonde curls outline his scrawny face. He big brown eyes and long eyelashes remind me of Andrei.

I can take care of you, Pavlik, I say silently, fighting back the tears that threaten to roll down my cheeks. *I will love you and I will protect you.*

As I approach him, Pavlik freezes and stares at me, blinking. His father's shirt looks more like a long dress on him.

The poor boy doesn't have any children's clothes. I will make him some.

"Hi, Pavlik." I wave at him.

Pavlik smiles at me and waves back. He takes a few steps toward me, raises his tiny arms, and says, "Up."

I grin at him and pick him up, hugging him close to me, and whisper, "Don't worry, Pavlik. Everything will be all right."

CHAPTER 31
FAIRY TALES

Over the past sixteen months, Ruslan has managed to get Lyuda and me a second pair of used stockings and some cloth to sew new underwear, shirts, and trousers for all four of us.

Even so, I still keep all my belongings packed and neatly folded in my pillowcase, ready to go at a moment's notice. All my extra thread is now gone from its spools, most of it spent sewing and fixing my clothes, Pavlik's, and Lyuda's. My graduation dress still hangs loose on me, but it doesn't seem as long as it once was.

Did I get taller? I sometimes wonder even though everyone except little Pavlik still towers above me.

"Guess what?" Lyuda whispers to me one morning. "The Germans surrendered in Stalingrad."

I feel myself smiling, warmth spreading all over my body despite my toes freezing through my sandals in the winter snow. It is Lyuda's turn to wear the boots now, though the two of us are snuggling in our shared coat as we walk from the house to the mill. "Do you think it will be over soon?"

"Let's hope so, but let's also keep our feet on the ground," Lyuda responds.

When we step into the mill, we take off the coat to make sure we don't trip on it or damage it in any way. Three cotton sacks full of grain await us today, each weighing about forty kilograms, based on the size of them. Lyuda picks one of them up and hands it to me, carrying two sacks all by herself.

I heave the sack up on my shoulders and follow Lyuda up the slippery, creaking steps to the top. Twice I almost slip, silently cursing Ruslan for not letting us borrow his winter boots while we work.

"Here, hand me your sack," Lyuda says when I am at the top of the steps. Lyuda's own sacks are already on the ground next to her.

I heave, ignoring the spreading pain in my shoulders, and lift the sack over my head, handing it to Lyuda with one hand, while gripping the shaky railing with the other.

"Thanks," I say, panting when I step onto the top floor next to my friend.

Lyuda helps me to untie the sacks, and we pour the grain down the chute to be minced by the millstones.

"You go ahead and take care of Pavlik," Lyuda says. "I'll finish up here."

I grin at her. "Really? Are you sure you don't mind?"

Lyuda waves me off. "Go on. It's my turn anyway. You can take the next shift." When I hesitate, feeling too guilty to leave her to work the mill by herself, Lyuda shoos me toward the steps. "Go. I'm sure Pavlik is already asking about you."

I hug her and descend the steps, careful not to trip. We've been living here for nearly a year and a half, and in all this time, I've never missed an opportunity to play with Pavlik, if I'm able. I carry him on my shoulders each day, play chasing games with him, and am teaching him to draw all the things I know how—stars, flowers, the sun, and a house. I recite all the stories I know for him, from memory—*Cinderella, Puss in Boots,* and *Little Red Riding Hood.*

Sometimes I ask Lyuda to help me act out the stories for Pavlik. "And then the prince brought the crystal slipper to Cinderella," I narrate, as Lyuda hands me one of my raggedy summer sandals.

I then slip the sandal onto my foot and continue, "And as she put it on, the prince saw that it was a perfect fit."

"All thanks to her fairy godmother and some potato juice magic," Lyuda sometimes adds, and the two of us laugh.

One night, after we acted out Cinderella, Pavlik said, "I want p'tato juice magic."

"Aww, my sweet boy," I said to him, patting his head, "I'm afraid you're a little too young for potato juice."

Pavlik stared at me then with his big brown eyes, his pupils dilating as he pleaded, "When I'm bigger, you let me have p'tato juice?"

I laughed. "We'll see."

I smile at the sweet memory as I run back toward the house before my feet can turn purple from the cold inside my sandals and my patched stockings.

Once I make it back to the house, I find the little boy kneeling outside in the snow.

"There you are." Pavlik waves at me. "Look what I drew."

I am shivering from the cold, and my feet feel numb,

but I still squat next to him. Pavlik is holding a stick—a piece of a dead branch—and drawing in the snow. He's drawn a house—a simple square with a triangle roof, a door, and two windows, just like I showed him.

He's also drawn a sun in the sky, a few trees outside the house, and five stick figures. Two of them are standing next to each other on one side of the house. "That's Mamo and *Tato*," Pavlik says.

He points to the other stick figure, one standing by herself. "That's *Titka* Lyuda." And then to the remaining two figures, a little one and a bigger one, holding hands, "And that's me and you."

My eyes well with tears. "Thank you, my sweet boy. Thank you."

～

LATER THAT EVENING, Ruslan walks in with a small basket of potatoes and oranges.

Must be a payment he received for another load of grain, I think. My mouth waters. *When was the last time I had an orange? It must have been at least four years ago.*

And sure enough, after he places the basket on the wooden dinner table, Ruslan turns to me and Lyuda. "Time to grind another one."

"Now? Can't it wait until the morning?" Lyuda asks. "It's dark and everything is covered in ice."

Ruslan shakes his head. "We're supposed to sell five hundred kilos of flour in the morning, and then we have more orders coming."

"Fine," I say with a sigh. "It's my turn to go up."

Lyuda shakes her head. "Nah. You have a kid on your lap. I'll go."

I glance down at Pavlik, curled up like a kitten on my lap, in a deep sleep. I beam at Lyuda. "Thank you. I owe you one."

Lyuda winks. "I'll hold you to it." She pulls on our shared coat and winter boots. "Don't eat all the oranges without me. They're my favorite," she says and walks out the door.

Ruslan lights a log in the fireplace and steps away to his room. I am left alone with Pavlik, asleep in my lap. I smile at the little boy, feeling a warming sensation spread from my face, down my throat, to my heart and stomach.

Funny, such a small moment. But so sweet. Sweeter than oranges. Sweeter than candy. Yet bitter, too. We will have to leave one day, and will Pavlik even remember me then? Will he ever see his mother again? Who will take care of him if we leave?

Pavlik groans in his sleep, perhaps from a bad dream.

I pat his head. "It's okay, Pavlik. Everything is going to be okay."

He shifts and pulls one of my hands toward him. He nuzzles his face in the palm of my hand and turns to his side, so that my hand now serves as his pillow.

Is it that the sweetest moments come in the face of deep sorrow or is it that we cherish peaceful moments in the midst of violence?

Whatever the answer is, I am grateful for this magical experience. For the warmth of a house with a burning fireplace. For the warmth of a small child asleep on my lap. And for the warmth of my best friend, willing to share winters and summers, coats and hard floors, as well as smiles and sorrows with me.

A loud crash makes me jerk, my heart pounding in my chest.

Trying not to wake him, I gently pick up Pavlik off my lap and lower him onto the ground. The little boy stirs for a moment and then falls back asleep on the cold floor.

Another crash comes, and then a piercing scream.

Lyuda's scream.

And then silence.

I bolt out the door, my stocking-covered feet sinking in the snow down to my ankles.

I dart toward the mill. A dark figure lies outside it in the fresh snow.

"Please don't be Lyuda. Please don't be Lyuda," I mutter to myself as I run.

I stop suddenly. Not wanting to get any closer.

Not wanting it to be true.

I take a hesitant step closer to the figure, still lying motionless. I am shaking, not daring to cry or scream.

As I take another step closer, I gasp, recognizing the familiar boots.

I gulp. My lips tremble. Everything around me feels frozen in time.

I kneel next to her, "Lyuda?" And then I yell, "Lyuda!"

She doesn't move.

"No, no, no!" I cry. I flip Lyuda onto her back and shake her. "Lyuda? Lyuda, get up."

But Lyuda isn't moving.

CHAPTER 32
AFTER THE FALL

"What happened?" Ruslan asks.

He is panting. He must have run after me, but I didn't notice him until now.

"I... can't. She's not moving," I manage to say.

My hands are trembling over Lyuda's motionless body.

"Let's bring her inside," Ruslan says.

He squats down, keeps his knees bent, lifts Lyuda up, and carries her inside the house.

I follow him, my mind galloping with every possible scenario.

Is she going to die? Is she going to be disabled forever? Will I survive on my own? Will I be able to take care of her and myself?

No, don't think like that. So long as she survives, then so will I. Remember the survival pact.

Ruslan lays Lyuda down on Pavlik's bed.

"Bring me the blankets from my bedroom," he says to me.

I do it without questioning him.

Pavlik walks up to me, rubbing his eyes with his tiny fists. "What happened to *Titka* Lyuda?"

"She's just a little sick, honey," I say, trying not to look at him. I hate lying to him. "She'll be all right."

I pull both blankets off Ruslan's bed. They are warm and heavy, not like the thin one Lyuda and I have been sharing at night, as we sleep on the cold floor, wishing we could have three or four more blankets just to get warm.

By the time I return with the blankets, Ruslan has already taken off Lyuda's coat and boots. I hand him the blankets and help him to cover Lyuda with them.

Ruslan grabs Lyuda's wrist, checking her pulse with his index and middle fingers.

"Will she be okay?" I ask, desperate to know but also dreading the answer.

"Well, she's got a pulse. Not much else we can do in the nighttime."

I let out a breath of relief, sit next to Lyuda, and grab hold of her freezing hand. It reminds me of shoving my hands into icy water.

I lean closer to inspect Lyuda's face. Her hair is damp from the snow and stuck to the side of her head in clumps. When I move some of the hair from her pale face, my hand comes away dark with blood. My heart is pounding, but I try to keep my breathing steady.

Remember what Lyuda says. Keep your feet on the ground. Now is not the time to panic. Slow down and help her.

I take a few slow breaths, gently turn Lyuda's chin, and tilt her head to the side. Just behind her temple is a deep bloody gash.

"Ruslan, look," I say. "She's bleeding from her head. How did I not see that?"

"Go get me a wet towel," Ruslan says to me and then turns to Pavlik. "You're sleeping in my bed tonight. Now, go to sleep."

"Why?" Pavlik whines.

"I said go. March!" Ruslan says and points to the door.

Pavlik mumbles something under his breath and stomps out of the room.

Ruslan gazes up at me. "Are you waiting for an official invitation from Stalin? Go get me a wet towel, girl."

"Sorry," I mutter, and then run to the kitchen, grab a towel, dip it into the bucket of water, and bring it back to Ruslan. "Here you go."

He presses the towel to Lyuda's wound. As he does, she moans and squeezes her eyes.

A moment later, she blinks them open. "Hey, Mouse," she says in a raspy voice.

"*Slava Bogu*," I manage to say, "how are you feeling?"

Lyuda licks her chapped lips and then takes a long breath before she answers, "Almost drunk." Her voice is strained, and she is slurring some of her words as she speaks. "The room is...spinny. And my vision—it's like that time when we had the vodka."

"I'll get you some water," Ruslan says and walks out to the kitchen.

"We need to call a doctor," I say.

Lyuda sits up and grabs my hand, glaring at me. "Do *not* call the doctor. Under any circumstances. Remember what Yuriy told us. What Rita told us. We need to stay under the radar."

I nod. "Okay. You just rest tonight then."

Lyuda falls back onto the bed.

Suddenly, she groans, contorts, and screams.

I bite my lip from how tightly she is squeezing my

hand, but I don't let go. "What is it? What's wrong?" I ask.

"My...feet," Lyuda puffs.

She clenches her entire body, squinting her face and squeezing both of my hands now.

Oh, Bozhe. What is happening?

I manage to pull one of my hands from Lyuda's grip and lift the blanket off her. "Let me see."

Lyuda's feet and ankles look swollen. "I'm going to take your stockings off," I warn.

She nods.

I free my other hand too and slowly pull her stockings down. As I begin taking them off her feet, she screams in agony.

Ruslan rushes back toward her, spilling some of the water on the floor as he runs inside. "What happened?"

"Her feet are very swollen," I say. "Look."

Lyuda's feet are both twice their usual size and dark red. Not the ordinary pinkish-red my feet tend to turn from the cold, but the color of the inside of a beet root.

When Ruslan attempts to touch them, Lyuda screams as if he's cut her with an axe.

"We need to get her a doctor," I say.

Ruslan shrugs. "It's the middle of the night. We can wait until the morning. She's probably just badly bruised."

"I can't move them!" Lyuda shouts, her voice panicked. "They feel numb, but they hurt at the same time."

She is sweating now and shivering at the same time. "I can't..." Lyuda gasps a few more times and passes out again.

"Oh, *Bozhe!*" I shake her. "Lyuda!"

Nothing.

I check Lyuda's pulse. I can barely feel it.

"Something is wrong, Ruslan," I say, looking up at him, pleading. "Something is very, very wrong."

Ruslan shakes his head. "At worst, maybe she has a broken bone but there's not a lot a doctor can do right now."

How can he be so selfish? What if she dies?

I get to my feet, step toward Ruslan, and get up on my tip toes. "You listen to me," I say, poking his chest. "This is not normal. This is not a case of a broken bone. She needs a doctor. And you're going to get one. Right now."

"That's not what I signed up for when I agreed to take you in," Ruslan says, folding his arms across his chest.

I open my mouth to yell at him but remember my father's words as he used to shake his finger at me. *Good girls don't get angry.*

I take a big breath to steady my voice. "Ruslan. She needs a doctor. Please get a doctor."

I stare at him, pleading with my eyes until he grunts and storms out of the room, mumbling something under his breath. The front door slams behind him a moment later.

"Mouse?" Lyuda whispers.

I grab her hand. "What is it?"

"Something isn't right. I'm scared." Her eyes are bulging, her lips are the color of light blue chalk, and her grip is as weak as her pulse.

Please don't die, I silently plead with her, but I don't say anything out loud. Instead, I climb in bed next to her and hold her.

I have just started drifting to sleep when the front door opens and slams shut again.

"Where is the patient?" the doctor asks in Russian.

But there is no mistaking it—his accent is German, and he does not sound pleased.

CHAPTER 33

THE DOCTOR

I glance down at Lyuda, asleep in my arms, her forehead covered in sweat. I hate having to wake her up, but I have no choice. I shake her awake, just in time before Ruslan walks in, followed by a tall frowning man, wearing a grey coat.

"Here she is, doctor," Ruslan says. "I will be in the kitchen if you need me."

I get up to greet him. "Hello, doctor. Thank you for coming."

The doctor ignores me and approaches Lyuda. "I will need to examine you. But first, I need to see your papers."

"Here," I say, pulling Lyuda's birth certificate out of her pillowcase.

The doctor inspects the paper. He slides his finger toward the line that says *Nationality: Ukrainian*. He nods and seems satisfied. He hands Lyuda's birth certificate back to me without saying another word.

Does he treat all women like we're invisible or is it just me?

The doctor takes out a stethoscope from his bag and

listens to Lyuda's lungs and pulse. He takes her temperature, examines her pupils and ears, and inspects the gash on her head.

He then uncovers her feet. I fight my impulse to yell at him when he lifts up one of her legs, causing Lyuda to shriek from the pain.

"Mhm," the doctor says to himself.

He places her foot down again and then picks up the other foot by her ankle.

"Ahh!" Lyuda cries out, tears bursting from her eyes and streaming down her face.

Leave her alone, you paskudnik, I want to yell. Or at least want to ask the doctor to be gentler. But I can't risk him leaving, so I bite the inside of my lip instead.

The doctor presses on the bottom of Lyuda's feet and then pulls on each of her toes, one at a time.

"Does this hurt?" he asks before pulling each one, his voice devoid of any concern or emotion.

Lyuda's body jerks and contorts with each motion. I watch, feeling as helpless as I did during the executions. I clench my fists and grit my teeth but force myself to be still, to bear witness to Lyuda's pain.

Finally, the doctor is done. "Get the man," he orders.

"What's wrong with her?" I ask.

"Get the man," the doctor repeats in a flat tone.

I purse my lips, nod, and go to get Ruslan. When I return with him, the doctor is writing something on a piece of paper.

"So? How is she?" Ruslan asks.

The doctor doesn't answer until he is finished writing. He then looks up at Ruslan. "After you bring me back home, bring her to the hospital in Vinnytsia."

Lyuda and I exchange glances.

Whatever you do, stay away from Vinnytsia, Yuriy and Rosa Viktorovna both warned me. *How bad is she that she needs to go to the main hospital in the city?* I wonder.

"Vinnytsia?" Ruslan whines. "Now? It's nearly midnight."

The doctor shrugs. "You can leave her here if you'd like."

Ruslan breathes out with relief. "Oh, good. Thank you, doctor."

"Yes," the doctor says, as he packs his medical instruments back into his travel bag. "She will likely lose function in both feet and will need to have them amputated or she will die of an infection. Unless, that is, you bring her to the hospital immediately. But ultimately the choice is yours."

"Oh, *Bozhe!*" Lyuda cries, although I'm not sure if it is from the pain or from the doctor's prognosis.

I turn to Ruslan. "You need to take her right now. Please. I will watch Pavlik, and I will mind the mill. I will take care of everything. Just please. Go."

Ruslan sighs. "Fine. But you two," he points to me and Lyuda, "you owe me big. I did not hire you to be sick."

The doctor hands Ruslan the note that he had written earlier. "Give this to the chief doctor in the emergency room. He's my colleague and he'll know what to do."

I glance down at the note he wrote in German:

Patient fell. Likely concussion. Signs of compartment syndrome in both feet. Treat immediately to alleviate pressure and prevent necrosis.

After that, if she can walk, let her walk. If she cannot, order to have her shot.

Ruslan shoves the note into his pocket, clearly

unaware of what it says. He picks up Lyuda and carries her out. I follow them, carrying the blankets.

Ruslan secures Lyuda in the back of his wagon as I wrap her in blankets and whisper, "Lyuda. Listen to me. You're going to be okay. You hear me? Remember our survival pact. You understand?"

Lyuda nods. "I'm scared, Mouse," she whispers.

"Me too," I admit. "But you have to pull through." I kiss Lyuda's forehead and hop off the wagon.

I run after it for a few minutes, my feet sinking in the snow, until I can no longer follow.

Please be okay, Lyuda. Please be okay.

CHAPTER 34

JUST SURVIVE SOMEHOW

I work non-stop from the moment that Ruslan and Lyuda leave for the hospital, running back and forth between working the mill and watching Pavlik at the house. Ruslan returns in his wagon nearly twelve hours after he left, but Lyuda is not with him.

"Where is she?" I demand. "How is she?"

"Easy, girl," he says. "She was admitted to the hospital."

The doctor's note flashes before my eyes. *If she can walk, let her walk. If she cannot, order to have her shot.*

"Did they say if she'll be okay? Will she walk again?"

Ruslan shrugs. "How should I know? I'm not a doctor."

"Fine," I huff, "I'll go to find out myself."

"Where are you going? There's work to be done."

"I finished it all while you were away," I respond, and then add, "and I'm taking my payment with me."

Before he can argue, I shove two slices of bread, a potato, and an orange into my coat pockets, step outside, and walk toward the very city I was told to stay away from.

I pull up the hood of my coat as I walk. It feels strange wearing the coat without sharing it with Lyuda. The coat feels so much larger now. Emptier.

I don't like it.

My mind is spinning, playing out every possible scenario—what I would do if Lyuda dies, how I would take care of Lyuda if she were to lose both of her legs. I imagine bringing Lyuda food and water in bed and working for the both of us. That would be fine. I am used to hard work. *Anything will be fine, so long as Lyuda is alive.*

"Just survive somehow, my friend, and we will figure out the rest," I mumble as I walk, pretending that Lyuda can hear me.

Something crunches under my foot. I jump back, glance down and feel a wave of nausea wash over me.

I'd stepped on a hand. A human hand. It's the kind of white that looks almost blue. Corpse white.

My heart is pounding, and my hands are trembling as I sweep the snow off the unmoving hand.

I gasp and crawl back. The hand is still attached to a person. A boy of about fifteen. A dead boy covered in snow. He is naked. His body lies on top of other naked bodies, also covered in snow.

Bile travels up my throat and I vomit on the side of the road.

After a few minutes, I stop heaving, my breathing stabilizes and I approach the mass grave again, thinking back to the one Frida described in Babin Yar.

I check to make sure that no one can see me before I cover the boy as best as I can under the blanket of snow, letting him rest with dignity.

"I'm sorry. I'm so sorry," I whisper to the boy and to the hundreds of other people stacked carelessly into the mass grave with him—stacked as if they are garbage to be thrown away rather than human beings. These were once brothers, sisters, children, and parents. People who laughed at funny jokes and cried when they felt sad.

"I'm so sorry," I keep repeating as I walk twelve more kilometers to the hospital. "Why did I live and why did you die? Why did I get lucky, and you did not?"

I find myself wishing that I could give them something. A proper burial. Anything. But if I did that, I'm sure I would be caught.

"Stupid Mouse," I chide myself. "Always too meek and scared to do anything."

I blame myself all the way up to the white columns of the city hospital, and through the white hospital doors, and up the hospital steps.

The smell of alcohol overwhelms my nostrils as I run up to the front desk. "Romanova, Lyudmila Aleksandrovna?" I ask the receptionist, panting.

The receptionist, a young woman barely older than Lyuda with short brown hair, checks the list in front of her and looks up at me. "Third floor. First room on the right."

I am halfway up the stairs before I realize that I never thanked her.

Bad Mouse, I scold myself. *Where are your manners?*

By the time I enter Lyuda's room, my stomach hurts from the shame and guilt. Lyuda is still as pale as she was last night, and her lips are still chapped with bits of dry blood on them. Both of her feet have been cut open and stuffed with cotton to prevent bleeding.

"Hey, Mouse," Lyuda says, her voice a barely audible whisper.

I burst into tears and hug her as tight as I can. "I'm sorry. I'm so sorry. It's all my fault. It was my turn to go. It should have been me."

"Shh," Lyuda whispers into my ear. "That's your Jewish guilt talking. Just have some potato juice and loosen up a bit, will you?"

I giggle despite myself. "Glad to see you still have your sense of humor."

"That's the one part of me they couldn't surgically remove if they tried."

I chortle, plop on the bed next to Lyuda, and empty my coat pockets onto the nightstand. "I brought you some food. You need to eat. You need strength to get better."

I hand Lyuda a slice of bread.

Lyuda shakes her head. "Can't. I feel so nauseous that just seeing food makes me want to throw up."

I sigh and hand Lyuda a glass of water from the nightstand, but she waves me away. "Can't drink anything. Really nauseous. Sorry."

She tries to sit up and groans in pain.

"Don't," I say. "Just lie down."

Lyuda doesn't argue, which is unsettling.

"What do the doctors say?" I ask.

"That I'm lucky Ruslan brought me in when he did. They needed to cut my feet open to relieve the pressure and they'll probably stay cut open for a few days, maybe a week, and then they'll sew me back up."

"And after that?" I ask.

"When the swelling goes down, hopefully I can walk again, and hopefully the concussion heals by then too."

"You have to heal. And you have to walk again," I say.

I tell Lyuda about the doctor's note. "So, you see, you have to eat. You have to get better. Your life depends on it." *And my life depends on you,* I think, but don't say it out loud.

Lyuda takes a deep breath and nods but doesn't say anything in response.

I try handing her the bread again, but Lyuda refuses both the bread and the potato.

"Fine. How about an orange?" I ask, feeling exasperated. "It has *askorbinka*. Vitamin C. It's good for your health."

"Seriously, I have a splitting headache," Lyuda says. "If I chew on anything, my head will explode."

"I have an idea," I say.

I peel the orange and break it into individual slices. It smells sweet and the sticky juice on my fingers makes my mouth water.

I hand one of the slices to Lyuda. "Here. You don't have to chew it. Just bite into it and suck the juice out of it."

Lyuda sighs. "Fine. It does smell good."

She tries a slice.

And then another. In a few minutes, she has finished the entire orange, looking less pale now. "Are there any more?"

I shake my head. "Not today, but I will bring you more tomorrow. Just concentrate on getting better."

Lyuda smirks. "Survival pact?"

I smile in return. "Survival pact."

Lyuda nods. "I'll do my best."

CHAPTER 35
THE MOVING SNOW

On the way back to the mill, I walk with a bit more bounce in my step even as my stomach rumbles. I left the potato and one of the bread slices with Lyuda despite her objections. I just need her to get stronger. I'm saving the second slice of bread until I get back to the mill.

When I pass by the mass grave again, I pause, taking a moment of silence for all the people buried there—murdered and humiliated simply for which God they prayed to and for one word listed on their paperwork.

Jewish.

My vision blurs again.

I shake out my head and count. *One. Two. Three. Four.*

I take a few slow breaths, and my vision comes into focus once again. I say a silent prayer in Yiddish for the dead and bend down to honor the snow, as well as the bodies buried under it.

The snow moves.

I gasp and shake my head to make sure I'm not hallucinating from hunger and exhaustion.

But the snow moves again and underneath it is a faint grunt.

"Oh, *Bozhe*," I stutter and run toward the moving snow, shoving it aside with my bare fingers.

A small hand clamps around mine.

"Oh, *Bozhe*. Oh, *Bozhe Moi*," I cry out.

Stupid Mouse. Someone can hear you.

I spin my head around, but don't see anyone else.

I turn back to the small hand, gripped around my wrist, and dig around it with my other hand. A second hand grips my other wrist, and I pull.

He is about eight or nine years old. Unlike the corpses around him, the little boy is dressed in a sweater and long pants, both of which are filthy and soaked. He is emaciated. His skin is ashen, and his eyes are bloodshot.

The boy is trembling and staring at me, wide-eyed. He lets go of my wrists and steps back, shivering.

"Were you..." I struggle to find the words, "were you hiding under the corpses?"

The boy nods.

I clasp my hand to my chest. "Oh, *Bozhe Moi*. You poor thing. You must be freezing. Here. Come with me."

I reach for him, but he jerks away.

I hold out my hands, palms up. "I'm not going to hurt you."

The boy continues to back away.

"Okay. Okay. I won't come any closer."

I pull out the remaining slice of bread from my coat pocket. "Take this." I extend my arm toward him. "You need it more than I do. Take it."

The boy stares from me to the bread, and back to me again, but does not approach.

"Okay," I say. "I'm going to leave it here and walk away. All right? And you take it. Please eat."

I place the bread on the melting snow and back away from it.

The boy waits until I am far enough, then checks his surroundings, and slowly creeps toward the bread. He grabs it and bolts into the pine forest, his tiny figure melting into the darkness.

CHAPTER 36
THE LAST JEW IN VINNYTSIA

The sound of laughter fills my ears as I make my way toward Ruslan's house. It's been so long since I've heard genuine laughter. Occasionally, Lyuda and I will share a laugh, and Pavlik will let out a giggle. Yet, I am more used to the sounds of gunfire than those of genuine laughter.

I squirm all over, thinking back to the boy who crawled out of the mass grave. *Is it proper to be laughing at a time like this?*

Stepping through the doorway, I spot Ruslan and his friend Igor. He's a large, muscular man with a dense brown beard and shifty eyes that dart back and forth as he speaks.

Ruslan's voice booms, interrupting my thoughts. "Mouse!"

"Please don't call me that," I say sternly.

"Why not?" he chuckles. "It's your nickname."

I refrain from saying what I'm thinking. *Only Lyuda can call me that.* Instead, I just give him a cold stare.

Ruslan shrugs. "Whatever, come join us. We're celebrating. A toast."

He hands me a white enamel mug half filled with vodka and a slice of a pickle.

I put the mug down on the table but bite into the pickle. It's sweet, salty, and sour, all at the same time. Not as good as Babushka's pickles, but I'm starving, so it will do.

"What are we celebrating?" I ask with my mouth full, trying to play nice and hoping to get another pickle slice.

"This," Igor says and slides a newspaper page toward me.

I force myself to swallow the piece I am chewing, so as not to choke or spit it out.

Taking up half of the page is a black and white image that captures immediate attention. *The Last Jew in Vinnytsia*, the headline boldly declares at the top of the page.

The photograph captures a group of around thirty German military personnel, identified as members of the Einsatzgruppen, a special death squad within the SS.

The Einsatzgruppen are standing solemnly around a ditch filled with bodies – yet another mass grave. In stark contrast to their rigid and uniformed appearance, a lone man kneels before them wearing traditional Ashkenazi Jewish garb – a black jacket over a white shirt, with a heavy coat draped across his lap. One of the Einsatzgruppen members casually points a gun at the man's head, displaying an expression of indifference and disinterest on his face.

"The title ain't fully true now, is it?" Igor says, leaning so close that I can smell the vodka on his breath.

"What do you mean?" I ask, squeezing my fists together under the table.

Igor flips the newspaper to another page and points at the text there. "Says here that this picture was taken from last year. They're just using it in this article. But if you read here," he points to another paragraph on the same page, "they say that just last week, they found more kikes, hiding in people's attics and cellars and the like."

My mind flashes to me and Lyuda hiding in Yuriy's cellar. This must mean that there are more people like him out there, *heroes*—willing to risk their lives to save us.

Igor continues, "But now, I guess, they say they found them all and put them in the ground where they belong."

"How many?" I demand, trying to conceal the tremble in my voice.

Igor squints at me. "How many what?"

"How many Jewish *people* did they kill in Vinnytsia?" I intentionally stress the word *people*, but Igor just shrugs, clearly unaware of the weight of his words.

"Oh, *ya ne znayu*. I can't say for sure," he says. "Maybe around twenty-five thousand."

I swallow down my rising nausea and try to maintain my composure.

Ruslan adds with a laugh, "They were like cockroaches, weren't they?" He playfully nudges Igor's arm. "Well, at least they got rid of all of them now." He leans back in his chair and closes his eyes, seemingly at ease.

I shoot him a glare. *How could you?* I scream in my mind. *I expected this from Igor, but not from you.*

I stand up and start pretending to tidy up the dishes.

How can someone bring you new clothes, give you food, wish you a Happy New Year, and even make sure you have a blanket at night--and then turn around and celebrate genocide?

As I head toward the front door, Pavlik runs up to me with his blonde curls bouncing on his head.

"Up," he says, holding his arms up to be carried.

I take a deep breath and lift him up, trying to calm my racing heart.

"I made something for you," Pavlik says with a smile.

I force a smile in return, still reeling from the events of the day. "Oh really? What is it?"

Pavlik points to his bed, and I carry him over to it. As soon as I set him down, he crawls under his bed and pulls out a crumpled piece of paper from underneath. It's a government document announcing that the new currency will be called a *karbovanez* instead of rubles, and that all rubles must be exchanged for karbovanez. One of the examples on the form shows a smiling girl, and below her image is a stamp with an eagle perching over a swastika.

So now our money will have a Nazi symbol on it, I realize, feeling tense all over.

Pavlik turns the announcement over and hands the paper to me. "I drew this for you."

I freeze as I study the back of the paper. Like the picture he'd drawn in the snow yesterday, this one also depicts a house and people in front of it.

There are also heart symbols drawn in the sunny sky. And snowflakes.

And swastikas.

"This is for you," Pavlik repeats, grinning at me.

"Thank you, Pavlik," I manage to say.

With a forced smile, I fold the paper and tuck it under my arm. "I have to go now," I say, not waiting to see if he will start crying.

But as I walk out the door, I can feel my own heart wailing inside of me.

CHAPTER 37
ORANGES

After a week of working at the mill without Lyuda, I can barely take a step without excruciating pain in my lower back. My legs shake as I put weight on them when I get out of bed in the morning. I will myself to the front door and stretch out my back while holding onto the door handle.

My back gives a slight crack. I grunt from the pain and make my way out the front door. Over the past week, I got in the habit of only standing still when there is something nearby that I can lean on, like a wall or chair.

But nevertheless, I keep working. No breaks. And today, I am determined to make it back to see Lyuda again.

At the end of the day, when I am done with all of my work, I march straight to Ruslan.

"Ah, so you *do* exist, Mouse," Ruslan says with sarcasm in his voice.

I tilt my head up at him. "First, don't call me Mouse. Second, what do you mean that I do exist?"

He shrugs. "I just mean that I've hardly seen you at all today. You must have started at the mill before dawn. Working like a goddamn bee. I honestly think more things are getting done with you working here by yourself than it was with the both of you. Perhaps Lyuda should fall more often."

As I stare at him, my cheeks burn, and my nostrils flare up.

Ruslan waives at me dismissively. "Oh, relax, Mouse. Learn to take a joke."

I bite my bottom lip to stop myself from saying what I really want to say.

Remember what Papa said. Good girls don't get angry, I remind myself and address him as calmly as I can. "Ruslan, before I leave to see Lyuda, I want to bring her some oranges."

Ruslan nods and offers me one. "Here. You two can share this."

I shake my head. "You don't understand. She's still recovering and can only eat oranges at the moment. I need as many as possible to help her heal."

Ruslan gives me a smug look and speaks in a condescending tone, like adults do when they want to belittle children. "No, you don't understand. You work for me, not the other way around."

What is wrong with you, you pitiful excuse for a man?

I want to scream but I take a deep breath and remind myself: *Good girls don't get angry.*

I try again. "Ruslan, please. She needs them to survive."

He smirks. "You don't dictate what I do or how much food I give you. If it weren't for me, you'd be an Ostarbeiter right now."

My head throbs as I whisper through gritted teeth, trying to control my anger, "Is that so? Well maybe we'll volunteer for it then. According to the posters, the Ostarbeiter are paid and fed better than we are."

Ruslan raises his eyebrows at me. "What are you talking about?"

I can't believe it's working.

"You heard me," I say, remembering Rita, the kind woman who gave us the coat and boots.

I step closer to him, standing tall with newfound confidence. "You need me. And you need Lyuda. There aren't many young workers here who can run the mill and take care of your son like we do. So, if you don't give me all of your oranges right now, I'll volunteer both of us for the Ostarbeiter the day she leaves the hospital."

Ruslan stares at me in silence.

"That's what I thought," I say.

I can't believe I actually did it.

I take all four oranges and put them in my coat pocket. "And one more thing. Don't ever call me Mouse again."

I storm out and slam the door behind me.

Maybe good girls DO get angry when they have to, I think, and feel a satisfied grin spread across my face.

I PRACTICALLY SKIP on my way home from the hospital. Lyuda looked much better today, and she ate all the oranges.

A gruff voice halts my steps. "Stop."

I spin around. A man in an SS uniform approaches me, speaking with a thick German accent. "Documents."

"Yes, of course," I say and hand him my papers.

The man inspects my birth certificate and shoves it into his pocket. "You need to come with me."

CHAPTER 38
EXAMINING
THE CATTLE

With a rough tug, the man pulls me with him. We walk for what feels like a half hour, until we arrive at a small clinic that I've never seen before, and he shoves me through the heavy wooden door. The sudden change in temperature is jarring, the air inside somehow colder than outside.

Fear clenches my stomach as I inspect the dimly lit room. *Oh, Bozhe, what's going to happen to me? Did he realize that the papers are fake? Is he going to shoot me?*

I hold my breath against the overwhelming stench of the clinic – a mixture of human waste and decay. My eyes scan the walls, adorned with chipping paint and crawling with cockroaches. A shiver runs down my spine as I take in the cracked floors, covered in dust and dried excrement.

"Is that you, Otto?" A gruff voice echoes from another room.

"Yes, Doctor Voigt," Otto responds in German. "I brought another one."

"Send them in," Doctor Voigt commands.

Otto turns to me with a stern expression, barking orders in Russian for me to enter the room. My legs shaking with each step, I follow him into the unknown.

Just like the hospital, this clinic also has electricity. The harsh overhead lights make me squint and cause my eyes to water. Slowly, the room comes into focus—a stark white space with a single metal examination table in one corner and a writing desk at another. My heart races as I take in the scene before me.

Standing in the center of the room is a tall man with sharp features and cold, grey eyes. He wears a stiff, knee-length white coat that is stained in multiple places. His arms are crossed against his chest and his thin lips are pressed into a hard line. A magnifying mirror rests on his forehead like some kind of gruesome headband.

The doctor beckons for me to come toward him. Otto's rifle presses against my back, urging me forward as I comply, too scared to resist.

With heavy brute force, the doctor unbuttons my coat and tosses it onto the floor. *My coat!*

My heart pounds in my chest as I try to make sense of what is happening.

The doctor then makes me remove my boots, my dress, and finally my undergarments. Panic sets in as I realize how vulnerable and exposed I am.

Will they rape me? Kill me?

I try to cover up my breasts and sex organs with my hands, but the doctor slaps them away and points toward the exam table with a grunt.

My legs buckling under me, I walk over to the corner of the room as if in a daze. The cold metal of the exam table sticks to my skin as I climb up onto its surface.

What is he going to do to me?

Fear and uncertainty swirl through my mind as I lie there shivering on the dirty, stained table.

So cold!

Is he going to cut me open?

I heard of Nazis torturing some people, just to study them. Is that what's going to happen?

I look around the room. *I can try to grab his magnifying mirror, break it, and stab him, or hold it against his neck and order the other one to give me his rifle.*

Before I can do anything, Doctor Voigt walks up to the table, his hefty presence even more imposing now. I am trapped in between him on one side and the pale wall on the other. The already small room feels even smaller, and I am struggling to get a breath in, making it clear to me that as much as I want to act, to fight back, my body will not cooperate now.

The doctor slides the magnifying mirror to his eye. I squint from the glare as he examines my eyes. He then checks my ears and teeth, all the while keeping a painful grip on the different parts of my body. He moves my head and my limp arms and legs, up and down, and side to side as he needs to, leaving stark marks on my skin that will surely turn into bruises.

This exam, it's what we did with cows. Am I just a cow to them? Like livestock?

"Otto, take notes," the doctor orders.

Otto nods, puts down his rifle, and sits behind a desk. He pulls up a sheet of paper and a fountain pen.

A fountain pen! I've always wanted one. Even to hold one would be incredible.

I silently scold myself, *A fountain pen, really, Maria? That's what you're focusing on right now?*

"Take this down," the doctor says and begins

dictating in German. "Brown eyes with dilated pupils that do not constrict, suggesting signs of fear and chronic stress." He takes my pulse with his index and middle fingers. "Pulse is 148 beats per minute. Breathing rate is 26 breaths per minute. Teeth have some plaque and signs of dehydration and neglect."

He coughs without covering his mouth and a splash of his saliva lands on my naked breast. I squirm slightly but force myself to otherwise remain as motionless as possible.

The doctor continues, "She is extremely thin. Quite disgusting actually, and her ribs are showing. The breasts —" I shriek as he squeezes them, "are too small to feed a child if she's even able to have one."

He shoves my legs apart with his callused hands and before I realize what he's doing, he shoves two of his filthy fingers deep inside me.

"Quiet," the doctor hisses in Russian to stop my screaming and continues to dictate to Otto in German. "Pelvic exam is okay, but she desperately needs a bath."

"No children?" The doctor asks in Russian, and after I shake my head, he asks, "When was your last period?"

I count in my head, trying to remember. "A year and ten months ago."

The doctor narrows his eyes. "And you've never been pregnant?"

I shake my head again. "Virgin," I explain in Russian, my lips trembling. "I'm a virgin."

Is that true?

Am I still a virgin after what he just did?

The doctor nods to Otto in German. "Add that she's a virgin and severely malnourished."

"Yes, Doctor," Otto says, continuing to write.

The doctor squeezes my biceps so hard that my eyes water as he continues dictating. "She has some muscle, so she's likely to be able to do physical labor but some of her muscles are atrophied, probably due to malnutrition and dehydration."

The doctor lets go of my arms and turns to Otto. "All in all, she's quite abysmal, but she'll do."

What does that mean? "Will do" for what?

"What will happen to me?" I manage to ask him but the doctor walks out of the room without another word.

"Be grateful," Otto says to me in Russian. He collects all his notes and swings his rifle around his shoulder. "You've been selected for the Ostarbeiter."

"No!" I bolt up, covering myself with my hands. "He said that I am malnourished, weak, and abysmal. I won't be any good."

Otto stares at me. "Ah, you understand German. Good for you." He pulls up a camera on a tripod from behind the desk. "Hold still."

I stare as Otto takes a picture of me, without any concern that I am still naked. He then adds, "No, you aren't good for the breeding programs. Besides, you aren't Aryan anyway." Then he throws my clothes at me. "But aside from that, you'll do as an Ostarbeiter. So be grateful. Your choices were to be selected or to be shot. Now, stay here."

With that, Otto walks out of the room.

"Wait! My papers!" I shout after him. "What about my papers?"

But Otto doesn't respond, he just closes the door behind him.

I jump off the exam table and hurry to get dressed. I run toward the door, push it open, and step out into the hallway. I stop when I see an armed SS guard standing there, a man who wasn't there before.

The man doesn't even bother taking off his rifle, like he knows that I won't fight or run. He just shakes his index finger at me, like I am some naughty child, and motions for me to go back inside the exam room, his face deadpan.

I stare at him for several seconds, unsure of what to do. But after weighing out my options in my mind, I sigh, bow my head, and walk back inside the exam room.

What am I going to do? What's going to happen to me now? How will I let Lyuda know? I glance down at my boots. *How will I give her the boots back? And the coat? She will need them when she gets out of the hospital. If she gets out of the hospital.*

I grip my hair with both hands in realization. *What if Ruslan thinks I left? I threatened to. Why did I do that? What if he hires someone else like Fedka did? And then Lyuda won't have a job. She'll starve. She'll die of cold and starvation, and it will all be my fault.*

I take off my coat and boots, and step outside of the room again, this time barefoot. I cringe at the cold, sticky ground under my feet and clench my teeth before I address the guard in German.

"Listen, I understand that I am going to be taken as an Ostarbeiter. But my friend doesn't know that, and she needs these clothes." I point to the boots and coat. "Can someone please bring them to the Vinnytsia central hospital and give these to Romanova, Lyudmila Aleksandrovna? She goes by Lyuda."

The guard shakes his head and silently points for me to get back to the exam room. The absence of any emotion on his face makes me feel colder than the icy winter air on my shivering feet.

I clench my jaw and return to the exam room again. I pull on my boots and cuddle my coat against my chest for comfort. The coat still smells like Lyuda. I close my eyes, pretending that I am hugging her. That way, with my dress, still embroidered with reminders of my family, and with my coat pressed tightly to my chest, I won't have to face this alone.

CHAPTER 39
THE TRAIN
TO NOWHERE

O tto returns sixteen-thousand two-hundred and twelve seconds later. I count each one.

I hop off the table when he enters the room. "My documents! Please, give me my documents."

Otto shows me a piece of paper. "This will be your document now."

I unfold it. It's not my birth certificate but a new piece of paper. It has all the same information as my forged birth certificate, plus new material. This one has my photograph, the one Otto took earlier, but thankfully with just my startled face. Two stamps surround my photograph, each one featuring an eagle standing over a swastika. My stomach churns at the sight of these symbols on my permanent paperwork.

Otto yanks the paper away from me, pockets it, and pulls out a square, blue badge made of cotton. At the center of the badge, the letters OST are stitched in white over the blue background.

Otto uses two safety pins to attach it on the left side

of my graduation dress, but not without running his hands over and squeezing both of my breasts first.

"What?" he barks when I yelp in pain.

"Nothing," I mumble.

"I thought so. Now, come with me," he says, and drags me out of the room by my arm.

Where is he taking me? What will they do to me? What will happen to Lyuda?

I consider speaking in German to Otto and asking him where he's taking me, to see if he is more willing to answer in his native tongue but decide against it.

Just survive somehow and get back to Lyuda.

The realization that I will have to survive without Lyuda feels like a gut punch.

I scream inside my head. *I don't want to! I don't want to live without her.*

I imagine wrestling Otto for his gun.

Whether I shoot him, or he shoots me, it must be better than whatever will happen to me now.

I make a small gesture toward the weapon but the image of Lyuda's stern face makes me pull back.

No. You're safe for now. Remember the survival pact.

Otto drags me outside of the clinic and down the snow-covered road.

I try to put on my coat, but Otto won't let go of my arm.

"Don't protest," he hisses at me in German, squeezing my arm hard enough that I know I will bruise again.

We walk for about ten more minutes until we come to a cattle car train. A few of the wooden cars have small windows lined with barbed wire, but most don't have any windows.

Three armed guards pace around the perimeter, each

holding a German Shepherd on a leash. The dog closest to me is emaciated. He growls at me, making me jump.

Otto laughs and then addresses the guard holding the dog—a tall, thin man with four silver pips on one side of his collar and the double lightning SS symbol on the other. "Here's another Ostarbeiter for you, Sturmbann-führer Jeckeln."

Jeckeln nods. "Do you have her paperwork?"

Otto reaches into his pocket and pulls out the same document he showed me earlier. Jeckeln examines it and hands it back to Otto. He then walks around me, still holding onto the dog's leash, and inspects me from all angles.

Like cattle.

He halts in front of me, staring me up and down, and brushes his straw-colored hair with his fingers. He has thin mustache, and his eyes are cold and impersonal, the color of the sky on a foggy day, devoid of warmth or kindness.

"Cabin two," Jeckeln orders.

"Yes, Sturmbannführer Jeckeln," Otto says and drags me toward the train.

"Wait." I struggle in Otto's grasp.

Jeckeln lets go of his dog, who pounces next to me and let out a terrifying growl. I freeze and stop squirming, as Jeckeln points a pistol at me.

"Please," I beg. "Please. I just want to know where we are going."

"Nowhere," Jeckeln says. "Now get on the train before I shoot you."

"Relax, Axel," Otto says to him in German. "She's like a lamb. Very obedient."

"It's Sturmbannführer Jeckeln to you," Jeckeln

corrects him, but with a strange smirk on his face. "Like a lamb, you said? Tell you what, throw her in cabin three instead."

"Yes, Sturmbannführer Jeckeln," Otto says and drags me toward the third car, then up the slippery train steps, and inside the tiny, windowless cabin.

The pungent smell of wet hay fills the small wooden space, mixing with the sharp odor of animal waste from the caged chickens and goats in the corners. Otto shoves the paperwork into my trembling hands before stepping outside and slamming the door shut behind him.

Although I always wanted to ride the train, this was never how I pictured it. The unnerving cabin offers little comfort as I sit alone in the cramped space, surrounded by the sounds of rustling hay and shifting animals. With no windows to let in natural light, darkness envelops me.

Beethoven's sonata is beginning to play in my head.

"No," I say out loud and shake my head from side to side.

One. Two. Three. Four.

I take a big breath and feel my way around until I find a corner and slide down onto the ground. I wrap my coat around my legs and arms like a blanket.

Lyuda, whatever happens, please stay alive. Just survive somehow and I will try to do the same.

The cabin door flies open once again, creating a flash of light, and two more women are shoved inside. Someone else slams the door shut on the outside and everything goes dark again.

"Oh, *Bozhe*. Oh, *Bozhe Moi*." one of the women whimpers.

"Hey, it's okay," I say.

"Who's here?" the second woman asks.

"My name is Anna," I say to match the name on my papers. "What are your names?"

"I'm Oksana," the first woman says with a sniffle, and I realize that she is crying.

"I'm Irina," the second woman says. She sounds a little older than the first. "I can't see anything."

"I'm going to reach out and guide you to the corner," I say. "It's drier and a little warmer here."

I place my coat on the ground and get to my feet. I hold onto the wall with one hand and reach out into the darkness with the other, until I feel someone else's hand grasp mine.

"It's okay," I say when I hear Oksana gasp. "I've got you. See if you can hold Irina's hand since you're standing close to each other, and I will guide you both here."

"Okay," Oksana says, sounding a little calmer now.

I guide both of them, gently pulling Oksana's hand closer to me in the corner. The two women slide onto the floor next to me with Oksana in the middle.

"I'm so cold," Oksana says. I can feel her shivering.

"I have a coat that we can all share as a blanket, but we are going to have to cuddle up close to each other," I reply.

All three of us scoot close and I spread the coat around the three of us. It's barely long enough to cover all our legs. My chest and arms are much colder now than when I had the coat to myself, but my heart is warmer for the company. We shiver together in silence, aside from the occasional clucking of the chickens and the distant sounds of the other cabin doors slamming.

"How many people do you think they're bringing?" Oksana asks.

"They are probably going to try to get the train full," Irina says.

"And we are all going to be transported like those chickens," Oksana replies.

"Like cattle," I correct her.

'What's the difference?" Oksana asks.

I sigh. "None, I guess. Either way, they don't see us as human."

The three of us sit in silence again. Someone is sniffling to the side of me—one of the girls is crying. Oksana, I'm guessing, based on the location of the sound.

The train jerks and starts moving.

"Where do you think we're going?" Oksana asks and squeezes my hand.

I squeeze back. "When I asked, they told me we're going to nowhere, but based on the Ostarbeiter paperwork I received, I'm guessing we're going to Germany, but I can't be sure."

"So, I guess the only thing we know for sure is that right in this very moment, we are okay," Irina says.

I ponder that for a few moments.

It's somewhat true. Things overall are worse than I could have ever imagined. And yet, they also could have been worse. I could have been shot along with Babushka on the very first night of the occupation. But for some reason, the SS that came to my house let me go. *Was it just because I gave him some aspirin, or does he actually have a heart?*

I could have ended up in one of the mass graves. But because Yuriy risked his own life to hide me and Lyuda and forged our documents, we both survived, at least so far.

I could be facing the horrors of this trip alone, but I've

been joined by two other women facing the same experience. And if we all have to face the same fate anyway, a fate I wouldn't wish on anyone, then I am grateful that we are facing it together.

Grateful and guilty.

Why did I get to survive, and other people did not? My mind flashes back to Andrei.

Why did I get lucky when over 60,000 Jewish people have been killed so far? Or maybe more by now? How many Jewish people will die altogether? Why did my brother and Babushka have to die, and I survived? And what happened to Papa?

I think back to the little boy I saw climb out from a pile of corpses a few nights ago. *I wonder if he's okay. I wish I knew his story. His name. I wish I knew if he'd survived. He's someone's son. Someone's baby brother. And he might be all alone in this now.*

I squeeze Oksana's hand again, unsure if it's to comfort myself or the other girl. Oksana squeezes back and lays her head on my shoulder.

CHAPTER 40

TORMENTORS
AND PROTECTORS

Based on the rhythm of her breathing, Oksana soon falls asleep. I close my eyes but can't fall asleep for a long time.

I'm so sorry, Lyuda, I silently plead. *I should have been more careful. And now, you won't have the coat or the winter boots.*

I need you to promise me that you will get better. Promise me that you will survive, Lyuda. And I promise that I will do all that I can to survive too.

I start drifting into a dream. A memory.

The older boys have stolen my shoe again.

"Give it back," I yell, but my tiny six-year-old voice can hardly be heard over the sounds of the boys' laughter.

"Maksim, catch," Sergei shouts and kicks my shoe like a soccer ball.

I run after it. "Give it back," I shout again as I run toward Maksim.

Maksim smirks. He lifts the shoe above his head, so that I have to jump up to try and reach it, then throws my shoe into the trash. He leans over and puts his face right up to mine.

"Climb in and get it, you little bitch," Maxim says.

My lower lip quivers. "You're mean," I say in a barely audible whisper.

"What did you say?" Maksim roars and pulls both of my braids.

"Oww, let me go."

But Maksim drags me toward the trash. "Let's put you where you belong, you kike pig."

"Let go!" I scream again.

Pavlik's growl comes from behind me. "Get. Your filthy hands. Off my sister."

Maksim releases my braids, and I spin around to see my brother's towering figure.

He is fifteen, about the same age as my tormentors, but much taller. Pavlik spits out the freshly plucked straw he was chewing a moment ago and steps toward Maksim.

Maksim raises his hands and takes a step back. "Pavlik, man. I'm sorry. I didn't know she was your sister. I wouldn't have if I—"

Pavlik takes another step toward him. "So, if she wasn't my sister, then it would be okay for you to bully little girls?"

"Watch out!" I shout as Sergei lunges at Pavlik from behind.

Pavlik spins around and in one move elbows the other boy in the gut.

"Oww," Sergei cries out, holding his stomach as he falls on the ground.

Pavlik turns back to face Maksim. He grabs the front of Maksim's shirt and lifts him up. "Stay away from my little sister and tell your cronies to do the same. Don't touch her, don't talk to her, don't even look at her, or you'll have to deal with me. Understood?"

Maksim nods.

"Good," Pavlik says and releases him.

"Thank you," I manage to say when Pavlik fishes out my shoe from the garbage.

"I'm your brother, Maria," he says, as he helps me to retie my shoelaces. "I will always look out for you. Do you understand? Always."

CHAPTER 41
LILACS AND PIANOS

I sit up with a gasp. My face is wet; I must have been crying.

"Is it time to get up yet?" I whisper to Lyuda.

Lyuda.

The reminder makes my insides twist and burn.

Lyuda is the hospital. Alone.

And I—

I'm on the train to nowhere.

Down the corridor, there are doors slamming—opening and closing.

I elbow Oksana. "I think something is happening."

In the darkness, I hear Oksana wake Irina, and the three of us huddle together, quiet and motionless, save for the still moving train.

We all gasp in unison when the door to our cabin bursts open and three men walk inside. I squint my eyes, because the harsh light from the men's lanterns makes it nearly impossible to see.

I recognize Axel Jeckeln, the same SS who threatened me before we boarded, as well as the other two SS that I saw with him then. *Was it yesterday? It's hard to tell without any external light.*

"Inspection," Axel says in Russian. "Each of you, get up and stand in a different corner. Face the wall."

None of us move, frozen by the sight of the armed SS.

"Now!" Axel shouts, pointing his gun at us.

Irina and I jump up first. Oksana is still on the floor, shivering. Irina and I help her up and lean her against the wall before we spread out to the opposite corners.

I face the wall adjacent to the one where the three of us slept.

"Raise your hands and spread your arms and legs," Axel commands from behind me.

Why is this necessary, when they already inspected us at the clinic? I wonder but do as he says anyway.

Axel's quick and gruff hands pat me down. I wince. My arms and legs are already raw from the doctor's exam, and I know full-well that I will have more bruises from Axel's brute force.

He squats behind me as he pats down my legs.

Then he pulls up my dress and rises back up, lifting my dress over my head, and then pulling down my stockings and my underwear.

What's happening?

I feel the hard barrel of his gun press against my thigh.

No.

Not a gun.

And then there is a piercing pain between my legs, like I'm being stabbed there over and over.

Oh, Bozhe. Is this rape?

I squeeze my eyes shut.

The pain won't stop.

How long will it last? When will it be over?

Quick. Think of something else. Anything!

Celebrating Lyuda's birthday.

No, thinking of that seems wrong at a moment like this.

Little Pavlik's drawing.

Wrong again.

Maybe I can just imagine something, even if it's not real.

The inside of my body hurts so much!

I clench my jaw to keep myself from screaming, and picture myself in a garden full of lilacs.

Okay, I think I can do this.

I walk up to the lilacs. I smell each one.

And now a piano appears, right there in the garden.

I am the one in charge of my body now. And I want to play the piano.

It's my choice.

I sit at the bench and put my fingers on top of the keys.

Beethoven Sonata #14.

I speed up and slow down as I wish. And with each note I play, the smell of lilacs grows stronger.

I squeeze my eyes shut even harder and switch to a different piece—a crescendo in B flat. The scent of the lilacs envelops me—white, rose, and purple lilacs, their smell is both sweet and overpowering. My sonata evolves, accelerando: smells of mead; allegro: sweet, sweet honey; presto, prestissimo in C major.

I stop playing, reach out to grab a magical bloom—and in a flash the flowers disappear, and I collapse onto the harsh ground.

CHAPTER 42

WHY DO WE BLEED?

"Anna. Anna, are you okay?"

I force myself to open my eyes, but everything is just as dark with them open as it is with them closed.

"Are you okay?" Irina asks again, shaking me.

"I... I don't know," I mutter.

I sit up. My head is spinning. "Oof."

I nearly fall back down on the ground.

My lower abdomen aches and pulsates, as if someone is twisting my insides round and round, nonstop, like bad monthly cramps, but worse.

Much, much worse.

Something is wet between my legs.

I feel around—there's sticky and viscous liquid. It smells like rust. Or metal.

Blood.

"I'm bleeding," I say. "Why am I bleeding? I haven't had my period for nearly a year and a half. Why am I bleeding now?"

Irina sighs in the darkness next to me. "Girl, it's not

that kind of blood. Do you know anything about women's bodies?"

Irina doesn't say it in a condescending tone, but the phrase reminds me of Natasha's comment on the night of the German final, about getting pregnant.

"My Mamo died when I was ten," I say, noticing the familiar lump that forms in the middle of my throat as I speak. "She died in the famine, the Holodomor. So, I guess, she never got to teach me."

"Poor girl," Irina says.

As the coat is draped over my shoulders, I feel two sets of arms wrap around me in a gentle embrace. Irina, I presume, cradles my head against her chest while Oksana rests her head against my waist.

A wave of emotion washes over me at this small act of kindness, and I sob uncontrollably. My body trembles as tears pour down my face, but the women continue to hold me, making me feel safe for the first time since I was separated from Lyuda. Eventually, exhaustion takes over and the warmth of their bodies and the soothing sound of their voices lull me into a peaceful slumber.

I dream of Axel and of Rita, the woman who gifted us the coat and the boots. In my dream, Axel smirks at Rita. "What's worse than being dead?"

At this, Rita spits back at him, "You're not a woman. You wouldn't understand."

CHAPTER 43

SNOWDROPS AND WEREWOLVES

Over the next day, I get to know Oksana and Irina better, at least by the sounds of their voices. I learn that Irina is twenty-four, although judging by her low, confident tone, I would have guessed she was older.

Irina is married and has two small children, who as far as she knows, are at home with her parents. Irina's husband was forced to join the Red Army under the threat of desertion. Her older brother attempted to flee from the Army, but was caught, arrested, and eventually shot by Stalin's secret service, the NKVD, in a prison massacre.

"At first, when the Germans came, I was grateful," Irina says. "I even baked fresh bread and brought it out for them with salt, treating them like honored guests. My four-year-old daughter picked fresh flowers and handed them to the SS. We all thought they would be our liberators. My neighbor even had a poster of Hitler with a quote, *Hitler the Liberator,* in his house.

"I was so stupid. I thought my husband would be

coming home." She spits on the ground. "I welcomed the wolves before they ate us. How disgusting is that?"

"You didn't know," I say, holding her hand. "We don't always know who the good people are until bad things happen."

I learn that Oksana, whose shrill voice sometimes creates ringing in my ears, is twenty-one and was caring for her ailing mother before she was taken. Oksana used to walk to Vinnytsia at least once per week to get the proper medicine for her mother because there was only one pharmacy that had the medicine she needed.

"The thing is," Oksana says, "over the past year, I'd noticed something. On the way to Vinnytsia, I'd walk through Stryzhavka, through the pine forest there. And I'd see the SS supervising the Soviet Army prisoners. Apparently, they were building some kind of a secret house."

"What kind of house?" Irina asks, sounding intrigued.

"Not sure," Oksana says. "But it must have been important because they'd never let anyone linger for too long. But the rumor is that they're building it for a werewolf."

"Werewolf?" I ask and sit up. "Those aren't real."

"I know," Oksana says, "I overheard one of the SS talking about it. I don't speak German, but I could have sworn I heard him say *werwolf*."

My mind flashes to a year and a half ago when Lyuda and I stayed with Rita and her husband, the auxiliary policeman.

What was it that Rita had said? *"I overheard my husband talk about some kind of a wolf. A big, strong wolf that kills people."*

Could this be the same wolf? I wonder. *Are the Nazis*

using some kind of supernatural weapons to invade other countries? Could there really be a werewolf in Vinnytsia?

We are all thrown to the side when the train comes to a sudden stop. The chickens cluck, making a ruckus, and I almost throw up a piece of the raw egg we'd all shared a few hours earlier.

"Why are we stopped?" Oksana whispers.

"Huddle together, girls," Irina says. "Whatever happens, we stay together."

I nod even though we are still in full darkness. I cling to the other girls, my heart pounding.

I can hear the other cabin doors slamming open and shut again.

Are they coming to rape us? I can't survive that again. I will jump on his rifle and force him to shoot me if he tries it.

No, just survive, I silently remind myself. *Remember the survival pact. No matter what happens, you have to get back to Lyuda.*

My heart is pounding so much I can feel it in my throat, almost as if it wants to jump out of my mouth.

Is this it? Are we in Germany now? Are we going to be sent to work in a death camp? Or are they going to shoot us all now? Is this when I'm going to die?

The aggressive light slashes at my eyes a thousand times worse than it had yesterday. I shield my face.

"Fresh air stop," Axel commands. "You need it. Your cabin smells worse than a pigsty."

I shudder. I can barely see him, as he's standing behind the blinding light. I clench and tighten my entire body as the place he violated throbs all over again.

"Outside! Now!" he shouts.

Irina jumps up to her feet. Oksana and I follow her lead.

Squinting with one eye at a time to minimize my pain from the ravaging light, I follow Irina, pulling Oksana's hand behind me. I hold onto the train wall with one hand and Oksana's hand with the other as I descend the slippery steps.

My legs shake as I step out onto the snowy ground. I'm not sure if they are shaking from the cold, fear, or atrophy.

I haven't been able to fully stand up on my feet since Axel...

I glance at him. He is talking to another armed man outside in the snow. He is gazing absent-mindedly at the rest of the train passengers.

Can he even tell me apart from the other girls? I wonder. *Or is it how some people can't tell one cow apart from another? Though I could always pick Moo-Moo out of a thousand.*

Someone's hands wrap my coat around me.

"Put this on or you'll catch a cold," Irina whispers into my ear.

I glance at her. This is the first chance I've had to study her. Irina is tall. Taller than Lyuda even. She is thin and has long brown hair tied in a messy braid. Her blue eyes have bags and wrinkles under them despite her young age. Her long-sleeved grey dress is covered with stains and patches.

"But what about you and Oksana?" I ask nodding toward the other girl, who, I now realize, is barely taller than I am and like Irina, also has long brown hair.

"Don't argue with your elders," Irina says.

I nod and put on my coat. "Thank you."

My eyes still throb from the light and the blinding

reflection of sunlight in the crystalline snow. My head is pounding with pain. It feels both heavy and unwieldy.

I peel my eyes away from the snow and glance around. There must be about four dozen passengers on this train. Most of them are young women and girls; some look about twelve or thirteen, while the oldest is probably Irina's age. Every single one of them is hunched over, covered in dirt. Many of them have matted hair, and some have blood on their skirts.

Did Axel and the other guards visit them too? Or do some of these girls still get their periods? I wonder.

All of the women have the same, sullen look of hopelessness in their eyes. They remind me of Moo-Moo. And Mamo before she—

I shake my head. *Stay in the present moment.*

I glance farther away, taking in the view. There is an empty, snow-covered field ahead of us. And just a few meters beyond the last of the passengers, there are tiny, white, tear drop-shaped flowers hanging from their arched green stems like small bells.

Snowdrops.

The first flowers of spring, their presence indicating the end of a vicious winter. I smile, remembering picking them with Babushka.

Hope, Babushka used to say. *Snowdrops mean hope.*

Vivaldi's *Spring* plays in my mind, in the way that my mother would play it when we practiced together.

I indulge in the memory for a few seconds and then shake my head to refocus on the present moment again, as well as on the flowers in my line of vision.

"Hey—" I start, intending to show the snowdrops to my new friends.

Someone screams. There's a lot of commotion, and the passengers crowd together.

I get onto my tip toes to see over the rest of them. One of the youngest girls has collapsed onto the ground.

Axel runs toward the crowd and elbows his way toward her, gun in hand, while the other SS remain in place.

"What happened?" Axel asks in Russian.

The young woman standing next to the girl who collapsed is saying something to Axel, but I can't hear the details. Axel lowers his gun and holsters it. He kneels down to check on the girl and yelps in pain when the girl kicks him in the balls.

I hear Axel curse as he falls to his knees and see one of the women tackle him. "Run, Lena!" she yells at the young girl, who jumps up to her feet and bolts.

Several other women rush to assist in tackling Axel on the ground and the second SS hurries over to aid him.

"Go after her," Axel yells to the second man, while fighting off the women.

I am standing motionless, watching the scene unfold.

"Hurry," Irina whispers into my ear.

I glance back at her, confused.

"What are you waiting for?" Irina hisses. "A special invitation? Run! Let's go."

My eyes widen in understanding. *This is our chance.*

I take one last look at Axel, just in time to see him point his pistol at the woman who tackled him.

I take off after Irina and Oksana. I don't stop when I hear the gunshot behind me. I just keep running.

CHAPTER 44
ON THE RUN

Twice, I trip over my long coat, and twice I slide into the swallowing snow. The second time I fall, my ankle twists at an awkward angle, and I cry out in pain.

Irina, who is about ten meters ahead, turns back and runs toward me. "Oksana! Help me to lift her up."

Oksana returns as well, and they sling my arms around their shoulders and hoist me up.

I try to protest. "Leave me. You should run ahead."

"Shut up and keep moving," Irina says. "We are all going to make it together."

I tighten my jaw, trying to ignore the sharp pain in my ankle, and almost fall again when Oksana trips over my coat.

"Take it off. It's only slowing us down," Oksana demands.

"Okay," I agree. "But we should hide it, so they aren't able to track us."

"I'm pretty sure our footprints in the snow will make it easy for them to track us," Irina says and pulls my coat off. "Just hold the coat with one arm and lean on me with the other." She turns to Oksana. "Run ahead and find us a place to hide. Somewhere where our footsteps won't betray us."

Oksana nods and takes off ahead.

"You really think there's somewhere they won't find us?" I ask, trying not to whimper from pain.

"I guess we'll see," Irina says, out of breath. "Maybe at least she'll make it out alive," referring to Oksana.

I gulp, thoughts firing at me like flying bullets. *It's all my fault. People are always risking their lives for me. It was my turn to go up to the mill that night; if it wasn't for me, Lyuda wouldn't have gotten hurt. And now Irina is risking her life for me because I didn't think to take off my coat when we first started running.*

"Look," I say, panting, "you should run ahead too."

"Shh," Irina says, putting her finger to her mouth. She crouches down, pulling me down with her.

I strain my ears and then I hear them.

Dogs!

"Run!" I whisper to Irina.

'Together," Irina whispers back and pulls me up with her.

"Girls, over here!" Oksana shouts from up ahead.

Irina and I sprint toward her, and toward a small overpass that crosses a narrow river up ahead.

"Hurry. Get under it," Oksana instructs.

Irina mumbles something about it being a terrible plan, but we don't have any other options. All three of us slide down under the overpass and hide in the mud next to the water, huddling together.

Above, we hear barking and voices, but I can't make out what they're saying.

Then everything goes quiet.

Oksana squeezes my hand and we stare at each other, holding our breath as if we are under water.

There is a slight rustle right above us. And then a low growl.

"*Fass!*" Axel shouts.

And before we can even scream, four dogs pounce on us.

Forceful paws knock me over to my side. Hot drool lands on the back of my neck. I manage to cover my face with my coat just in time before dagger-like teeth bite into the flesh on my right shoulder. The dog pulls, dragging me around like a ragdoll.

I yank my shoulder, once, twice, and in spite the searing pain, finally wriggle it free. But the hound finds a new grip on my hip, its teeth stabbing into my skin like four jagged knives.

Sweltering pain spreads over my entire right side. I try to cry out, but the air seems to have left my lungs.

I'm dead, I think to myself, gasping from the sweltering pain. *This is it. I'm going to die.*

"*Anhalten. Setzen,*" Axel commands.

The dog releases its grip and steps off me. I am shivering uncontrollably, despite the fact that even the smallest movement sends agonizing spasms down my spine and leg.

"Get up this very second or you will die," Axel orders.

My hands are still shaking as I pull the coat from my head and look up at him.

Axel is standing over me, pointing his gun at my head. Another SS, not the one I saw outside earlier, a new one, is standing next to Axel, also pointing his gun at me, ready to shoot. Four dogs are sitting on the snowy ground behind them, blood dripping from their mouths. They look obediently at Axel, awaiting further instructions.

"You will all either walk yourselves back to the train or you will be shot," Axel says.

I am still shivering as I slowly get to my feet, trying not to look at the pool of blood under me, painting the snow scarlet.

To my side, Irina and Oksana both struggle to get up as well. Irina is bleeding from both of her arms, her leg, and her neck. She looks like she is about to faint. She must have been attacked by two dogs, judging by her wounds.

Oksana is bleeding too but it's difficult to assess the extent of her wounds because, unlike Irina, Oksana is barely moving. Her hair hangs loose over her face, sticking to her cheeks.

Oksana stares at the dogs with a look of ultimate terror, visibly too traumatized to move.

Irina manages to get to her feet. She is swaying from side to side, and then collapses onto her knees, panting.

Bang!

I scream and fall on my knees too.

Oh, Bozhe! He shot Irina.

Irina gasps several times, gurgles, and then stops moving.

"Last warning," Axel says. "You two either walk yourselves back to the train or I shoot you right here."

I glance over at Oksana, who is also kneeling and is staring at Irina's body but still failing to move.

Axel aims his gun at her.

"Okay!" I shout.

It works. Axel turns back to face me. *They point their guns at whoever is speaking.*

"Okay," I repeat, forcing myself to get back up again. "We will *both* go back to the train." I make sure to put stress on the word *both*.

I pick up my coat, which is now stained with patches of blood.

Should I just leave the coat here? I wonder. *The blood will never come off and I will never be able to look at it without remembering Irina.*

No, I argue with myself. *It's all I have left of Lyuda. This and the boots. I have to keep it.*

I squeeze the bloodstained coat closer to my chest.

The dogs growl but don't move as I walk past them and approach Oksana.

"C'mon, we have to go back," I say.

If Oksana understands me, her facial expression doesn't show it. She is still staring at Irina's motionless body, unblinking, as if trying to understand what happened.

I lean down, keeping my knees bent, throw Oksana's arm around my shoulder and pull her up to her feet. My ankle still throbs but I manage to put weight on it anyway.

It's that or we'll both be shot.

Oksana leans her entire weight on my injured shoulder and allows me to lead her back without uttering a sound. I pull her with one arm and carry my coat in the other.

I try not to look at the dogs walking next to me because every time I do, I see Irina's corpse flash in front of my eyes and it makes my knees buckle. I try to block out the searing pain in my side, shoulder, and ankle. Instead, I stare straight ahead, also ignoring the throbbing in my eyes from the bright reflection of the sun in the blinding snow.

My stomach churns when I see the train coming up ahead. *I was so stupid to think we would be free.*

The rest of the people are already gone, presumably ushered back inside by the third guard who is pacing back and forth in front of the train.

"Just a little bit farther," I say to both Oksana and myself.

There is a dark object lying in the snow ahead of us. The stabbing pain behind my right eye makes it difficult to make out what it is. But as we step closer, I gasp when I realize what I am seeing.

Lena, the little girl who ran away earlier, now lies curled into a ball, her clothing torn, her flesh mangled. She is not moving.

I shiver, remembering the feel of the dog's sharp teeth on my shoulder.

"Just look straight ahead, Oksana," I say. "We're almost there."

I nearly slip on the ice-covered steps but catch myself and pull Oksana up too. We walk into the familiar foul-smelling car and collapse onto the ground.

Axel walks in after us. "You two will either heal and walk like you're all shiny and new by the time we arrive in Germany, or you will be shot just like your friend back there."

He slams the door, and we are in the dark once more.

CHAPTER 45
THE SILENT PRAYERS

Oksana and I cry in the darkness and hold each other until we can speak again.

"We need to dress each other's wounds," I say, grunting as I sit up.

"I can't see anything," Oksana says, her voice shaking, "but I feel like I'm bleeding all over. And I can't get the image of Irina's body out of my mind."

"Hold my hand. Sit up," I say and pull Oksana up into a seated position. "There. Now just feel my hand in yours. Just focus on the feel of it. Breathe. Right now, in this very moment, we're okay."

Oksana squeezes my hand and whimpers, "That's what Irina said the other night."

I hold Oksana's hands in both of mine. "I know. And we survived. We owe it to her to stay alive."

Oksana takes a deep breath, and I feel her shudder.

"Okay," she whispers. "What do we need to do?"

"Hang on." I let go of Oksana's hands and tear two big chunks of fabric from the skirt of my dress. "Here's one piece of cloth and I'll hold on to the other." I place the strip of fabric into Oksana's hand. "There. Now, guide my hand to where your injuries are, and I'll feel for which need to be tended to first. Then, we'll switch."

ABOUT AN HOUR LATER, we are done. Still weak, sore, and shaky, I manage to lie down again, though the hard floor and the extent of my wounds make it impossible to get comfortable.

The two of us cuddle up under the coat, using it as a blanket. A few minutes later, Oksana's breathing slows, as she is drifting into deep sleep.

Good, I think. *She needs sleep to recover.*

My mind flashes to the stillness in Irina's face.

I'm sorry, I whisper silently. *I'm so sorry.*

I try to calm my breathing, but my thoughts attack me like throwing knives.

It should have been ME. Irina slowed down to help ME. Lyuda got hurt because of ME. Yuriy was probably sent away because of ME. I should have just died on that very first night when Natasha brought those Nazis to my house.

I close my eyes and replay the first execution in my mind—the look on Babushka's face. And Andrei. Sweet Andrei.

I open my eyes again. Somehow, in spite of the darkness, keeping my eyes open keeps the flashbacks away.

Lyuda, I pray silently, *I don't know if you can hear me, but I just want you to know that I'm alive.*

I probably don't deserve to live. It's not fair that so many innocent people are dead. Like Lena, the little girl from the train, who just wanted her freedom. And Irina, who tried to save Oksana and me.

Oksana stirs and groans in her sleep. I pat her head the way I used to comfort little Pavlik, Ruslan's son, when he had a bad dream. "It's okay, Oksana. Everything is going to be okay."

Oksana's body shifts and I feel her exhale and relax.

I can't die now. Oksana needs me.

A realization spreads over me, making me shiver. *Is this what Lyuda used to do for me?*

I feel a familiar twinge of sadness in my throat at missing Lyuda.

You know, Lyuda, I silently say, *there have been so many times that I've thought about ending my life, especially in the last few days, being without you.*

It would be easy to just tell one of the Nazis that I'm Jewish and have them kill me. But then I remember our survival pact. And somehow, it makes me think that if I survive, maybe you will survive too.

It's stupid, I know. But it's all I have. So, if by any chance you can hear me, I want you to know that I'm alive, and I hope you are too.

CHAPTER 46

GERMANY

A loud boom rips through the air, startling me awake.

Oksana's hand grips my arm as she screams, "They're shooting again!"

"Oh, *Bozhe!* Are you sure?" I ask, my heart racing.

The room falls silent for several minutes before another deafening sound echoes through the walls.

I duck down and cover my head, bumping elbows with Oksana as she does the same.

We wait in tense silence for what feels like an eternity before something drips onto my forehead. I jerk upwards, wiping the liquid off.

It's wet, but not sticky. *It's not blood.*

I bring my hand to my nose and smell it. *Water.*

In a shaky voice, I whisper to Oksana, "It's raining. I think it's a thunderstorm."

I hear her exhale in relief next to me.

We open our mouths, trying to catch and swallow the droplets of rain, savoring every drop.

Slava Bogu for the rainwater. I hadn't realized how dehydrated I was.

After a while, I wrap my coat around us to shield us from the rain—catching pneumonia is the last thing we need right now. And even though I know it's coming, every clap of thunder or sudden turn of the train still makes my heart race. But it nearly jumps out of my chest when the train comes to a complete stop.

I take a sharp breath, feeling Oksana's heart and mine pound as one while we embrace, dreading whatever is to come next.

Our breaths hitch when the train car door suddenly slams open, flooding the dim space with harsh light. My eyes sting from the sudden brightness as Axel Jeckeln enters the car. I grit my teeth and lower my gaze, noticing the dirt and dried blood caked on his boots.

How many people's blood have you spilled, you paskudnik? I wonder, remembering the other SS, the one from Babin Yar.

Axel spins his revolver around his finger, taunting me. "So, what will it be? A walk or a bullet?"

I glare at him and swallow, trying to suppress a sudden urge to spit at his feet. I can't imagine anyone more repulsive, anyone I despise more than Axel in this very moment.

Papa's words replay in my mind. *Good girls don't get angry*.

What do you even know about girls? I shout back at him in my mind.

"We'll walk," I reply to Axel through gritted teeth. I get up into a crouch and help Oksana to her feet as well.

Axel eyes me up and down, pausing to cast a lingering

eye on the ripped skirt of my dress. He smirks. "Follow me."

He walks out the door. Oksana and I trail behind him, stepping out into the damp air. It's still sprinkling but the rain has mostly stopped, leaving the ground wet and slippery. Oksana stumbles on the wet train steps and nearly falls, but I grab her arm at the last second to steady her.

"It's okay, I've got you," I reassure her with the best smile I can muster.

All the other passengers are off the train and at the platform already. They all look lost and dazed. Axel and his two guards are there too, as well as six other men in uniform. Each one has the double lightning SS insignia on their collars. Their ranks vary, except for one man whose collar bears two oak leaves on each side instead.

I stare at the SS with the oak leaves, feeling my mouth go dry. *Why is he here?* I wonder. *Do they always have higher-ranking officers meet the new Ostarbeiter or only when some have tried running away? What are they going to do to us?*

As the sun dips below the horizon, the March fog creeps in and engulfs the city. The armed guards in front of us are barely visible through the haze. One of them, a short man with a mustache and bald head, holds a list in his hand. His collar is adorned with two silver pips and two silver stripes, marking him as another high-ranking SS officer. He surveys the new arrivals with a look of disgust on his face.

"Repugnant, aren't they? Filthy, putrid, unkempt, uncivilized," the SS remarks to Axel with disdain.

"What do you expect, Sturmscharführer Fuchs?" Axel says, folding his hands behind his back. "They're not Aryan. They're swine."

"Right," Fuchs replies. "Well, let's divide them up, shall we?"

I squeeze Oksana's hand.

"What?" Oksana asks. "What are they saying?"

"They are going to divide us up. My guess is that they need different people at different jobs."

Oksana's eyes grow wide. "No. I want to go with you. I'll die if I'm alone."

I try to think of comforting words for her, but I feel just as lost and helpless as she seems to feel. *Did I look this scared when Lyuda was helping me?*

My mind flashes back to when Lyuda held me close and spoke soothing words as I panicked. Her gentle touch and calm voice were like a warm blanket around my anxious heart. *"You'll be okay...Everything is going to be okay."*

I glance over at Oksana one more time. *Oksana needs me just like I needed Lyuda then. She needs something to hold on to.*

I pull Oksana closer and whisper in her ear, "Listen to me. Whatever happens, you have to promise me that you'll survive."

Oksana stares at me. "I can't promise you that. Look at what they did to Irina."

"Promise me," I say in a stern whisper. "Let's make a survival pact. No matter what happens, we survive for one another. Okay? Promise me."

Oksana takes a big breath and nods. "Okay. I promise."

We hold hands until Fuchs comes up to us. Like Axel, he looks us up and down, consults the list in his hand, and shakes his head. "Too skinny for the factory. Too ugly to be nannies. Too weak for agriculture." He scratches his forehead. "What am I going to do with these two?"

Axel turns to the officer with two oak leaves. "Oberführer Müller, would you like me to just shoot them?"

I squeeze Oksana's hand again but motion for the other girl not to say anything.

Oberführer Müller, the highest-ranking officer, who up until this point has been silently observing the Ostarbeiter distribution from the back, steps forward. He looks to be in his fifties and appears sleep deprived, judging by the bags under his eyes.

He approaches me and Oksana and tilts his head from side to side as if considering his options. "I'll take one of them. My wife has been asking for more help around the house. This will be a nice surprise for her."

He points at me. "Put that one in the car and shoot the other one."

I gasp. "No, please," I shout in German, no longer trying to hide the fact that I can speak it.

Axel and Müller look taken aback, as I continue, "You don't even have to pay us. Just please don't separate us."

"Why did you think you were going to get paid?" Müller asks with a look of sincere bewilderment. "Your life is your payment."

"You can feed us half the normal portions," I plead. "You'd get two workers for the same cost of food."

Müller folds his arms around his chest. "A quarter portion is standard for Ostarbeiter actually."

Some of the other SS sneer as they observe this interaction.

I shake my head four times in barely detectable movements, and a strange sense of tranquility washes over me. Then, I turn to Müller and speak in a tone so calm that it surprises me, "With all due respect, Oberführer Müller, you can always decide to shoot one of us at a later time."

"That part is true," Müller says and all the men around him laugh.

"Right," I continue. "So, you don't have anything to lose. You said that your wife needs more help. I can guarantee that my friend and I will do everything around the house to make your wife happy."

"And if you can't?" Müller asks, raising his eyebrow.

"Then you can still shoot one of us," I reply.

Müller grins and turns to Axel. "Load them both up in the back of my car."

CHAPTER 47
A REUNION

Once we arrive at Müller's residence, he gives us a quick tour of the house. The place is like a royal palace – with running water and electricity, it feels luxurious compared to the housing arrangements that I'm used to. There are two floors, a fully equipped kitchen, a formal dining room, a library, two bathrooms complete with toilets and bathtubs, and five bedrooms.

Do people really live like this? Does having all of this luxury make people act better or worse toward one another? Are people more likely to hurt others when they are deprived or when they have too much?

As I follow Müller through the house, my eyes catch a glimpse of a bowl filled with neatly stacked oranges on the kitchen counter. Their sweet scent fills the air, and I can almost taste them on my tongue.

Did Lyuda ever get more oranges? I wonder. *Did she survive?*

I look away to keep the memories of Lyuda out of my mind and follow Müller who shows us to the bedroom we will be sharing and then how the faucets in the bathtub work. He hands us each a new dress with a square blue OST badge with white letters stitched on it, and a pair of used, but clean, underwear and stockings.

"This is your uniform now," he says to us, pointing at the clothes. "You are to take good care of it."

I nod and he continues, "My wife, Hannah, though you should call her *Frau Müller*, she gets up early. She will need breakfast, and she will want to see a clean house. And my name is Kurt Müller, and you are both to call me Herr Müller."

"*Ja*, Herr Müller," I say.

Oksana bows her head even though she clearly doesn't understand much of what he said.

I'm going to have to teach her German if we are to survive.

"There are five other Ostarbeiter in the house," Müller says. "In the morning, they will show you what needs to be done. And I do hope that I made my position perfectly clear—do what you're told, or I will have you shot."

"*Ja*, Herr Müller," I say.

I elbow Oksana, who bows again, pretending to understand him.

"Good," he says, nodding. "Now, go wash up. You both smell disgusting."

"*Ja*, Herr Müller." I bow and pull Oksana with me to the bathroom.

I relay Kurt's instructions to Oksana and teach her a few essential phrases in German.

"Just remember to say '*Ja*, Herr Müller' when speaking to Kurt and '*Ja*, Frau Müller' when addressing Hannah."

Oksana looks confused. "So, I must always use their last names? No first names?"

"No. Only surnames."

"And what about patronymics?"

I shake my head. "No, Germans mainly use titles and surnames. We should not address them by their first names, and unlike Russian or Ukrainian, there are no patronymics in German."

Oksana nods. "I understand. And thank you. Without our survival pact and your guidance, I wouldn't have made it this far."

"We both got lucky to have each other," I reply with a slight smile.

Following Herr Müller's instructions, I turn on the water and fill the bathtub. Oksana takes her turn to bathe while also washing her train clothes in the tub. As I wait for my turn, I sit on the bathroom's black-and-white patterned tile floor, clutching my coat and new dress to my chest, fighting exhaustion. When Oksana finishes and changes into her new clothes, she leaves to go to our new room.

I finally get into the bath and offer a silent, thankful prayer in Yiddish. For months, I have only been able to take occasional sponge baths due to the lack of plumbing at Ruslan's place and the freezing temperatures of the lake during winter.

The warm water envelops me like a comforting embrace, but I would trade it all for one hug from Lyuda.

I gently scrub away dirt and bloodstains from my skin and dress. The bites from the dog still throb on my body, and my hip stings from the injury, but the warmth of the water soothes some of the discomfort.

The water is murky and brown, but I feel cleaner than I have in months.

I dry myself off with a towel before putting on my

new Ostarbeiter uniform. It is a gray dress with a white collar and sleeves. It hangs loosely on me, but I can use the belt sewn into it to adjust the fit.

I hang up my graduation dress to dry and examine it. It is still wet and torn at the bottom, so it's hard to tell whether all the stains have come out of it, but there are several new holes that will need patching.

My fingers trace over the embroidery on the dress—a clef note for Mamo, a black spade for my brother, a tiara for Papa, and the sewn-in pink ribbon for Babushka.

My chest is bursting from longing to see them. All of them. Any of them. For a moment, my mind flashes to Babushka's eyes right before—

No!

I shake my head four times. *Stay here. In the present.*

I focus on the silky sensation of Babushka's ribbon on the tips of my fingers. Some parts of it are scratchy and less smooth than they used to be, and a part of it is starting to come loose, as is the button in the back that holds the dress together.

I need to ask Frau Müller for a needle and some thread to fix these.

I run my fingers from the ribbon over the stitching again, and over the button. *It's all I have left of them.*

I squeeze the bottom hem of my torn dress as if clutching my family's hands like I used to when I was a small child.

I let go and swallow hard, suppressing my tears. Then, I gather my coat from where it lays on top of my boots. It's still stained with blood.

Bad Mouse, I chide myself. *Lyuda wouldn't have let the coat get dirty. And she wouldn't have allowed Irina to get killed.*

I carry the coat toward the bathtub and gently scrub the blood spots with my hands, trying not to get the entire coat wet, so as not to damage it.

But no matter how hard I try, the blood won't come off and soon my own hands are covered in it.

I have blood on my hands, I think as I scrub harder. *Irina's. Oksana's. And probably Lyuda's. And it's all my fault.*

My vision blurs and I struggle to catch my breath. I fold over in shame, feeling like my entire body has been put through a meat grinder.

I'm sorry, Lyuda. I'm a terrible friend. I'm so sorry.

There is a familiar sonata playing in my mind.

No! I shake my head. Hard.

No! I'm staying right here. Oksana needs me. Lyuda needs me. I'm not going anywhere.

After I finish, the coat is still marked with stains, but it's significantly cleaner than before. I pick up my boots and tiptoe down the hallway, feeling more self-assured now.

I will get through this. I will help Oksana survive this and I will make it back home to see Lyuda again. Everything is going to be okay.

"Maria?" a gruff, familiar voice calls from behind me.

My heart jolts, as does the rest of me.

It can't be him. Can it?

I spin around.

But it is—Sergei, the man from my hometown. This is the same man who used to torment me as a child, and who tried to coerce me into marrying him before the SS arrived in Vinnytsia.

"So," Sergei says with a one-sided sneer. "Does Kurt know that you're a kike?"

CHAPTER 48

BERCHTESGADEN

I slip into the small bed next to Oksana as she snores beside me. The windowless room is filled with a musty smell and only holds a child-sized bed, a small dresser with one drawer for each of us, and a single chair.

Despite being exhausted and finally having a real bed to sleep in, I am unable to get comfortable. My shoulder, hip, and ankle are still aching from the dog bites and my fall. My mind is racing after running into Sergei.

Before leaving him alone in the shadows, I tried repeatedly to deny his allegations. I told him over and over that my name is Anna and that he must have mistaken me for another girl. But Sergei only laughed at me.

"I've got you now, you little kike," he said with a disturbing grin. "Maybe I couldn't get you in Vinnytsia, but I've got you now. And you'd better do what I say, or I'll tell them."

What should I do? I wonder. *I should run. I can sneak outside the back door and just run.*

But I know that I can't. *I can't leave Oksana. She needs me now.*

I think back to what Kurt explained to me and Oksana on our drive to his home. "If you try to run, it will be easy enough for someone to check the OST registry. Any Ostarbeiter caught running away will be shot."

"Sounds more like slavery than a job," Oksana whispered to me when I translated what Kurt was saying.

"Quiet," I whispered back. "Remember what he said back at the station. Our payment is our lives. We need to be careful."

Oksana squeezed my hand. "I'm scared, Anna. Whatever happens, please don't leave me."

"I promise," I said, knowing that I meant it.

Now, as I lay in the cozy, warm bed, even knowing that I have clean clothes and will be fed regularly, I still have never felt more threatened or vulnerable.

What will happen if Sergei tells on me? And if they kill me, will they kill Oksana too?

I try not to toss around too much, to let Oksana rest and sleep through the night. *Maybe at least one of us can get some sleep, and I need Oksana to remain as calm as possible tomorrow.*

I don't complain when Oksana rolls over and drapes the one blanket we share over herself, leaving me exposed and shivering. I hug myself tightly, reminiscing about how Lyuda and I used to cuddle up for warmth in Fedka's barn or on Ruslan's floor. Taking a deep breath, I look up into the darkness and silently pray. Not to God, but to my best friend, as if pleading with a guardian angel.

Lyuda, I'm so sorry,

It's all my fault. You are stuck now without boots. Without a coat. And without a friend.

I see now how much you did for me. How much you put your own needs and emotions aside to care for me.

I'm so sorry and I'm so grateful.

I promise to take care of Oksana the way you did for me. I promise not to give up on our pact. And I promise to make it back to you.

Until then, please hear me, Lyuda. Please survive.

I close my eyes, trying to force my mind to rest, knowing that tomorrow will be as dangerous as hiding from the Nazis in Yuriy's cellar.

Eventually, I drift off into a restless slumber filled with nightmares of ferocious dogs chasing me. The sound of their snarling sends shivers down my spine, and I scream as their sharp teeth sink into my flesh.

"Anna. Anna, you have to get up now," someone says, shaking me awake.

I spring up, shoving the other person off me, taking in quick breaths as my eyes widen and my heart races. It feels like I am drowning all over again, only without Lyuda's caring arms to rescue me from the vicious waters.

"It's okay. It's okay! It's me, Anna. It's Oksana."

As my vision begins to focus, I see Oksana sitting on the edge of the bed next to me. It takes a few moments for my mind to catch up and remember where I am.

I'm in Herr Müller's house. We're Ostarbeiter now.

Sergei!

"*Bozhe!*" I finally say.

"Bad dreams?" Oksana asks.

I nod.

Oksana extends her hand to me. I grasp onto her hand and allow her to assist me out of bed. "Thank you."

My graduation dress and coat are already laid out on the chair beside the bed.

"I brought them in from the bathroom," Oksana says. "Your dress is almost dry now but your coat—"

As she lifts it up, I let out a gasp. The coat is still stained, now with a pinkish, vomit-like shade covering the right side and back.

Four bite-sized holes are visible on the same side. *How did I not notice them last night?*

"I know that you love this coat," Oksana says. "And I know you tried to clean it. But I think it might be time to throw it out."

"No!" I protest, gripping the coat tightly as if it were Lyuda herself.

It's all I have left of her.

Oksana shrugs. "Fine, do as you like. But I think we need to get to the kitchen. I heard voices. People are starting to wake up."

I pause to take a breath and give a small nod. Once I finish spreading the coat carefully over the bed to finish drying, I squeeze one of the tassels attached to its waistline. *I will fix you later.*

I readjust the soft grey belt of my new dress, smooth out my collar, and glance up at Oksana, who is wearing a dress almost identical to mine. Now that she's had a bath and it's morning time, I can see that she has long, light brown hair, lighter than it seemed to be when I first saw her on the train. Her hair has been neatly plaited in a long braid that hangs down her back.

I stare at the OST patch sewn on the right side of Oksana's chest, then look down at my own. The blue and white square serves as an eerie label, one that represents our new identities.

I went from being stamped from birth in my paperwork to being stamped with a patch now, I realize, feeling my jaw clench tight.

"Let's go," Oksana urges.

We head to the kitchen together. The other Ostarbeiter are already there—Sergei, as well as one other man, and three young women. Just like me and Oksana, they each wear a blue OST badge with white letters on their attire.

"Good morning, *Maria*," Sergei says in Ukrainian, placing a special emphasis on my name.

"My name is Anna," I respond loud enough for everyone to hear. "Like I told you yesterday, you must have me confused with another woman."

"Oh, I don't think so, my dear," he hums with a sideways smile.

"No, it's true. Her name is Anna," Oksana says coming up to him. "And I'm Oksana."

"I'm Sergei," he says, and kisses Oksana's hand. "Very pleased to meet you."

I bite my lip to keep myself from saying anything when Oksana blushes and giggles.

"Leave them alone, man. The girls just got here," the other OST man says to Sergei.

He is tall, taller than Sergei, and muscular. And like Sergei, he also has thick stubble on his face.

The man introduces himself as Viktor and gestures toward the three young women beside him. "This is Svetlana, Zoya, and Kamila."

I wave at everyone before asking, "Are all of you from Ukraine?"

Kamila, her blonde hair tied back with a blue ribbon to match her bright blue eyes, responds in Russian, "I am from Poland." She looks to be about my age or younger.

"I'm from Ukraine, from Lviv," Zoya says, adjusting her brown braid. She looks about 30 years old. She is plumper and shorter than most of the other women but still taller than me.

Zoya points at a tall, thin young woman, who is quietly scrubbing the silverware by the kitchen sink. "That's Svetlana, but she prefers to be called Sveta. She's from Donetsk."

I quickly observe Sveta, noting that she seems uninterested in being a part of the conversation.

"We have been mostly speaking Russian between ourselves and trying to learn German as we go," Viktor says.

"Well, Anna is fluent. She can teach us all," Oksana says.

"Oh, perfect," Kamila says, clapping her hands. "Then we can talk to the cute German guys that come to the house sometimes."

"Exactly," Oksana chirps. "Anna is amazing."

I feel my cheeks flush, but before I can say something self-deprecating, a stern-faced woman strolls into the kitchen. She isn't particularly tall, perhaps just a few centimeters taller than I am, but her stoic expression and ramrod-straight posture make her look taller and more intimidating. She reminds me of my first-grade teacher, who used willow branches to whip misbehaving girls. Or girls who talked too much. Or girls who asked too many questions.

This must be Frau Müller, I think to myself.

Like her husband, Frau Müller looks to be in her early fifties, judging from the grey hairs visible in her tightly pulled bun, as well as the severe lines etched around her piercing grey eyes.

She wears a long brown skirt and a white shirt with brown patterned squares. There is not a single wrinkle in her clothes, not a single stitch out of line.

"*Guten Morgen*," she states in German.

"*Guten Morgen*," Viktor, Kamila, and I say in unison, as the rest of the Ostarbeiter bow their heads.

"I am Hannah Müller. You are to refer to me as Frau Müller," she says, addressing me and Oksana, "and I expect you to behave and to follow my instructions at all times."

"*Ja*, Frau Müller," I say, elbowing Oksana to say it too, and then adding, "We understand."

Hannah examines me closely, tilting her head to the side. "What is your name, girl?"

"My name is Anna, Frau Müller," I respond, trying to sound as formal as possible. "I am honored to make your acquaintance."

Frau Müller raises her eyebrows. "You are fluent in German?"

"*Ja*, Frau Müller," I reply, trying not to let my nerves show. My heart is pounding in my chest as I make sure to only use German and not mix in any Yiddish words. "I studied German in school back in Ukraine."

Hannah nods. "Good. You can help the others improve their German." She turns to Viktor and Sveta. "Viktor, show Anna how I like my house to be cleaned. Sergei and Svetlana, show the other new girl how to garden."

Viktor and Sveta both exchange glances and reluctantly nod at Frau Müller. I notice that Sveta has turned pale, and Viktor gives her a gentle nod as if to reassure her.

"Zoya and Kamila," Hannah continues, "you will oversee cooking of tonight's dinner. We will have several very important guests. I will give you the menu and I expect everything to be prepared and cooked properly."

Zoya shrugs, clearly not understanding what Hannah said, so I translate into Russian.

"*Danke Schön*, Anna," Hannah says. "Why don't you also help Zoya and Kamila serve dinner tonight? Since you are fluent in German, you can help to better entertain our guests."

"*Ja*, Frau Müller," I respond.

Hannah nods and then turns to face everyone. "I expect everything to be clean and for supper to be ready by 18:00 hours. Some of the most important Schutzstaffel officers from the area will be here tonight, and if you embarrass my husband, he will not hesitate to send you to the camps, where you won't be treated so kindly."

Sergei snorts. "I thought the camps were just for the dirty Jews." He sneers and winks at me.

But no one else laughs. I squeeze my fists together so tightly that my nails dig into my skin.

Hannah studies Sergei without blinking or speaking, her arms clasped in front of her.

Finally, she speaks. "Are you one?"

"Am I what?" he asks, raising his eyebrow.

"Are you a dirty Jew?" she asks, still not blinking.

Sergei gulps and shakes his head. "No."

"It is *No, Frau Müller* to you," she says in the same stoic tone. "Learn your manners."

"But—" he tries to argue, but Hannah gives him such

a piercing stare that he takes a step back. "I'm sorry, Frau Müller."

She squints her eyes and stares at him for a few more breaths before she marches out of the kitchen, as stern and collected as when she first walked in.

"You heard the lady," Viktor roars in Russian. "Everyone, get to your posts." He points at me. "Anna, you're with me."

I follow Viktor but not before he exchanges another glance with Sveta. He nods at her, and she nods back, takes a big, exasperated breath, and follows Sergei on what must be the way to the garden. Oksana follows them out without saying a word.

Viktor leads me toward the front door and outside. As we step through the door I feel as if I have been transported inside a fairy tale. The sun is at its full glow, and unlike last night, I can see the city now.

The Müller residence sits on a hill, overlooking an azure-blue lake, which still has pieces of ice floating in it, like shimmering dance floors. Silver ice crystals glisten like diamonds over the soaring pine trees. And in the far backdrop of this enchanted view, I can see the stunning pinnacles of snow-covered mountains.

I draw in a breath. "Oh, *Bozhe Moi*. I've never seen mountains in person before. Only in picture books." I crane my neck to take in the views. "They're beautiful." I turn back to Viktor. "Where are we?"

"Berchtesgaden," he answers.

"It looks like a resort."

I stand up on my tippy toes to study more of the view. I imagine bringing Lyuda here and showing her around. *She would love it.*

I find myself smiling for the first time in many days.

"It *is* a resort," Viktor says. "Hitler's personal vacation house is here. His *dacha*, if you will."

That news snaps me out of my daydream. "Hitler visits here?"

Viktor nods. "All the time." He pulls out a broom, dustbin, a mop, and several rags out of the outside supply closet, and hands them to me. "Here, grab these."

I feel bile build in my throat. *Hitler visits here? How could a place so beautiful also be a home to such a monster?*

I follow Viktor back into the house and help him to sweep the foyer.

"Where in Ukraine are you from?" I ask, trying to take my mind off the horrendous fact that I now share a city with Hitler.

"From Ovruch City originally," he says, lifting a bronze hat rack, sweeping under it, and placing it back down. "I moved around a bit when I joined the Army."

I look up at him. "You fought in the Red Army?"

Viktor looks down at his hands and then rubs the sweat off his face with the palm of his hand. "Yes. Before we were captured."

I accidentally knock over some of the shoes from the shoe rack that I am dusting. "Sorry," I mumble and hurry to stack the shoes back on the rack. I glance back to Viktor and whisper, "You were captured? By the Germans?"

He nods. "They brought us to a work camp near Kolo-Mykhailivka and put us to work."

My head spins. "Wait. Kolo-Mykhailivka? I lived near there for the past year and a half. That's not far from my hometown, from V—" I stop myself. *What if Sergei tells on me? He'll have more evidence if everyone knows we're from the same hometown.*

Viktor nods but doesn't press me to tell him anything

further. "Small world." He moves over to sweep the lounge area.

I follow him, dusting the shelves with one of the rags. "What did they have you do there, in Kolo-Mykhailivka?"

Viktor stops sweeping. He looks around to make sure no one is watching us and then whispers, "We were building something—essentially a secret house."

Oksana's words from the train ring in my mind. *They were building some kind of a secret house... they're building it for a werewolf.*

"Viktor," I say, wringing my fingers, "this might sound really strange, but does the word *werewolf* mean anything to you?"

Viktor glares at me. He pales and his eyes widen. "How do you know about it?"

So, it's true? I wonder. *There's a werewolf in Vinnytsia? The Nazis are using supernatural powers to fight the war?*

I step toward him. "Viktor, please tell me. What did they build?"

Viktor eyes me suspiciously. "You are asking too many questions."

"Viktor, tell me, please. I need to know," I beg.

Before I can move or scream, Viktor slams me against the wall and I drop the rag I was holding. His eyes narrow, his chest heaves up and down. "Are you a spy, Anna?"

My entire body goes stiff. *Is he going to kill me now?*

I try to wriggle out of his grasp. "A spy? No. Please. Let me go."

But he presses my shoulders against the wall with more force with each word he says. "It's just a little peculiar that on your first day here, you get assigned to work with me. You are fluent in German, and you know a hell of a lot about *Werwolf*." He says the last word in German.

I am starting to panic. "Viktor! Stop, you're hurting me. Let me go. Please."

He watches me but doesn't move, like he is in a trance. His chest is still heaving. He isn't blinking.

"Please let me go. I swear, I don't know anything. There were rumors around Kolo-Mykhailivka about some wolf. Or some werewolf. That's all I know."

Viktor studies me for a few moments and then releases me. He rubs his face with his hands and we both try to catch our breath before he addresses me, "I'm sorry. It's just... you never know who's a real friend or who's sent here to kill you, you know?"

I nod, trembling. Then I turn to walk out of the lounge, my heart pounding loudly in my chest.

"It's a bunker," Viktor calls after me.

I spin around. "Huh?" And then I pace back toward him. "What do you mean?"

Viktor shakes his head. "*Werwolf*. It's Hitler's bunker. It's called *Werwolf*, which is German for "werewolf." The bunker is the wolf's lair, Hitler *is* the wolf. He intends to attack from within it—destroy the Soviet Army and everything around it and claim his power over Europe."

For a few moments, I can't take a single breath. My legs tremble. It feels like the floor is collapsing underneath me.

Hitler is going to blow up Vinnytsia, and everything in his path.

I shudder.

Lyuda! What will happen to Lyuda?

My legs can't hold me any longer, and I collapse onto my knees. "So, that's it then? He won?"

Viktor kneels next to me, pretending to scrub a spot on the floor with another rag, and whispers, "Not necessarily."

I look over at him. "What do you mean?"

"There weren't supposed to be any witnesses," Viktor says and hands me the rag I dropped earlier. "When we were all finished building the bunker, the SS told us to dig a large hole in the ground. When we were done, they executed about a quarter of the prisoners."

I bring my hand to my chest. *Oh, Bozhe. I know where this is going.* I think back to the mass graves I'd seen.

Viktor nods at me and wipes some more sweat from his forehead. "Then they had us dig another hole. And then another." He scrubs every spot on the floor around him with force. "And when we were done digging the last hole, we were the only ones left."

I gasp. "They had you dig your own grave?"

Viktor nods. "They did the same thing to Jews in Ovruch. They had them dig a large pit, supposedly to preserve the beets for the winter. And then—" he trails off.

I release a slow breath. "How did you get away?"

Viktor shakes his head as if trying to get the image out of his mind. "I ran. When they started shooting. Word of advice, if ever you are getting shot at, run in a zigzag fashion. That way, you're less likely to get hit."

He slams a spider, squishing it to the ground with his bare hand before sweeping up its corpse into the dustbin. "Unless of course, you're being bombed, in which case, you just need to find a shelter, because you can't outrun the bombs."

I stare at him. *And I thought I had it bad.*

Victor continues, "Anyway, when they started shooting, I fell and pretended to be dead. And then, when I got the chance, I ran again."

Images of Frida and the little boy who crawled out of the snow-covered corpses flash before my eyes. I shake my head to stay in the present moment. "And then what happened?"

Viktor sighs. "I knew it wouldn't be long before I was captured, so I ran to the local church. I told the priest there about the *Werwolf* and he said that he'd try to get the word out to the Red Army."

"And how did you end up here?" I ask, scrubbing a different spot on the floor.

"I wanted to give the priest the maximum chance of getting to the Red Army, so it was important that I didn't stay there and risk drawing attention. The priest gave me some civilian clothes, and I left right after. I saw an OST train and I volunteered."

I stare at him in disbelief. "You volunteered?"

He nods. "I did. And I have to tell you—I'm grateful. I'm getting food. It's not a lot, but it's something. It's more than I ever got in the Army, and it certainly beats being a war prisoner."

Grateful? I think to myself as I scrub the floor. My stomach curdles at the thought of it.

Sure. I have food. A bed. And a new dress. But I have no choice about being here. My life is not my own. I am away from my family. My city. My...Lyuda.

My throat aches at the thought of her. *And I should be grateful?*

I skip a spot of dirt on the floor in a silent act of defiance.

CHAPTER 49

DINNER

We are all allowed to have a quick supper before the guests arrive. I nearly inhale my soup—a thin broth with a few sad-looking vegetables. My stomach growls as I slide the baked potato into my pocket for later.

"How's my hair?" Kamila asks Zoya while we are setting the table for the guests.

Zoya studies her. "You need to brush it more if you want to catch a good man."

Kamila runs off in the direction of the Ostarbeiter bathroom, presumably to check her reflection in the mirror.

"You. New girl. Anna. Help me," Zoya demands.

I walk over to the table and help Zoya arrange the silverware, plates, and glasses.

Kurt and his guests arrive a little before six o'clock—four SS men I have never seen, and Axel Jeckeln.

I glare at him, feeling a gripping pain down in my lower stomach, and then a cold shiver throughout my entire back. I would much rather scrub toilets a thousand times than be on dinner duty tonight. The bile comes up my esophagus, and I almost throw up my soup, disgusted at having to see *him*. Having to look at *him*. Having to serve *him*.

Axel gives me a quick wink and then turns to Hannah. "Good evening, Frau Müller. I've brought you some red wine."

Hannah replies, "Thank you. What a kind man you are, Sturmbannführer Jeckeln."

I clench my jaw tighter. I try to focus on the silverware and counting to keep myself from screaming.

Eighteen forks for six men.

Six glasses.

Six knives.

I take a big breath and focus on serving.

"He's so handsome," Kamila whispers to me and Zoya after we all slip into the kitchen.

"Who? Herr Müller?" Zoya asks.

"No," Kamila giggles, "Sturmbannführer Jeckeln. You know, *Axel*."

The words are out of my mouth before I can stop myself. "He's a rapist."

The other two women gawk at me, seemingly at a loss for words, until Kamila finally replies, "Well, I've been working here for six months, and he's always been nice to me."

"Maybe you should stop making things up just to get some attention," Zoya chimes in.

"Exactly," Kamila agrees. "You barely know him, and we know him well. He would never do that."

"Right," I reply, with a bitter taste in my mouth. "Never."

"If my Vanya had been half the man that Axel is,

maybe I wouldn't have had to volunteer to be an Ostar-beiter," Zoya snaps. "I know a good man when I see one. Now, do your job."

She hands me a plate of buttered bread and sends me back out to the dining room.

Lyuda, I pray, *help me get through this. Please help me get through this evening. Please help me to get back home.*

CHAPTER 50
UNCIVILIZED

My hands shake as I serve dinner to Herr Müller and his guests—bread, boiled potatoes, roast beef and mixed vegetables, followed by fruit salad, coffee, and marmalade.

Axel watches me with a lecherous smile. When I hand him his coffee, he winks at me again, and I freeze, staring at him.

"It is improper for young ladies to stare at and congregate around men," Hannah hisses in my ear, making me jump. "Do not let me catch you doing it again."

I stare down at the floor. "*Ja*, Frau Müller."

I can hear the men sneering at the dinner table.

Help me get through this, Lyuda.

Finally, the guests depart, although I can't help but feel like Axel's eyes linger on me a bit too long before he walks out the door.

In the kitchen, Kamila and Zoya are both giggling and whispering to each other, and I try not to let my mind wander to what they could possibly be saying about me.

As I walk back toward my room down the long dimly lit corridor, I squeeze my fists and replay the events of the dinner in my mind.

I wish I could just punch him.

I envision myself swinging at Axel and watching as he collapses to the ground, trembling with fear. I would yell at him with each additional punch. *This one is for Irina. And this one is for me. And this one is for all the women you hurt. And this one is for all the people you killed.*

"Well, well," Sergei says, making me jump, then runs up next to me. "If it isn't the whore of Vinnytsia. Or should I say, the kike whore of Vinnytsia?"

I feel a chill and then a flash of heat on my face. "What? What are you talking about?"

He grabs my arm and glares at me. His nostrils flare and his chest heaves as he says, "Don't lie to me. I saw the way that you and Axel looked at each other during dinner. How dare you sleep with him, you whore?"

"Let. Go." I pull my arm away.

I turn away but Sergei grabs my shoulders and slams me against the wall with such force that my vision blurs for a moment.

"You. Will. Respect me," he growls through gritted teeth. "Your kike brother isn't here to protect you now."

His nose is touching mine and his eyes focus on my lips. He leans closer.

My stomach churns. *Don't kiss me. Please don't kiss me.*

His lips creep closer to my own.

I pull my lips back and spit at his mouth.

"Bitch!" he yells.

He lets go of me and takes a step back. He wipes his mouth, a look of disgust spreading across his face.

A satisfying warmth washes over me. *I should have done that a long time ago.*

I sneer at him.

"Are you laughing at me?" he roars. "How dare you?"

There's a loud crack when his fist meets my nose. Warm blood pours down my face.

He punched me!

I pinch my nose and raise my head, trying to protect my new dress from getting blood on it.

Sergei takes a step back, breathing heavily now.

Is he going to hurt me again? I take a small step back, feeling the wall behind me.

Is he going to kill me?

"Let me see it," Sergei says, taking a step closer to me again. His voice sounds quieter and more apologetic now. He pries my hands off my face. "Tsk, tsk, tsk. Look at you." He takes out a handkerchief out of his back pocket and starts wiping my face.

I try to pull away but there is a wall behind me, and Sergei towers in front of me.

Nowhere to run.

His enormous hands bring my face closer to his. "I don't ever want to hurt you, Maria." His tone is sing-song, as if he is comforting a small child. "I love you. You know that, don't you? I just want to take care of you."

"What's going on here?" Viktor's voice booms in the hallway.

Sergei turns his head to face him but keeps his hands over my nose. "Not your business, Vitya," he barks, referring to Viktor by his informal name. "Keep walking."

"Is that blood?" Viktor asks, taking a few steps closer. "Anna? Did he hit you?"

Sergei's hands tighten around my face. Even if I

wanted to nod, I wouldn't be able to right now. So instead, I stare at Viktor.

Help me, I plead silently, hoping that he will be able to read the terror in my eyes.

"Take your hands off of her," Viktor demands.

Sergei's fingernails dig into my cheeks, and I flinch. This seems to set him off, because Sergei clenches his hands even tighter, and forces his forehead down against mine, to keep me from moving. "I said, keep walking," Sergei repeats without looking at Viktor.

The next moment, Sergei yelps, his greasy hands ripped away from my burning face, as Viktor grabs a hold of Sergei's shirt and pulls him off me. Viktor then slams Sergei's face against the wall. Then he spins him around and towers over Sergei. "Stay away from her. You understand, you dog? Stay away from all the women in this house."

Sergei laughs and licks a small trickle of blood at the corner of his lip. "You're going to pay for this, you son of a bitch."

"What is going on?" Hannah's voice roars at the end of the hall.

All three of us straighten up and I try to clean my face with Sergei's handkerchief as much as I can.

Hannah strolls toward us, her hands clasped behind her back, her lips curled in disgust. She stops about a meter away, glaring from one man to the other and shaking her head. "Fighting. How disgraceful. How... uncivilized."

"Sorry, Frau Müller," I say.

The two men lower their heads.

Hannah takes a big breath, folds her arms in front of her chest, and continues, "In case you have forgotten, my husband works directly for the Führer. One word from me and he will not hesitate to send you all where you belong."

She takes a step closer to me. "Now, I might expect such brute behaviors from the men, but I expected better from you, Anna. If I catch you causing drama between these men again, you will wish they had sent you straight to the camps."

I am shaking all over but force myself to nod. "*Ja*, Frau Müller."

Hannah stares at me for a moment longer and then leaves without saying another word.

"See what you caused?" Sergei snaps at me.

I wince, expecting another blow, but it doesn't come.

Viktor has grabbed Sergei by the front of his shirt again. "I'm warning you, Sergei. Leave Anna alone, and the other girls too, or you'll regret it. I used to eat punks like you for breakfast in the Army."

Sergei pushes Viktor off him, cackling now. "Oh, you shouldn't have done that, Vitya. You should not have disrespected me like that."

Viktor snorts. "Just get out of here unless you want me to smear the wall with your blood."

Sergei storms down the hallway, muttering to himself along the way.

"Thank you," I manage to say, still covering my nose with Sergei's handkerchief. "And I'm sorry."

Viktor raises his eyebrow. "Sorry about what?"

"Causing this fight."

Viktor takes a step closer to me. "*You* did not cause anything. *He* did," he says, pointing at Sergei's retreating figure at the end of the hallway. "Now, let me take a look at your nose."

I lower my handkerchief.

Viktor studies my face and whistles. "Yep. Your nose is definitely broken. Are you struggling to breathe through it?"

I nod. I glance down at the handkerchief and realize, to my horror, that it is soaked with blood and is starting to drip onto Hannah's rug.

"Keep your face down, not up, to prevent the blood from going down your throat," Viktor instructs.

I tilt my head down. "What happens if I get some blood in my throat?"

"You might swallow it, which can upset your stomach and cause you to vomit. Trust me, keep your face tilted down."

"Okay." I hold out the bloody handkerchief to Viktor. "Is this normal? I am losing a lot of blood. Am I going to die?"

Viktor puts his hand on my shoulder. "It's okay. Noses bleed a lot. I've seen people bleed way worse and they were perfectly fine afterward."

"Really?" I can't believe anyone could bleed more than this and actually survive.

"In the first few months, when I joined the Army, we were taking fire everywhere," Viktor says. "One of my Army buddies got his arm blown off."

I gasp. "Oh, *Bozhe*. Was he okay?"

Viktor nods. "I used my belt as a tourniquet—tied it around the stub, tied a stick into the knot, and cranked it like a faucet to stop the bleeding."

"And it worked?" I ask. "He survived?"

"Yes," Viktor says. "So, don't worry. You'll be fine. But I do need to fix your nose for you, like we did in the Army, otherwise it won't heal properly, okay?"

I nod. "Okay."

Viktor takes a step closer to me. "I'm going to need to put my hands on your face and push your bones into place. It's going to hurt. A lot. It will bleed more for a while and then it will stop. But it will heal better that way. Okay?" I nod and he continues, "Let me know when you're ready."

Something about Viktor letting me know what to expect and asking my permission makes me feel safer and calmer. My nose still throbs but I feel less afraid now. *It's my choice.*

I take a big breath through my mouth and nod. "Okay. Ready."

Viktor places both of his enormous hands on my face and pushes with his thumbs. Something cracks. I scream and collapse onto my knees, tears pouring out of my eyes and blood gushing from my nose like a fountain, staining my dress, despite my efforts to protect it.

"You're okay," Viktor says kneeling next to me. "It's going to heal, and you'll be all better. And the next time Sergei or anyone else tries to touch you, you fight back, you understand?"

I glance up at him. "How?"

Viktor points to my hand. "Lift your hand up like this." He shows me and adds, "You can use the heel of your hand to punch him in the nose like this."

He pulls my hand gently toward his own nose to demonstrate. "You hit him here like this and it will break his nose."

I feel myself grinning. "What else can I do?"

Viktor points to my forehead. "If he's ever this close to you again, you can headbutt him in the face. It will hurt you, but it will hurt him more."

I nod. "Anything else?"

"If all else fails, you just kick him in the balls."

I imagine Sergei collapsing on the floor, clutching his groin, squealing in pain, and I giggle.

"I can show you more tomorrow," Viktor says. "For now, go wash up, okay?"

I nod and hurry to the bathroom to wash my face.

Lyuda, I think excitedly, as I watch the water in the sink turn scarlet, *you'll never believe it, Lyuda. I got beat up. But I'm learning to fight now. I'm learning to fight back.* I glance at my bloody reflection in the mirror and break into a smile.

CHAPTER 51
WARPED

Oksana is already asleep by the time I return to our shared room. It takes a long time for my nose to stop bleeding and just as long for me to wash out the blood from my clothes and the handkerchief.

Oksana shifts in her sleep and rolls over, turning her back to me.

I sigh, thinking back to snuggling up with Lyuda in the barn. I would trade this bed for a night in the hay and the comfort of my best friend. Or better yet, if Lyuda could be here, and Sergei wasn't, my life would be perfect, because even being a slave would be okay if Lyuda was here.

I wrap myself inside our shared coat, which is finally dry, and imagine snuggling with Lyuda for warmth and safety.

I miss you, Lyuda, I pray again. *I feel so lost without you. I don't know how we survived but I know that I stayed alive because of you. Because of our pact. Because you saved me. And not just in the river. You save me each and every day.*

And I just hope you know that I'm still alive, so that you stay alive too.

Please stay alive, Lyuda. Remember our pact. Please stay alive.

Somewhere in between my prayers, I fall asleep.

When I wake up, my head is pounding like it did when I drank too much potato juice with Lyuda.

Lyuda.

Remembering her, my chest aches more than my head does.

"Oh, *Bozhe*, Anna! What happened to you?" Oksana gasps. She must have just woken up.

I don't answer her because talking or moving my face in any way sends a shock of pain throughout my entire head. I force myself out of bed and to the bathroom.

Unlike last night, when I see my own reflection in the mirror now, it scares me.

The face looking back at me is gaunt and sullen. My eyes look as if I painted them with black tar underneath. My swollen nose looks too big for my face. The bridge of my nose is caked with dried blood in several places.

"I don't want to talk," I manage to say to Oksana after a few moments of silence between us.

Oksana furrows her brows. "Fine."

The curtness of her voice reminds me of Frau Müller, but my head hurts too much to care about appeasing her right now.

I follow Oksana out of the bedroom, down the hall, and to the kitchen to get ready for our morning responsibilities.

I'm not sure what reaction to expect from the other Ostarbeiter, but I am in no way prepared for what happens when Oksana and I enter the kitchen. Zoya and Kamila rush over to us, their faces full of concern.

"Oh, *Bozhe*, Anna," Zoya says. She rummages in her apron pocket and pulls out a small white pill. "Take it. It's an aspirin. It will help with your pain and the swelling."

I take it and nod in gratitude.

Kamila hands me a cup of water. My mouth hurts too much to open it, but I force the pill between my swollen lips and swallow it.

"How are you feeling?" Kamila asks.

"I don't think she wants to talk about it," Oksana intervenes.

"Don't worry, dear. You don't have to say a word," Zoya says and pats my arm. "Sergei already told us what happened."

I nearly choke in astonishment. "He... he did?"

Kamila nods. "Yes, everything—about how that brute, Viktor, attacked you in the hallway."

It feels like I've just been punched in the nose again. "What? That's not—"

"I'm just glad Sergei was there," Kamila interrupts. "Poor man got hurt too but he said it was worth it to save you. He clearly loves you so much. It's so romantic!"

Zoya nods. "I wish my Vanya was more like him. All he was good for was getting drunk and getting beat up by Germans when they took over the factory, where he worked. Now, Sergei—he's a real man."

Kamila agrees, "You should marry him, Anna. He's perfect for you." She winks at me. "And if you don't marry him, I will."

"I thought you loved Axel?" Sveta asks. Her voice sounds bitter, but Kamila doesn't seem to notice.

"Axel is great and very handsome," Kamila goes on,

"but Sergei is great too. He's nice, honest, and he can protect me."

"There you are," Sergei says, striding into the kitchen and running up toward me. "I was so worried about you."

If I thought my face looked bad, Sergei's face looks like he was attacked by a brigade. His nose is even more swollen than mine. He has multiple bruises under his eyes. His bottom lip is swollen. And his arm is in a sling made out of an old rag.

Kamila gasps. "Sergei, you poor man. You look so hurt. Can I get you some water? Or bandages?"

Sergei shakes his head. "Thank you, Kamila. I'm hurt. But the pain was worth it to save Anna."

"What a man!" Kamila coos.

"He seems wonderful," Oksana agrees.

"Let's give the lovebirds some room," Zoya says and tries to usher the other girls out of the kitchen.

"Are you okay, Anna?" Sveta asks. "Do you want me to stay with you?"

I shake my head. "No. You go. I need to talk to Sergei alone."

"So romantic," Kamila says again, and Oksana giggles as they walk out of the kitchen.

Is it smart to be alone with him? Will he hit me again? I wonder as the other women walk away.

No, he won't hurt me. Because if he does, then everyone will know exactly who he is—a wolf, pretending to be a sheep.

When I am left alone with Sergei, I say to him, "You lied. How could you do that?"

Sergei's eyes widen. "What are you talking about?" He feels behind my head. "My poor girl. You must have gotten a concussion when that thug slammed your head into the wall. Don't you remember?"

My head pounds in confusion. *What's happening?*

Sergei holds my hand with his uninjured one. "Don't you worry about anything now. He can't hurt you anymore. I took care of everything."

My mind swims. *What is he talking about? Am I losing my mind?* My headache is turning into a migraine. "What are you saying, Sergei?"

He brushes my hair behind my ear. "Don't worry, my dear. I told Herr Müller everything—about how Viktor attacked you last night and about how he attacked me when I stood up for you."

My vision blurs again; my reality is splitting. *Am I dreaming? Is this real? Am I not remembering correctly?*

I shake my head four times from side to side. It hurts but it also helps to clear my head.

No, I'm not wrong, I realize. *He's being manipulative.*

I clench my fists. "What did you do?"

I must have spoken louder than I intended to, because Zoya pokes her head around the corner. "Everything okay?"

Just then, the other three girls follow Zoya and return to the kitchen. Sveta is eyeing Sergei and me, and Oksana is smiling at the two of us.

Sergei gives me a smile that turns my stomach. He puffs up his chest, and stares at me as he speaks in a voice loud enough for everyone to hear, "I did what I had to do to protect you and all the other girls here. I won't have anyone hurting the woman that I love or any other women for that matter, even if my life is in danger as a result."

"Aww," Zoya murmurs. "What a man."

"Thank you for always looking out for us," Kamila says and puts her hand on Sergei's arm. "It's really nice to know that during such an awful time, someone is there to protect us. Besides," she adds, now addressing the rest of the Ostarbeiter, "I never trusted Viktor."

"Me neither," Zoya agrees. "He was always barking orders at everyone and hiding out in his room when he wasn't working. He was a loner, and he was weird. I should have known that there was something wrong with him."

Kamila is still holding onto Sergei's arm. "Well, in the last three months, since you got here, I've felt like I can actually sleep at night. And now you've made sure that we're all safe once and for all."

"It's what I do." Sergei smiles down at Kamila.

I feel a wave of nausea and a cool shiver. *Oh, Bozhe. He's twisting reality, and everyone believes him.*

"What happened to Viktor?" I manage to ask, trying to keep my voice steady.

Zoya gives me a weak smile. "Don't you worry about him anymore, Anna. Herr Müller had him sent to the camps this morning, so that he can't hurt you or any of us."

Oh, Bozhe! Viktor! "Excuse me," I mutter and hurry out of the kitchen.

"Don't do it," a small voice whispers behind me in the hallway.

I spin around to see Sveta behind me, wringing her hands together. Her eyes are red and swollen.

"Don't do what?" I ask.

"Don't run off to tell Herr Müller the truth. That is what you were about to do, wasn't it?"

I stare at her for a few moments, and then pull her into a quiet corner and check that we are alone before asking, "How did you know?"

Sveta lowers her gaze, her hand-wringing more erratic now. Finally, she looks back up at me and whispers, "Because what Sergei tried to do to you last night, he already did to me."

My mouth falls open. *He raped her?* I grab Sveta's hands. "Oh *Bozhe*! Sveta, we *have* to tell someone."

Sveta shakes her head. "Sergei is a wolf in sheep's clothing."

I nod. "I know." *So, I'm not the only one who knows this about him.*

Sveta continues, "He's charming. He gets everyone to like him and to trust him. He pretends to be innocent. Viktor was the only one who ever saw through his lies. After Sergei attacked me two months ago, Viktor was the only one who believed me. He warned Sergei to stay away from me after that."

"And did he?" I ask. "Did Sergei stay away from you after that?"

Sveta nods. "I think Sergei was always afraid of Viktor, so he listened to him, in a way. But after Viktor threatened him, Sergei started spending a lot of time with Herr Müller, and whenever possible, with Herr Jeckeln too."

"Axel Jeckeln and Herr Müller? Sergei spends time with them?"

Sveta nods. "They like him, and they listen to him. They don't question what he tells them."

I rub my temples. "But we have to help Viktor. They sent him to the *camps*. I mean, don't you care about what happens to him?"

Sveta furrows her eyebrows. "Viktor and I are in love. We were planning to get married."

I gasp. *They loved each other. And now, because of me, Viktor was sent away.*

Sveta lets out a shaky breath before she continues, her voice starting to break as she speaks, "Viktor made me promise that if anything ever happened to him, I was not to try to rescue him because he didn't want me to die. He made me promise that whatever happened to him, I was to survive."

They had their own survival pact, I realize.

Sveta continues, "So, yes, I do very much care about what happens to him." She straightens out her dress and stands a little taller. "I don't know where he is, and I don't know if he'll ever be back. I don't know if I'll ever see him again."

"I'm so sorry," I say and hug her.

She hugs me back.

My stomach churns from guilt. *It's all my fault,* I tell myself. *If it wasn't for me, Viktor would still be here, and Sveta would be happy.*

Flashes of Sergei's face swarm in my mind—when he stole my shoes and threatened to throw me into the garbage, when he tried to force me to marry him, last night after he punched me, and when he taunted me in the kitchen this morning.

He was never a good guy, but was he always this cruel? Is this in his nature or did the war make him worse? Is it making all of us worse?

"We should go back," Sveta says, pulling away and dragging me after her.

When we walk into the kitchen, Hannah is already there.

"There you are," Hannah says, addressing me and

Sveta. "I will not say it again. I do not tolerate tardiness. Let this be a warning to you both."

"*Ja*, Frau Müller," Sveta and I say at the same time.

Hannah stares at my face and walks over to me. "Sergei's told me what Viktor did to you. He's been dealt with, and I will not tolerate any more inappropriate behavior between the Ostarbeiter. Understood?"

"*Ja*, Frau Müller," I manage to say, although I'm not sure what it is that I am agreeing to now.

"Very well," Hannah says, seemingly satisfied. "Anna, you are to accompany me to the market." She stares at my face again. "Under normal circumstances, I wouldn't take any of my Ostarbeiter in public looking like this." She motions toward my face. "But I need someone who speaks enough German to help me today."

She pulls out a white handkerchief from the sleeve of her dress and hands it to me. "Keep your face covered as much as possible. Now, go grab your coat."

My coat, I think in horror as I hurry toward my room. Given what Hannah said about my face, I doubt she would allow me to wear my coat anywhere in public with her.

When I get to the bedroom, I examine my coat again. It's stained dark red and putrid pink in multiple places and the holes in it are more visible than I initially realized. I run my fingers over its soft leather, now hardened after being exposed to the rain, snow, and blood.

I caress one of the red tassels that hang from its waist.

"What is *that*?" Hannah's voice pierces the room.

I spin around. "It's... it's just my coat, Frau Müller."

Hannah's lips curve down in disgust as she points to the pinkish-brown spots on the coat. "Is that—blood?"

I nod. "Yes, it's from the dogs, but I can fix—"

Before I can finish my sentence, Hannah yanks the coat away from me so hard that only the tassel I was holding a moment ago remains in my shaking hand.

"I'm throwing it out," Hannah says. "It is uncivilized for Ostarbeiter to have clothes like that. Or for anyone to have clothes like that. What will people think of our household? What will they think of my husband?"

No! I fall to my knees. "Please, Frau Müller. It's all I have left. Please! I will hide it. Just please let me keep it."

"Get up," Hannah hisses. "You will do as you are told. This coat is getting thrown out. You will wear the clothes that you are given, and you will be grateful for them. Now, clean yourself up and meet me outside by the car."

With that, Hannah storms out of the room, taking the coat with her.

My face hurts too much to cry, but my heart hurts too much not to.

I'm so sorry, Lyuda, I pray silently while gripping the red tassel in my hand. *I lost our coat. I lost you. I've lost everything.*

CHAPTER 52

FINAL WARNING

I stare out of the car window, ignoring the cold and refusing to put on the brown fur coat Hannah shoved at me before we left the house. Prior to that, I hid the red coat tassel under the bed, along with my torn graduation dress.

I wish I still had my needle and thread. Then, I could sew the tassel into my dress, so that I would never lose it.

I tense all over, despite the sharp pain that spreads around my face whenever I clench my jaw.

I hate Hannah now. *She took the last piece of me. There's nothing left.*

I vow to never let anything happen to my graduation dress and my remaining treasures—the coat tassel and my grandmother's ribbon.

I will hide them. I will guard them with my life. Or I will die with them.

We spend most of the drive in silence until Frau Müller tells the driver where she wants him to stop. The driver gets out of the car and opens the door for Hannah and me, and we both step out into the sunlight.

Hannah turns to the driver. "Meet us here in thirty minutes."

"*Ja,* Frau Müller." The driver nods, gets back in the car, and drives away.

"Put on your coat," Hannah says. "I don't want you getting sick and spreading your disgusting germs all over the house."

I glare at her and put on the coat without saying a word. The new coat feels warm, heavy, and lonely all at the same time.

What would Lyuda think of me wearing this hideous new coat without her? I wonder, fighting back tears.

I keep my head bowed to the cobble ground, determined to speak as little as possible.

"Follow me," Hannah says.

As we approach the bustling outdoor street market, my senses are overwhelmed by the abundance of color and aroma. The vibrant hues of oranges, turnips, and radishes spill out from carts and wooden crates, enticing us with their ripeness. Despite the early hour, the market is already teeming with shoppers, mainly women bundled in long winter coats, some accompanied by children, others alone.

In front of us, a vendor slices open an orange to display its freshness to a customer. The sight of the juicy flesh makes my mouth water, a longing for the tangy sweetness that I can only recall as a distant memory. My nose is too broken for me to smell anything. But I can remember just how sweet they taste.

"Cover your face. You look revolting," Hannah reminds me.

I cover up my face with Hannah's handkerchief, leaving just a small opening to be able to see.

Hannah hands me a blue cotton bag. "Hold this."

I nod and Hannah fills it with turnips and then gets in line to pay.

I stand in line next to her and glance around.

It's jarring to see a place so beautiful, so alive, so untouched by war. A place that has not been destroyed by bombs and grenades. A place that does not have blood and corpses scattered on the streets.

My gaze shifts to the scenic mountains covered in thin layers of snow at the top, the blossoming gardens, the beautiful blue lake, the historic churches and castles I can see in the distance. I can hear waltz music playing, although I am not sure if I am truly hearing it or if it is playing inside my mind.

It feels like something out of a fairy tale.

Like Cinderella.

I swallow so as not to vomit at the thought of it.

It's like there are two realities, one in which I am living through a second genocide after the Holodomor famine. And the other, the one with castles and beaches. And vacation homes.

Hitler's vacation home.

The juxtaposition of the two realities sickens me to my core. It's hard to imagine that this place is Hitler's second home. I am not sure what I imagined his home to be like, but if I had to guess, I would have pictured something more like a dungeon. Or an underground tunnel.

Or a bunker.

Werwolf.

The thought of Hitler stepping foot in my hometown, onto Vinnytsia soil, makes me feel sick and makes my head pound even more. Determined to make the most of this interlude from house chores, I focus on counting the people in the line in front of us—twelve—and then refocus on the trees, castles, and the mountains.

The town is truly breathtaking. In fact, it is the most beautiful place I've ever seen, more peaceful than any town I could ever imagine.

That is, with the exception of the SS patrolling.

I watch them escorting a prisoner. I glance over to the side to find three figures—two SS and a prisoner between them—being led. The person in the middle is thin, his head shaven.

My heart stops as I recognize his profile.

It's my brother.

Pavlik!

I drop the bag of turnips I was holding and run toward him, barely aware of Hannah's furious commands to stop. My head feels like I am under water again. All I can see is Pavlik's terrified face.

The SS yell something in German and one of them points a gun at me, but I can't make out what he is saying.

"Pavlik," I say as I get closer.

I gasp when I realize that instead of Pavlik, the person standing in front of me is a young girl of about fifteen. Her head has been shaved. She is so emaciated, that I can see the outline of her ribs poking out through her tattered shirt.

I shiver and step back, feeling hot and cold all over my body.

The girl's blue eyes are glassy and glossed over, no life left in them.

"How dare you interfere with official Schutzstaffel business? Come with me now." The sharp command of the SS finally breaks me out of my trance.

"Anna!" Hannah shouts behind me.

I spin to see Hannah running toward me. "I'm sorry, Sturmmann," she says to the SS, using his title and holding up a turnip. "This is my new Ostarbeiter. She dropped this and ran to retrieve it. She's still learning German, as well as her manners."

Why is she lying? I wonder.

Hannah points at me. "She's like a wild animal, this one." She slaps me across the face, her palm hitting my already injured nose and cheek. "Don't you ever run without permission ever again."

I bite my lip so as not to cry out in pain. My ears buzz, my cheeks burn, and my nose vibrates with pain.

Did my nose break again? I wonder, forcing the tears back into my eyes.

The Sturmmann lowers his weapon. "You need to train your Ostarbeiter better. Wouldn't want her to be mistaken for a Jew or something."

Hannah shakes her head. "Don't worry, Sturmmann. I will not allow her to step out of line again."

She grabs me by my ear and pulls me toward the car. "Come, you stupid girl."

I whimper but don't argue.

She's so awful, I think, squeezing my fists. *She's just like the rest of them. They're all the same.*

Hannah drags me for several blocks before finally letting go of my ear. "What were you thinking? How stupid are you? Do you want to die?"

I lower my head again. "I'm sorry, Frau Müller," I say, my voice breaking.

"This is your final warning," Hannah says. "One more step out of line and I will have my husband deal with you. Him or Sturmbannführer Jeckeln. They will not tolerate your nonsense the way I do. They'll send you straight to the camps."

I cringe at the mention of Axel's name and nod, but I do not respond.

CHAPTER 53

BLACKMAIL

I wipe the late spring sweat from my eyebrows and stare at the lilacs in front of me. *I hate gardening.*

Even though the white and lavender blossoms are enchanting to look at, the cloying scent makes me sneeze and my eyes swell. I set down the pruning shears and use my sleeve to rub at my irritated eyes. Another sneeze erupts, and I reach for a handkerchief to blow my nose.

Ever since that dreadful trip to the market two months ago, I have been stuck with garden duty.

Frau Müller knows about my allergies. Why is she forcing me to do this?

I march back to the house to refill the orange watering can before returning to tend to the blooming carnations, yellow and red tulips, and bright pink peonies. After another refill, I water the violets and bell-shaped lily of the valley flowers.

"I think you're overwatering them," Oksana says.

I turn to face her. "I probably am. I hate gardening. Always have."

"At least you're not dealing with horse manure every day," Oksana argues. Her face and dress are covered in dirt from the stables.

"I would gladly switch with you. I'm used to working in stables. And I'm not allergic to them. I can barely keep flowers alive. I truly don't see the point of most of them. Whenever I try to ask Frau Müller to allow me to switch tasks, she just curls her lip and says, 'You will do the task to which you are assigned,—

"—and you will be grateful for it'," we both recite together, rolling our eyes at the familiar saying.

"Maybe it's a punishment," Oksana suggests. "You know how she is."

"Wouldn't put it past her," I agree, thinking back to Frau Müller throwing out my coat. "The woman is pure evil."

Oksana nods. "She's almost as bad as Axel."

I drop the watering can, spraying water all over the dirty sandals Frau Müller gave me a month ago. They were an ugly shade of hospital-white and about three sizes too big. I grunt and pick up the now empty watering can. "No one is as bad as Axel."

"I said *almost*," Oksana says and sticks her tongue out at me. "I gotta get back to the stables. See you at supper."

AT DINNER TIME, I sit next to Oksana, as usual, doing my best to avoid Sergei. He's been ignoring me for the past two months, both of our bruises finally healed now.

With Viktor gone, he probably knows that he has no one to blame for his bad behavior, I think to myself, feeling a twinge of relief, and then a hot flash of guilt. *What is the*

316

matter with you, Mouse? Another man is probably dead now because he stood up for you. You can't possibly be happy about this.

Sergei is currently engaged in a conversation with Kamila, who is showing off her new hairband. It's red satin, ruffled together to form small roses around the top.

"It's a beautiful as you are," Sergei tells her, and Kamila's cheeks blush the shade of her hairband.

"Thank you," Kamila giggles and shows the hairband to the rest of the Ostarbeiter. "Isn't it beautiful? Frau Müller gave it to me today for my good work. She's so kind."

"She really is," Oksana says, smiling at Kamila.

What? I feel like I am being punched again. *I thought she agreed with me about how awful Frau Müller is. Was Oksana just pretending with me before? Or is she pretending now?*

Confused, I grab my baked potato and get up from the table.

"Are you okay, Anna?" Oksana asks.

"Fine," I respond without looking at her.

Although I usually try to walk the hallways with Oksana to avoid any chances of being alone with Sergei, I just want to get to my room and be with my thoughts now.

I scurry out of the kitchen, clutching the potato in my hands, and dart down the corridor.

"Good evening, *krasavitsa*," Sergei says, pouncing in front of me from around the corner.

I jump, dropping the potato on the ground. I curse under my breath, seeing that the potato split into pieces.

"Tsk, tsk, tsk," Sergei utters. "Are you stealing from

the kitchen, Maria? Herr Müller will not be happy to hear that."

I gape at him. "What? No, of course not. I didn't steal this. I saved it for later."

Careful, I remind myself. *I need to be very careful what I say to him. He can twist my words.*

He shrugs. "I've been looking for you anyway. Come with me. We need to talk."

He grabs at me, but I rip my arm away from him and step back. "Come where exactly?"

I notice a flash of anger in his icy blue eyes, but just as quickly as it appeared, it is gone, replaced by a vulturine smile. He takes another step toward me, and I flinch when he strokes my hair.

"Look, Maria. I'm a gentleman. I wouldn't hurt you. I just want to talk. After all we've been through together, can't we just sit in my room and talk?"

I shake my head. "I will not go to your room. I don't feel safe being alone anywhere with you."

He frowns. "And what about how *I* feel? Does it not matter how *I* feel and what *I* want?"

I shake my head. "Whatever you want to say to me, you can say tomorrow in the kitchen in front of everyone."

"Fine," he says, all traces of insincere kindness gone from his face now, "I'll just announce in front of everyone that I know your real name and your secret. You wouldn't want me to talk about that *with everyone*, would you?"

I stare at him for a few moments, unsure what to do or say. *I should have known he'd do something like this.*

I squeeze my fists together. "What do you want?"

He smiles again, but his smile doesn't reach his eyes.

"That's better." He grabs both of my hands and bends down so that we are eye to eye.

I try to pull my hands away, but Sergei squeezes harder.

"Look, it doesn't have to be this way," he says. "I love you. I don't want to fight with you."

He squeezes my hands so hard that I bite down on my lip, so as not to cry out, as he continues, "Some might say you're not the prettiest girl in the world, but I never cared about that. And I don't care that you're a kike either. Doesn't bother me. I'm willing to look past all that. I'm a good guy and I just want to give you a good life."

He stares at me with his hungry gaze. "So, what do you say, *kotyonok*?"

The corners of my lips pull downward and my stomach churns in repugnance.

"Let. Me. Go," I manage to hiss as I squirm to get out of his grip. "I'm not your kitten. Leave me alone."

His cheeks flush and his eyes widen in surprise.

He grabs me by my shoulders and shakes me like a ragdoll. "Are you seriously breaking up with me right now?"

My brain is spinning. *Did I do something to lead him to think that I was his girlfriend?*

I shake my head. *No, he is twisting things again.* I fire back at him, "We were never together."

Sergei's slap comes so quickly that I have no time to react. I freeze in shock, my ears ringing.

I cover my stinging cheek with my hand.

Sergei roars at me, saliva dripping from his mouth, "How could you say that? After all we've been through?" His nostrils flare and he isn't blinking now.

He's going to kill me, I think in horror.

"What is going on here?" Hannah shouts.

She dashes down the hallway and toward us, glaring at me. "What's this? What's going on here? Have you forgotten that you are on your last warning?" Then she notices the smashed potato on the ground. "And what's this?"

"She's been stealing from your kitchen, Frau Müller," Sergei says, pointing at me. "I caught her and was trying to convince her to return it. That's what we were arguing about. Please forgive me if my attempts to protect the integrity of your home awoke you from your sleep."

Sergei bows his head, but Hannah isn't looking at him. She is staring at me.

"Is this true?" Hannah demands.

My entire body is shaking. There is pounding in my ears and face, but I still somehow manage to shake my head. "No, Frau Müller. Please believe me. I didn't steal this potato. I kept it from when I was given it at supper."

Hannah furrows her eyebrows. "Why would you do such a thing?"

I shrug. "I haven't always known when my next meal would be. So, I've learned to save my food."

Hannah takes a breath, as if thinking it over.

She's going to send me to the camps, I think.

Hannah turns to Sergei. "I see no issue here. So, perhaps it is you who is starting fights and breaking the peace in this house?"

Sergei scoffs. "Me? How could you even think that?"

But Hannah holds out her hand. "Save it. I'm tired and I don't have time for your dramatics. It's not the first time you've cried wolf. Next time you sound a false alarm, I will have you dealt with."

I am both stunned and relieved at the same time. *Hannah believes me? She sees him for the wolf that he is?*

Sergei's face goes as red as fresh blood. There is a vein pulsing in his neck. "False alarm?" he roars. "Dramatics? Me?" He points at me. "Did you know that she's actually a Jew?"

Both Hannah and I gasp.

Sergei's face breaks out into a vicious grin. "That's right! Her real name is Maria Furman and she's a Jew."

CHAPTER 54
BEHIND CLOSED DOORS

Hannah squints her eyes and takes a step closer to Sergei. "What did you just say?"

"You heard me!" Sergei shouts, and points at me again. "I know her. She's a Jew. A dirty little Jew. So, call Herr Müller immediately. Tell him! Tell him she's a Jew!"

I squeeze my eyes shut. *Lyuda. Goodbye, my friend. I'm sorry.*

Smack!

I open my eyes wide to find Sergei clutching his cheek, where Hannah's handprint still shines in red.

"Don't you ever, EVER repeat such vile nonsense again," Hannah says, her gaze as sharp as her tone. Her mouth is twisting as if she has just smelled something foul.

"But—" Sergei tries.

But Hannah interrupts him, "When you spout lies like that, you put all the Ostarbeiter in danger, along with the people who employ them. So, let me make this perfectly clear. If you ever say something like this again, I will have my husband send you to the camps."

Sergei's eyes widen. He takes a step back but doesn't argue.

Hannah beckons me to follow her. "You. Come. Now."

Barely able to catch my breath, I follow Hannah down the hall and into the library, aware of Sergei's furious gaze as I walk past him.

"Close the door and sit down," Hannah orders when we step into the library, and sits down behind a wide office desk.

I do as she says and sit across from her.

"Talk," Hannah orders.

"What would you like me to say?" I ask, my voice shaking.

Hannah folds her arms across her chest. "The truth. All of it. And I don't need to remind you that you had your last warning two months ago, and at this point, you might as well be on the next train to you know where."

But can I trust her? I wonder. The image of Hannah ruthlessly ripping my coat away still burns me from the inside.

If I don't tell her the truth, what can I say?

A series of possible lies flash across my mind. *I can tell her that Sergei is lying just to get back at me. Or that he's delusional and that I simply look like someone he knows but that I'm not actually her.*

But when I glance up at Hannah, the sternness in the woman's face lets me know that if I were to lie to her, Hannah would know.

She did protect me just now. And at the market. But did she do it for me or for herself?

I gaze up to the ceiling. *Lyuda, help me. I don't think I have another choice. Please protect me.*

I glance back at Frau Müller and nod. "It's true. My name is Maria Furman. And I am Jewish."

I pause to check for Hannah's reaction. But her expression is emotionless. She simply nods for me to continue.

I take a breath. I am not sure where to start, so I tell Hannah about how Natasha brought the Nazis to my home. And then about the executions. And Yuriy. And my brother, Pavlik. And Lyuda. And the Babin Yar Massacre. And the photograph of the last Jew in Vinnytsia. And then about being put on the train to Germany. And the dogs.

Hannah doesn't say a word while I talk. She listens without interrupting. She just shakes her head on occasion.

When I finish my story, we both sit in silence for what feels like years. And even though I will likely be sent to my death now, it feels good to share my truth without having to hide who I am or betraying my heritage.

Finally, Hannah says, "I forget how many Jews died in the Kristallnacht. Ninety? One hundred, maybe?" She huffs. "We all knew about the Kristallnacht when they destroyed windows, stores, and property. I always knew that the people involved in Nationalsozialismus, or the Nazis, as you call them, were extreme. They told us that the camps were for working."

She swallows before she continues, "But I didn't know about the mass murders. It's so hard to believe. And yet seeing your face, hearing the details of your story—no one would make something like that up. And it makes more sense than what we were led to believe. I didn't realize that the SS were so—" She gazes up and spins her wrist in circles, clearly struggling to find the right word.

"Uncivilized?" I suggest.

"Inhuman," Hannah says, looking into my eyes now. She takes my hands in both of hers. "I am sorry about what you and your people have endured."

I feel a lump swelling in my throat. I swallow to push it down and force a smile. "You didn't know."

Hannah shakes her head. "But I should have." She squeezes and then lets go of my hands. "And to be honest, a part of me knew that there was more violence out there than we were told, especially against Jewish people. Kurt wasn't supposed to tell me, but he let a few things slip." She lowers her head. "And I shushed him. I guess, in a way, I did not want to know. But in that, I too am complicit."

It feels as if the rock that has been pressing on my chest over the past two years has suddenly lifted. A feeling of warmth spreads over my chest where all my grief had been.

I am still not sure if I can trust Hannah completely. And now that Hannah knows everything, I am even more vulnerable than before. But even so, having someone listen to my story, having someone just bear witness to my pain, makes me feel more at peace.

I nod. "Thank you, Frau Müller."

"You know," Hannah says, "a few years ago, the SS were issued an instruction to impregnate their wives, as well as all the single Aryan women they could find. They said that it was an honor for women to be considered for this, *Lebensborn* it is called—*the Fount of Life*."

My eyes widen as Hannah continues, "Kurt... err... Herr Müller and I discussed our options. I was already too old to get pregnant. We only ever had one child, Elizabeth. But she died when she was four months old."

I reach out to hold her hand, but Hannah pulls away, dabbing at her eyes with her handkerchief.

"Anyway," Hannah continues, "Kurt told me one night that some of the SS were instructed to divorce their wives and marry younger women in order to procreate."

I gape at her. "That's horrible. But...he didn't leave you?"

Hannah shakes her head. "He said that if they tried to make him, he'd retire rather than to leave me." She gives me a rare smile. "He's a good man. Even for Hitler's servant."

I am not sure how to respond to this. "I didn't realize there were good Germans out there." The words come out of my mouth before I can think about what I am saying and who I am saying it to.

Sheepishly, I glance up at Hannah, readying for a blowback.

Hannah smirks. "I guess prior to meeting you, I never knew there were good Jews out there either. In our stories, the Jews are the big bad wolves. But you're clearly not a big bad wolf."

I shake my head. "It's easy to make someone else the villain if you never have to look them in the eyes."

Hannah nods. "We hide behind our laws to salvage our conscience, but many laws are just as flawed as the people who wrote them."

I nod too. "Like the laws that legitimize rape, for example?"

Hannah nods and then stares at me. "Is that... is that what happened to you? Sergei? Did he—"

I shake my head. "Not me. Svetlana. He tried to with me, but—" I trail off.

Hannah leans forward. "But someone else did."

I squeeze my fists and nod, staring at the square patterns on the rug, trying to get the image of Axel Jeckeln's smirking face out of my mind.

Hannah gasps. "Sturmbannführer Jeckeln? Is that why you act so strange when he's around?"

I jerk my head up in surprise, unable to say a word. *How does she know? What will happen to me now?*

Hannah nods. "It's all right. You do not have to answer."

I nod.

Hannah leans in closer to me. "That coat I threw out-" I cringe at the mention of it, as Hannah continues, "It meant something to you, didn't it?"

I nod.

Hannah sighs. "I saw it in your face that day, but I couldn't stop myself. I'm so trained to comply with what others think to be right, that I forget to do what I know to be human. I realize now that they aren't always the same thing. I am sorry, Maria. Is there anything I can do to replace it?"

I shake my head but avoid her gaze. It still hurts to think about it.

"In that case, is there anything I can do to help?" Hannah asks.

I consider it for a moment. "I need a sewing kit and a pair of scissors."

"I can do that," Hannah says.

She gets up, walks up to a brown wooden cabinet, and opens the side door. She pulls out a small orange pouch, closes the cabinet door and walks back to the desk.

"Take it," she says, handing the pouch to me.

I unzip it. The pouch has several spools of thread— black, white, and brown, two needles, and a small pair of orange scissors. It even has a small silver thimble.

This must be what it feels like to discover long lost treasure. I beam at her. "Thank you, Frau Müller. I'll bring it back tomorrow morning."

"Call me Hannah when we're in private, and I will call you Maria then. In front of others, we'll still have to be formal, and I will call you Anna."

I nod and smile through the tears that are welling up in my eyes. "Thank you, Hannah."

It feels both strange and liberating to call her by her first name.

Hannah nods back at me. "Meet me in the kitchen in the morning."

"Yes, Frau Müller...err...Hannah," I respond.

"On time, Maria," Hannah adds as I am exiting the study.

I nod again and step out the door, clutching the sewing kit pouch in my hands.

After I close the door behind me, I pause and look around. No sign of Sergei.

I unzip the pouch again and remove the small orange scissors. I grip them in my hands, just in case, and hurry back to my room.

I exhale with relief when I make it back there without running into Sergei or anyone else. Oksana is already asleep, but she left one of the lamps on for me.

I kneel, pull my graduation dress from under the bed,

and unfold it. A small red tassel falls out from inside of it. I pick up the tassel and examine it.

It's all I have left of Lyuda. This and the boots.

I run my fingers across the embroidery of the dress. Some of the rose threads are coming loose, as is the back-clasp button and the pink ribbon that once lived on Babushka's keys.

I take a long, quiet breath, and begin to sew.

CHAPTER 55

A GARDEN GRAVE

"Did you sleep at all?" Oksana asks when she wakes up the next morning.

I am still sitting on the floor admiring my finished work. "Not really, no."

Oksana rolls out of bed. "Where were you yesterday? I was worried."

Can I really trust her? I wonder about Oksana. *She agreed with me about Hannah being evil and then with Kamila about Hannah being good. What kind of a friend is she?*

"I'm sorry," I say, "I had to talk to Frau Müller about something, but everything is fine. She lent me her sewing kit. See?"

I hold up my new purse for Oksana to see.

I managed to use every part of the dress. I cut the body of the dress into squares, and used the fabric with the embroidered roses, clef note, spade, and tiara for the outside of the purse. I still had enough fabric left to line the inside of the purse and make a small interior pocket. I cut and folded the sleeves the long way to create two thick and sturdy straps.

The straps are long enough to wear across my shoulder, so that I don't have to hold the purse in my hands. I sewed the dress button, the pink ribbon, and the tassel on the inside of the small pocket to make sure that I never lose them.

Now, I'll always have everything with me, unlike the things from my pillowcase.

"It's beautiful," Oksana says.

She runs her fingers across the purse as the two of us make our way toward the kitchen. "This was your dress, wasn't it?"

I nod.

"You embroidered all these rose stitches yourself?" Oksana asks.

I shake my head. "Babushka did most of it."

"She's very talented," Oksana says.

Was, I correct her silently, my chest feeling heavy at the weight of the past tense.

When the two of us enter the kitchen, we are met with sharp looks and scowling faces.

"How could you?" Zoya asks.

"How could I what?" I ask, confused.

"We know what you did," Kamila says, "so don't try to deny it."

Oksana looks from Kamila to me and back to Kamila again. "What happened?"

"Oh, you know," Zoya says. "Anna is just starting drama again. First, she was spreading rumors about Herr Jeckeln. Then, apparently, Viktor attacked her and that's why he was sent away. Now, she's spreading rumors about Sergei."

Oksana turns toward me. "Wait, what happened with Sergei? He was so nice."

"He *is* nice!" Zoya says to Oksana. "He is a good man. What I don't understand is why your friend is making up lies about him."

Oksana raises her hands. "Hey, don't put this on me. Anna and I barely know each other, we only met on the train. I don't even know what happened."

How could she? Does she just side with whoever is most convenient for her to side with? I thought she was my friend.

"What happened?" Sveta asks upon entering the kitchen.

"What happened was that Anna told Frau Müller that Sergei supposedly attacked her last night," Zoya snaps. "And so, Herr Müller sent him away this morning, probably to some camp to die."

Sergei is... gone? I stare at the floor as a wave of guilt washes over me, churning deep inside my stomach. *Will he die because of me? This isn't what I wanted. I just didn't want him around me.*

Zoya towers over me, shaking her finger at me. "What's next, Anna? You're going to say that Herr Müller attacked you too?" She rolls her eyes. "God forbid we look at you wrong, and you're going to say that we abused you as well?"

"Wait, that's not—" I try, exasperated.

"I hate to break it to you, Anna," Zoya interrupts, "but you're not so beautiful as to have all these men fighting over you."

"Leave her alone," Sveta says. "You're lucky that you didn't know Sergei that well. He had you fooled. He wasn't as innocent as you think, Zoya."

"See what you're doing?" Zoya snaps at me. "You're creating all this drama and division around you."

I tighten my grip on the straps of my purse and stifle a scream. *Even when he's not here, no one believes me. I can't even say anything.*

"Enough," Hannah says as she steps into the kitchen.

All five of us snap into line formation and straighten up, awaiting orders.

"Zoya and Oksana, you're running the kitchen today. Kamila and Svetlana, you're on house cleaning duty. Anna, you're in the garden with me. Let's get to it. Anna, follow me."

She grabs an empty bucket from the kitchen storage cabinet and heads out.

"*Ja*, Frau Müller," I say and follow her.

On my way out, I shoot a quick glance at Oksana, who looks down, avoiding my gaze.

What is her problem? I thought we were friends.

Hannah steps out of the house, opens the outdoor supply closet, and fills the bucket with gardening tools.

"What happened to Sergei?" I ask and follow Hannah to the garden.

"Don't you worry about him. Kurt transferred him to work at a factory. He is only living and working with men now."

I let out a sigh of relief. *He's okay.*

"I see you made a new purse," Hannah says.

I pull out the sewing kit from my purse and hand it to Hannah. "Yes, thank you for lending this to me."

Hannah nods. She places the sewing kit in the bucket and removes some of the gardening supplies, placing them onto the ground. She hands me a set of gardening gloves and puts a pair on herself. "Today, we are going to garden together."

I frown. "I'm afraid I will be a disappointment to you. I am terrible at gardening. My mother and my grandmother both had green thumbs. I used to joke that they were garden witches. They tried to teach me, but it didn't work. I couldn't even grow marigolds at home, and I've been doing a terrible job with your garden over the past few months."

"I have noticed," Hannah says, "and there's a reason I've been putting you in the garden since the day after we returned from the market."

"What do you mean?" I asked.

Hannah takes a breath. "I saw the way you looked at that girl, the one you mistook for your brother. I know grief when I see it." She beckons me to come closer. "You see this tree?" She points to a small tree with pink blossoms growing from it. "This is a dwarf apple tree. I planted it five days after my daughter died."

I glance from the tree to Hannah, and back to the tree again. I want to say something comforting to her but can't find the right words. So, I nod instead, a wave of my own grief swelling inside my throat.

Hannah walks up to the tree, unfolds a small pocketknife, and cuts one of the blossoms from it.

"Gardening isn't about being *good at it*," Hannah says and hands me the blossom. "It's about giving life. Especially in the face of death."

Her words make me reflect about what Babushka used to teach me, the message finally sinking into my heart now.

Remember that gardening isn't about being good at it. It's about creating life and helping it grow. It's about listening to what the plants want. It's about talking to them and caring for them.

I nod in understanding, caressing the blossom with my fingers.

Hannah pulls out a cold, damp, green pouch from the bucket and hands it to me. I untie the blue yarn around it to reveal a few small seeds.

"Today we are going to plant an apple tree for your brother."

My eyes sting with tears of gratitude and a warm, tingling sensation spreads across my entire chest.

Hannah continues, "And then, we will plant a flower for every Jewish person that was killed in your country."

A thin film of tears blankets my eyes, as I blink them away in disbelief. "Really? Wow. But that's...thousands."

"Can you give me a rough estimate?" Hannah asks.

"About thirty thousand in Kyiv and about twenty-five thousand in Vinnytsia. Viktor mentioned people getting killed in Ovruch and Lutsk, but I don't know how many. A thousand maybe? So, at least fifty-six thousand." Saying the number out loud gives me a chill.

Hannah nods. "Then you and I are going to plant fifty-six thousand flowers. As a grave, or a memorial. A life for a death. And every time there's another killing, we are going to plant life once again."

I nod in understanding. "All right. But this will take months."

Hannah kneels down. "Then I guess we'd better start."

CHAPTER 56
ONCE MORE
WITH GUSTO

I grunt as I pull out another weed. Even through my gloves, my hands still burn and ache, as do my knees, back, and elbows after hours of weeding. The ground is still wet and chilly from yesterday's rain, and my skirt, boots, and stockings are covered in mud.

Over the past two years, I've been tending to the garden like a nurse to a sick patient. I learned that I don't have to know much about gardening.

"Just listen to the plants. They'll tell you what they need," Hannah has told me on a number of occasions.

I have learned to listen. Some plants shrivel if they aren't getting enough sun. Others if they are getting too much of it. My eyes still swell with spring allergies and my back aches, but none of it matters. I am on a mission now. I have a purpose.

A life for a death, Hannah said that day in the garden nearly two years ago, and I haven't stopped gardening since.

I've planted trees—four apple, two walnut, and five orange trees. I've planted berries—strawberries, raspberries, and gooseberries. And most of all, I've planted flowers—roses, tulips, marigolds, and snowdrops. Many, many snowdrops. In February, earlier this year, we had nearly five hundred of them—four hundred and eighty-two. I counted each one.

I wipe my face with the sleeve of my grey Ostarbeiter dress and glance over to the new sunflower seedlings that are just beginning to raise their tiny heads out of the soil.

Two weeks ago, Hannah handed me a small pouch of sunflower seeds and told me to plant them. "They will make for beautiful sunflowers this summer," she said.

Sunflowers.

I smile, remembering Lyuda surprising me with them, and our moonlit picnic outside of a royal palace in Nemyriv.

I'm so sorry, Lyuda, I pray to my friend while pulling weeds. *It's been months since I've last talked to you in this way. But please know that I think of you every day.*

I can't believe it's been over two years since I've seen you. It feels both shorter and much, much longer at the same time.

I wrap my hands around the base of one of the weeds and yank, but it doesn't budge. I try again. After a few more tries, I stop. I realize my hands are too small to get a good grip while kneeling. I straighten up, stretch out my back, and take a wide stance with my feet. Then, I bend down again, wrap my hands around the base once more, take a big inhale, and pull it out on the exhale. The weed comes out with its roots.

My eyes burn and my arms ache, but I am not going to stop until I am done.

You know, Lyuda, in these last two years at Berchtes-gaden, I have seen Hitler twice. He was far away, but I could still see him and his horrible mustache. Both times I picked up a rock to throw at him and both times I didn't actually do it.

I think I'm a coward.

I live in this very nice house. I have a roof over my head, I have a bed. I share it with Oksana, but it's a warm bed, nonetheless. I have food. Not a lot but more than you and I usually had. And I should be grateful. Though it is hard to be grateful knowing that I can't leave. And I can't have anything of my own, other than my dress, which I've turned into a purse now. Sometimes it feels like I'm living in a golden cage when I would rather fly and be a free bird.

Or a Mouse.

I actually really miss you calling me that.

I sigh, brush off some of the soil from my dress, get up and stretch again. I can see mountain tops in the distance.

Sometimes, Lyuda, I look at the beautiful lakes, castles, and mountains, and I feel guilty because you are not here.

I feel guilty whenever I enjoy an orange or a bowl of warm soup.

I'm getting along better with the other Ostarbeiter, especially since Sergei was sent away. It was hard at first, but Sveta told the other three the truth about Sergei, about what he did to her. And I mentioned that he attempted to do it to me. They seem to believe me now and support me.

Zoya, she's the oldest Ostarbeiter here, she and I have been taking care of the other girls—Kamila, Sveta, and Oksana. It's kind of like we are parenting them together. I'm still helping the others with German, although the four of them are almost fluent now. I know I'm not the oldest, or even the second oldest, but given everything I've been through, I feel like I've lived for a hundred years.

Lyuda, I don't know if you are still alive, but since I am, I assume that you are too. I remember our survival pact always. It is what keeps me alive.

I hear the Allies are pushing back and are starting to make more of an offensive. I pray this war ends soon. It's been nearly four years since it began. I remember thinking it was too long when Yuriy told us to plan for six months. I never imagined it would last this long.

Please be safe, Lyuda. And one day, I pray to be able to come home and see you again.

After I complete my prayer, I kneel again to inspect some of the tulips that are starting to peek through the soil. "Good morning, my beautiful," I greet the tulips.

"*Dobroye utro, krasavitsa,*" comes a voice from behind me.

The voice makes my skin crawl before I even fully realize who the speaker is.

Is it really him? It can't be.

I spin on my knees and shield my eyes from the sun.

It's him.

"What are you doing here, Sergei?"

He looks older now. Not just two years older, but at least ten years older than the last time I saw him. His hair is greying. He is much thinner, his face gaunt and ashen. His grey shirt has the same blue and white OST patch stitched onto it, as all the other Ostarbeiter do, but his is faded and worn – it must be the same patch and shirt he'd worn two years ago.

He kneels next to me. "I'm just stopping by to deliver a package to Herr Müller, but I just had to make sure I saw you."

"What do you want, Sergei?" I ask, refocusing on the tulips.

"What do I want?" He sounds offended. "We haven't

seen each other in two years. I got sent away because of you and this is all you have to say to me?"

"If you're here to make a delivery, then just do it and go," I respond, inspecting the soil without looking up at him.

Sergei leans even closer now. I can smell the sweat coming from him. "I already met with Herr Müller this morning. And he told me that Frau Müller has been very angry with you for messing up her garden." He points to the weeds.

He doesn't realize that Frau Müller was the one who instructed me to pull them, I realize. *There just isn't any limit to his lies. Did I ever used to be so naïve that I blindly believed him?*

Sergei continues, "Apparently, Frau Müller said she hates what you've been doing with the garden, and she's fed up with you. She's thinking of having you sent to the camps."

I smirk. "Is she now?"

Sergei nods. "Yes. But don't worry. Now that I'll be making weekly deliveries here, I can put in a good word for you with Herr Müller. He trusts me."

Weekly deliveries? I curse under my breath. *Not again. I thought I was finally free of him.*

I take a breath and get up on my feet. "I am sick of your manipulations."

Sergei jumps up to his feet too. "How could you say that? We haven't seen each other for two years. All I've done was think of you and try to find my way back to you. And this is how you treat me? Aren't you glad to see me?"

I am so astounded at his questions that I find myself laughing. "No, I was glad you were away."

Sergei cackles. "Don't be stupid. All I've ever done

was to look out for you. No one else has ever done that for you. You can't trust Hannah. Or the other girls. You need to stay as far away from them as possible unless you want to be sent to the camps."

I roll my eyes at him. "Honestly, Sergei, this is pathetic, even for you. The only person I need to stay as far away from as possible is *you*."

I turn to go back to the house.

"Hey!" he shouts behind me. "Don't you dare walk away from me!"

I clench my jaw and keep walking.

"Stop, I said!" he roars behind me.

I speed up but don't respond. *Just get inside,* I tell myself silently. *Get to where the girls are. He won't hurt you in front of them.*

I grunt in frustration when he jumps in front of me.

"You've got some nerve walking away from me." His chest heaves as he speaks. "You have absolutely no respect for me."

Two years ago, I might have been afraid of him. But now I simply don't have the time or energy to be afraid. And besides, there are far worse things than Sergei in this world.

I look him right in the eyes and say, "You're right. I don't have any respect for you."

He shakes his head. "You've changed, Maria. You used to be such a good, quiet girl. And now—"

"And now I can see right through you," I interrupt. "You're a coward. And a rapist, just like Axel. You are a small, pathetic man."

Sergei gapes at me, his cheeks burning red. "You bitch!" he snarls.

He pushes me onto the ground and falls on top of me, his hands tightening around my neck.

Everything inside me jolts into high alert once I realize that I can't breathe.

I thrash and struggle underneath him, like when I was drowning and struggling to find firm ground. But Sergei's hands hold firm across my neck, his eyes staring intently into mine.

My vision begins to tunnel. *Is this how I'm going to die?*

A memory of Viktor flashes in front of my eyes. *"Use the heel of your hand to punch him in the nose."*

I pause, gaze at my intended target, and punch him in the nose with the heel of my hand, just like Viktor showed me.

"Oww!" we both yell at the same time, but the sharp pain in my wrist is worth the look of surprise in Sergei's eyes. He lets go of me and rolls onto his back, gripping his face.

"You punched me!" he yells, indignant, blood pouring out of his nose, staining his shirt and hands. "You actually punched me!"

"Yes, and that's the least of your problems," I respond and run to find Hannah.

CHAPTER 57

TRAITORS AND SYCOPHANTS

W hen I tell Hannah what happened, she immediately calls her husband to join the two of us in the study. She informs him of Sergei attacking me and the fact that he'd previously assaulted Sveta.

During their conversation, I shift in place several times, too anxious to stay and too anxious to ask to be excused.

Kurt might be sympathetic, I reflect to myself, *but he is still a Nazi. A high-ranking Nazi.*

"He is unhinged," Hannah is saying to Kurt. "Who knows what to expect from him?"

"Don't worry," Kurt reassures her, his tone firm and tender at the same time, "I will make sure that he will not make deliveries here anymore. I will report him to his supervisor."

"Thank you, dear," Hannah responds.

I observe their interaction from the corner chair. I don't have a chance to witness the two of them interacting too often. There is kindness in their exchange. A kind of gentleness that surprises me.

My stomach churns in a familiar guilty fashion. *If it wasn't for me and Sergei's obsession with me, Viktor would still be here. And everything would be peaceful. And all of this chaos wouldn't be happening right now.*

No. I stop myself. *If it wasn't for Sergei, Viktor would still be here. All of this is happening because of him, not because of me. Everything was peaceful when he was gone, and everything is worse again now that he's back.*

I'm unable to sleep all night, and the next morning, I am lightheaded from worry and exhaustion. The house is on lockdown after what happened with Sergei.

"Any sign of him?" Oksana asks when she enters the kitchen.

I shake my head and stifle a yawn.

Oksana stretches her hand across the table and grips mine. "Don't worry, Anna. I'm sure Herr Müller won't let anything happen to you."

I smile at her. In the last few years, I've learned that Oksana likes to reassure everyone. Even though it is still sometimes confusing when Oksana contradicts herself, I see now that her intentions come from a kind place.

I'm lucky to have such good friends now, I think to myself.

Someone rings the doorbell, and Oksana runs to answer the door.

I hear voices in the foyer and then Oksana's worried yell, "Herr Müller? Come quick!"

Both Kurt and Hannah rush to the foyer, and I follow them there.

When I turn the corner, my heart jumps into my throat.

Oksana ducks into the corner and out of the way. Kurt and Hannah have their arms folded across their chests. Axel Jeckeln is in the center of the room with Sergei and two other SS with submachine guns. Sergei's face is swollen, and his shirt is stained with blood.

"Ah, Sturmbannführer Jeckeln," Kurt says, and then points to Sergei. "Good. You found him. I'm glad you brought him back. But you might as well take him with you. He's not allowed at this house, as I have ample evidence that he is a threat to the other Ostarbeiter, as well as my wife."

"You misunderstand," Axel says, his face stern and devoid of emotion. "We are here to arrest you."

Herr Müller makes a sound in between laughing and choking. "Arrest me? Arrest ME? How dare you? I am your superior."

Axel shakes his head. "Not anymore. We have evidence to believe that you and your wife have been conspiring with the Soviets to kill the Führer."

"What?" Hannah spits, stepping forward.

"That's right," Sergei says, "and they wanted me to pass messages between them and the Soviet Army. But I am loyal to the Führer. Heil Hitler." He salutes.

"Get them out of here," Axel orders, nodding toward Kurt and Hannah.

One of the SS grabs Kurt and the other is handling Hannah, twisting her hands behind her back.

I run toward her. "Hannah!"

The two of us lock eyes and Hannah shakes her head

for me to stay away. A sharp memory of Babushka shaking her head the same way flashes in my mind, burning in my chest with anguish.

No!

"Stay away from me, you Hitler-lover!" Hannah shouts at me.

I stop mid-step.

Hannah turns toward the SS and screams at them, ignoring her husband's attempts to silence her. "Killers! Murderers! All of you! Do you know what is happening in Poland? In Ukraine? In Latvia? There are death camps. Mass executions. Gas chambers. They are killing millions of innocent people. Including children. In broad daylight. And you work for them, you are complicit, and you—"

Bang!

Bang!

Smoke.

Red.

Everything blurs and the Moonlight Sonata begins to play somewhere in the confines of my mind.

CHAPTER 58

TRANSPORT

M y ears are still ringing from the gunshots, and the accompanying Beethoven's Sonata. Hannah and Kurt are lying on the ground.

They're dead! Both of them are dead.

A small trickle of blood flows from each of them, connecting in the middle, like two hands desperately finding each other in the darkness.

I shiver, my eyes darting around in a daze. The SS drag Kurt and Hannah's bodies out of the house. Oksana is whimpering in the corner, looking as shocked and confused as I feel. The other three women huddle together in the doorway.

"Attention, Ostarbeiter," Axel announces. "You will now be relocated. You have ten minutes to gather your belongings. If you are not in my car in ten minutes, you will be shot."

The devious relocation announcements posted in Kyiv prior to the Babin Yar massacre flash in my memory.

"Where?" I manage to ask. "Where are you taking us?"

"My home," Axel says. "Out of the kindness of my heart, I've decided to bring you with me rather than— well, you figure out the rest."

There is a loud scream inside my mind, but I make no noise. None of the women do.

"Thank you, Herr Jeckeln." Sergei says. "Or Axel. May I call you Axel?"

Axel glares at him but does not respond.

Sergei continues, "So, now you will all be working for Herr Jeckeln, and I will be in charge of all of you."

"Right," Axel says. "I'd forgotten that we agreed to that."

Bang!

Sergei's body slumps onto the ground.

I am lightheaded and numb all over.

"Take care of him too," Axel says to the other SS, pointing to Sergei's body. "You know what to do."

Axel turns toward me and the other Ostarbeiter. "Now, unless you all want to end up like your friend here," he says, pointing at Sergei with his smoking pistol, "I suggest you load yourselves into my car. And do not try to run. Do I need to remind you what happens when you try to run?" He says the last part directly to me.

I shake my head and slowly walk up to Oksana. I bend down and help her to her feet.

"It's like the dogs all over again," Oksana whispers, trembling as we walk.

I nod and motion for the other three women to follow us. We gather our belongings as quickly as we can, and then all five of us cram ourselves in the back of Axel's car.

Nobody says a word during the car ride. The other women are crying, but for me, everything feels much clearer now, more in focus. My thoughts slow and I feel calm—a kind of unsettled calm, a kind of calm I've never felt in my entire life.

Shouldn't I be devastated right now? I wonder. *Why am I not crying? Why am I so relaxed right now? Am I a heartless person like the Nazis are?*

I guess I should be feeling guilty about feeling as serene as I do, but somehow, I don't care anymore how I'm *supposed* to feel.

When we arrive, Axel brings us inside his two-bedroom house at the edge of Berchtesgaden. His house smells like cigarettes, mold, and rotten food.

He ushers the five of us into one of the rooms—a small and dark bedroom with a window and two narrow beds.

"This is where you sleep," he says. "I expect you to cook and clean today and get ready for tonight."

"What's tonight?" Kamila asks, her eyes wide and her voice trembling.

"The same entertainment we had on the train," he says, and winks at me before walking out of the room.

So strange. I should be terrified right now but that's not at all what I feel. I am not sure exactly what I am feeling, but it isn't fear. It's more like serene anger mixed with excitement.

There is a warm buzzing in my chest and stomach.

What is this? I ask myself.

After a moment, I feel a flash of understanding.

Vengeance.

An image of my grandmother flashes before my eyes.

"*When it comes down to it, I hope you'll choose to be more like the Night Witches.*"

Sorry, Papa. I guess I was never meant to be a "good girl" after all, I think, and find myself grinning.

CHAPTER 59
MONTHLIES

"What did he mean about the same entertainment as you had on the train?" Kamila asks me.

Oksana and I exchange looks, then inform the other women about what happened on the train.

"Anna," Kamila says, "I feel terrible for not believing you before. You tried to tell us, and I didn't listen."

I wave my hand at Kamila. "Don't worry about it." I glance at all four of them. "We will all need to trust each other now and work together if we are going to survive this. And we *are* going to survive this."

"But what can we do?" Sveta asks.

"Zoya and I will think of something," I say but I have no idea what to do.

We all turn to Zoya, who is curled into a ball on the floor, her legs pulled under her. She is speechless and motionless.

I walk over to her. "Are you okay?"

Zoya stares at the cracks in the white wall when she speaks. "Raped? We are going to be—"

I sit next to her and put my hands on Zoya's face. "Look at me."

Slowly, Zoya shifts her gaze toward me, and I continue, "We are all in this together. There's five of us and one of him."

"But he has a gun," Zoya whispers. "I saw what one person can do with a gun. Even an unloaded one. One of them beat my husband for being late to work. He beat him with the butt of his gun." She pulls my hands off her cheeks and squeezes them. "Vanya was drinking again. He didn't know that the Germans had taken over his factory. He couldn't walk ever again after that day."

Kamila sits on the other side of Zoya. "That's terrible. I had no idea. Was that why you decided to volunteer for the Ostarbeiter?"

Zoya nods. "I thought I could send money to my kids while they lived with Vanya's mother. He moved in with her too. But there's been no money to send back." She shakes her head. "I try not to think of it. But we are just prisoners here. We can't leave. We have no choices. No power. Nothing."

Sveta kneels next to one of the beds and motions for Oksana to join her. All five of us are gathered together now.

"We might not have many choices," Sveta says. "But Anna is right. We are stronger together. And if we have any chance of surviving this, it's by working as a team, not by giving up."

I nod. "Exactly. And in the meantime, let's focus on chores. It will help us clear our minds and keep Axel from suspecting anything." I look around the room. "Kamila, I need you to help me in the kitchen. We are going to look for anything we can use to protect ourselves."

Kamila nods as I continue, "Oksana and Sveta, you two need to clean the house, but also find any escape routes you can—loose doors, windows, anything."

"Okay," Sveta says. Oksana nods.

"And Zoya, I need you to rest," I say.

"But—" Zoya tries to argue but stops herself. She nods. "Okay."

"You're not the same person," Kamila says to me as we walk into the kitchen together.

"What do you mean?" I ask. I've already begun searching through the kitchen cabinets looking for anything that can be used as a weapon.

Kamila leans over the kitchen table, studying me. "What I mean is that when I first met you, you were—"

"Mousey?" I suggest as I inspect a butter knife and shove it into my purse. *It's dull, but better than nothing.*

"Yes. Exactly. Mousey," Kamila says.

I pull out a steak knife from the cutlery drawer.

Much better. I pocket it too.

"And now?" I ask.

"And now, it's like you've become a bear. A petite one, but a bear nonetheless."

I smirk, feeling a thump of excitement in my chest. "Well, it's time for this little bear to eat the big bad wolf."

Kamila giggles.

A memory of my brother teaching me to play cards flashes in my mind. *"This game is about strategy, about knowing your opponent. And so long as you play the cards in a smart way, you can win just about any match."*

"So, what are we making for dinner?" Kamila asks.

"I think we are having chicken," I say, nodding toward the chicken coop visible through the kitchen

window. "And then we are going to play some games."
My mouth curves into a sideways grin.

AFTER WE FINISH PREPARING DINNER, Kamila and I leave the
cooked chicken on the kitchen table and return to our
shared bedroom where Oksana and Sveta wait for us. In
my hand is a jar filled with warm, sticky blood I collected
from the chicken before we cooked it.

"You really think it will work?" Oksana asks.

"If it doesn't, then we attack him on my signal," I say,
smearing chicken blood on each woman's thighs and
legs.

When I am finished, we sprawl out on the beds and
wait.

I jerk upward when Axel swings the door open.
There's part of me that still fears him, but there is a new
part too—a part of me that's excited. A part that feels in
control as I squeeze the handle of the steak knife that I
hid under my pillow. A part that's ready to avenge Irina,
Hannah, and myself.

I moan, as all the other girls do, pretending to be in
excruciating pain.

"What is this?" Axel shouts. "Why are you all covered
in blood?"

"We are on our monthly cycle, Herr Jeckeln," I groan.

Axel furrows his eyebrows. "All of you? At once?"

All five of us nod.

"When women all live together, their monthlies
synchronize," Oksana says. "Everyone knows that."

Axel raises one of his eyebrows, pauses, and lowers it
again. "Right. Of course. I know that," he says—though

his voice is less confident now. "But no matter. I don't mind a little blood. Go wash up and get to it."

Nobody moves.

Axel stares from one woman to another. "What's going on? Why aren't you moving? Do you want to get shot?" His voice is shrill now and his ears are turning red.

It's working, I think, trying to hide my smile. *He's feeling embarrassed and less confident.*

But out loud I say, "Herr Jeckeln, with all due respect, the issue is not with the blood."

He glares at me. "Well, then what is the issue?"

"The issue is that when women are on our monthly cycles, we carry a lot of bacteria. And if the bacteria were to get on your penis," I shrug as if explaining the world's most obvious facts, "well, your penis could get infected, of course. And in the worst case," I pause, waiting for him to lean in, and when he does, I deliver the punch line, "in the worst-case scenario, the doctors might need to amputate it."

Axel's lips curl in disgust, and he jerks away from me. "What? No. That's preposterous."

"Well," I continue, pretending to be more interested in the hem of my blanket than in looking at him, "surely, a smart and educated man such as yourself knows how women's bodies work." I glance up at him. "You *do* know how women's bodies work, don't you?"

"Of course, you can always ask your friends if you don't believe us," Sveta adds. "They might know more."

Axel looks absolutely deflated. "Well, of course I know that," he snaps. "It's just... how long do these monthly periods last?"

All five of us stare at him with a rehearsed, synchronized gaze of disbelief. "They are called *monthly* periods,

Herr Jeckeln," I say. "I imagine that a man of your status knows what that means."

Axel lowers his head. "Right. *Monthly*. A month." He sighs. "And... and this is *all* women?" he asks, looking at me.

All five of us nod.

Axel nods too. "Right. Of course. Obviously."

He looks around at all of us. "Well, you just get cleaned up. It smells like a dead animal in here."

"Of course, Herr Jeckeln," I say. "One thing though."

"Yes?" he says through gritted teeth.

I pretend not to notice Axel's consternation, but inside, I am overjoyed. "In order for us to become a healthy and a viable choice, truly deserving of a powerful Aryan man such as yourself, we are going to need some things."

Axel's eyes widen, "How dare you?" He charges at me. "You forget that you work for me, not the other way around."

I nod and continue, trying to make myself seem as demure as possible, remembering what Natasha would do whenever she was flirting with a boy she liked. "Of course, Herr Jeckeln. You are absolutely right. You are our Master, and we serve you."

"And don't you forget it," Axel says but he appears to be pacified.

I continue with a smooth, melodic tone, "It's just that if you look at cattle, for example, you need to take good care of your cattle in order to use them and make them truly worthy of your consumption."

On the last word, I bite my lip, looking him right in the eyes and giving him a coy smile.

Axel coughs. "Right. Ahem. Consumption. What do you need?"

That's right, I think to myself. *You do treat women like cattle, you sick, twisted man.*

I hand him a small piece of paper. "Just some food to restore our bodies to their proper functions and some medicine for your protection, of course."

Axel snatches the paper from my hand. "Fine. You will have it. But in a month when you're all done bleeding, if there are any other delays, I will put every one of you out like a sick cow."

"Yes, of course," I reply. "Thank you, Herr Jeckeln."

"Thank you, Herr Jeckeln," the other four women repeat with a smile.

Axel nods, walks out of the room, and slams the door.

I grin at the other girls who look back at me with a mixture of relief and expectation.

"What's next?" Zoya asks, as if reporting for duty.

CHAPTER 60
ESCAPE PLAN

Over the next few days, I keep a sealed jar of chicken blood in our shared bedroom, just in case Axel decides to check and see whether we are still bleeding. However, since that night, Axel has been completely disinterested in me and the other Ostarbeiter in the house. Aside from asking when our monthlies will end, he barely talks to us and doesn't step into our bedroom or even go near it.

Funny how the sight of blood after murdering people doesn't offend you, I reflect when Axel rushes to wash his hands after touching a chair I'd previously sat in, *but the thought of women's cycles repulses you.*

I find myself smirking. *Does this mean that I am the big wolf now and you're scared of me because of your ignorance?*

Once I feel confident that Axel will leave us alone for the time being, we start to prepare for our escape during the day, while Axel is away at work. Oksana and I take a trip to the market to study the city and plan out our route.

Lyuda, if you can hear me, help us get out of here alive, I pray as Oksana and I read all the headlines we can find about the ongoing war.

It sounds like the Allies are getting stronger. They seem to be making progress in Austria. I hope they come here. I hope they will cross over to Berchtesgaden.

I pray to everyone now. *Babushka, Pavlik, Mamo, Papa, Lyuda, anyone. Please send the Allies here to Berchtesgaden to rescue us.*

Back at the house, I help the others make use of the pillowcases, taken from the pillows on our beds, to make supply bags. I stuff my purse and each pillowcase evenly with aspirin, bandages, and non-perishable foods, like walnuts and baked sunflower seeds.

Sveta, Kamila, and Zoya spend the day cleaning, cooking, and searching Axel's house from top to bottom for anything we can use.

Kamila finds an old, dusty map of Berchtesgaden in his study. "Doesn't seem like he'll notice it's gone," she says with a big smile, "but we can use it."

"Great thinking," I respond, and we gather around to pour over it. "We need to get to Austria," I say, pointing to the German-Austrian border. "That's our best chance to get to the Allies."

I try to put the horrible memories of me and Lyuda fleeing to Kyiv out of my mind.

"We can try going to Hallein," Oksana says, tracing the escape route with her finger.

I nod. "And if anything happens, we can try Dürrnberg as a backup option." I turn to face the rest of the women. "We'll refer to Hallein as Rendezvous One and Dürrnberg as Rendezvous Two. We all need to memorize these routes, in case we can't bring the map with us, or in case we get separated."

The other four women nod.

~

TWO DAYS before our planned escape, Axel comes into our room. "All of you. Outside with me. Now."

"What's going on?" Oksana whispers to me.

"Not sure," I whisper back and tuck the steak knife I have been hiding under my pillow into my purse.

We step outside to find another man standing in front of Axel's house. The man must be a photographer because he is holding onto a camera, propped on a spindly-legged tripod. The camera has a glass lens and several knobs, and black bellows sag around it like an old accordion.

"What is this?" I ask.

"No questions!" Axel snaps and turns to face us. "This photographer will take pictures of you now. He will take some pictures individually, one of the entire group, and some in groups of two. Make sure you smile and look happy in these pictures, or I will be angry. And you don't want me to be angry."

The other four women look to me for instructions.

I nod and say, "*Ja*, Herr Jeckeln," and the other four women mirror my reaction.

"Right over here, ladies," the photographer calls.

Over the next hour, the photographer takes several pictures of us smiling and posing, some of each of us separately and several in pairs. He takes a few pictures of me and Oksana and others of me and Kamila, as well as one picture of all five of us.

When the photographer is finished, Axel tells us all to get back inside. "And don't go anywhere."

"But what about the market?" I ask.

"No more trips to the market," he snarls. "I will be going to the market from now on and you are not to leave. Do you understand?"

He pushes us all inside and slams the door shut. There's a dragging sound, as he is moving furniture, likely a dresser, outside of the door.

"He's barricading us in," Kamila whispers. "Why?"

"Something is happening and it's making him nervous," I reply. "I say we take no chances. We escape tonight. Things are getting more dangerous, and we don't gain anything by waiting an extra day."

The other four nod in agreement.

I continue, "Remember our rendezvous point and our back-up plan. Review them and memorize what you haven't already." I point to each location on the map once more. "Make sure everything you need is in your pillow-case. And be ready."

CHAPTER 61
MUTTERBÄR

When Axel returns later that evening, I can hear him arguing with another man outside of our window. Axel sounds drunk.

"Just look at these pictures, Vogel," Axel says. "They are good-looking girls. I'm sure you'll be happy with one or more of them."

We all cluster around the window – out of sight, but within hearing distance. "Is he trying to sell us?" Zoya whispers.

"Is selling Ostarbeiter even allowed?" Oksana asks.

"If they can rape and kill Ostarbeiter, I don't think they care if we're sold or not," I respond.

"I don't understand," Vogel says. "If you like them so much, why are you getting rid of them?"

Axel huffs. "You wouldn't believe how expensive living with five women can be. Even if you're feeding them Jew rations."

I squeeze my fists.

"I hear that," Vogel said, "and that's why I just do

Lebensborn—I only impregnate the racially valuable Aryan girls. I get praised for it and I don't mess with the Ostarbeiter. Plus, if you ever got an Ostarbeiter girl pregnant, you have to make sure they get an abortion, and that they get sterilized afterward. It's a pain and a half. Why bother when you can just impregnate Aryan girls instead?"

We all exchange glances.

"Did you know this?" Oksana whispers.

I shake my head. I remember Hannah briefly mentioning Lebensborn to me, but she never said anything about how the Ostarbeiter women are treated if they get pregnant.

"Look, Vogel," Axel tries again, "I respect you. I won't even charge you. Just take one of them. Or two. I don't really care."

"Can't do," Vogel replies. "With the Soviets on our tail and the Americans on the other side, plus the Brits to boot, it just seems too risky to have a distraction right now."

They argue some more, but I stop listening. I look over at them–the four women who are all counting on me to survive. Oksana, whom I first judged to be spineless, now so resourceful and ready to fight alongside us all. Zoya, who was gruff and stern, now so warm and caring. Kamila, whom I initially dismissed as only interested in getting married, but who I now realize, is the kindest and most loyal one of all of us. And Sveta, who barely talks, and yet is one of the bravest people I've ever met.

Hey, guess what, Lyuda? I say silently. *I guess I am a bear now, a Mama bear—Mutterbär. And no one will mess with my cubs.*

"Sisters," I say out loud. "We are all sisters. Be ready for anything tonight but know that we will all survive this together."

We grab each other's hands and form a circle.

CHAPTER 62
THE TRAIL OF DEATH

I t's somewhere around midnight when I wake up the others.

"We are going now," I whisper.

Nobody argues.

As soundlessly as possible, I open the window.

"I'll go first to make sure it's safe," I whisper.

But before anyone has a chance to respond, the door bursts open and Axel stumbles in carrying his submachine gun.

He is swaying from side to side, and even at several meters away, I can smell the cheap beer on his breath.

"Outside," he barks, slurring his words. "Now."

I nod to the other women, and we walk outside in a single file line, with Axel in the rear. I make sure to hang back to remain as close to him as possible.

"All right," he says when we are all in his dimly lit backyard. "You have all caused me enough stress and money. It's time to say goodbye."

This is it! I realize. *Now or never. Don't hesitate.*

He raises his gun.

"*Davai!*" I shout.

Within the fraction of a second that it takes the disoriented Axel to glance in my direction, I pull out my steak knife and move to stab him in the arm.

But Axel is faster. He drops his gun wrestles the knife away from me.

Don't lose your nerve. Keep fighting.

"Was this your plan?" He snarls at me and throws the knife where I can't reach it.

I grab a hold of his other arm, pull him down sharply, and headbutt his nose. He cries out and covers his face with the other hand, blood gushing down his nose and dripping through his fingers.

Don't stop now.

I take a step closer and knee him between his legs as hard as I can.

Thank you, Viktor, for teaching me, I think as Axel howls and collapses onto the ground.

All of this happens in mere seconds, and now my sisters close in on him too. Zoya kicks the gun further away from him. Kamila kicks him on his side, Oksana kicks him in the stomach. Then all five of us are kicking him until he stops moving.

I press my hand over my mouth to silence the guttural primal scream of fury and liberation that's building inside of me.

It's over, I realize. *We are free. Lyuda, we are free!*

It takes a few moments for us all to catch our breaths.

"Is he dead?" Zoya asks, panting and pointing at Axel.

I check Axel's neck, feel his pulse, and shake my head. "No. He's just knocked out." I get up to my feet. "We need to go. Now."

I grab the knife and shove it back into my purse.

"I'll get our things," Sveta says and runs inside as Oksana and Kamila search Axel's pockets for anything useful.

"Hey, look at this," Oksana says and shows me a picture she has just pulled out of Axel's pocket. It's a picture of all of us smiling.

I grimace in disgust at the smile the five of us were forced to share and the photographs none of us wanted taken. I shake my head and shove the photo into my purse. I'm not sure why I do it, only that I don't want Axel to have it anymore. I don't want him to have any part of me ever again.

When Sveta returns with our pillowcases, we all huddle together. "Sisters," I say, "let's all promise each other that we will survive together. Survival pact."

"Agreed," they say in unison.

I nod. "Let's go."

They nod back and follow. We creep out of the backyard and onto the dimly lit street. It's more secluded than I expected it to be. Just a man walking his dog, but no other people.

We all wrap our sweaters around our dresses, to hide our OST letters, and proceed to the path toward Rendezvous One.

We walk in silence for about ten minutes.

Lyuda, I'm coming home. I hope I am, anyway. Please keep me safe and please stay safe too.

A loud siren makes me freeze mid-step. We all cover our ears.

"What's happening?" Oksana mouths over the noise.

"It's an air raid," Sveta shouts. "We are about to get bombed."

"Run!" Zoya shouts.

We run, clutching our belongings to our chests.

"Where are we going?" Sveta shouts.

"Rendezvous two," I shout over the air raid siren. "We need to get out of the city as soon as possible!"

What if I'm wrong? I wonder. Don't think about that now. They are counting on you. Don't let them see you being indecisive.

Giant birds fly above us in the sky in an angled formation.

No, not birds.

Planes.

There is an unnerving whistling sound.

And a deafening—

Boom!

We all fall to the ground as a bomb explodes not far behind us. My ears ring so loud, I'm pretty sure I'm going deaf.

Get up! These girls are counting on you!

I force myself up and yell at others to do the same.

"We have to keep moving!" Zoya yells.

"No," I argue.

Kamila, Oksana, and Sveta stare from me to Zoya, unsure of what to do.

"Viktor told me," I shout, unsure if they can hear me, if their ears are ringing as loudly as mine, "he said that if we're being bombed, we need to find a shelter. We can't outrun the bombs."

"Which way?" Sveta shouts.

I look around. More planes are flying toward us.

With a trembling hand, I point in the direction of the planes, "We have to go back to Axel's house."

"What? No!" Zoya shouts. "Are you crazy?"

"Trust me!" I shout. "They are less likely to go to the

places they've already bombed." I point toward the eerie orange glow of the city, now on fire. "Our best bet is to run back. Axel's house has a cellar; we can hide there."

"But he also has guns," Zoya argues. "He literally tried to shoot us just now."

"I hate this even more than you do," I say, "but we are safer there than out here getting bombed."

"Are you sure that's our best choice?" Kamila asks.

I'm not sure, but I nod anyway.

I hate this so much. I thought we were free of him.

Another explosion.

We all fall down again.

My vision swims to another world. *A world where everything is okay.*

I shake my head. *No. I have to stay focused. My sisters need me.*

"Let's go!" I shout, motioning for the others to follow me.

No one argues with me now. The girls follow me toward the bright orange flames of the burning buildings and toward the nightmare from which we just escaped.

The air is filled with debris, shrapnel, and the terrifying screams of the wounded, but the five of us keep running.

Another explosion.

We fall.

And we get up again.

We run.

The ground quakes with a cacophony of explosions. The air is heavy with smoke and soot. I cough, but I keep on running.

Lyuda, help me! I scream in my mind. *Babushka! Mamo! Pavlik! Help us to get out of here alive!*

Another explosion. We fall again.

"Get up!" I shout at the rest of them. "We're not far. Keep going."

Zoya screams.

"Help!" Sveta shouts. "Anna! Help!"

I turn back. Zoya's leg is torn off at the knee.

"Oh, *Bozhe*," I yell. "Oh, *Bozhe Moi*. Zoya!"

I run to Zoya and fall to my knees. *It's all my fault. She's hurt because of me. She's going to die because of me.*

No! I scream at myself internally. *No one is going to die here today. Get yourself together.*

I untie my purse with impatient, trembling hands, and pull out the bandages. I apply pressure to the gushing wound, but the bandages just soak through. The wound is too large and there's too much blood.

This won't work.

Then I remember something else Viktor told me. I pull on the belt from my dress and rip it. I then tie the belt around Zoya's knee, pull the knife out of my purse, slip it inside the knot and turn it, like turning off a faucet. Just like Viktor had explained two years ago.

Thank you, Viktor, I say in a silent prayer. *You've saved our lives more than once.*

Zoya howls in pain, but the makeshift tourniquet works to slow down the bleeding.

"Oksana, help me to lift her," I order.

"Leave me," Zoya groans, tears streaming down her face. "I'm going to die anyway. I'll just slow you down."

"Shut up, Zoya," I bark. "No one is dying. Not today." I nod to Oksana. "Ready?"

"Ready," Oksana yells back.

We place one of Zoya's arms around each of our shoulders, heave as we lift her up, and run.

Six more times, we fall. And each time, we get back up, helping each other to stand. Sveta and Kamila help Oksana and me to lift Zoya again, and again, and we keep running.

It's my fault that Zoya lost her leg. I made the wrong choice. Viktor would have known what to do.

No time for this now. Lyuda's stern voice shows up in my mind. *Focus on surviving, Mouse. Keep going.*

I take a big exhale and keep running.

At last, we reach Axel's house. He's not outside where we left him.

"Take over for me," I order Sveta.

She does, her hands shaking as she holds Zoya up. I walk inside the house first.

"Axel?" I call out, my voice barely audible over the sound of sirens and explosions.

No sign of him.

Sveta and Kamila carry Zoya inside to the kitchen and set her down on the floor.

"Go check the cellar to make sure we can all fit and figure out how we can get Zoya down the stairs."

Sveta nods and Kamila lifts the cellar door, and the two of them disappear down the stairs.

The air is thick with the acrid stench of smoke and destruction, each distant explosion vibrating through the cracked walls.

I crouch beside Zoya, tightening the provisional tourniquet above her knee where her leg used to be. Zoya's pale face glistens with sweat, her breaths shallow and uneven. Oksana huddles next to us, clearly exhausted.

The back door bursts open.

My heart stops as Axel Jeckeln strides in, his smile as

sharp as the submachine gun strapped around his shoulder. There's a trickle of blood on his face, his hair is matted, and his eyes are gleaming with malice.

"Well, well," Axel sneers. "Like rats in a hole. Did you really think you could escape me?"

Axel's gaze sweeps the room before landing on Zoya's mangled leg. He lets out a low, mocking laugh. "Seems one of you is already halfway to death. How considerate. Try not to bleed out on my floor."

My body moves before my mind catches up, stepping between Zoya and Axel.

"Leave her alone," I hiss, my voice trembling but unyielding.

He lunges, faster than I could ever expect. I yelp as his hand pulls at my hair, and the blade of his knife presses to my throat.

Where did this knife come from?

"Let's see how brave you are now," he murmurs, his breath hot against my ear. "I'm going to savor every bit of this." Just then, he notices the open cellar door. He drags me over to the door, kicks it shut, and stands on top of it, trapping Kamila and Sveta in the cellar. I hear the girls pounding on the door.

I struggle, panic surging in my chest as the edge of his knife bites into my skin. I pull at Axel's arm, at the gun strap, at anything. The strap loosens, and the gun clatters and slides across the floor as Axel's grip on me tightens.

I wish I could see all the girls, my sisters, one last time, but Axel's knife is at my throat. He's spun me, so that my back is to Zoya and Oksana. All I can manage to say is, "Remember the survival pact—"

A shot rings out.

Axel's body jolts, and I feel warmth and wetness

spread down my back. I fall to the ground as his grip loosens; I turn and watch blood flowing from a wound in his neck as he gasps for air. A few centimeters lower, and the bullet would have gone through him and hit me too.

I scramble backward, away from him. Axel stumbles and falls away from the cellar door. It flies open and Sveta and Kamila rush out. We all stare at Axel as his body twitches and then stops moving.

My eyes dart to Zoya.

The gun—Axel's gun—is in Zoya's trembling hands. Blood pours from her wound, pooling around her, but her eyes burn with fierce determination. Her lips move, a whisper barely audible over the ringing in my ears.

"Survival pact."

The weapon slips from Zoya's grasp as her strength gives out. I crawl to her, pressing my hands against the wound, desperately trying to staunch the bleeding.

"Zoya, stay with me!" I cry out, my tears mixing with the blood on my hands.

Kamila, Sveta, and Oksana rush to my side, their faces illuminated by the dim light. Zoya's breathing grows fainter, her eyelids flutter, until she passes out.

The sirens blare again.

"Let's drag Zoya to the cellar," I command, refusing to let the tears come. "Let's move."

CHAPTER 63

ON THE TRAIN AGAIN

We spend the next two days hiding out in the cellar. On the third day, Sveta, Kamila, and I venture upstairs to assess the situation.

Axel still lies motionless, his lifeless eyes staring into nothing.

I avert my eyes from him and step out of the door.

More than half of the city has been bombed.

All around us, buildings have been shattered, glass blown out, and in some places, fire still burns.

It looks a lot like Kyiv now, I reflect, my chest feeling heavy at the thought of it. *No one deserves to experience this. No one.*

Zoya has been going in and out of consciousness the entire time we have been here. It's truly a miracle she is still alive.

"What's that?" Sveta asks pointing in the distance.

I get up onto my tiptoes and I see them—tanks and other armored cars with white stars painted on the side.

Americans!

Kamila runs toward them and waves. "Over here! Help us!"

Everything else is a blur.

Several men come inside, climb down to the cellar, pick up Zoya, and carry her off to get treated.

There is shouting, talking, and crying.

I haven't allowed myself to dream of this moment, a moment when I'd be a free person again. Now that this moment is here, I am too exhausted to feel the weight of it. It still doesn't seem real.

I talk to one of the American soldiers in my broken English. He introduces himself as Martinez and tells me that Oksana, Kamila, Sveta, and I will be put in armored cars and transported to Austria to meet the Red Army and Zoya will stay behind to be treated by medics.

My eyes water. *Thank you, Lyuda. Thank you. I know you sent help somehow. I'm coming home now. Please be alive.*

On our way to the armored cars, Martinez points at our badges. "What are you doing? Take those OST badges off and throw them away. And destroy any paperwork that shows that you were an Ostarbeiter."

"Why?" I ask, still in a daze from the events of the past few days.

Martinez appears stunned. "Why? Because you'll be arrested for treason. Some of the Soviet soldiers are known to rape and kill the Ostarbeiter. The lucky ones go to prison."

"What? That's ridiculous!" Oksana says.

Martinez shrugs. "You do as you like. I'm just telling you what I've seen them do to the others. The Red Army views you as a traitor. They'll say that you could have fought for your country and died a hero but if you worked for the enemy, then *you are* the enemy."

"But it's not like we wanted to do it," I snap. "Don't they understand? The Nazis forced us. It was slavery."

"I agree with you," Martinez replies. "I'm just looking out for you is all. But do as you please."

"Unbelievable," I mutter and share what he said with the others.

I collect everyone's OST badges and documents, and Martinez helps us to burn them.

"There it goes," Oksana says. "The last reminder of our OST days."

I don't want to remember my OST days, I reflect with a bitter taste in my mouth. *But I will forever remember the friends I've made.*

"Where's Kamila?" Sveta asks.

I spin around. "She was just here."

"She's okay!" Kamila shouts from around one of the armored cars. She runs back toward the rest of us. "I just spoke to one of the medics. They said that Zoya is okay. She had surgery and will take a few days to get well enough to travel, and then they will put her on a train home to Ukraine."

"Poor Zoya," Oksana says. "She and her husband are both disabled now."

"They are alive, and they have each other," Kamila says. "Zoya is strong, and just because she is missing a leg does not mean she wants to be pitied."

Oksana blushes. "Right, of course. I'm just glad she's okay."

"Who's going to Poland?" Martinez asks.

"Me!" Kamila says. "But I'm going to stay until Zoya is ready to get on her train home. Someone should be there when she wakes up after her surgery."

"Then we should stay too," I say.

"No," Kamila says. "You all go. I got this."

I consider this for a moment, "Are you sure?"

"Completely," she says with a wide grin.

We all hug.

"I will never forget you. Never," Kamila says to the three of us.

She kisses each of us on both cheeks and runs off.

"So, are you excited to go home?" Oksana asks after she, Sveta, and I board the train to Ukraine. We find a train car where we can all sit together, with me and Sveta sitting opposite Oksana.

Sveta nods but I take a long breath before I answer, "I'm not sure. I'm happy to go home but I'm also afraid of what I will find or whom I might find dead." I push thoughts of Lyuda out of my mind. "In some ways, while we are on the train, both realities exist, and this fact is both scary and comforting at the same time."

Oksana laughs. "Did you learn that in a philosophy class?"

I shake my head. "Physics. This is called the Schrödinger's cat thought experiment."

Oksana raises her eyebrow at me but doesn't comment.

I take a few moments to look out the window. This is my second time being on the train, but the first being on a *human train*. This one has seats, tables, and windows. This was the experience I often dreamt of, yet now, I doubt I will ever want to ride the train again.

My stomach growls. I slide my hand inside my purse

and take out some baked sunflower seeds left over from our escape preparations.

"Would you like some?" I offer them to the other girls.

"Thanks." Oksana smiles and tosses a few seeds into her mouth. "And thanks for not being a kike about it." For a moment I am too shocked to respond. Oksana has never used that word before.

Is she serious?

I suck in a breath and then let out a long exhale. "That's a very offensive word, Oksana."

"What do you care? You're not a kike," Oksana says.

"It's still a rude word," Sveta interjects. "We should never use it."

I stare at Oksana without saying anything.

Oksana meets my gaze and gasps, nearly choking on her seeds. "You are, aren't you? Sergei *was* telling the truth. About all of it."

I'm so tired of hiding who I am. I grip the side of my seat. "Not everything he said was true, but yes, I'm Jewish, if that's what you mean. My name is Maria, and I am Jewish."

For a moment, both Sveta and Oksana just stare at me.

Why did I do that? I chide myself, and then correct myself, *No, I'm tired of being called Anna, tired of lying, even if they hate me for who I am.*

But Sveta grabs my hands. "It doesn't matter. None of it does. Jewish, Orthodox, atheist, whatever. None of it matters. After all we've been through, we are all sisters now, just like you said a few days ago." She turns to face the other woman. "Right, Oksana?"

I smile at Sveta and look back to Oksana, who is now

staring out the window with her lips pursed. She doesn't say anything.

"What are you doing?" Sveta asks Oksana. "How can you be like this?"

Oksana doesn't respond; she only looks out the window in silence.

After all we've been through, she still only sees me by a word printed on my birth certificate, I realize. *Will any of it ever change?*

"I'm so sorry about her," Sveta says. "That's not right."

I shake my head. "It's fine." I force myself to smile. "So, what are you most looking forward to eating once you get home?" I ask Sveta in order to change the subject.

Sveta starts chatting about the soup her mother used to make.

I nod, pretending to listen but I can't stop beating myself up for sharing the truth.

Stupid. I'm so stupid. Telling people that I'm Jewish is never smart. And it will never be safe.

CHAPTER 64

MARIGOLD

When the train arrives in Vinnytsia, Oksana, Sveta, and I disembark, and I watch Oksana walk away from the platform without saying a word to me, without ever turning around.

How could she? Did all of it mean nothing? Our survival pact? Everything we've been through together? Was she only nice to me because I helped her?

Then I have another, more sobering thought. *Or maybe she didn't actually need me, maybe it was me that needed someone to take care of in order to survive.*

Sveta hugs me and hops back on the train, now headed to East Ukraine, to Donetsk. She makes me promise to try and get in touch once I am settled. I agree, although a part of me is scared to do it. *Would Sveta eventually treat me like Oksana just did? Or worse?*

When I look around, I wonder if I've gotten off at the wrong stop. My city, my entire city, is completely unrecognizable.

Most buildings are gone, destroyed, or burned to the ground. Piles of soot and unmarked graves with crosses over them populate what used to be the city grounds. There is nothing but spread-out trees and vast nothingness surrounding it, as far as I can see.

I walk among the ashes and the rubble, pausing now and then to examine bits of brick and stone as if they were headstones in a cemetery. The whole city feels like a giant graveyard now.

I make my way back to my old neighborhood. And even though I'm not surprised to find charred rubble where my house used to be, it still cuts a fresh wound into my pounding heart.

Memories of Babushka pour into my mind. And Pavlik, and Mamo, and Papa. And Moo-Moo. I stumble around the perimeter of my ruined home fighting back tears.

It's gone. All of it is gone.

Among the char and the wreckage, I see a small speck of orange and gold.

"What's that?" I say out loud.

I kneel down and remove the debris around it before recognizing it—a single marigold growing right where I'd planted it four years ago. I stroke its petals, wishing the flower had tiny hands I could clasp into my own.

You grew, little one, I silently say to the flower, *you actually grew. Babushka would have been so happy to see you.*

"Mouse?" a familiar voice calls from behind me.

My heart leaps into my throat, making my eyes water. I whirl around.

A woman in a long brown dress waves at me from up the road.

Could it be?

"Lyuda?" I whisper.

My best friend beams and waves again.

"Lyuda!" I shout and run to her.

I hug her as tight as I can. She has the same comforting smell she always has. She doesn't smell like anything in particular. She just smells like Lyuda.

I close my eyes, afraid to open them, afraid that it's all a dream, afraid that Lyuda will disappear from my life again. We just stay like that for a while.

When we finally part from our embrace, both of our eyes glisten with tears. Lyuda looks both older and unchanged at the same time. She seems a little shorter, or perhaps she is slouching. She is much thinner. Her hair has streaks of grey in it. Her eyes appear more tired, but they still shine as bright as ever.

"I prayed to you," I say, sniffling. "I don't know if you heard me. But I prayed to you like you were my guardian angel. By thinking of you, that's how I survived. It's probably stupid, I know."

Lyuda shakes her head. "Not at all. I did the same thing."

My heart flutters. "You did?"

Lyuda nods. "I thought of you every day. I even talked to you. Talking to you even when we were apart, and our survival pact, that's what helped me get through it all." She is beaming now. "Is that—" she points to my purse, "your graduation dress?"

I nod and pull out a single red tassel from it. "I've still got our boots," I point to the boots I'm wearing, "but I lost our coat. This is all I have left of it. I'm sorry."

Lyuda hugs me again. "You're back. That's all that matters now. You are so much more important than any coat."

I sigh in relief, and then ask, "How did you find me?"

Lyuda smiles. "After you didn't return to the hospital,

I just knew in my heart that you were taken. I also knew that you were still alive because of our pact. I knew it because it kept me alive too. When people started to come back a few weeks ago, I decided that I would come here every day to wait for you. I figured you'd wind up here eventually."

"And you? How did you survive?" I ask.

"I'll tell you everything. But first, come with me. I'll show you the reunification house where I'm staying. There are many people who are displaced staying there too. It's quite full, almost twenty-five of us so far in just one room, but I suspect they'll make room for one more."

CHAPTER 65

BRICK BY BRICK

We hold hands as we walk, and I sometimes squeeze Lyuda's hand, afraid that she might disappear, worrying that this is all too good to be true.

Lyuda squeezes back. "Is it true that there are castles in Germany?"

I nod.

Lyuda smiles. "Does this mean that you became a proper princess like you always wanted?"

I shake my head and giggle. "Princess? No. I became a bear instead. A Mutterbär."

Lyuda laughs.

"Tell me," I say. "Tell me everything."

Lyuda fills me in on what I missed over the past two years. "Once I got out of the hospital, I was able to stay with Ruslan. He was so relieved that I was back to take care of Pavlik, that he even started helping at the mill."

"Brilliant." I grin at her.

"Oh, and get this," she adds. "Apparently, Hitler had some kind of a secret bunker built right outside of

Vinnytsia. Can you believe it? He called it wolf—something."

"*Werwolf*," I say.

"That's it!" Lyuda exclaims. "Anyway, I guess he had all these plans to attack Ukraine and then Russia from there. But get this, some soldier found out about it and tipped off a priest, of all people, and the priest managed to get the word out to the Army."

I stop walking. "It worked?"

Lyuda laughs. "It did. Our army went to attack the bunker in hopes of destroying it, but the Nazis destroyed it themselves because they didn't want the bunker to fall into Soviet hands."

"Brilliant." I smile, thinking of Viktor. "Just brilliant."

"Come on, keep walking." Lyuda pulls me with her. "I have so much to tell you. Do you remember Frida? That woman who survived the Babin Yar massacre?"

I nod.

"Well, I just found out that she will be testifying against the main SS that orchestrated it all."

"I hope she gets justice," I say as we walk around another batch of rubble. "Oh, have you heard anything from Yuriy?"

Lyuda shakes her head. "Sadly, no. No one's heard from him since he was taken."

"Maria?" I hear another familiar voice call out to me, this one shrill and full of spite. "Is that you?"

My eyes narrow, my shoulders tense, and my cheeks burn like an ignited flame. I turn around and glare at Natasha, who is standing in front of two sidekicks—a man and a woman I've never met.

I guess her gang is getting smaller.

"I can't believe you actually came back," Natasha

snarls and takes a step closer. "Just look." She gestures wildly around. "Look at what you did to our city!"

I feel like my breath has been knocked out of me. "What *I did*? I only just got back here. "

"Don't try to deny it," Natasha spits back. "It's because of people like you that the Nazis came here in the first place. And now look at our city, and all the people that died, because of *you*." Natasha takes a step closer and points at me.

My nostrils flare with fury but not fear. Four years ago, her wrath would have left me speechless. But not anymore.

I walk up to her so that we are eye to eye. Natasha seems shorter than I remember. And shabbier. Her dress is plain, and her hair lacks its usual silk ribbons.

I smirk.

"What?" Natasha asks, her eyes narrowing as she speaks. "Why are you laughing at me? You need to apologize for what you've done."

I shake my head and smirk again. *You don't look so scary now.*

Natasha growls, "Apologize, I said!" She looks like a little pouting duck, puffing its feathers, trying to make itself look intimidating.

The image makes me burst out laughing. I glance over to Lyuda who is chuckling softly.

"Apologize!" Natasha roars.

The man standing behind Natasha approaches her and grips her by the arm. "Let's go. You're embarrassing me," he says in a harsh whisper.

Natasha huffs and turns toward him. "You're my *husband*. It's your job to stand up for me."

"Let's go," he hisses. "You are causing a scene."

He drags Natasha away without ever looking at me.

I shake my head and wipe the laughter-induced tears from my eyes. I'm glad that Natasha doesn't scare me anymore, but I also feel sad.

War or no war, some will never see Jewish people as people, I realize with a bitter taste in my mouth.

The woman who was standing next to Natasha a moment ago comes up to me. "Hi. I'm Lilya." She grabs my hands and holds them in her cold and clammy ones.

I jerk back a little, but not enough to pull my hands away because she's gripping them too tightly. *Why is she touching me? What does she want? Is she going to hurt me?*

"I'm sorry about my sister-in-law," Lilya says. "She doesn't understand."

My hands shake and tingle at the same time. I nod.

Lilya continues, "I lost a lot of Jewish friends in the war. I don't think it's right, what happened. We all lost a lot. And I am sorry about how Natasha treats you. I want you to know that it doesn't matter if you're Jewish or not. We are all Ukrainians."

"It's fine," I say and pull myself free. Lilya smiles at me and walks away.

Is it fine? I ask myself.

Lilya's comments unsettle me, and I find myself wishing that I could hide my Jewish heritage forever, that I could have my forged documents back, so that no one would ever know. *So that my being Jewish is just for me.* But then I chastise myself for that thought. *What is the matter with you? These are your roots. People have died for you to be able to be true to who you are. Besides, Lilya is right. Ukrainian people suffered too. We are all in this together. Just like you and the Ostarbeiter were.*

I try to keep the thought of Oksana from my mind.

"C'mon, let's keep walking," Lyuda says, pulling my arm.

We walk for a while in silence until we approach one of the few buildings left standing in the city. It has four stories, though most of the windows are missing. I follow Lyuda up the stairs to the third floor.

We step inside one of the apartments. It's crammed end to end with tables covered in bowls full of bread and strawberries and jugs of water.

"Maria!" Another voice calls my name.

I whirl around. "Papa!"

I jump into his arms, crying, feeling like a small child all over again. "Papa!" I manage to say in between the sobs, in every language I can. "*Tato! Tateh!*"

It hurt so bad to think about him over the past four years, that I hardly did. In some ways, I buried him. Yet now, he is here.

Papa hugs me back tightly, then pulls back and pats me gently on the head. "I'm so relieved you're alive, my little one. My wonderful girl."

"Papa?" I say, pulling away from him, feeling a twinge of guilt churning in my stomach. "I must tell you that I am no longer the good girl you remember. I get angry. So very angry."

Papa smiles at me. "That's good." He squeezes my hands in his. "I get angry too, *moya dorogaya*. With everything that's happened, how can we not? Being angry and fighting back—I realize now that it's how we stay alive."

I let out a big exhale of relief.

Papa pulls my hand, still not letting me go, as if scared to lose me again. "Come, let's get you something to eat."

When I sit down to eat some bread with Papa, he tells

me about how he escaped the Nazis and joined the Red Army.

As we talk, Lyuda comes up to us with two Army soldiers in full uniform. "Maria, I want you to meet my husband, Grisha," she points to the man on the left.

I raise my eyebrows and jump out of my seat. "Husband? When did that happen?"

Lyuda giggles and looks up at Grisha with adoring eyes. "Two days ago."

"Congratulations," I say, my heart full at witnessing her happiness.

I give Lyuda a hug and shake Grisha's hand.

Lyuda points at the other soldier, the one standing next to Grisha. "This is Peter. They served together. He is Jewish too."

Peter is gigantic, although to me, most people appear tall. He bends down to be at my eye level. His eyes are the kind of mixture of blue and green that I can't remember ever seeing before.

"Hi, Maria," Peter says. He runs his fingers through his black curls and smiles at me. He holds two strawberries in his other hand and hands them both to me. "Please have some."

Our fingers touch when he hands me the delicious-smelling fruit. He smiles and I find myself beaming back at him.

Papa gets up and offers his seat to Peter. "I need to go help with the dishes," Papa says.

Papa helping with dishes. That's incredible.

Peter sits in his place. His smile sends warm, tingling sensations up my arm and down the middle of my back.

"Have you been able to locate your family?" I ask, sitting back down.

He shakes his head, his smile fading. "Gone. All of them. The Nazis—"

I instinctively reach for his hand, noticing how tiny my hand looks in his. "I'm so sorry, Peter."

Peter glances around the room. "It's hard to believe it. Six million Jewish people—all gone. Ninety thousand just from Vinnytsia. Gone. All of us here today—we just have each other now." He looks up at me. "But it's a start."

I nod and squeeze his hand. "Yes. It's a start."

PETER PROPOSES to me the next day.

"I've seen enough death for a lifetime," he tells me when he gets down on one knee. "I survived because I learned to trust my instinct. And my instinct tells me that I want to spend my life with you, if you will have me."

I smile at him. There's a sense of warm ease whenever I am around him, just like when I am around Lyuda.

Is it foolish to get engaged so quickly? I wonder. *No. War changes things. I don't want to wait to live. Not anymore.*

One week later, we get married, with Lyuda, Grisha, and Papa attending the ceremony. Peter kisses me on both cheeks, and I know in my heart that he's the only man I ever want to kiss for the rest of my life.

The day after our wedding, Peter and Grisha drive to the city to get bricks and foundation materials. They deliver them to the lot where Lyuda, Papa, and I wait for them. The same lot where our house used to be.

"We will help you build your house, and then you can help us build ours," Lyuda says.

My eyes well up. Looking at all four of them, my

family, there's a spreading warmth of gratitude throughout my entire body.

"Ready?" Peter asks me.

I smile and nod at him, "Ready."

He smiles back, the same shy and playful smile he only has for me. "Which part of our home do you want to start with?"

I think about it for a moment, "A garden. I want to start with a garden."

EPILOGUE

*pril 13, 1995, 2:55am, on the train from Moscow*

RAIN POURS down the moonlit windowpane as the train rocks from side to side. A blasting sound has just jerked me awake, and for a moment I forget where I am, but the motion of the train jogs my memory.

My bunk creaks when I roll over, a motion that sends a spasm down my back. The sharp pain reminds me of the sensation of sharp teeth ripping away pieces of my flesh. I can still feel the dog's hot breath on my exposed skin, and I realize I must have been dreaming.

I close my eyes and replay the images in my mind.

Guns.

Screams.

Bodies.

I shake my head hard, left to right, four times. It has been some time since I've had nightmares this intense.

Perhaps it's because of the train. This is the first time I've been on a train in fifty years.

No, not fifty.

Forty-nine years, eleven months, and three days.

"How long do you think till we get back to Ukraine?" I ask Peter.

There is no answer.

I turn in my bunk to face him. "Peter?"

I stare at the empty space next to me and sigh. His side of the bed has been empty for over six months now but I still forget sometimes, and I call out to him when I have bad dreams.

I reach under my pillow, pull my cotton purse toward me, and count.

Button. One.

Ribbon. Two.

Tassel. Three.

I exhale in relief and turn my attention to my sleeping family, their faces lit by the moonlight. No one will ever hurt them, not while I am still breathing.

I hug Peter's pillow to my chest and burrow my face in it. I can still smell the fleeting lilac scent of his cologne. I take a deep breath, relieved that I thought to bring the pillow on this journey. The scent goes up my nostrils and into my heart.

A few tears fall and they sting my cheeks on the way down. I wipe them away, take a breath, and force myself to lay down and close my eyes. Closing them is always the hardest part. Like a projector screen, my eyelids seem to invite moving pictures of my past.

Guns.

Screams.

Bodies.

Then the flashbacks morph into a replay of yesterday's meeting.

My family stands in line for hours before we finally reach the front of the line at the American Embassy in Moscow. The representative standing there addresses us without looking up.

He yawns and checks his watch. "Name?"

"Maria Furman."

"How many of you are here today?"

"Five. Me, my daughter, my daughter's husband, and their two children."

"Why are you seeking refugee status in the United States today?"

My lips tremble. Don't cry, *I tell myself, and then to the representative, "We have been targeted. Our lives are in danger. If anyone finds out—"*

The representative yawns again, and I lose my patience.

I point my finger at him like a gun barrel. Even standing on my tiptoes, I barely reach his chest, but he still steps back and takes notice of me for the first time.

"You," I say, still pointing my finger at him. "Listen. This might be just a day job to you but for us, this is life and death."

An hour later, we huddle together in the Embassy lobby, our immigration documents in hand, before stepping out onto the freezing streets of Moscow.

"We can't tell anyone we're moving to America," I tell my family. "We can't risk anyone seeing these documents or anyone finding out."

The train jerks, snapping my attention back to the present. I take a few breaths to settle my pounding heart.

In just four months, we will be moving to America. I can't believe I have to leave Ukraine again. I thought it was all behind me.

What will I bring? How can I pack my life of fifty years

into two duffle bags? I can't bring what's most valuable. I can't bring the desk that Peter and I made for our son, Yuriy. Or the bed, where our daughter, Sofia, slept. Maybe I can bring the children's drawings. But the wall dents and scratches that are filled with memories, I can't bring those. I can't bring my home. And I can't bring my husband.

Even though it feels like being forced to leave all over again, this time, it's my choice. This time, it's to protect my family.

They say there's no antisemitism in America. They say we can worship openly, that we can attend synagogues and wear the Star of David around our necks. They say we can post a mezuzah on our doorposts. But a part of me fears that it's all too good to be true.

Is there really a single place in the universe where people can truly be free? Where everyone has compassion for one another regardless of which god we worship, our faith, place of birth, or history? I hope to find it in America, or else, I hope to live to see it in this world.

~

SEPTEMBER 2000, New York, NY: German reparations hearing

WHEN I GET off the train, my head is spinning. "Are we in Germany?" I ask Peter.

"No, Mom, we are in New York," Peter responds.

No, not Peter.

It's Yuriy. My son, Yuriy.

Peter is dead. Has been dead for many years now.

I swallow my tears.

And Lyuda? Where is Lyuda?

I strain to remember.

Living with her adult children now.

A bark makes me jump.

A police officer holding a German Shepherd by the leash walks by me. He is carrying a machine gun.

Dogs.

Flashbacks of the biting hounds play like a horror film in my mind.

Dogs.

Irina.

Train.

Axel.

"And do you have any documents that prove that you were in Germany?" a tall blonde man with glasses asks me. His nametag reads *Steve.* He holds a blue pen in his hand.

I don't respond. *How did I get here? Who is he? How does he know I was in Germany? Is he going to arrest me now?*

I stare at him, trying to remember if I've ever met him before because everyone looks both familiar and like a complete stranger at the same time.

"She has dementia," my daughter, Sofia, says.

"No, I don't," I argue. I glance around. "And where's Peter? Where's your dad? I haven't seen him yet this morning."

"It's okay, Mom," Sofia whispers and hands me a small black purse.

The purse has roses stitched on it, as well as a clef note, a spade, and a tiara. I run my fingers across it, letting out an exhale of relief, my heart rate slowing down now as I feel the inside of the purse.

Button. One.

Ribbon. Two.

Tassel. Three.

Sofia pulls a letter out of her own purse and hands it to Steve. "Here is the note from her doctor. My brother and I are here to speak on her behalf."

Steve adjusts his glasses and flips through the pages of the letter. "I see. Did she work in Ukraine?"

"Teacher," Yuriy says. "She was a chemistry teacher."

Steve nods. "And how did the Nazi invasion impact her life?"

"Her grandmother was executed," Sofia says. "Her brother was killed in action."

Steve shakes his head. "Many people die in wars. That hardly qualifies your mother for benefits."

"She was enslaved," Sofia protests, her voice shaking now. "She was kidnapped and forced into a slavery, as an Ostarbeiter."

Steve leans forward. "And does your mother have the official Ostarbeiter paperwork? Something with her name and picture?"

Sofia shakes her head. "She had to destroy it after the war. Otherwise, she would have been imprisoned."

Steve drums his fingers on the blue pen he's holding. "Well, do you have *any* proof that you mother was even there?"

Sofia pulls out an envelope from her purse and hands it to him. "This is all I have."

Steve opens the envelope and pulls out a photo, the back of which features my handwriting, "The girls and I in Berchtesgaden, spring 1945."

Steve examines the picture for a few moments before he responds. "I can't accept this," he says, and points to the picture. "Look at her face here. She looks way too happy to be there. I'm sorry, these benefits are only for those people who actually suffered in the war."

He stamps the word *Denied* on my paperwork.

I pull the picture toward me.

It all comes back to me now.

The train.

Hannah.

Axel's house.

The forced smiles in the posed pictures.

The bombings.

Oksana's deafening silence on the train back to Ukraine.

I shake my head left to right. *One. Two. Three. Four.*

A moment of clarity washes over me. My power returns to my frail bones, along with the familiar certainty that I will never allow anyone to hurt me or my family ever again.

I stare up at Steve with a defiant smile. "May you never feel as *happy* as I did during that time. You wouldn't survive it."

I grab the picture and walk out the door.

AFTERWORD

I have wanted to share my grandmother's story since I was a small child. All four of my grandparents were Holocaust survivors. All of them, along with my other elderly relatives and neighbors, were full of stories about the impacts of the war. The hospital I often visited as a child for the plethora of the health conditions I struggled with was erected atop the area that served as a concentration camp, just a few miles from the personal bunker built for Hitler during WWII, called *Führerhauptquartier Werwolf*.

The majority of this novel is based on true stories—my grandmother's experience and other people's too, whose stories I wanted to honor. For example, I based the character of Frida on two different women—Frida Michelson, who actually survived the Rumbuli massacre, and Dina Pronicheva, who survived the Babin Yar massacre. Dina Pronicheva later courageously testified against the SS involved in the massacres. I wanted to honor both women in this story.

The character of Lyuda was based on an actual friend of my grandmother's and was named after my own best friend in Ukraine when I was growing up. Most of the events that occur in this novel between Maria and "Lyuda" are factual, to the best of my knowledge, including their suicide plans, forged documents, them nearly being sold out to the Ostarbeiter by the Ukrainian policeman, their shared coat and winter boots, and their work at the mill, as well as Lyuda's accident.

The two did not, to the best of my knowledge, travel to Kyiv, nor did they witness the Babin Yar massacre. I added this part to shed light on the details of this horrific event. The Babin Yar posters, requiring all Jewish people to appear under the pretenses of being relocated, are word-for-word exact translations of the actual posters. The Ostarbeiter propaganda poster, and the doctor's note are word-for-word translations as well, with the exception of the doctor's diagnosis.

Maria's experiences at her school—using a mop to help her classmates during the German final, being sold out by her classmate who brought the Nazis to her doorstep, many of her experiences as an Ostarbeiter, being attacked by dogs when she and other women fled from the train, being betrayed by a man from her home-town, and protected by a woman she worked for—are also all true.

Sadly, my grandmother being denied reparation benefits because she looked "too happy in this picture" is also true.

The chapter about Maria running into a little boy buried under the corpses of a mass grave is based on my paternal grandfather's brother, Grisha, who hid under corpses on several occasions when he was twelve years old to escape from the Nazis, while looking for food to help feed other people in hiding.

The Night Witches that Maria's grandmother mentioned in the very first chapter were indeed real. They were some of the most badass women in history. Although the timeline in which they're mentioned here isn't exactly accurate, as they didn't form until 1942, I wanted to pay tribute to these courageous and powerful women.

The Last Jew in Vinnytsia was not a newspaper article but a photograph found after the war. The title, *The Last Jew in Vinnytsia,* was handwritten on the back of the photograph. It's one of the few historical pieces of evidence depicting the mass killings by the *Einsatzgruppen*, the SS death squads, shedding more light on the horrors of the war in Vinnytsia.

Parts of the Pechersk Lavra Cathedral were indeed destroyed during WWII; however, some scholars believe that it happened at a later time than depicted in this book.

The quote, "Just survive somehow," mentioned a couple of times in this novel is an homage to "JSS," an episode of "The Walking Dead," which depicted the horrors of being a lone survivor, of losing one's loved ones, and facing a world full of monsters on your own.

Speaking of quotes, I named Maria's cow Moo-Moo in honor of a famous Russian short story, *Mumu,* by Ivan Turgenev.

I named one of the main villains of this book, Axel Jeckeln, after Friedrich Jeckeln, a Holocaust perpetrator, who orchestrated the Babin Yar massacre, and many others. I did so to bring light to the horrors of his actions, as well as to give my grandmother and the other Ostarbeiter the opportunity to defeat him, even if in fiction.

Finally, I do not know the name of the man who

forged my grandmother's papers, but I am forever grateful to him for saving her life and the lives of many others. I named him Yuriy in this novel because it is my uncle's name (my grandmother's first-born), and I imagine she might have named him after someone very significant in her life.

There are many reasons why I wanted to write this book: to share my grandmother's story, to give a voice to the millions of people who died in Ukraine, and to address the growing issue of antisemitism. I've found that outside of Ukraine, most people don't know about the mass murders, the famine (the Holodomor), and the torture that Ukrainian people endured. I've also found that most people don't know about the Ostarbeiter, the forced enslavement of Ukrainian people during WWII. Many people don't know about the Babin Yar massacre, as well as many other massacres that took place in Ukraine.

Unfortunately, I have found that fascism still exists all over the world, from people openly wearing swastikas to people denying the Holocaust, to people oppressing others based on who they are or where they come from. I decided to write this book to honor my grandmother's voice and the voices of many others affected by this horrific time in our history, including myself.

I truly think that most people are not evil. I do, however, think that sometimes people might not understand how their behavior might affect others.

When I was fifteen years old, my (then) partner, let's call him *Ben,* had a friend whom he jokingly called "Nazi Dave." When I asked Ben about his friend's nickname, he said that he used it to distinguish "Nazi Dave" from his other friends, several of whom were named Dave as well.

When I first met "Nazi Dave," he wore a silver swastika ring on his middle finger and had a swastika tattoo on his shoulder. He was always nice to me, but he never knew that I was Jewish. I never told him. I wonder how he would have treated me if I had.

On one occasion, "Nazi Dave" said to me, "The Nazis had the right idea, am I right?" and winked.

I don't remember the context of that conversation, but I will never forget how that phrase made me feel.

Ben, on the other hand, knew that I was Jewish and was aware of my family history. And when I privately told him that being around "Nazi Dave" made me uncomfortable, Ben replied, "Oh, he's just joking. Don't take it personally. That's just how he is. He's harmless."

"But I'm harmed," I tried to argue. "This was harmful."

"Are you on your period or something? You're extra moody today," Ben said, and changed the subject.

I was left with my thoughts about whether I was being unreasonable and blowing the whole thing out of proportion.

After all, Dave was just joking.

Back then, I didn't know what intergenerational trauma was or what PTSD was, or that one could develop one from the other. Back then, I didn't have the words to stand up for the six million people who were savagely executed, as well as the loved ones they left behind.

This kind of microaggression doesn't only happen to Jewish people. It happens to all people, especially those who have a lot of history of being oppressed and who have experienced long-standing intergenerational trauma. BIPOC people, women, LGBTQIA+ people and many others have sadly been transgressed against in ways that cut deep and do a lot more damage than the person inflicting such damage might actually realize.

I was twenty-one when my grandma, Maria, on whom this book was based, died. I was devastated. "Anthony," a friend of a friend, called me to offer his condolences and asked if we could meet up.

I agreed, and when we met, I told him my grandmother's story and some of what she meant to me.

"So, is that why you and your family moved to the United States?" he asked.

I nodded and told him about my family's experiences of antisemitism. When I mentioned that some of the kids in my school in Ukraine bullied me by calling me a "*zhid*," an equivalent to the word *kike* in English, Anthony interrupted.

"Well, you know that the word *kike* is actually not an offensive word, right?"

I stared at Anthony, an Italian Catholic boy with dark blonde hair. I blinked for a while before I was able to respond, "Um, what?"

"Oh, right. You're an immigrant, so you probably don't know this," he said to me. "Let me explain it to you. The word *kike* actually started as a way to identify Jews when they immigrated to Ellis Island. The word actually comes from Hebrew, or perhaps Yiddish, or one of those Jewish languages. Anyway, it means *circle*. You see, customs would draw a circle on their paperwork instead of an X, because they weren't Christian. So, the word *kike* just means circle and it's really a form of respect, if anything."

"Are you serious right now?" I asked, my hands trembling.

"I'm just saying that you're taking this word all

wrong. You just didn't know what it means, that's all. But clearly, it's not an offensive word. It just means *circle*."

I got up from the bench. "I gotta go," I said, and speed-walked away from him.

Anthony followed me for almost a mile, trying to convince me to see his point of view.

Feeling both desperate and threatened, I ran into a café, where my good friend, Matt, often hung out.

Please be here. Please be here.

Thankfully, Matt was there. He sat in his usual corner seat, sipping his tea.

"Help me," I whispered and slid into the seat next to him.

A moment later, Anthony walked in and sat down opposite me. The two guys had not met until now.

Matt glanced from me to Anthony and back to me again. "What's going on?" he asked me.

I opened my mouth to answer but Anthony answered instead. "Bro, help me out here," Anthony said to Matt. "I'm trying to get her to understand that the word *kike* is not an offensive word. It actually comes from a Yiddish word—"

"Stop," Matt said, holding up the palm of his hand. "Just. Stop."

"But listen, I'm just—" Anthony tried again.

But Matt interjected, "Look, *Bro*. You need to go." Matt pointed to the door. "Now."

Anthony shook his head, got up, and walked out, muttering something about people being *too sensitive*.

I'm so grateful that my friend, Matt, was there that day, and beyond grateful that he was able to stand up for me. This is how people—friends and strangers alike—can stand up for others. By calling out inappropriate behavior or standing up for the person who is being oppressed, we can stand against hate and intolerance and support peace.

As this book is being released, my home country of Ukraine enters its third year of bravely fighting off the horrific invasion from Russia. I've seen a tremendous amounts of parallels between what my grandparents experienced during WWII and what the people of Ukraine continue to go through. The spirit of Ukrainian people, the kindness so many of them showed during WWII (by risking their lives to hide Jewish people), and also the incredible courage that they show today, is truly unmatched. It is my dream that we will someday live in the world where we will not have to hide our identities, and where we will all be able to love and care for one another.

And above all, may there be peace.

ACKNOWLEDGMENTS

This book would not have been possible without some truly incredible people. First and foremost, I'm incredibly honored to have known my maternal grandparents, Maria and Peter, and my paternal grandparents, Emma and David. All four were Holocaust survivors. Their courage and their stories made this book possible.

In addition, I am very grateful to have been able to consult with the daughter of my grandmother's best friend during the war (the one whom the character of Lyuda is based on). This book would not have been possible without all of her support and input.

I was also incredibly grateful to have been able to consult with Dr. Anton Masterovoy about Ukrainian culture and history as well as the following books, which I highly recommend for anyone interested in learning more about the Holocaust:

1. *The Harvest of Despair: Life and Death in Ukraine under Nazi Rule*, by Karel C. Berkhoff
2. *I Survived Rumbuli*, by Frida Michelson
3. *The Shoah in Ukraine: History, Testimony, Memorialization*, edited by Ray Brandon and Wendy Lower

I am very grateful to Dr. Alex Tievsky, who consulted with

me about the most likely diagnosis Lyuda would have had due to the injuries in her feet.

Of course, this book would not have been possible without the inspiration and support of my amazing book coach and editor, Erin Michelle Gibes. Thank you for all the fairy dust.

This work would not have been possible without the support of my amazing husband, Dustin McGinnis, who held me every time I broke down when researching, outlining, and writing this book.

From the bottom of my heart, a big thank you to Sherry and Rich, thank you so much for being my Jewish Fairy Godparents (and now becoming my adoptive parents) and for supporting me the way you always do.

I am also incredibly grateful for the amazing support of my dear friends—Chase Masterson, Alex Tievsky, William Blumberg, Philip Sharp, Travis Langley, Travis Adams, Jill Stoddard, Sasha West, Paxton Alyssa, Shawn Johnson, Jonathan Maberry, Happy Malla, Kiere Eichelberger, Erika Coco, Kage Ryan, Boo Clay, Johnnie McDuffie, Star Dell'Era, Diane Pendragon, Justin Zagri, Liana Minassian, Michelle Lopez, Annabelle Mebane, Asher and Isabel Johnson, Olga Shvartsur, Marina Triner, Matt Bartels, Eugene Zusman, Robin Buckwalter, Matt and Shannon Miller, and Lora Innes. Thank you for believing in me, even when I didn't believe in myself.

I'm over the moon grateful for all the support from Andrew McAleer, a wonderful editor from Little, Brown, who helped me get started with my writing career. Thank you, Andrew, I wouldn't be where I am now if it wasn't for you.

A big thank you to my wonderful therapist, Dr. Carla Payne, for helping me process my own intergenerational trauma. Thank you for your support and encouragement with this book.

If you felt moved by this book and would like to help people affected by the Holocaust, please consider donating to your local Holocaust Museums, such as the United States Holocaust Memorial Museum, https://www.ushmm.org.

ABOUT THE AUTHOR

Dr. Janina Scarlet is a Clinical Psychologist, author, and a creativity coach. She immigrated to the United States at the age of 12 and later, inspired by the X-Men, she developed Superhero Therapy to help patients with anxiety, depression, and PTSD.

Dr. Scarlet is the Founding Director of Divine Feminine Publishing, a small publishing press, focusing on producing books where at least fifty percent of the characters are women.

Dr. Scarlet is the recipient of the Eleanor Roosevelt Human Rights Award by the United Nations Association for her work on Superhero Therapy. She regularly consults on books and television shows, including HBO's *The Young Justice*. She was also portrayed as a comic book character in Gail Simone's *Seven Days* graphic novel and was interviewed for Marvel's *MPower* television series about the Scarlet Witch. Dr. Scarlet works at the Trauma and PTSD Healing Center in San Diego, California.

THANK YOU FOR READING THIS BOOK

For information about our books and our authors, please
visit:
Divine Feminine Publishing
www.divinefeminine-publishing.com